THE
UNTANGLED
CASSIE BLACK

Book Three

of

The Cassie Black Trilogy

TAMMIE PAINTER

The Untangled Cassie Black
Book Three of The Cassie Black Trilogy

You may contact the author by email at
Tammie@tammiepainter.com
Mailing Address:
Daisy Dog Media
P.O. Box 165
Netarts, Oregon 97143, USA

First Edition, May 2021
also available as an ebook

ALSO BY TAMMIE PAINTER

What Readers Are saying About the Trilogy...

The Undead Mr. Tenpenny is a clever, hilarious romp through a new magical universe that can be accessed through the closet of a hole-in-the-wall apartment in Portland, Oregon.

—**Sarah Angleton, author of *Gentleman of Misfortune***

Man oh man, did I love this book! ...The plot was great, and got even better as things progressed.... I think the biggest pro of this book is the characters.

—**Jonathan Pongratz, author of *Reaper: Aftermath***

...suffused with dark humor and witty dialogue, of the sort that Painter excels at...a fun read for anyone who enjoys fast-paced, somewhat snarky, somewhat twisted, fantasy adventures.

—**Berthold Gambrel, author of *Vespasian Moon's Fabulous Autumn Carnival***

I was unable to put this down when I started reading it. The author combines humour with a fast paced murder mystery all packed into a funeral home.

—**Amazon Reviewer**

It's a bit "Pushing Daisies" meets Hogwarts, which makes the novel a fun and entertaining read. Great wit too.

When I saw the book title…my first thought was, "another zombie apocalypse". A wonderful surprise greeted me with an entertaining story that was written with humor, a great story line and new twist on the undead.

Wow and wow again! I absolutely loved this book! You get such a feel for the characters and the story is so fast paced you don't want to put it down.

The whole story was a bit of wild ride, but it was a ride I wanted to stay on all the way through! There is mystery that actually kept me guessing, there's humor, magic, and a unique storyline.

AUTHOR'S NOTE:
TOWER TERMINOLOGY

As with *The Uncanny Raven Winston*, the majority of this book takes place in the Tower of London. The Tower of London has many towers...which is a little confusing, so let me again explain how I use the term "Tower" in this story.

The Tower of London is a large complex that includes walls, living quarters for the Yeoman Warders, and structures like Wakefield Tower, Salt Tower, and the White Tower (the castle that started it all).

As in *The Uncanny Raven Winston*, I use the word "Tower" by itself only when referring to The Tower of London as a whole. Other towers within the Tower are referred to by name.

I don't know if this is helping dispel the confusion, or adding to it, but there it is.

If you'd like to see an excellent map of The Tower of London to get an understanding of the layout (of the non-magical bits, anyway), take a gander at the one provided by the Historic Royal Palaces website at:

www.hrp.org.uk/media/1587/tower-map-2018.pdf

This book is dedicated to my mom for always having an encouraging word even while I'm having a writer's meltdown.

And to my dad for all his dogged attempts to open the ebook versions and for earning the silver spittoon in Typo Hunting.

"Magic is not about passion or anger or the power of friendship. Magic is about control, focus, and being able to concentrate when you're drowning to death."

—Ben Aaronovitch, *The Hanging Tree*

THE
UNTANGLED
CASSIE
BLACK

LET ME CATCH YOU UP

Morelli here. So the last time you were hanging out with that dimwitted tenant of mine, she'd gone and gotten herself into a huge heap of trouble. When I heard about it, I wasn't a bit surprised. Always figured she'd end up on the wrong side of a problem.

So here's the deal in case you ain't just read that second book of hers and you might've forgotten a few things.

The Queen of Mistrust, who's already been on this loop-the-loop ride of trying to sort out whether Alastair's a two-faced jerk or not, had gotten her panties in a twist seeing Alastair kissing Olivia. She'd also failed a pretty important test and faced the risk of being booted from the magic community (should we be so lucky). And so, as Black tends to do, she went and had a knee-jerk reaction that landed her right where the Mauvais wanted her.

This girl, I tell you. Makes me glad I never had kids.

'Coz not only did she get herself in a tricky situation, she got Tobey and Alastair in a bind. Literally. And when she walloped the Mauvais, he tumbled into a hidden portal. Along with Alastair and Tobey.

Like I said, the girl's a nitwit. That cat of hers has more smarts than she does.

But, you know, you lose some, you win some. Because while she did lose two people, she also found two people…her parents. Not sure if that evens up the balance sheet, but I'm gonna guess not.

Anyway, when you last saw her, she was running down the hallway of an abandoned building calling for her mom. Which I suppose is kind of touching. Except it's Black we're talking about, so I'm sure she'll screw it up somehow.

So that's it. I'll let you loose with the story. I've got to go whip up a BLAT for that boss of hers. Great guy that Mr. Wood. Man after my own heart. Can't believe he actually likes that nitwit tenant of mine.

Speaking of, if you see her, tell her the rent's due in three weeks, five days, and sixteen hours.

CHAPTER ONE
THE AFTERMATH

Enough with the comments from the TV-binging troll. It's me, Cassie, and yes, you did last see me running down a hallway calling for my mother. Something I believe I've only ever done in my dreams.

Let me just be clear, my parents were in awful shape. They hadn't been washed in what smelled like months, they appeared to have been fed the bare minimum to keep them alive, and they had been drained to the point that even a nineteenth century lobotomy victim would have seemed a MENSA genius in comparison. I recognized myself somewhere in my father's emaciated face, but I didn't for a moment fool myself into thinking they knew me. There wasn't even a spark of awareness.

And so I left them behind in that abandoned building. Probably easiest for everyone if we just let them wither away and die.

I'm kidding. Do you actually believe I'm such a monster? Wait, don't answer that.

I did leave them, but only to race back to the Tower to get help since I knew, even in a big city like London, a young woman escorting two drooling, stinking imbeciles down the street is bound to draw unwanted attention.

Olivia, not once questioning what I'd been doing out of the Tower, immediately called in the magic medics, told them where to go, and what they'd find. I went with them. First, I had to see my parents brought back with my own eyes; and second, I wasn't ready to face Olivia's scrutiny.

It wasn't a pretty sight. My parents fought, spreading their filth across the people who were trying to help them. They cried out in fear, and my heart broke at the sound. Finally, one of the medics gave up playing Mr. Nice Guy. He hit them with a Stunning Spell and we whisked them back to the Tower.

They were then rushed to the Tower of London's medical ward — yes, located somewhere in the White Tower. Seriously, the place is a wonder of the world. After a few attempts to jump start their recovery failed miserably, Olivia pulled me aside and insisted I meet with her and Mr. Tenpenny in her office while we let the medics do their job. Once seated, with scones and tea served up despite the late hour, I told them what had happened.

Dressed in perfectly tailored, dark grey slacks and a crisp, dove grey shirt, Mr. T abandoned his stiff upper lip and broke down in tears when I told him about Tobey. Of course, being British, he begged apologies for his foolish behavior, took all of three minutes to compose himself, then asked for the full story.

"Alastair told me he'd detected you on the lock," Mr. Tenpenny said once I'd finished, "but not that he'd found that address. I'm not surprised he went after you. I would have insisted he do so had I known what you were up to, but he should have taken backup. Still, how did Tobey get there?"

"I'm not taking any responsibility for that. I did use him to get out of the Tower." I darted a quick glance to see Olivia's reaction to my escape. Her face remained disconcertingly unreadable. "But I had no intention of him going anywhere beyond the galleries of the V & A. I ditched him at the cafe. He's the one

14

who followed me to the building where the Mauvais was." I paused. Flashes of memory returning to me in harsh detail. "I said some awful things to Alastair. I thought he was helping the Mauvais, but now I'm not sure. I just don't know what to think. They were there together when I arrived. There was the whole Vivian thing, the donuts the morning of my draining—"

"Which he explained to you," Mr. T scolded. "Cassie, this mistrust needs to be tamed as desperately as your magic does."

"Does it? Is it really so far-fetched? He made the watch. He was a close ally of the Mauvais. He—" I wanted to bring up the fact that Alastair was the last person who'd been near me on the day I was kidnapped, but I knew from the exasperated expression on Busby's face that he would only make excuses and say Alastair's name had been cleared from that case long ago. "My point is, every time I start to trust Alastair, some new piece of information comes along and eats holes in that trust. It doesn't take an overactive imagination to think maybe he was leading me on, luring me in to either hand me over to the Mauvais or give my power to him. Then, seeing him and Olivia, well, that was the final straw."

Mr. Tenpenny shook his head. I hated the disappointment overflowing from such a simple gesture. I was about to redeem myself by telling him some confidence in Alastair had eventually won out. After all, I did give Alastair a hit of my magic in the form of an absorbing capsule. You know, right before he got yanked through a portal to who knows where. But Olivia cut me off before I could salvage my already-tarnished reputation.

"I don't understand. What exactly did you see between me and Alastair?"

"You and him," I started, my throat suddenly resistant to saying out loud what I'd witnessed. I took a gulp of tea, then forced the rock-like bolus down my throat. In a rushing surge of words, I said, "You and him groping each other on this desk. His face buried in your neck. You groaning with pleasure."

"Cassie," Olivia said, her face completely impassive as if I'd just informed her Alastair ate a toasted cheese sandwich for lunch yesterday, "I'll put this as bluntly as I can and hope it gets through that surprisingly thick skull of yours: I don't like men in that way. I have never kissed Alastair other than in greeting, and if he tried to put his lips anywhere near my neck I'd probably slap him. No offense, he is devilishly good looking."

"Then how did I see that?" My voice trailed off as I recalled the Mauvais morphing into Tobey for just the briefest moment back at the building. I told them about it. "Could he have morphed into you, Olivia? Is that what I saw?"

Not that the idea of Alastair making out with the Mauvais was anywhere near a comforting thought.

Mr. T and Olivia exchanged a meaningful glance.

"Don't do that thing where you have a secret conversation with your eyes," I said. "It's really annoying."

"You're already aware that we suspect the Mauvais is somehow gaining power, and that we worry he's gaining it from someone within HQ?" Olivia asked. I nodded as I bit into an orange-and-almond scone. "It's the only way he can have gained enough strength to morph into Vivian, to make the portal he escaped through, or to do any of the tricks he's used lately. At one time he may have been pulling magic from your parents, but from the state of them, that source had to have been exhausted years ago."

"He did mention having Tobey under some sort of BrainSweeping Charm. He said he used it to convince Tobey to carry absorbing capsules with him when we were in the file room together. Maybe other times as well," I added doubtfully, thinking of our lunch at the Museum of London, plus all the times Tobey had found me wandering the Tower grounds. Had he sought me out because he was under the Mauvais's influence? I should have known Tobey Tenpenny wouldn't willingly have wanted to spend time with me.

"But that doesn't explain how he got the capsules once they'd been filled," said Olivia. "Tobey certainly wasn't leaving the Tower to deliver them to him; the gnomes would have commented on such frequent comings and goings."

"It had to be whoever is working with him," Mr. T said distractedly. "Still, it doesn't explain how he had enough strength to do a Morphing Charm."

He shook his head in frustration. But I think I knew the answer to that. Alastair had told me that, thanks to the watch's influence on my magic, my power could easily replenish itself. It's one reason I bounced back so quickly when Runa drained me. Well, that and the four donuts I'd inhaled just before the draining. With this unique quirk to my magic, if the Mauvais could get even just a small amount of it, it would grow, and he wouldn't need much to boost his power. Of course, that power boost would only be temporary since transfusions of magic were tricky business, but if he had a steady supply of Cassie Juice coming to him...

I explained my theory to Olivia and Busby.

"And when did you say you saw this, um, *event* between Olivia and Alastair?" Mr. T asked.

"It was the day before my second test, when those dark clouds came in. I left this office, then Tobey was in the hallway. We ended up in front of the office door, and then I saw, well, you know."

"That day. The corridor was rather dark?" said Olivia.

"It's not like this hallway is well-lit to begin with, but yes, the clouds made it even darker."

"That would have helped," commented Mr. Tenpenny. "Even if he didn't have the strength to do the Morphing Charm with exactness, in such dim lighting he wouldn't need it to be perfect."

"There's still the matter of you seeing something that didn't happen," Olivia said, dipping a lemon scone into a bowl of melted chocolate. "As a Magic, he couldn't have done a BrainSweeping Charm on you." She took a bite of the scone, magically clearing away the chocolate that dripped onto her desk with a swish of her index finger. She then nodded as if she'd just figured something out. "A Mirage Hex. It's the only thing that makes sense."

"But I don't understand how he could have done a Mirage Hex on Cassie. That requires not only being near the person, but touching them as well. That touch, that connection, it's the only way to hone in on a person's mind. It's not a spell you can do at a distance. What happened when you were in the hall? Did he get close to you?"

"He touched me, ran his fingers along my cheek. Then he showed me what was going on in here. After I saw, or thought I saw you two, I hit him and—" I swallowed hard, feeling a little foolish after just showing my jealousy over Olivia and Alastair, "—he kissed me," I said, grimacing and most definitely *not* adding just how intense that kiss had been. Nor that I hadn't exactly resisted it.

Mr. Tenpenny's face took on a horrified expression of utter shock. "That's— You shouldn't— You and Tobey—" Damn, I hate it when I say something that makes him revert to Zombie Speak.

As Mr. T sputtered out additional sounds of disbelief, Olivia told him, "Calm down, Busby. It wasn't him." To me, she explained, "The touch, the kiss, that's the textbook setup for the Mirage Hex. I suppose resisting it, or at least recognizing it, is something we should have trained you in."

"Yeah, I suppose that might have been good to know," I said, grabbing another scone and slathering it with marmalade.

"I'll admit, we've gotten a little out of practice with our defensive training. As for the Mirage Hex, Alastair and I were in the office together, I believe we were discussing your upcoming test. When the Mauvais touched your cheek, he gained insight into your mind. Unlike a Confounding Charm, a Mirage Hex digs deep into your emotions to conjure what you'll see. Was it his suggestion you look in here?" I nodded, my mouth too full of citrusy goodness to speak.

"That was likely when the Mirage Hex was put on you. Then when you and he," she fluttered her hand vaguely, "did what you said you did, not only was he getting a strong dose of power from you, but he was also sealing in the hex to twist your memory of what you'd just witnessed. He made you see something you were worried about, fearful of. You can't create an image out of thin air, but if Alastair and I were standing near to one another, he could have used that as a starting point."

"He read my mind?"

"The spell read your mind. It's not quite the same."

I suddenly felt like my brain needed a good cleaning with a stiff toilet brush.

"Were there other occurrences when you saw things that didn't accord with what should have been happening?"

"Well, not exactly seeing things. More like not seeing things."

I told them of the missing files and of the scent of Alastair on the drawers where those files should have been.

"Those were likely just Confounding Charms, perhaps placed on the room itself. They can work on sight and smell. They don't require as much strength as a Mirage Hex, but neither is the Confounding Charm a simple spell," Olivia said, as if pondering the Mauvais's tactics. "It shows just how much power he's gained."

"If he was already casting the BrainSweeping Charm on Tobey," said Mr. T, "the Mauvais could have also been using him as a spell carrier for the Confounding Charm."

"Carrier?" I asked.

"It's like the virus I told you about. I haven't heard it being used on an Untrained, but I suppose it's not impossible. You essentially infect a person with a spell, and it passes to another person. Being in close quarters like the file room would have helped. As does your already being a strong absorber. Another argument for—"

"I know, I know. Taming my magic."

"And taming that mistrust," Olivia added. "He may have already known you suspected Alastair, and if he was BrainSweeping Tobey, he would have known what files you were most keen to find. Infect Tobey or the room itself with a form of the Confounding Charm and that would have caused you to see what you expected to see. Or in this case, not see."

"But what would have been the point of all this trickery? If he wanted me to find him, why not make it as easy as possible?"

"I can't guess the Mauvais's thought processes, but I imagine it was to keep seeding doubts in your mind, to really strike at the heart of your power." As I'd learned, doubt makes a Magic less effective. Magic requires self-confidence, something I'd never been in good supply of. "The Mauvais knows if you trust Alastair, if you dare to care for Alastair, your magic will be indomitable."

"Love conquers all?"

"I suppose so, yes. I know it goes completely against your nature, but you need to find a way to trust Alastair, and to gain confidence in his feelings for you. And perhaps yours as well," Olivia added knowingly.

Trust and confidence. If magic was Popeye, those would be its cans of spinach.

My stomach twisted as my mind played over the scene of Alastair falling through the window. I had to get him back. And Tobey too. You know, for Mr. Tenpenny's sake. But this was all getting a bit gushy. A change of subject was in order.

"And my parents? What will happen with them?"

"They're very sick. As we feared, they have been extracted. Luckily, I've recently been pushing research on some new techniques that might help. I can't make any promises, but you did save them. The Mauvais is likely on the run and won't be foolish enough to return to that building. He abandoned them, which means they would have starved to death within a few days given how thin they are. The unsanctioned extraction aside, he deserves to be punished for keeping any person in the conditions they were."

"I'll gladly volunteer to be the first in line for that. I wouldn't be amiss to a bit of witch burning." Mr. T and Olivia passed distressed looks to each other. Maybe the community was still touchy about the whole send-them-back-to-the-fires-of-hell thing. "What? Too soon?"

"I think it's time you know a little more about who you are," Olivia said smoothly.

"Please don't tell me I have a magic uncle and six siblings to save, too."

She handed me a slip of rough paper.

"Read it."

21

CHAPTER TWO

PROPHECIES & PORTALS

The folded sheet bore the yellowing color of old parchment. Its edges were browned and unevenly trimmed.

I unfolded the note. At a glance, the script, arranged in six lines of text, was a form of calligraphy with chubby letters and fanciful capitals. The words, which had been written in dark purple ink rather than the traditional black, read:

Black bird ends the wicked dark.

Black bird ends the master of time.

Only the Black will have the heart.

Only the Black will bring the light.

When the Black bird reverses, it succeeds.

And the end of evil a Black bird will bring.

With every line, my gut churned like an off-balance washing machine. All those quickly hushed references to a prophecy. Of people mentioning something I was meant to do. They couldn't really believe this crap, right?

"What is this?"

"Banna wrote it."

I placed the paper on desk and pushed it back toward Olivia.

"Well, she sucks at poetry."

"She wrote it three hundred years ago," said Olivia. "It was her first."

I was about to comment that maybe she shouldn't have rushed to publish her first work, but Mr. Tenpenny was already saying, "Cassie, you don't understand."

But I did. I did understand and I did not want the knowledge. The past month had been a whirlwind of learning and of fear and of confused emotions. I did not need another layer added onto that. He must have seen the distress on my face because he stopped talking.

Olivia, however, kept right on explaining. "Banna has given a fair number of prophecies. Very few have been wrong."

"So what do you expect me to do now? Find Alastair, rescue Tobey, and then kill the Mauvais because of some stupid piece of paper?"

"Pretty much," Olivia said cheekily. "But not tonight. Alastair has your strength and we have the watch, so we have a little time." In response to my scolding look, she gave an apologetic half-grin for her accidental play on words.

"The best course of action will be to find where that portal led," said Mr. T. "We'll need Runa for that. I'll put in a call to her straight away."

For the first time since I'd stepped into her stone-walled, tapestry-lined office, Olivia lost some of her composure. Her cheeks darkened and her hands fidgeted. One might almost think she was flustered.

"Look," she said after clearing her throat, "I know this is a lot to take in, but we all need some rest, we need a plan, and we need to root out who within our ranks is helping the Mauvais. So, to your room, Cassie. Tomorrow we begin."

* * *

23

Despite any sleep I managed to get being plagued by dreams of getting sucked into a black hole that was actually the gaping mouth of Devin Kilbride, things felt oddly normal the following morning. A full English breakfast appeared on my table, Winston stopped by to beg some toast and sausage, and Nigel strolled around the grounds below, speaking to himself and probably reciting his usual historical inaccuracies.

But there was also an underlying sense of something being off. Even though the population of the Tower was only down by two residents, a new emptiness filled the place.

And if you ever tell anyone I missed Tobey Tenpenny, I will turn your fingernails into cockroaches. I'm not entirely sure I can do that, but have no doubt, I will try my hardest.

As soon as I'd finished all but the final bean, the tray of food popped into oblivion and a note on fine stationery took its place. I was to go down to Olivia's office as soon as possible. Could none of these meetings take place in my room?

I dressed, I tamed my hair, then I left my room to wind down numerous staircases and wander through endless hallways to reach Olivia's center of command. Already waiting were Busby, Rafi, and Banna. While the guys wore somber expressions, Banna held her head high. Big Audrey Hepburn sunglasses as dark as the black hole from my dreams covered her eyes and most of her cheeks.

"Have a seat, Cassie," said Olivia. I took the empty chair next to Rafi rather than the one next to Banna. I knew on some level that everything she had done during my test had been part of protocol, but I still couldn't forgive her for the viciousness of her testing methods. My skin still ached and itched at the memory of her vacuuming my magic out of me. Without realizing I had ever started, I told myself to stop scratching my forearm.

"We've a couple more that should have already arrived,"

Olivia continued, "but they can be caught up later. I think our first step is to sort out where the portal may have led to."

"Actually, I think the first step is for me to ask how my parents are doing. When can I see them?"

"Simon and Chloe are stable," Mr. T said with cautious warmth. Which meant they were stable, but showing no signs of improvement. "And when the others show up, they will be a big help in determining the long-term prognosis. We'll go see them as soon as we're done here."

From the hallway came heavy steps.

"That must be them," Rafi said in a tone that seemed far too amused for the situation. He watched Olivia, so my eyes also went to the dusky-skinned woman who could normally have had her picture in the dictionary next to the word "poised." But what I saw, and what was clearly entertaining Rafi, was Olivia pushing her braids over her shoulders, then bringing one cluster back to the front. She was also shifting in her chair, looking for all the world like someone had tossed itching powder into her tights.

"Mr. Olivia, sir," said Chester in his deep, yet surprisingly soft voice. Rafi shook his head — training Chester out of the habit of calling everyone *Mister* or *Sir* had been the bane of his elvish existence. "Runa Dunwiddle and Eugene Morelli are here. You said to let you know when they arrived."

"Yes, Chester. And if you could now step out of their way, they could indeed arrive," Rafi said gently while making a step-aside motion with his hands.

"Oh right, sorry."

Chester moved his bulk out of the doorway and in stepped my landlord, who looked relatively small in comparison to Chester's broad frame. Close on his heels came the Portland community's medical maven, pharmaceutical fancier, and Cassie curmudgeon: Dr. Runa Dunwiddle. She was dressed in, I'm not kidding, a black, A-line skirt and a pink blouse with a frill down the front. I struggled to recall having ever seen Runa out of her white lab coat. The image wouldn't come, but even so, I was pretty sure her usual attire was more jeans and t-shirt than flounces and frills. Even her glasses, which hovered just above her head, gleamed as if they'd been given a recent polish.

As Rafi thanked Chester, Olivia stammered out a greeting, to which Runa mumbled something about how convenient it was to have the international portal open again in Portland. The doctor then fussed with her skirt before she perched on the seat next to Banna while Morelli plunked down in the chair next to mine.

"Rent's due in—"

"I know," I said through gritted teeth, but when I glanced over at him, he was grinning.

"So, back to where we left off," said Olivia, who, now that she had an agenda to get to, seemed more her usual self. "Cassie, can you tell us anything about what you saw when Alastair and Tobey fell through the portal?"

"No, not really. I didn't even know there was a portal. I expected to find them all smashed to bits on the pavement below." Mr. T winced at that. "I tossed a stapler through, but didn't see a thing other than the stapler there one second and gone the next. Should I have been able to see inside it?"

I recalled traveling from Portland to London via Corrine Corrigan's delivery system portal. I'd hoped to catch a glimpse of Big Ben when it opened, but the only thing I'd seen was darkness.

"No, the fact you didn't see anything helps us narrow down what kind of portal it was. That's part of why we've brought in Dr. Dunwiddle. She's one of the Magics most knowledgeable in portal science. Runa," and here Olivia's voice cracked slightly, "could you explain?"

Runa's round cheeks turned the color of a cayenne pepper, but this didn't affect her ability to lecture. "Long-distance portals use a different dynamic than short-distance ones. If the Mauvais had traveled to another part of London, or within the U.K., you would have seen something even if it was fuzzy. But your being unable to see inside means he's crossed at least the Channel if not an ocean."

"Is there any way to figure out exactly where the portal went?" asked Banna.

"It's difficult, but not impossible. With some study of the portal records and various particle signatures, we might be able to figure it out."

"Particle signatures can be unreliable," Banna noted.

"And they'll only tell us where he went first," Rafi said. "Not where he went after that or where he currently is."

"I didn't even think about that," I blurted. "They could have traveled anywhere since last night. Merlin's balls, we're never going to find them."

Mr. Tenpenny made a noise almost as if he had indigestion.

"Thanks for that, Captain Compassion," said Morelli, nudging me with his meaty elbow.

"Nothing is impossible," Olivia said, bringing us back to order. "We can at least try to narrow down his starting point and perhaps extrapolate from there where he's headed. Now, the other reason we've brought in these two is for their medical expertise. Dr. Dunwiddle and Mr. Morelli can both work toward healing your parents. Chester's healing abilities have already done excellent work at getting the Starlings' electrolytes stable and slowing any further damage from malnutrition, but he can't keep it up without rest. Mr. Morelli can take over whenever Chester needs a break."

"Wait," I turned to Morelli, "you're going to be *here*? What about Mr. Wood?"

"Don't worry, I'm not staying. I'm only popping in occasionally as needed. With the Portland portal back open, we don't have to wait for Corrine's schedule." I recalled having to wait for Chester to open the door when we'd first arrived to the Tower. It seemed like a year ago. "And Wood is doing well. His cast will be removed any day now. The Norm doctors are scratching their heads over his bone-knitting capabilities," he added with a knowing grin.

I can't say Morelli was my favorite half-troll on the planet, but I did appreciate his dedication to helping and healing my boss. I hoped that would be a point in my favor when Mr. Wood had to choose between me and Daisy, who had usurped my job duties while I was busy taming my magic, fighting off evil, and well, misplacing people.

"As for you, Cassie. There's still the matter of you failing your test."

I couldn't help but groan. What with all the parent rescuing, wizard fighting, and people losing I'd nearly forgotten I was supposed to be extracted. My test with Banna the Hoover supposedly proved that I couldn't control my power and was therefore a threat to Magics everywhere. As such, the only solution anyone could come up with was to extract me. Personally, I didn't think that showed much creative problem solving on the part of HQ, but no one had asked my opinion. The extraction must be the third reason Runa was here, and why she was dressed so finely. Getting rid of me must be like Christmas, her birthday, and graduation day all rolled into one big celebration.

"More than one Magic has argued your case." Olivia glanced between Morelli and Busby. A pit formed in my gut at the thought of the third person who should have received her knowing look, the one other person who had spoken up for me:

Alastair. "But the matter has not been fully settled. However, under the circumstances, I have demanded a stay in the ruling. One, I think we are going to need your power in the coming days. Two, from what you reported last night, we can no longer deny that someone has been passing the Mauvais magic. If we extract you, I worry that power would be too easy to hand over to the Mauvais in one convenient package."

"I thought magic didn't work like that." I'd been told magic couldn't be kept in a Tupperware dish and passed on to another Magic.

"It doesn't work like you think," Runa said. "But from what I hear, you've seen yourself that magic can be transferred. You passed some to Alastair before you lost him." She shook her head in exasperation. "I still can't believe you lost two entire humans."

"She does exceed all expectations, doesn't she?" Morelli chimed in.

"Could we focus a little less on my failings and a little more on Olivia's very important speech? And I didn't exactly *give* Alastair my power; I filled the absorbing capsule he brought with him," I said, then realized I'd just proven Runa and Olivia's point. My extracted magic, handled properly, could be easily packaged into a heaping helping of yummy absorbing capsules and given as a treat to the Mauvais.

"For now, you will continue training," said Olivia. Not exactly what I wanted to hear, but far better than being extracted. "I know control is in there somewhere, so you need to take this seriously," she said with grave significance.

"More than seriously," Banna added. "Yes, there's the matter of your test, but you've also defied the rules and you lost two people with your foolishness. I think it's only fair to tell you a tribunal has taken up your case to evaluate not only your magic control issues, but also the threat your magic poses if the

Mauvais captures you. They will make their decision within the week."

I didn't need to ask what would happen if I lost my case.

"And, who knows, the tribunal may decide to test you again," Busby said with strained optimism. "Which is why you must focus on your training. In the meantime, no more skulking around trying to solve whatever mystery you've created for yourself. Train. Visit your parents. And stay within the Tower."

"Stay? I can't go home?"

When Morelli had mentioned the Portland-London portal being open again, of being able to go back and forth with ease, an urge to go home had hit me like a sucker punch to the solar plexus. I just wanted to check in on the world I'd left behind. I mean, what about Pablo? What about Daisy stealing my job? What about making sure Mr. Wood remembered his very dedicated employee still existed?

"We don't think it would be safe," said Mr. Tenpenny.

"But you think the traitor is someone in HQ. I'm not exactly safe here either, am I?"

"She does have a point," Banna said, looking up from the notes she'd been jotting.

"We'll evaluate your situation," Olivia said while passing a cool glance over Banna. "If you need to go home, you will go with Morelli or Chester or someone else who can provide protection. Now, I believe that's all we have to cover this morning. If you'd like to visit your parents, Dr. Dunwiddle and Mr. Morelli are headed that way."

CHAPTER THREE
MAGICAL ENZYMES

"Mister" Morelli fell into step with Runa, and as we climbed the stairs the two discussed various ideas on how to treat my parents. The others — Rafi, Olivia, Banna, and Mr. T — also came along with us, so I'm not entirely sure why we couldn't have just met in the White Tower's hospital ward in the first place.

Built way back around the year 1100, the White Tower might look like it only has a handful of floors to the magically-challenged observer, but once you get inside — assuming you're a Magic, of course — you discover an unknowable number of levels, corridors, and rooms, an open air tennis court on the roof, and even, on a lower level, a swimming pool I'd yet to try out.

"Chester told me they were doing a world better," Rafi said as we stepped out from the stairwell. His soothing scent of sandalwood was knocked aside by the hospital ward's powerful fragrance of cleaning solution and bleached laundry.

"Given the condition they were in," said Busby, "anything might be considered an improvement."

When we neared my parents' room, several Magics who I recognized from the night before were standing around magnanimously hemming and hawing over what could be done. At the sight of Runa and Morelli, their murmurs — which I'd bet you anything were little more than boastful speculations — went silent. The group stepped aside, moving out of the room's threshold while making excuses of places they needed to be, spells they needed to cast, and the like.

What I saw when they cleared the way, well, it wasn't what anyone would call a miracle, but after the state my parents had been when I'd last seen them, it was surprising enough to make me stop in my tracks.

My mom sat in a plush chair that had been placed between her bed and the window. She wore a short-sleeved, pale blue top. The neckline gaped, not because it had been designed that way, but because my mom's shoulders were so thin a clothes hanger would have given the shirt more shape. Her arms and chest showed fresh bruises from her struggles with the medics the night before, but most of the discoloration was the purplish-yellow of fading bruises. Fury flared in me over the Mauvais's vicious treatment of his pets. When I glanced to Mr. T, his jaw showed the same tension I felt tearing through mine.

But that's not what had left me dumbstruck. Rather than the screaming, poo-flinging chimp she had been, Chloe Starling was now calm and clean. Her dark brown hair had been brushed back from her face and tied into a ponytail that made her look young despite the disturbingly dark circles hanging under her eyes. She wasn't doing anything, just sitting and staring into space and quietly, distractedly humming the same tune I'd heard coming from her when I found her.

The nurse attending my parents was a husky white guy with shaggy black hair. When he glanced up to see who'd come in, I barely had time to notice one of his eyes was blue and the other brown before he quickly returned his attention to the task at hand: trying to get my dad to eat something that looked like it might have come out of a dirty diaper. Wisely enough, Dad —

who was resting in his hospital bed — kept dipping his head away from the spoon every time it came near him. This saved him from eating the *poo du jour,* but meant he had a thin layer of the stuff on his cheeks and forehead.

"How are they doing, Jake?" Olivia asked after introducing us.

"As you can see, his reflexes are pretty sharp, but other than that there's been no change since Chester did his work last night," Jake said, surprising my ears with his Canadian accent.

As Olivia had mentioned, my parents had been extracted by the Mauvais. An extraction, in case you've forgotten, not only leaves you with no magic, but also wipes out large portions of the regions of your brain that allow you to do amazing things like speak, think in a logical manner, and feed yourself.

"Chester's work," the nurse explained to Runa and Morelli, "and the nutrient boost we gave them does mean they're now able to hold themselves upright. There's also enough of them in there somewhere that they signal when they need to use the loo, for which I am immensely grateful, but they don't seem to have much more cognitive function beyond that. There's no speech capabilities. They do little more than mumble a word that sounds like *white* or *wipe,* maybe *whine.* We still can't tell if it's indeed a word or just us hoping it's a word. They also enjoy humming that tune," he said, indicating my mother.

"And their magic?" Runa asked.

"None really. Or at least no accessible power. But our tests have shown there's still some residual cellular magic."

Again, a little refresher in Magic biology, every living creature has magic deep within its cells, but only Magics — and a few very clever animal species — can tap into that magic. We call that *accessible* magic.

"It's better than nothing," Runa said, mostly to herself. "If the cells had been completely wiped, there'd be nothing we could do. If the inaccessible magic is still there, we might be able to coax it back to being accessible. Chester can work on healing their bodies, but a transfusion of magic is the only thing that's going to kick start their cells and get their minds to heal."

"You really think a transfusion will work?" I asked Runa, cruel sarcasm adding an accusatory, waspish tone to my words. Mr. Tenpenny touched my arm and told me to hush, but I shook him off. "Sorry, but you weren't here last night. You haven't—" I bit off my words, knowing what wanted to spill out next wouldn't help anyone.

One of the first things that was attempted after we got my parents back to the Tower was to call in other Magics, including the ones you just saw loitering around. It had been hoped that they could transfuse some of their own magic to Simon and Chloe. It wasn't done in the belief that the Starlings would suddenly pop back into magical self-awareness. It was done because if they had magic, accessible magic, to tap into, they would heal faster. Normally, intact Magics will avoid extracted Magics as if they were highly contagious medieval lepers. But my parents were heroes of a sort to the magic community, which meant in this case, volunteers were easy to find.

And so, like some Midwest revival, there was a lot of laying on of hands, and for a few moments my mom did have a spark of life in her eyes. Those eyes met mine and I don't know if it was just wishful thinking, but I swear there was that brief slackening of the face and widening of the eyes a person gets when they recognize someone.

But just as fast as it appeared, it was gone. Turns out my parents were like magical sieves. You could pour magic in, but it flowed right back out the holes that had been poked into them.

"Are you really in any position to question me?" Runa said, a bit snippily, but not harshly. "Normal transfusion techniques can't be used on Magics who have been extracted. However, there is an old technique I've been researching that might do the trick. It fell out of use, but I think it's our best chance. *If* you would cooperate."

"Me?" And then I recalled her telling me something about magic transfusions sticking better between relatives. At the time, I didn't think I had any relatives, so the information rolled right out of my brain as useless.

"And him," she said, pointing to Rafi.

"Wait, am I related to Rafi?"

"Yes, he's your long-lost brother. You can see the resemblance," Morelli said sarcastically. Although Rafi and I did both have black hair and we were both tall and slim, that's where the similarities ended. Rafi had rich, warm-toned skin, whereas the covering over my bones was more the color of bleached flour. And Rafi's trim frame moved like a cat trained in ballet, whereas mine bumbled about like a buffalo hoping for a spot on the roller derby team.

"Rafi, maybe you could explain," drawled Mr. Tenpenny. "I don't think I can handle this clever banter much longer."

"Certain elves, like yours truly, can serve as magic conduits."

"More like magic enzymes," Runa clarified. "If your magic is sent through Rafi and into your parents, it's carried more efficiently and should bind better than just sticking it into them directly. Your being a close relative increases our odds greatly. There's no guarantees, though. No offense, but your parents are a bit leaky. Now, if you'd like to be useful for once..." She trailed off and pointed to her patients.

Since Jake had just resumed his attempts at feeding my dad, and since my mom was still calm, we decided to start with her. Rafi placed one hand gently on her bony shoulder and used his other hand to hold mine. His skin was as warm as its coloring

35

and I hoped my mom found his touch soothing on her bruised and battered body.

At a signal from Runa, I concentrated on giving my magic. Since I'm an over-the-top absorber, giving isn't the easiest thing in the world for me, but it helped to picture my last moments with Alastair, when I fought my own doubts and threw him enough magic to fill the absorbing capsule, turning it from red to purple. The mistrust, the accusations, the utter hatred for him I felt when I first saw him with the Mauvais popped into my mind as well, but I tried my best to visualize the full capsule glowing violet from within.

"That's enough," someone said. I can't tell you who. The voice sounded very far away. My hand instantly went cold as Rafi let go.

And then the pain rushed in. A burning, itching pain like I'd just shoved my hand into a cluster of poison oak into which someone had tossed broken glass.

"Here's the ice," came a smooth, posh accent that sounded like something straight out of a Masterpiece Theatre program. Busby grabbed my wrist and plunged my hand into a bath of ice water. It didn't stop the pain, but it did slow it down.

"Did it work?" I grunted.

Morelli was leaning over my mom and sniffing her. Which sounds like a bizarre thing to do to someone, but all Magics carry a signature scent that varies by who's doing the smelling. If my magic made it into my mom, she should smell like me. Over time, I later learned, once the magic in her cells got its motor running, my scent would fade and hers would take over.

"Faint. Hardly any," he said, standing up straight again.

"Cassie was pushing hard," Rafi said. "Even her memories were coursing through me. Do you really think Alastair was helping the Mauvais? That he was betraying you?"

Morelli shot me a strange look. Surprise? Disgust? Nah, that's how he always looked when dealing with me. Or maybe that was just how his face was arranged.

"Not now, Rafi," Banna snapped, the ozone tang of her magic suddenly stinging my nostrils. Rafi made a motion of zipping up his lips. "Dr. Dunwiddle, do you really think this is going to work? There is a reason why it fell out of use."

I watched my dad. There was no sign he had any idea what was being said, but his eyes were lolling back and forth between us as if watching a tennis match. At least it proved there was something in there.

"It'll take time for us to build up their ability to retain magic," Runa said, her voice brusque, annoyed. Believe me, after stirring up Dr. D's annoyance on many occasions, I recognized the tone. "Before their final extraction, the Mauvais could have drained them several times, forcing their power to recharge in between sessions. Their cells have been overused and need to rebuild their ability to hold onto magic. But, yes, I do think with several more applications it could work."

"But that will exhaust Cassie," said Mr. T.

"I'm willing to eat all the cake in London if it will keep me able to donate. But isn't there any way to speed it up?" I asked, my hand starting to go numb from the ice bath.

"The watch," Busby said, then handed me a towel. I dried my hand, then wrapped the towel around it to warm the poor appendage.

"Well, go get it then. Use it on them. Get them better." I'd never admit it, but I was desperate to see that look of recognition again in my mom's eyes.

Mr. Tenpenny shook his head regretfully.

"Not like that. It's not the watch's presence that would heal them, but its absence."

"I'm not in the mood for riddles, Mr. T."

"They've really had too much stimulation," said Jake. He'd wiped my dad's face clean and Pops had fallen into a quiet slumber in which I hoped for his sake he was dreaming of eating a large pepperoni pizza. My mom was still in her chair, but her chin now rested on her chest. The nurse was slipping a neck pillow over her shoulders and shifting her head into a more comfortable sleeping position.

We took the hint and left the ward, leaving Runa and Jake behind to tend to their patients.

CHAPTER FOUR

D SPELLS

Since my room was located only one floor down from the hospital ward, the moment we left my parents, I seized the chance to avoid a trek all the way back to Olivia's office.

"Meeting in my room?"

To my surprise, everyone agreed to my suggestion. Everyone except Rafi, who claimed he had to make sure Chester remembered he was supposed to help the cleaning pixies take care of a gang of rats who were trying to establish territory in the White Tower's pantry.

As we reached the door of my room, a chime came from Morelli's back pocket. He reached for his left butt cheek and pulled out his phone. Why does everyone's phone but mine work in this place?

"Look guys, I gotta go. Wood's about done with his PT and he'll need a ride. Can't believe I gotta be seen driving a Prius."

"Monster truck more to your taste?" I asked.

"A monster truck for a half-troll. Good one," he chuckled. "Nah, what I'd really like is a Tesla. State of the art. All electric. It's the way of the future."

"So profound of you."

I opened the door to my room and let the others in, but Morelli still lingered in the hallway.

"I thought you had to go."

"Look, Black, we need to talk. That thing Rafi said about you and Alastair. You need to know some things."

"If I had known Rafi was going to read my mind and blurt out what he found—"

"Ah hell." Morelli had his hand on his right butt cheek, and cursing when you're in that position means you've either messed your pants or your wallet has been stolen. Or that you've just discovered a pouch in your back pocket, which Morelli apparently had. He held it out to me. "Look, can you take this to Runa? I collected a few things she asked for and forgot to give them to her."

"Why wouldn't she just get the things herself?"

"Some things require going to special sources." He jutted the wallet closer to me. "Go on. Nothing in there will kill you. Not quickly, anyway."

I warily took the packet. It was a trifold leather pouch, slightly larger than your average-sized romance novel and held shut with a leather thong that wrapped around a button on the front flap.

"What's in here?"

"Just stuff."

"What? Is there eye of newt in here or something?" I was only teasing, but Morelli's lips tightened and I caught a whiff of his magic's gingery scent. "Black market eye of newt?" I teased.

"There's also frog saliva, bat claw, and chameleon skin, so leave off about the eye of newt. It's an overrated ingredient anyway, more for flavoring than anything." His phone chimed again. "I really gotta go. We're talking later, Black."

"Looking forward to it."

As Morelli jogged down the hall, I entered my room and set the pouch on the suitcase rack in the recessed closet alcove located just past the entryway. The bed was indeed unmade, but thankfully, I didn't see any hint of dirty underwear. I also didn't see any hint of Banna and wondered where she'd disappeared to.

"Okay, so the watch," I said as I plopped down on the edge of my bed and pulled my legs up to sit cross-legged. "By its absence, do you mean destroying it?"

"In a manner of speaking, but—" Mr. T started to say.

"I don't think there's any room for buts here," Olivia said, cutting Mr. Tenpenny off and making me smirk since there were clearly three butts in the room.

"But," I said, drawing out the word to get the conversation rolling, "if we destroy the watch, we destroy him, right?" Olivia nodded. "Then we just figure out where the portal led to, jump in, and get Alastair and Tobey. If we do it right now, we can have them back by lunchtime."

Yeah, I don't know what breed of optimistic fairy invaded my brain, but to be fair I had been under a lot of strain over the past forty-eight hours, so I suppose a little personality lapse shouldn't have been a surprise.

"Cassie," said Busby, "please understand I'm in as much of a hurry to get Tobey out of the Mauvais's clutches as I believe deep down you are to get Alastair, but it's not that simple."

"Of course it's not. It never is with you people." Forgetting I wasn't sitting in a chair, I slumped back, teetered a moment with my legs kicking out for counterbalance, then righted myself. I know, I really am the Queen of Cool, aren't I?

"This is very complex magic we're talking about," said Olivia. "But we're fairly certain destroying the watch's essence would also destroy the essence of — that is, the magic within — the Mauvais. It would be like an instant extraction. You know of the plan Alastair developed, and of the three-strand problem we now face?"

I did. When Alastair built the watch, he put his magic into it to get the motor running, so to speak. When the Mauvais took possession of the timepiece, he also put his magic into it. These two strands wound together, binding in a way that meant they were nearly one. Nearly, but not quite. Alastair's idea had been to unwind his strand of magic from that of the Mauvais's. But before he could do so, the watch ended up in my coat closet, my magic got swirled into the mix, and our three strands made a braid that would only become more tightly bound if anyone tried to force them apart.

"But even braids can be undone if the ends are loosened." I said.

Mr. Tenpenny grimaced in that way people do when having to deliver bad news. "Matters have been further complicated."

"I don't understand."

But on some level, I did. From the very beginning, from the moment I pedaled away from Corrigan's Courier with the fateful package that contained the watch, I'd messed up any chance of easily destroying the damn thing. Then, when I pulled the watch's magic into me, that attempt to solve one problem only created another: my unmanageable magic levels. And in my most recent smackdown with the Mauvais, I'd hurled a hunk of magic back into the watch, turning the strands into a tangled clump. As was a habit of mine, I'd turned a small mess into a toxic waste dump by reacting hastily out of anger, frustration, and stubbornness.

"We have the matter of Alastair's, Devin's, and your magic coming together in the watch," said Mr. Tenpenny. "But we also have the issue that during your *interaction* with Alastair after your first test—" *shoop shoop* "—you would have exchanged some magic. That means some of your magic, which is also the watch's magic, which is also the Mauvais's magic is in Alastair."

42

THE UNTANGLED CASSIE BLACK

I didn't have the heart to confess I'd also given Alastair doses of my magic without his knowing it when I'd notice him flagging during our lessons.

"So you're saying if we destroy the watch, we might take down the Mauvais, but we'd also risk hurting Alastair? Extract him, if not kill him." I paused as the full consequences crept into my notoriously thick skull. "And me as well."

"Precisely," Olivia said. "And in much the same way, extracting you would remove your magic from the watch, leaving us back to the more easily solved two-strand situation. But I don't like the idea of leaving large packets of your magic lying around for anyone to take to the Mauvais." Oh, okay, so she had no problem turning me into a mindless imbecile? "Which is why, for now, I'm advising we set aside any gambles with the watch and go after the Mauvais directly."

"Even though you have no idea where he is," I said.

"There is that minor problem, yes. However, regardless of what happens with the Mauvais, at some point, the watch must be disarmed. If it continues to function, those who would use it to their advantage will continue to seek it out. You are responsible for the end of evil according to the prophecy and we assume that must mean destroying both the watch and the Mauvais."

I wasn't against getting rid of the watch, but the prophecy struck me as a load of whatever Jake had been trying to feed my dad. I didn't say anything, but I'm sure my disbelieving eye roll spoke volumes.

"Which is why," Olivia continued, "if we cannot find Devin Kilbride, you may be asked to assist willingly with the watch's destruction. And if you don't—"

"This was not discussed last night," Mr. Tenpenny protested.

"But she has to. Don't you see? Extracting her allows us to

destroy the watch. And destroying the watch will destroy the Mauvais. Problem solved."

"But it also risks destroying Alastair," said Mr. T.

"Um, and me as well," I said, seeing the need to remind them I was still there and in no mood to have my brain turned into mush just yet. "So, can we keep 'destroy watch' a little lower on the list of things to do? And what do you mean 'problem solved' if we destroy the Mauvais?"

"Olivia, I don't think we should—"

"Mr. T, my life has been torn to shreds by this man. I think I deserve to hear what I want to know."

"You have a bad track record of running amok with information once you have it," Mr. T said matter-of-factly.

"As if not having the information has ever stopped me."

Mr. Tenpenny shrugged. "True." He took a deep breath, then continued. "'Problem solved' refers to the reversal of D-spells once a person dies."

"D-spells?" I didn't know magic had bra sizes.

"There are three kinds of spells: destructive, constructive, and neutral. Known as D, C, and N," Olivia explained.

Busby cut in. "You worked at a funeral home." Wait a minute. *Worked?* As in past tense? Did Busby know something I didn't? "You've seen how, for the most part, mourners hold fond memories of the deceased. Even bad memories can be made light of unless the person was truly awful." I nodded in agreement. "Magic is like that, but only to an extent. The last several destructive spells a Magic has cast are reversed when that person dies."

"By destructive spells, you mean killing someone with magic?"

"Killing," he said, "or extracting. Which means his death would cancel out your parents' extraction. It's the easiest solution to return them to normal, but it's also the hardest as we have no idea where he's disappeared to." He shook his head, his face tight with annoyance and self-recrimination. "To think we had him right at our fingertips in Rosaria. We just have to hope your parents are still in range for the reversal to work."

"In range?"

"The rules allow the last thirteen of a Magic's destructive spells to be reversed," Olivia answered, the Rs rolling along with her underlying hint of a Scottish accent. "If fourteen or more are conjured, only the thirteen most recent spells, the ones *in range*, get undone. We refer to any spells older than those thirteen as being out of range."

"But my parents could already be out of range. I mean, how can we know how many spells he's cast since extracting them? And just how destructive is destructive?"

"Destructive means vastly affecting someone's life, or property if the damage is extensive enough. Magically breaking a teapot isn't considered destructive, but setting someone's home on fire is. D-spell magic is also called D.E.A.D. Magic. An abbreviation for death, extraction, annihilation, and damage." Olivia counted the words off on her fingers. "For example, his shifting to become Vivian was used for bad purposes, but it wasn't directly destructive. However, when he killed Busby, that was definitely destructive."

"Olivia, can you check the database of spells to get the exact number?"

"I checked last night," Olivia said. "He's done eight D-spells since his last Extraction Hex, so the Starlings are well within range."

"Wait, there's a magic database?" I asked.

"No, a database of magic. It sounds like a computer program, but it's actually just a large book. Whenever a negative spell is cast, it gets registered."

"By magic?" I said, imagining the book writing itself, not unlike a certain diary in a certain series that I am careful to never mention around Mr. Tenpenny.

"No, by the gnomes," said Olivia. "They sense negativity, which also adds to their usefulness as spies. When they sense D.E.A.D. Magic, they add it to the database under the person's name. Anyway, from what they noted, they sensed only one extraction performed by the Mauvais, which confirms that Chloe and Simon must have been in pretty bad shape if they could both be extracted with only one spell."

"Can they sense where a spell is performed?" I asked, hoping if the Mauvais, wherever he was, got up to some D-spell mischief, the gnomes could track him down.

"No," stomped Olivia's steel-toed boot on my hopeful thoughts. "The gnomes sense the nature of the spell, who performs it, but not who it's done to or where it's done."

"So," I said, pushing aside my irritation with all gnomes, "destroying the watch…tempting, but too risky. Are we agreed?" I breathed a sigh of relief that they both nodded their heads. "And if we destroy the Mauvais, that will reverse his Extraction Hex on my parents."

"Do not seek out the Mauvais, Cassie," Mr. T commanded flatly.

"I said 'we.' And," I said with sudden realization, "if we do knock him off, that would also mean you'd come back to life. Properly back, not just walking dead back."

"That would be nice. But this assumes we can stop him before he casts another six destructive spells."

I suspected Mr. T had the Mauvais murdering Tobey in mind when he said that, so I put on my very dusty cheerleader hat.

"The Mauvais's in hiding, right? He's not about to do anything that would draw attention to himself."

Mr. Tenpenny's weak smile showed a hint of relief.

"But there's still the issue of not knowing where he is," Olivia reminded us, just to make sure we didn't get too optimistic.

CHAPTER FIVE

BAD COMPANY

Most of the rest of that day was spent in a loop of Rafi and me trying to transfuse magic into my parents, me having my hand plunged into an ice bath, then spending an hour or so recuperating with hot tea and a magic-restoring pile of pastries, cakes, cookies, or other sugary treats from the ovens of Fortnum & Mason.

Everyone seemed hopeful that we were doing exactly the right thing. But the cycles of transfusions were exhausting me, and there were several times I had to bite back my grumpy comments that we didn't seem to be achieving a damn thing. By the time the Tower closed to tourists for the day, my parents still couldn't feed themselves, still couldn't speak, and still couldn't recognize me from a hole in the wall.

Once Runa had decided they'd had enough, she had me fill a couple dozen absorbing capsules that could then be steadily administered to them over the course of the evening. Exhausted and craving a five-pound bag of sugar, I headed to my room. I did want to get outside after being cooped up indoors all day, but flopping on the bed sounded far better than trudging down half a dozen stairwells to get to the lower level.

Actually, what sounded even better was dinner. Which happened to appear on my table the moment I stepped into the room. After a day full of junk food, the enormous green salad and steaming plate of gnocchi topped with fire-roasted tomato sauce sent my mouth watering. And I certainly wasn't going to complain about the large glass of red wine that accompanied it.

The food re-energized me, but the wine meant a nice bit of lounging in bed still sounded like the best course of action. Or, rather, inaction. Once good and flopped, I reached under the bed to dig out my borrowed copy of *The Principles of Physics and Magic* I'd fallen asleep with a few days previous. Something tried to spark in my soggy mind as I re-read the section on the Light Capture Charm. I even reined in a few stray photons to make a study light, hoping the exercise would stir the embers in my brain.

The Light Capture Charm works by pulling in photons. Quantum theory says all particles are entangled, meaning Photon A has a matching Photon B buddy somewhere out there in the universe. Most quantum physicists believe that whatever action happens to one particle happens equally to the other. But there's also the rogue few scientists who think the opposite action happens to the second particle. But no matter what, anything done to Particle A ends up breaking its entanglement with Particle B.

Regardless of how interesting I would normally have found all this, my concentration that night was about as hard to locate as the correct phone charger in a cluttered junk drawer.

In my distracted state, I ended up reading the same page about what might be happening to my photons' entangled friends at least five times. The only thing that would stick in my head was that I might be causing a sort of photon divorce, so I closed the book, shoved it under my pillow for later reading, and gave in to the undeniable tug to visit the hospital ward.

My dad was asleep, and my mom was once again in her chair,

looking like an emaciated doll. I wanted to see some spark of magic in her eyes, but there was nothing there. No recognition, no registering of the bustling activity around her, and no tune humming. I don't even recall her blinking.

When Runa came in and saw me sitting with them, she ordered her glasses back into the breast pocket of her lab coat. Apparently, this was done so she could fix a scathing look on me without anything getting in the way. Her hands went to her hips, elbows jutting out. Never a good sign.

"You can't be in here. Not without Rafi."

"Why? I thought it was good for catatonics to have company."

"Not your kind of company. We need Rafi for his conductivity, but elves of his sort also provide a sort of buffer to absorbing. It's going to be hard enough to get any magic to stick to them without you sitting there sucking it all back up. Unless, that is, you've suddenly gained control over that little problem." She placed a hand on my shoulder and instantly jerked it away. "Nope, you haven't."

Dr. D pointed to the main ward. I sighed, got up and, reluctantly conceding, loped my way out.

"I am improving," I said over my shoulder to Runa, who was following close behind.

"I'm glad to hear it, but you're still a danger to my patients."

"So, I can't see them at all?"

Why exactly should it matter to me? I hadn't seen these people in over twenty years. I had no conscious memory of them. There was no reason I should feel like something was being pulled from the roots of my hair at the thought of finally being so close to them, while also being unable to go anywhere near them.

At my slightly (okay, very) mopey question, Runa changed to a more gentle tone that, in all honesty, was more awkward and more difficult to accept than her usual gruff, berating one. "I know it's hard, but it's for the best. And you did good, girl. Going and getting them like that. Not many would. Or did," she added critically.

"Why didn't they? I mean, it only took me a few days to figure out where my parents were, and that was in addition to taking classes, being tested, and befriending a dead Beefeater," I said irritably.

Ever since finding out they might be alive, it had irked me to no end that no one had actively sought out my parents. Just as they hadn't scrambled to uncover Busby's murderer or to do a simple background check on Vivian. Magics certainly weren't crime-solving go-getters. If I ran the magical zoo, the first change would be making the police investigators a bit more proactive.

"Maybe you're more talented than you give yourself credit for." When I said nothing to this half-compliment, she continued. "I know it's a lame reason, but I think it was easier for many in the community to assume your parents were dead. Keep in mind, the rumors that they might be alive only recently began circulating. They'd probably have acted on those rumors more readily if not for the watch hunt and the Mauvais popping back into action. You can't really blame Oliv—" Runa's cheeks flushed redder than a cinnamon candy as she bit back the name. "That is, you can't blame HQ for making priorities."

"What's with you and Olivia?" I teased. "You two act like goofy teenagers around each other."

"And you think you're any better around Alastair?"

"At least I don't flip my hair around and risk bursting into flames from the heat in my cheeks." Runa laughed. More of a scoffing laugh than a you-should-become-a-comedian laugh. "What?"

"Yes, you do."

"Well, I certainly don't go around in frilly pink tops," I said, glancing down at the rosy frills exploding from the opening of Runa's lab coat.

Before Dr. D could reply, a storm of activity crashed into the hospital area like a rogue wave. Doors slammed open, Magics called out orders, someone shouted for a stretcher, while someone else ordered anyone within earshot to find a troll.

Runa and I traded uneasy looks. Then, as if reaching a silent consensus, we both dashed after a pair of magic medics who'd started a race down the stairs with a stretcher hovering along behind them.

CHAPTER SIX
UNEXPECTED RETURNS

"In there, now!" Rafi was pacing near the stairwell, his magic's sandalwood scent streaming off of him as he ushered the stretcher down the hall. His hair was dripping wet and he wore no shirt, but he did have a towel wrapped around his slim waist. "Get to the armory," he ordered the two medics. "We'll levitate the stretcher back up. Just get in there."

"What the hell happened?" Runa asked. I could only imagine a magical practice session having gone wrong — not that I'd know anything about that.

The medics whipped open the door to the armory and I immediately covered my nose. A stench like someone had smoked a cigar made of sewage hit me, but the others ignored it and rushed in.

"He— I don't exactly know," Rafi stammered as we rushed by the row of life-sized wooden horses where Chester joined us in our haste. "I'd just come out of the pool and Chester— Chester, you tell them."

Chester, sporting a tweed jacket over, oddly enough, a Mickey Mouse t-shirt, wore a confused expression. "I came and got you."

"No, tell them *why* you came and got me."

"Oh, that. I was in here and heard a crackling noise. My nose hairs tickled like when there's an electrical storm on the way. I rushed over to the noise. I was worried one of the cleaning pixies had jammed his finger into a light socket. They do that, you know. But no one was here. Then all the sudden he was here, and that's when I got Rafi."

"He's alive," called out one of the medics, "but he's not moving."

"Who?" I demanded, no easy feat given how much I wanted to keep the room's strange smell out of my mouth.

"Tobey Tenpenny," Rafi said.

I stumbled over my own feet. Tobey? He wasn't dead? Surprisingly, that filled me with a sense of relief. You know, for Mr. T's sake. Not because I was in any way concerned for the likes of Tobey Tenpenny. But if Tobey was back—

"Alastair?" I asked, my voice barely above a whisper.

Rafi shook his head. "Not when I left, but maybe by now."

Runa, unexpectedly fit for her stout appearance, wasn't showing any sign of exertion as we hurried along the collection of weaponry and the oddly placed wooden execution block. We rounded a display of swords and my heart plunged down into Olivia's office. Or possibly up. One could never tell in the White Tower.

I should never have let Rafi's optimism influence me. Pessimism. Cynicism. It's the only way to go.

Through the pair of medics and the first-aid team, I caught a glimpse of a single body. Not the lithe frame of Alastair Zeller, but the broad build of Tobey Tenpenny. And despite the medics tugging him to shift him onto the stretcher, he wasn't reacting.

"Did he—?" I started to ask, but the door to the armory banged against the wall as Mr. Tenpenny rushed in.

"Dear heavens. Tobey!" He started to run forward, but Dr. Dunwiddle blocked him. "Let me by, Runa."

She remained firm, her no-nonsense stare working better

than a Binding Spell. "He's alive and in good hands. Let them do their work and you can see him in the ward soon enough."

Chester squatted down next to Tobey and was gently patting his hands over Tobey's body. Trolls, even half-trolls, despite their clunky appearance, have the ability to heal physical wounds. Chester himself had fixed my hand after the Mauvais crushed it to bits; and as he mentioned, Morelli was currently moving Mr. Wood's healing process along at a slightly accelerated pace.

I was just wondering if Norms couldn't be repaired as quickly as Magics, or if Morelli was taking a slow approach to avoid suspicion, when Chester's hands paused over Tobey's ribs. After a moment, Chester nodded and stood. The two medics from the hospital ward then lifted the stretcher — magically of course, why use muscles when you've got magic?

"We'll get this up to the ward," said one of them, a woman with high cheekbones and straight, so-blonde-it-was-white hair. "Outside protocol, now. Someone will be there to receive the patient?" she asked, looking around. Runa said there would be.

It was twilight out. The tourists were gone, but wouldn't the resident Yeoman Warders and their families be awestruck by a floating stretcher, let alone an occupied one? I didn't have a chance to ask the medics, but I'm sure they had training for that sort of thing. Unless of course, placing BrainSweeping Charms on the Tower's inhabitants was common practice.

The question must have been written across my face because Rafi explained, "They use a Concealing Charm to blur the stretcher from view."

"I should go assist," Dr. Dunwiddle said. "In the meantime, seal this area off. I'll need to come back and inspect it to see if I can detect any sign of the portal Tobey was sent through." Then, with a forced smile straining her lips, she told Busby, "I've no doubt Tobey will be up and eager for visitors within the hour."

CHAPTER SEVEN

DEMANDS & ANNES

Let me just be clear, Runa's chipper tone did not instill confidence in me or in Mr. Tenpenny. Before I could ask if Mr. T wanted to grab some tea, or perhaps an entire cake, Chester bumbled up to us.

"His ribs?" Rafi asked.

"He has all of them. Humans have thirty-nine, right?"

"Twenty-four, I believe," said Rafi. Mr. T now looked painfully worried.

"Ah well, I'm sure he has all of those."

"But were any of those ribs broken?" demanded Busby. "Was he injured?"

"No, a few bruises and knocked out, but he's all in one piece. Inside and out." Busby's shoulders drained of tension.

"Then what were you doing?" asked Rafi. "Your hands, his ribs. Were you practicing the xylophone?"

"Just checking. I—" Chester abruptly cut himself off and smacked his palm to his forehead so hard I expected to see a dent in his brow.

"I was supposed to give you a note." He pulled a slip of paper from his shirt cuff. "Should I give it to Mr. Olivia?"

Rafi's face tensed. He looked to Mr. Tenpenny, who was eyeing Chester warily.

"No, hand it over. We'll take care of it. Good work, Chester."

"Thanks, Mr. Rafi." Chester made his goodbyes, and once he'd left, Rafi glanced between me and Mr. T.

"Read it. What are you waiting for?" I said.

"Someone's become demanding," Rafi said churlishly as he unfolded the note. He then read:

> *To HQ, I'm returning this pointless pile of flesh—*

"Bit rude that," Rafi commented. I suppose it might seem so, but clearly Rafi hadn't spent much time with Tobey.

"Rafi, please," Mr. Tenpenny pleaded. "This is most unusual. Where did Chester get this note from? I don't like that he said he was *supposed* to give it to us. But I would like to hear what it contains. Without commentary," he added.

Rafi began again:

> *I'm returning this pointless piece of flesh in a show of good faith. In exchange, I ask you to hand over Cassie Black. I know you can barely stand her, but to me she's quite valuable.*
>
> *I want her. You don't. It should be a simple deal, but I'm sure you'll find some excuse to make it difficult.*
>
> *So, to help you in your decision making, as a sort of catalyst, shall we say, I will bring destruction on one major city every second day until you hand her over. You have two days before the first tower tumbles.*
>
> *—Yours truly, Devin Kilbride*

"Tower? Does he mean *the* Tower?" I asked.

"No, he wouldn't strike HQ without getting possession of you first. But this is concerning," said Mr. Tenpenny.

"Understatement of the century," Rafi said, exactly what I'd been thinking. Despite Morelli's sarcasm, I wondered if we might not have been separated at birth.

"Enough with the jokes," Mr. T said irritably. "Were you not listening to what Olivia and I just told you? The death of the Mauvais will only take back thirteen D-spells. And here we have him stating quite clearly he intends to perform D.E.A.D. Magic. And to likely perform it more than once. If he makes good on this threat, if he performs more than just a few destructive spells, it pushes Simon and Chloe out of range."

"And it's also concerning because you don't want to hand me over to him?" I prodded questioningly.

"Yes, of course," he said, a bit too dismissively for my comfort level. "Look, I need to take this to Olivia. At least it will occupy me until I can check in on Tobey."

"If he's physically well, I'm sure he'll be back on his feet soon," said Rafi. "It's lucky for him he's a Norm. Makes him useless to the Mauvais."

"Have either of you forgotten Tobey isn't the only missing person?" I pointed to the note. "Is there any hint in there about Alastair?"

Rafi shook his head and my heart felt like it had been freeze-dried then pulverized into dust, leaving behind a hollow space in my chest.

Mr. T took the note from Rafi and strode wordlessly from the room. Rafi arched an eyebrow at me.

"So you decided you do care about him, despite what I saw in your head?"

"I'm still uncertain, but that doesn't mean I want the Mauvais tormenting him."

"But why would the Mauvais torment someone who's supposedly on his side?" Rafi teased.

"Don't annoy me with your logic, or I'll conjure another unicorn and sic it on you."

"Fair enough." He glanced down at himself. "I suppose I can't run around like this all day. I best get dressed." Leaving him to it, I headed toward the armory's entry. I'd barely gone three steps before Rafi called after me, "Still, I think you like him deep down in that icy little heart of yours."

I flung a Spark Spell at him, but he was already racing away, clutching his towel as he ran.

* * *

The next morning, I woke with my mind swimming in a list of chores that needed tackled: tame my magic, save Alastair, save the world, have breakfast.

Since eating was a task I could complete without any trouble, and since the waffles topped with strawberries that appeared while I was getting dressed sent my stomach growling with anticipation, I decided breakfast was the day's first order of business. Once I'd eaten all but a small crumb of waffle, I headed down to wander the grounds of the Tower of London just as the tourists started marching through the entry gates.

Less than a minute after stepping outside, my phone pinged its incoming messages. The first few were from Mr. Wood. While I was thrilled to see his leg had already been freed of its cast, I was not thrilled to read about Daisy taking readily to her job duties. A quick learner, hard worker, and unable to accidentally wake the dead? How soon would it be before I received a text from Mr. Wood telling me to find a new job? Then again, by next week I might be brain-drained and wouldn't have to worry about unemployment. Or anything, for that matter. Look at me finding the bright side of things!

I sent Mr. Wood a quick note reminding him not to push his recovery too quickly, to pay attention to his physical therapist, and not to eat too much bacon. All advice I was sure would be ignored. I didn't comment on the Daisy situation.

The next texts were from Lola. One expressing in all caps and plenty of celebratory emojis her utter joy over me finding my parents. The next was in all lowercase letters with an array of frowny-face and storm cloud emojis over the loss of Alastair and Tobey. Seeing it written out cast a new layer of angst over me.

But, before I could get too morose, I scrolled down to see Pablo with the caption: *I could use a vacation.* Somehow, Lola had wrangled him into a Carmen Miranda-style fruit hat and a grass skirt. He was sitting next to a margarita (a catnip margarita? I wondered) and the background was something straight out of a tropical islands wall calendar.

I texted back that it looked like he already was on vacation. I didn't have the heart to respond to her other two texts.

I strode away to get out of the shadow of the White Tower and into the morning sunshine — yes, London does have sunshine…occasionally. I'd just gotten my phone back into my pocket when Winston swooped down to the ground to hop alongside me.

This sort of behavior would normally have sent tourists flocking so they could prove to their Facebook friends that Tower ravens were perfectly tame. But Winston was a ghost raven. In my nervous chatter on the way to fetch my parents, I'd asked Mr. T about him. Apparently, the bird is visible only to the dead such as Busby and Nigel, a select few of the Yeomen Warders, and yours truly. It would be interesting to learn why that is. Maybe I could add it to my lesson plans. You know, as soon as I figured out how to thwart an evil wizard and avoid getting extracted.

Not long after Winston showed up, a chill tickled along my arms just before Nigel appeared beside me. Winston immediately crouched down and, with a burst from his spindly bird legs and a single flap of his sleek wings, leapt to perch on Nigel's shoulder. Since Nigel was also not visible to the Norm observer, I got out my phone and put it to my ear so I wouldn't look like I was talking to myself.

"Is it true?" Nigel asked, bouncing on the balls of his feet with glee. "Did you find them?"

I momentarily wondered who Nigel heard his gossip from. The gnomes? Other Magics? Ghostly intuition? I then chided myself. He'd been friends with my mom when she'd come to London to hunt down the Mauvais. I should have told him the news about my parents straight away.

"I did. They're not doing very well, but maybe Runa will let you in to see them."

"Oh, that would be delightful. Do you think she'll recognize me?"

"Nigel, I don't think she recognizes herself right now. She's been through a lot," I said, my throat catching on the final words.

"Well, I'm sure she will recover nicely. And you, I hear you got in a bit of a scrape."

"That's putting it mildly. I lost two people."

"But one's back now. That's good." I gave him a sidelong look. "Isn't it?"

"When we're talking about people, a fifty percent reduction in how many are still lost isn't seen as a real improvement."

"No, when you put it that way, I suppose not. But," he continued, his voice changing from empathy to tour guide positivity, "speaking of missing people, did you know Anne Frank hid here during World War II?"

"She didn't," I corrected as Winston shook his gleaming black head.

"Anne of Cleves?"

"Not alive in World War II."

"I *knew* she died in World War I."

And so began another history lesson with Nigel. To be fair, he had gotten quite solid in his facts from 1066's Battle of Hastings up to the Battle of Bosworth Field. I mean, not every detail, only those related to the Tower. After all, I was an armchair traveler, not an English historian. Getting him through Henry VIII's wives, though, was proving tricky.

"Just remember," I said after I related yet again the marital exploits of our Henry. "Divorced, beheaded, died. Divorced, beheaded, survived."

"Got it. So did Anne Boleyn's head grow back?"

"What? No."

"Then how was she beheaded twice?"

Before I could explain the Annes were two different people, and that the beheadings were actually a Catherine and an Anne (which I feared would only send me down a rabbit hole of explanation about Henry's triple dose of wives with the name Catherine), Chester came trudging our way. A happy grin stretched across his broad face.

"Mr. Cassie, I'm to tell you..." He trailed off and looked to the sky as if searching for the message in the wispy clouds. Winston clacked his beak, snapping Chester's memory to attention. "That Sir Tobey woke up."

"That was fast," I said, my heart racing with joy at the news. Again, not because I liked Tobey Tenpenny, only because he might have information about the Mauvais's location.

"Told you he was alright. I gotta find Mr. Tenpenny and tell him. Although I think Mr. Tobey already knows he's awake, so I don't know why I need to tell him."

"No, they probably mean Busby Tenpenny," I said. Between him and Nigel, I wondered if there was something in the London water that reduced IQs. "Look, I'll tell him, okay?"

"Sounds good. I could use a sandwich, anyway," Chester said with a shrug, then strolled off toward the Tower's cafe.

I told Nigel I'd catch up with him later and headed back inside. Since Olivia's office was only a few zigzagging corridors away from the White Tower's door for Magics, I began my hunt for Busby there. I told myself I was being logical, but the lack of stair climbing probably had more to do with the decision. My thigh muscles sent up a cry of joy when my ears picked up the sound of Mr. T's smooth voice coming from Olivia's office.

I was about to walk straight in when I caught what they were talking about.

Or rather, who.

CHAPTER EIGHT
KISSING COUSINS

"She did show remarkable bravery going in after them like that," said Mr. Tenpenny.

"She showed remarkable stupidity and look where that has led. Alastair gone, the Mauvais with a boost to his power, your Tobey lying in a hospital bed. And now some vague threat if we don't hand her over."

"But she did get her parents, and she still has the watch," said a soft voice with an Irish accent.

With the sunny day outside, the hallway was brighter than it had been when I'd witnessed — or thought I'd witnessed — Olivia kissing Alastair, but the corridor was still castle-dim. The interior of the office, however, was even darker than the hallway and lit only by the glowing, icy blue light of a Solas Charm.

"The watch," Olivia scoffed. Her heels were making a sharp *click-click-click* as she paced across the stone floor. "You mean the watch that should have been destroyed ages ago?"

"Olivia," said Mr. Tenpenny in the tone of someone begging for reason, "what's done is done. Or rather, not done. We can't go back and disarm the watch before Cassie's magic mixed into it. To do so now, it's far too risky."

"But will the tribunal think that, especially when they get

wind of this demand he's made? Banna, you're a part of it. What's the mood in there? Who else is on the tribunal's panel?"

Both my jaw and shoulder muscles tensed at the news that Banna was part of the very group who would decide my fate. The woman had never given any indication she didn't like me, but despite her warm, melodic voice, there was an unyielding aspect to her. She would not let emotions, hers or others, sway her opinion.

"You know I can't tell you that, but I'm afraid the mood is grim. They see Cassie Black's magic as a dangerous thing. Like letting a dragon loose in a barn full of hay. I can tell you this new threat won't help matters. I'm afraid unless something drastic happens, they will vote for extraction, and likely sooner than the seven days."

"They have to see it's a good thing the Starlings are back," Mr. Tenpenny insisted. "Surely that's a point in her favor."

"Breaking the rules, acting without any true forethought. These are what the tribunal will bring up."

"Then why even save the Starlings?" Olivia said curtly. She had stopped her pacing when Banna spoke, but now the *click-clacking* started up again. "Why didn't we just leave them in that building? What's the point of bringing them here? Their minds are completely gone."

"You can't punish her for trying," said Busby calmly but assertively. "We used to reward selfless Magics who would rush in to save someone without thinking of their own risk."

"Selfless?" Banna asked critically. "Do you not think she wasn't thinking of herself or her own wishes when she went after them? Did she stop to think of the danger this would bring to us all? Don't get me wrong, it was indeed a brave thing. I'm only repeating what will be said in the tribunal so you can mount your arguments." After a pause, she added, "If they allow any."

"If they allow any?" blurted Busby. "Of course they must allow arguments. They can't judge a Magic without allowing other Magics to testify on her behalf. It's precedent."

I made a note to myself to buy Mr. T a pint or two later that day.

"This is an unprecedented case, you have to admit that, Busby Tenpenny."

"There has to be some way to give her time," argued Olivia. Okay, I might have to buy her a drink too. "Or at least lessen the sentence. A draining, perhaps?"

Well, maybe not a full pint.

"I think we know the only way to save her is to do away with the Mauvais," said Mr. T. "We have this note. Maybe we can trace something in it. Allow me a team, Olivia. Put me back on the force."

Olivia made a sound as if about to speak, but Banna cut her off. "You know that can't be allowed."

"Then what other option do we have?" said Olivia, a hint of fire in her words.

"We must consider destroying the watch. That's the only way to destroy him. The tribunal has discussed it and we would be more than willing to take care of the timepiece."

"That risks killing Alastair and Cassie," Busby said flatly.

"There are risks," replied Banna, "but only a few people will be hurt. If we don't act, hundreds, thousands of people could die. And of course, Cassie Black need not be hurt. If we extract her first, her magic will no longer be bound up in the watch and she won't be harmed by anything we do to the thing. That then brings us back to Alastair Zeller's original two-strand concept of neutralizing the watch."

"But the prophecy," said Olivia. "If we take her magic, if we damage her mind, she won't be able to fulfill the prophecy. She

THE UNTANGLED CASSIE BLACK

could be the one to rid us of the Mauvais forever. Without her, even if we knock him down a notch, he may rise again. We need her to fully put an end to him."

"With her magic intact we're at more risk than ever." When no one replied to this, Banna continued, "Besides, from what you've told me, she doesn't even believe the prophecy is real, or that it doesn't apply to her, just like every other rule we've created. And it may not be that simple. We may not have time to wait for her to fulfill the prophecy."

"What do you mean?" asked Mr. T.

"If someone in the community is helping the Mauvais, the longer we keep the connection alive between Devin Kilbride and Cassie Black, the longer this person has to boost his power with that connection."

"Who is it? Has the tribunal any theories?"

"That I cannot say."

"I believe," said Mr. T, "possibly more strongly than anyone here, that the Starlings deserve a chance at recovery after what they've been through. And I'm aware it's a concerning situation with tough calls to make, but I will *not,*" Mr. T pounded his fist on the desk a single time for emphasis, "risk Alastair. Not after everything he's done. And I don't think it is in any way fair to extract Cassie for magic strength she didn't ask for. Would a few extra days, even an extra week, make any difference? Think about it, the Mauvais wants Cassie's power. If we extract her, we may never figure out who is helping him."

"You mean to use her as bait?" Olivia asked.

"Not exactly how I'd put it, but I suppose so."

"Fair point," said Banna, in a tone that made it clear she thought he was being ridiculous. "But keep a tight rein on that girl. She's too precocious by far."

"Precocious," said Olivia with a weary chuckle. Her leather

chair creaked as she finally took a seat. "Yes, that's one word for it."

"Lurking in hallways again?" Rafi whispered, scaring me so much I had to slap a hand over my mouth to keep from screaming.

"Do not do that," I hissed. He was dressed in a black t-shirt and black slacks. He must have been swimming again that morning since a hint of chlorine competed with the scent of his magic.

"Last time you lurked outside Olivia's office things got a little weird between you and a certain Tenpenny. You think you'd learn."

"Unicorns," I warned, and Rafi put up his hands in defense.

"Shall we? There's news to tell." Before I could respond or react, Rafi linked his arm with mine and dragged me into the office. "Guess who's awake."

Mr. T's face beamed brightly enough to replace the bulb at the Cape Meares lighthouse on the Oregon Coast. He practically tripped over his chair in his haste to get up. He jerked to a stop at the door, offered an apology to Olivia for his rudeness, and gave a little bow of his head when she waved him off.

Even behind her bug-eyed sunglasses, I could feel Banna watching me. Ignoring her despite the chill at my neck, I hurried after Rafi and Busby, who can be surprisingly quick for a dead guy.

* * *

Runa, now with lavender frills peeking out from her lab coat, bustled up to us the moment we stepped into the hospital wing. As we followed her back to one of the last beds in the nearly empty ward, she spoke in a hushed tone, making every effort to put up a roadblock to the traffic jam of questions trying to spill out of Mr. T's mouth.

"He's gone back to sleep, but he was awake and seemed coherent," Runa whispered once we reached Tobey's bed. "He's a little dazed, but that's to be expected."

Tobey's curtained-off cubby included a broad window that looked out over the exact same expanse of the Tower's grounds that could be seen from my room. And, I recalled, from Alastair's. On a side table next to the window stood a bouquet of bright white daisies. But what held my attention was the box of Moonstruck chocolates next to the flowers.

"Did he say where he'd been? Is there any clue as to where the Mauvais has gone?" As Mr. Tenpenny rattled out these questions, I stepped over and, while pretending to look out the window, slipped a truffle (okay, three truffles) out of the box.

"All he could say was it was rather dark and seemed to be underground because there were no windows."

"He said that much? That's a good sign, isn't it?"

"A very good sign," said Runa.

Seeing Mr. Tenpenny acting so non-British with his enthusiastic feelings of hope, love, and optimism was charming, but it was also plunging a hot knife of envy into my gut. Would anyone ever care about me like that? Would I ever have a family who gushed with heartfelt joy over me waking up for five minutes?

To hide the sting in my eyes, I popped a rum-infused chocolate into my mouth and scanned the charts attached to the foot of Tobey's bed. It detailed his reason for checking in (concussion and magical exposure), his vitals (normal), his current treatment (rest, and Chester as needed), and of course, his name: Tobey R. Tenpenny.

"What's the R stand for?" I asked through a mouthful of swoon-worthy chocolate. I expected something steadfastly posh like Reginald or Remington, but I hoped for something tease-worthy like Ranunculus or Rumpelstiltskin.

But Mr. T dashed my hopes and expectations when he answered, "Raven."

"Raven?"

"Yes, it's a family name. His father's name was Raven Tenpenny. I'm Busby Raven Tenpenny. Every branch of our family tree has a bird perched in it."

"Like Starling?" Rafi asked significantly.

"Yes, of course," replied Mr. Tenpenny, as if Rafi were a brainless dolt. "You know very well the name Starling goes back far longer than most names, even Raven."

"Wait, wait, wait," I said, mental gears smoking with how fast they were turning. "Are you saying we're related?" I pointed between me and Tobey and Mr. Tenpenny.

"Yes, of course," Busby said.

"And you didn't think to tell me?"

"It— I suppose it never crossed my mind. Or maybe I just assumed you knew. I mean, except for how thin you are, you and Tobey look quite similar. The height, the eye color, and the dark hair are common traits in our line."

"So Tobey and I are—?" I asked, fuzzy on the details of how family trees branched.

"Cousins of a sort. Your mother's mother was my sister."

"That's why you were so flummoxed when you heard Tobey had kissed Cassie," Rafi cried out, half laughing.

"I did not kiss her," said a faint voice from the bed.

CHAPTER NINE
LUNCH IN THE BUBBLE

It was true. Tobey didn't kiss me and I didn't kiss him. Even though we had. As Olivia had theorized, the Mauvais had likely morphed, sucked a bit of magic from me during an intimate moment I would very much like to forget, while also worming his way into my head to make me think Alastair had been groping Olivia. Magic is so complicated. And icky, now that I think about it.

Everyone thrilled over Tobey being awake and being able to speak, and this quickly wore him out before I could grill him about what had happened to Alastair, where the portal had led to, or where they'd been since going through. When it finally got to the point that Tobey was doing little more than snoring and mumbling in his sleep, Runa ordered us to leave, reminded me to come back later in the day to fill up some more absorbing capsules, then told Mr. Tenpenny she'd find him if anything changed. As we headed toward the hallway, the sound of my mother's tune caught my ears. Only this time, it was my dad doing the humming.

"Cassie, I think we need to talk," said Olivia.

And believe me, no good conversation ever started with those words.

"Now?"

"Unless you have plans."

Rafi, seeing his chance to escape another meeting, said he needed to get back to his office to make sure Chester had his schedule in order for the afternoon. I gave him a withering look as he practically skipped down the hall away from us.

"Your place or mine?"

"It's a nice day. How about we go outside? We can order up some lunch." The woman knew how to bribe me, that's for sure. "I need to first check all is in place in the armory, though."

As Mr. T, Olivia, and I trudged down the stairs to the armory, Olivia informed us the Yeoman Warders were demanding we buy them a pint for each complaint they were having to deal with over the armory being 'closed for renovations' twice in one month.

The armory looked the same as we'd left it. The rows of horses stood at attention — one still missing a small piece of ear thanks to an earlier magical mishap of mine. The execution block still stuck out like the ugliest of sore thumbs. And the cases full of swords and suits of armor still delighted any eye that loved shiny objects.

The one difference was the area where Tobey had been found. It had been roped off and four gnomes had been placed at the corners. I say *placed*, but for their sake, I do hope they were allowed to waddle in and get into position of their own free will. It must be annoying to be a gnome and having to endure humans lifting you up and sticking you in whatever dirt patch they pleased.

"New decor?" I asked.

"They're surveillance gnomes," said Mr. T. Or should I be calling him 'Uncle' Tenpenny now?

"Yes, I know that, but I don't think the Mauvais is going to keep using that spot to send us messages."

"Some days I do forget how little you know," said Mr. T in an exasperated tone, as if I was supposed to feel guilty for not absorbing every single fact of magic knowledge and culture over the past month. "Percival, Pinafore, Pinchot, and Petunia are highly sensitive and might be able to sense where the temporary portal that opened here came from."

"Another temporary portal?" I said. "Are they common?"

"They are. Often, in a time of high alert, we restrict main portals such as we did with the international one in Portland. This requires smaller, temporary portals to take up most of the slack. Temporary portals are also put in place when main portals have to be shut down for repair. The other common use for them is transport for a special occasion, such as a festival or sporting event."

Oh, if you knew how hard I was biting my tongue to keep from spewing, "Like a quidditch tournament?" you would wonder what kind of wondrously strong material my tongue was made of.

"And because they're typically built in a hurry without proper precautions being taken, these temporary portals often leave a trace of their source. Which is what these four are hoping to detect," said Olivia, casting a strange look over me as I kept my lips clenched firmly shut. "All looks in order here. Lunch, then?"

I nodded and we headed back toward where we came in.

"At least you got that stink out," I said, recalling the cabbage-cigar stench that had lingered in the air earlier.

"Stink?" Olivia asked.

"Don't tell me you didn't smell it? It was like the sewer had backed up."

"And you say you smelled it when we found Tobey?"

"Yeah, why?"

"It's something to consider," she said with dismissive finality, as if her very tone would cut off my questions. It didn't, but her tight expression, plus Mr. Tenpenny nudging me and shaking his head with a warning look in his eyes, kept me from pressing the matter any further.

Outside, there was only a hint of high clouds in the sky and the temperature was as close to perfect as you can get. And Olivia knew how to make the most of it. Once we reached a grassy spot, she snapped her fingers and a sort of bubble formed around us. It did nothing to block out the perfection of the day, but it did block out the chatter of tourists who, without realizing their feet were taking them instinctively around it, skirted around our enclosure.

"Patio Charm," she explained. "One of Rafi's inventions."

Another snap of her fingers conjured a plate of sandwiches along with a round bistro table to eat at and cushioned chairs to sit on. Included with the variety of sandwiches were cut fruit, cookies, potato chips, and mugs of ale. I wasn't about to complain about a little midday drinking.

Olivia took a few bites of an egg salad and watercress on wheat, then brushed the crumbs off her fingers.

"Busby, I think it would be best for you to explain."

"I'm not fully sure I grasp the concept, but I'll do my best." I guzzled half my beer. I figured I'd need it with the heavy way they were speaking. "The watch, I believe I told you Alastair had an idea of how it could be deactivated, but your coming along complicated things."

"Right," I said warily through my mouthful of ciabatta, basil, tomato, and mozzarella.

"The idea was that his magic and Devin's magic were both in the watch. Two strands. Two strands wound together aren't strong and can be teased apart if you're careful. Your magic coming in added a third strand, making a braid. Braids are incredibly strong, which is why the watch could no longer be easily put out of commission." I already knew this and didn't understand where Mr. T was headed. A cookie seemed a good way to cover up my consternation. "But if one of the Magics whose strand is in there dies, you are left with only two strands once more."

The cookie suddenly tasted of cardboard. Were they going to kill me?

"What are you saying?"

"The thing is," said Olivia, "the Mauvais sent back Tobey but not Alastair. That's concerning since Alastair is of no more use to Devin Kilbride than Tobey would have been."

"That's not true. Alastair has magic. The Mauvais could take his power for his own purposes, just like he did with my parents."

"Exactly," said Olivia, then paused, letting the significance of her statement settle in. When, after a few moments, I didn't suddenly say I knew precisely what she meant, she continued. "We believe Alastair has been extracted, if not killed. The Mauvais would have taken his power, then discarded him."

An image of an empty peanut shell being tossed onto the floor of a honky-tonk bar popped into my head.

"You thought the exact same thing about my parents."

"But Devin has a history with Alastair. In his mind, Alastair betrayed him. The Mauvais never took disloyalty lightly. He will have wanted his revenge for a long time."

"What does this have to do with the watch?"

"With Alastair gone, the three-strand problem is solved. We believe the remaining two strands — yours and Devin's — could now be unwound. If you pull your magic from the watch, we could then destroy the thing and destroy Devin Kilbride. The D.E.A.D. Magic reversal would then take place. It would prevent the destruction he's promised, as well as return Simon and Chloe to health."

"And reverse any destructive spells performed on Alastair. That could be the reversal mentioned in the prophecy," Mr. Tenpenny said, as if suddenly realizing just how great this whole idea really was.

"But you don't know if Alastair's dead," I said. "If he's not, messing with the watch, as you only just told me, risks killing him. Plus, if I try to pull my magic from the watch and Alastair is still alive, my magic could still be braided with the others. Not to sound un-heroic, but you're asking me to sacrifice myself on a pretty big supposition."

"We don't think it would work like that. You're such a strong absorber, we believe you could pull the majority of your magic out. You might be safe."

"Believe. Think. Might. This is all guesswork."

"Guesswork that could keep everyone safe. And all signs point to Alastair having been killed. He wasn't sent back. There's no mention of him in the note. Surely, the Mauvais would have used Alastair as a bargaining chip in this game he's playing if he still had that chip in his possession."

"Maybe Alastair escaped."

"He would have come straight here."

I was fuming. I was so angry even the food in front of me wasn't appealing. And given my appetite, that's saying something. Although I still carried lingering doubts about Alastair, I had mostly convinced myself he might not have been working with the Mauvais or passing him my power on the sly. Still, there also remained the Everest-sized mountain of questions I had about his role in my going missing as a child.

However, these questions weren't stopping Team Heart from taking the lead over Team Brain when it came to the matter of

Let's Risk Alastair's Life on a Bit of Guesswork. I mean, if anyone was going to kill the man who had possibly been my kidnapper, it was going to be me.

Kidding.

Sort of.

Regardless, the thought of him dead at the Mauvais's hand was too surreal to process. It was a concept that, even drawn out in a schematic, wouldn't make sense. Sort of like assembly instructions for IKEA furniture. But Busby and Olivia seemed more than ready to accept that Alastair had already breathed his last and we should just take a magic hammer to the watch to see what happened.

"When were you planning on running this little experiment?" I asked testily.

"We haven't gotten that far with the discussion yet," replied Olivia, "but with your tribunal underway, I think it's a good idea to try sooner rather than later. This is in your own best interest. Because as it stands, things are not looking good for you."

"So I've already been convicted."

"Believe me, Cassie," said Mr. T, "this is a far more direct solution than trying to figure out where the portal led and—"

Just then, the walls of our bubble began vibrating, creating a high-pitched whine that had me clamping my hands over my ears.

"Someone needs us," said Olivia, more annoyed than concerned by the prospect. She gave a flicking twist of her wrist. The food and tables disappeared. As did the chairs. Knowing what was going to happen, Busby and Olivia had stood. But they hadn't bothered to warn me. As such, I dropped butt first to the grassy ground.

I was about to curse at Olivia, but running toward the bubble was the nurse who'd been trying to feed my dad. Mr. Tenpenny's face turned a deathly shade of grey. I mean, he was dead, but he rarely revealed his little handicap. Now, he looked every bit the zombie he was.

"Something's happened with Tobey," he muttered to himself as the walls of the bubble vanished.

CHAPTER TEN
SEND HIM THROUGH

Do I need to mention again how sick I was of stairs by this point? If I'm crippled with arthritis in my knees when I'm old, I will blame it entirely on my time spent in the White Tower. Olivia, Banna, and I abandoned our unpleasant conversation and followed Jake to rush along the hard-tile hallways and up the stony stairwells. Again.

"What's happened, Jake?" Olivia asked.

"He's woken up again. More alert this time."

From ahead of me, I heard Busby suck in a quick breath of air, then release it in a great gust of relief.

In the ward, I felt a tug as I hurried past the side room where my parents were, but I pushed my desire to see them aside as Runa's warnings came to mind. Still, how many doses would they have to get before I could spend time with them? Would I have to keep a permanent distance even if they did recover? I set a goal then and there to pay closer attention to my studies, to work more diligently at getting my magic under control.

I told myself this resolution was for them, but somewhere inside, Team Heart was cheering that if I survived this with my mental faculties intact, controlling my magic would also allow me more time with Alastair. Unless, of course, Olivia and her HQ cronies killed him off first. I could also hope if this tribunal group saw me taking my training more seriously, they might reconsider extracting me. I know, who am I kidding?

Tobey had been propped up in the bed and did look more lively than before. I mean, he still looked like he'd only just stirred to life after hitting the snooze button several times, but he had more of an appearance that a brush of the hair and a cup of coffee might almost snap him back to rights.

Mr. Tenpenny stopped himself, then glanced toward Runa. She gave a single nod, and Mr. Tenpenny, Mr. Stiff Upper Lip himself, surged toward Tobey, leaned over the bed, and wrapped his grandson in an awkward hug.

"I thought we'd lost you," said Mr. T, his voice husky with his fight to tame those pesky emotions humans are prone to.

"I thought I'd lost me too," Tobey said, chuckling in that way people will do when trying to play it cool while having an internal meltdown.

"Let's try not to overwhelm him," Runa insisted as she glanced at Olivia, who had been staring fondly at Dr. D and quickly looked away. I smirked until Runa threw me a warning glower.

Mr. Tenpenny stood up, straightened his jacket, and squared his shoulders as if shaking off the display we were all never supposed to mention to anyone. Ever.

"Can you recall what happened?" Olivia asked. "Anything about where you were?"

"It was dark except for a really bright light at one point," said Tobey hesitantly. "And then there was the other light."

"It was dark except for all the lights?" I asked. "Are we sure he's mentally all there?"

"I see you're still as charming as ever. I meant there weren't any windows. It was dark, but there was one room down from where I'd been kept. It had a bright light in it. Maybe a workroom, I'd guess. The place, I don't know, there were wood beam supports and a hard-packed dirt floor, like an underground storeroom or an unfinished basement. Sorry, he wasn't exactly handing out floor maps."

"And he let you go? Did he hurt you?" Mr. T asked.

"A few punches, nothing much, until— I don't know, he started going on about getting rid of me, that I was pointless. No comments from you, Cassie. I think if it weren't for Alastair, I'd be dead. Sorry, Cass, I guess I was wrong about him."

"Alastair's alive?" I said, adding as much emphasis as possible to the question as I shot a glance between a very sheepish looking Mr. Tenpenny and Olivia.

"Yeah, he convinced the Mauvais I wasn't entirely useless. That you guys might pay more attention to demands attached to a living body than a dead one. The Mauvais kind of scoffed at that, but grudgingly agreed that Alastair had a point."

"And what's he doing with Alastair?" Runa asked.

Tobey shrugged. "Kind of just being a dick to him. Sorry." Tobey darted a look to Olivia, but she waved off his potty mouth. "Chastising him, belittling him, that sort of thing."

"Keeping his magic down," Mr. T said. "If he breaks Alastair's confidence, makes him feel like he's got no hope, Alastair won't be able to access anything but his weakest magic. He'll be unable to defend himself or escape."

"The capsule," I interrupted. "Did Alastair use the capsule yet?"

The still-doubting part of Team Brain chimed in that Alastair probably gave the absorbing capsule to the Mauvais. I told Team Brain to piss off.

Tobey shrugged. "I'm not sure what happened to it. There was talk of using it to get me back. I know the Mauvais didn't want to waste his power sending me. I don't think he's all that strong. I mean, he is, but in short bursts, then he has to build up."

"That would coincide with our theory," Busby said. "Without the watch he doesn't have his own strength. Or not much of it. He must get hits of magic from whoever's passing it to him."

"Right now he's likely parsing out the magic Cassie gave him when she was fighting him," Olivia said, and I recalled how pleased the Mauvais had looked when I'd thrown spell after spell at him, how little he did to defend himself, and how Alastair had begged for me to stop.

"Could be," Tobey said. "The Mauvais told Alastair if he wanted me sent back to you alive, he'd have to do it himself. I can't exactly go through portals on my own, you know." Tobey was a Norm, a person without magic, and needed a Magic to get him through portals. "So Alastair's idea was to give me the capsule to send me through. I don't remember much about how I got back, but it had to be the capsule. Cassie's magic brought me through, right? Otherwise how'd I get here?"

My shoulders slumped at this speculation. The capsule had been everyone's hope that Alastair would remain stronger than the Mauvais. Now the Mauvais had my magic, but Alastair didn't.

"And what about when you did come back?" Olivia asked. "Did you see anything? Anyone?"

"I don't know. That's when there was the bright light. I'm not sure if it was before I left, during the trip, or after. It almost seems like all three. I remember the brightness and a couple dark patches. Then, once it was fully dark, there was this rhythmic thumping coming from the ground, sort of like a bass beat. Sorry, that's pretty vague."

"It's an interesting observation," said Olivia, as if it totally wasn't. "It's just good you're back in one piece."

"But now Alastair, who seems to be very much alive," I said

pointedly as I looked between Busby and Olivia, "is on his own against the Mauvais without the capsule."

"I think he's also pulling magic from Alastair," Tobey said. "I mean, you guys always say he's a strong magic, but Alastair seems weakened around him."

"He could indeed be doing just that," Runa said, "which means Alastair will only be of use to him for so long."

"We've got to find the portal," I insisted.

"Or take our chances and destroy the watch," said Olivia. "I know it's a harsh call, but Alastair may not live much longer anyway."

"No," said Tobey in a sterner voice than I'd ever heard from him. "Alastair saved me. He deserves the same chance."

"No watch smashing," I said, arching an eyebrow at Olivia. "Agreed?"

"Agreed," she replied. "For now."

"But what about handing Cassie over to him?" asked Runa, who would probably have been the first to tie a bow on me and send me gift-wrapped to anyone who'd take me.

"We're not doing that either," I said.

"So you're willing to let cities be destroyed?" Olivia asked.

"If he gets his hands on me, the world will be under his power, right?" Olivia gave a half nod. "So, like I said, ignore the watch, find the portal, and let's get him."

"Wait," said Mr. T, "did the note say anything about how we're to hand over Cassie?"

"Again, that is not a topic up for discussion."

"No, I mean how would we get you to him if we don't know where he is? Tobey, did he mention this?"

Tobey shook his head. "He just said he would know when you decided, that Cassie would be brought to him the moment you were ready to give her up."

"Someone in HQ," I said. "If there's a traitor here, I'd bet whoever it is has a direct line to him. Like Tobey says, the minute you decide to hand me over, the Mauvais will know."

Which, I'm going to say flat out, was not a comforting thought.

CHAPTER ELEVEN
SANDS THROUGH THE HOURGLASS

I spent the rest of the day studying and practicing with an apprehensive Rafi. But after swearing I wouldn't think of unicorns (which then was all I could think about), we fell into one of my best practice sessions during which the membrane flowed readily from my fingertips and I even (mostly) fought off his whip-crack fast Binding Spell.

It made me wonder if I shouldn't have beer more often before training.

In my room that night, full of determination, I tried a Solas Charm. This is meant to generate a ball of light. Pure light that should match the color of the conjurer's eyes and give off no heat. But with my supercharged magic powers turning even the most innocent spell into a potential weapon, my orbs had a few thermodynamic issues and they often reflected the color of my mood rather than the color of my eyes.

Still, I'd had a good day of practice. So, hoping my control issues were nearly behind me, I focused on a good memory — that flickering moment of recognition from my mom — and said the word for the Solas Charm.

In the next instant, a hazel-green ball hovered at eye level about six feet from me. From where I stood, I couldn't detect any warmth, but I wanted to be sure. I stepped closer to what looked like a near-perfect Solas orb. My movement shifted the light closer to the window.

And promptly caught my curtains on fire.

Luckily, my electric kettle had enough water in it to douse the flames before any alarms went off.

The pride in my firefighting skills fizzled out just as quickly as my curtains when I thought of Alastair. The Solas Charm, while it did take a lot of concentration when you were first learning it, wasn't a spell that required a great deal of magical energy. The orbs the charm generated contained traces and could be used to signal your location to others when you were in trouble. But Alastair wasn't sending us that signal. Maybe he really was dead. Maybe once Tobey had been sent away, Devin Kilbride decided to go it alone.

No. I refused to accept that. The Mauvais would have sent his body back just to taunt us.

But what was the Mauvais doing to Alastair to make him too weak to get in touch with us? Then again, you did need to wrap your head around a few happy thoughts to make an orb, and with the way I'd treated him before he fell out of the world, I doubt Alastair had many happy thoughts readily at hand.

* * *

The next morning my breakfast was accompanied by another note. I suppose given the unreliability of my phone in any magic locale, it was the most reliable way to send me messages.

Since the Magics never hesitated to bang on my door at any time of night or day to bring me important news — or news they deemed important — I figured the note couldn't contain anything urgent. I set it aside, deciding that satisfying my hunger took priority.

Winston showed up just as I cut into my slice of bacon, and he had no qualms about devouring half of it, along with an entire triangle of toast and the full portion of blood sausage. Sorry, black pudding. Which does not make it sound any more appetizing.

Once his favorites were gone, Winston hopped on the note and began tearing at it. I really needed to talk to someone about a ghost bird's ability to interact so destructively with objects in the physical world. But before that, I needed to yank my letter from said bird. An act that earned me a nip on the forearm from his very sharp beak.

"No more treats for you if you keep that up, mister."

I opened the note. It would seem my brief stint at deciding my own schedule was over. I was to meet Banna in the practice room downstairs. And, thanks to my delay, I was already ten minutes late. I shoveled the rest of the eggs into my mouth, then jogged down the stairs for class time.

I wasn't looking forward to this lesson. Besides the fact that Banna loved to push me to control my magic and to find its limitations, as I now knew from my eavesdropping, she was one member of this mysterious tribunal. Any screw up would be reported to them and used against me. And, to be honest, sometimes her teaching sessions seemed utterly pointless.

I rushed into the practice room, stumbling over a throw rug just to prove haste and dim lighting do not mix. My nose prickled at the electrical scent of Banna's magic. Then, as my eyes adjusted to the darkened room lit only by the chilly gleam of her Solas Charm, Banna announced I'd be demonstrating my control by shifting the sands of an hourglass from the lower portion to the upper portion.

See? Pointless.

Her usual sunglasses were off, revealing her glacially blue eyes that matched the color of her orb. Eyes that showed she wasn't the least bit amused when I walked over and turned the hourglass over.

"What? Problem solved." I'm sure any professor of logic would have applauded my approach to the problem.

"This is meant to challenge you. Now, move the grains without touching the hourglass or," she added, "using a Shoving Charm to knock it over."

Damn, how did she know my next strategy?

I tried. Believe me, I tried. But moving those itty-bitty grains of sand with magic was like trying to lift a boulder with my scrawny arms. Something about their tininess made them slippery, and my magic kept losing its grip on them. It probably didn't help that I couldn't concentrate. I kept thinking of the Mauvais. Of Alastair. Of where in the world they might be. The more these distracting thoughts paraded along, the more annoyed I got with Banna.

She was supposed to know everything. Shouldn't she know where portals led to or how to fix my parents? But whenever I asked something non-sand related (which was everything), Banna made a *tut-tut* sound and pointed to the hourglass.

"You need to visualize them going upwards," she said in her lilting accent.

"No, I really don't. I have serious doubts that my life is going to depend on wowing people with a parlor trick."

"Fine, then what do you want to learn since apparently, even though I've been doing this for hundreds of years, I'm clearly not qualified to provide useful instruction."

I had a headache, I was already growing hungry again, and I felt like I needed at least another hour of sleep. But, recalling how quickly Banna could Hoover magic out of me if I irked her, I forced myself to keep an even tone.

"Look, you're a good teacher, but in case you've forgotten, there's a tribunal going on that might extract me soon. I don't exactly have time to focus on silly tricks. I need to be taught how to find a portal, or how to figure out where a portal traveled to even after it's vanished. I need to find Alastair."

"You need to start leaving these matters to Magics who know how to handle them. Had you mastered your own power, you could have learned more advanced magic such as portals, but right now, if you want to keep the tribunal happy, you need to master the basics."

The basics? I'd faced the Mauvais twice now and survived. For better or worse, I could bring back the dead if I was around them too long. I could execute a Shoving Charm with precision and force. I could both absorb magic and give it. I hated her judging me just because I couldn't shift some stupid sand grains or pass some stupid test — which I had indeed passed, but then Alastair kissed me and so my results were declared invalid. Then when I was tested again, I was put up against one of the originators of magic, possibly the most magic of Magics, who walloped me with everything her four-foot, eight-inch frame could muster. Which was a lot, let me tell you. In magic it would seem, size does not matter. So please don't lecture me about the basics.

Not being a complete moron, I did not say any of this. I merely glowered at her.

Banna shot visual daggers right back. She might have been so light sensitive any exposed skin would burn even under the glow of a full moon, but she wasn't going to cave in at the sight of my facial expression. Still, I had more useful things to learn, and better teachers to learn them from. I marched toward the door.

"Where are you going?" She threw a spell to latch the bolt on the door.

"I have things to do," I said, whipping my hand horizontally in the air and ripping the lock off the door — in all fairness, I'd only meant to unbolt the thing. Oops.

"We're not done here," Banna said.

I yanked open the door, turned around and flicked my fingers upward while giving my hand a little twist at the wrist. The sands in the hourglass not only started to flow upwards, they did it in a nice tornado-style funnel. Don't ask me why, but something about Banna's chastisement roused in me a need and ability to prove myself to her.

"Aren't we?" I said, feeling more than a little smug at Banna's expression of impressed surprise.

Unfortunately, just then, the top of the hourglass burst off and sand went flying everywhere, shooting out like a geyser and spraying Banna in a dusty haze. Okay, maybe I did need a few more lessons in controlling the volume of my magic.

I don't know if it was Gaelic or something much older, but Banna was clearly cursing me as she spit sand from her lips and brushed grit from her face.

CHAPTER TWELVE

MAKING REQUESTS

I made my escape from the practice room while Banna was busy with her sandy mess. My first thought was to take cover amongst the hundreds of tourists outside. I had just reached the exit when a jumbo jet-sized desire halted me in my tracks and set my feet to marching back toward Olivia's office. The desire was so furious even seeing Banna going into Olivia's workspace didn't stop me from my mission.

Both women looked surprised, and somewhat annoyed, when I walked straight in without asking or knocking. My stomach fluttered. I was afraid they'd say no, but if I turned tail and skulked out of the room, I'd look like an absolute loon. I gathered my courage and blurted, "I'd like to go home."

I didn't think this request was out of line. I mean, I'd been in the Tower for over two weeks. I might become a magical battery for the Mauvais soon, or I might be extracted by this mysterious tribunal. I should at least get to see my cat one last time. Plus, collecting some fresh underwear would be nice.

"That's not going to happen," replied Olivia. "You know very well that the Mauvais would love to get his hands on you. And we're all aware of your bad habit of going after him yourself."

"Look, the Mauvais is holed up somewhere. He's working his spells from a distance, not gallivanting around the world on his

Tour of Destruction." Which I then thought was the perfect album name for a death metal band, but I supposed Olivia would find that irrelevant. "Within these very walls, I've had magic stolen from me and a Mirage Hex put on me. Clearly, I've been no safer here than in Portland, so why not let me go back? I mean, what's the point of having these international portals if not to allow students to study abroad?"

"She has a point," Banna said, showing no trace of irritation over my sandy screw-up. Rather than darken the room, she'd donned an even larger pair of sunglasses than normal, she'd fully covered her skin in gauzy fabric, and she'd conjured her umbrella to hover just over her scalp. "Besides, if we let her go home, she can damage things there instead of here. But more importantly, it would keep her away from the Starlings while they recover."

"That's true. Runa—" And here, Olivia's hands started fidgeting with the papers on her desk. "That is, Dr. Dunwiddle needs to see how well the initial round of transfusions stick, but she worries that Cassie's presence might be hindering that."

"So I can go?" I asked. Inside my shoes, my toes tapped with impatient excitement.

"You can go." *Yes!* "But—" Of course there was a *but*, "—when you do, you will go with someone. Not alone." She paused, drumming her fingers as she considered who to send. I was hoping she'd say Rafi. After all, despite having nearly killed him, we got along well. "Since you'd be going to your apartment, and he's—"

"No," I said with dread, "not him."

"Do you want to go home or not?"

I sighed, my shoulders slumped, and I rolled my eyes. This was an indignity even I shouldn't have to endure. "Yes."

"Good. I'll send Eugene a message. He'll be waiting for you when you're ready."

As ever, my comings and goings were going to be monitored by Morelli. My life just couldn't seem to jump off that hamster wheel.

"I can be ready in fifteen minutes."

"No, sorry—"

"You just said I could," I said, cutting Olivia off. She couldn't really be going back on the offer already.

"If you'd let me finish. It's not even dawn yet in Portland. The portal stays closed at night except for urgent matters and for Sunday traffic. So gather what you need and meet Chester at the portal in," Olivia scanned a sheet on her desk, "an hour. Oh, and I believe Runa needs you to fill some more capsules before you go."

"So soon?" I'd just filled a couple dozen before holing up in my room the night before.

"Yes, those have all been emptied. Jake must have misunderstood the dosage. She needs to talk to him about it, but she's been so busy with everything. Maybe you could remind her when you see her."

"Because Runa just loves me telling her how to do her job." Olivia gave me a look that told me to do it anyway. I was about to leave when a thought struck me. "I don't exactly know where the portal is."

"Right, I forget, this is still only your first time in London and that you came in via the delivery portal. Just come back here in forty-five minutes and someone will show you the way." I told her I would, then turned to leave. "Oh, and Cassie," Olivia said just as I reached the door, "promise me you won't go after the Mauvais on your own."

To be honest, if I knew where the Mauvais was, I'd already be hunting him down. But since I didn't have a clue what corner of the world my nemesis had tucked himself into, not going after him was an easy promise to make. Still, I kept my

93

fingers crossed when I promised her I would behave.

I threw a few items into my satchel, then wondered why I would want to go home. This was the Tower of London, where English breakfasts and heaping mounds of sandwiches and sweets magically appeared, where plates kept refilling as long as you ate every last bite. My apartment had never seen a full fridge, let alone a full plate of food. I'd have to keep track of the time difference to make sure I was back to the Tower by dinner.

Even after stopping by the hospital ward, I still had time to kill. On my way back to Olivia's office, I decided to take a quick tour through the armory, which remained closed to the public. The four gnomes stood unmoving, each concentrating with unwavering intensity on the spot where Tobey had appeared.

As I was leaving the armory, I caught sight of a head of flaming red hair and the owner of that hair hurrying down the corridor toward Olivia's office. An unexpected smile crept up my lips, and I called out, "Corrine!"

She halted abruptly, almost as if she'd run into an invisible wall. I never quite knew what my magic might do, and I briefly wondered if I had somehow accidentally conjured some sort of Shield Spell. But it turned out Corrine just had quick reflexes. She stopped, turned around, then her face lit up with delight.

"Cassie!" I took several quick steps on my long legs to catch up. Then, just to make me regret my joy at seeing her, Corrine wrapped me in her arms and squeezed me into a hug. I stiffened, and she backed off. "Sorry, I just— Oh, the things we've heard. Are your parents really back? Simon and Chloe. Did you meet them? How was it? I bet they're so proud of you."

I'm sure if my parents had a working brain cell between them, they'd be glad I got them to safety, but I don't know if proud is what they'd be of me. I was socially awkward, I found it impossible to trust most people, I lived in a dingy apartment, and I'd only recently been able to confidently make my rent on time. No, pride in me was probably not what they'd be experiencing.

"They're still not well," is all I said. "What are you doing here?"

"Oh, I had to pop by to deliver something to the Museum of London." She held up a package that was about the size of an unabridged dictionary. "Have you met Alvin Dodding?" I said I had. "He's such a charmer. Anyway, Eugene sent me a message saying you were coming back, but he couldn't get away just yet so he asked if I could I come get you. Are you really coming back to Rosaria?"

Rosaria being the name of Portland's magic community.

"Just for a visit. Apparently, they still want me here."

"And who could blame them? You're such a delight and so hardworking. Your studies must be going really well."

Delight? Me? Had someone slipped a spoonful of Delusional Drops into Corrine's coffee?

"My studies are, well, they're going. That's about all I can say."

"That sounds splendid. Now let's get ourselves to Olivia's office. Need to let her know you're in safe hands. You can run this little errand with me," she held up her package, "before we zip back to Rosaria. Although I would have liked to pop in somewhere for an afternoon tea. Well, maybe next time. It is hard to beat Gwendolyn's baking."

Once Olivia had seen I was in safe, albeit talkative, hands, she gave me a warning look that left no doubt I was to try no funny business while away from the Tower. I was certain every single gnome in the Portland area would be on Cassie Watch. Corrine and I then made our way through the labyrinthine passageways to get to the portal that would put us out near the Museum of London where she could hand off her delivery.

As we merged into the bustle of the City's business men and women, Corrine's unending stream of words slowed down only when her attention was pulled aside by a tea shop, a cookie store, then a bakery advertising a buy-one-get-one-free sale to clear up items before closing for the day. But Corrine was a woman on a mission and wouldn't be distracted by carbohydrates and caffeine. Well, not much, anyway.

At the Museum of London, Corrine used a Voice Modulation Charm to convince the stick thin guy at the front desk that Alvin Dodding was expecting us. With an arm that looked as if it might break if he waved it too vigorously, he made a languid gesture toward the stairs.

"Ah, Ms. Corrigan. You've brought me my goodies," said Professor Dodding as he leapt up from his desk chair to greet us. He must have forgotten to undo some of the effects of his Floating Charm because the leap sent him floating up five feet in the air. He grabbed the rungs of his bookshelf ladder and pulled himself back down. "Silly me. Always forgetting to dial that back. And Miss Black, still looking to steal that kiss from me?"

I smiled at his teasing and told him I'd try to control myself as Corrine handed over the package. I was dying to know what was inside, but curiosity be damned, the elderly curator merely set the box on a side table piled high with papers.

"Working on anything good lately, Alvin?" Corrine asked, pointing to the teetering stack of documents.

"Ah yes, it's what distracted me from undoing that Floating Charm. I've been considering revising a few sections of *The Making of the English Magics*. Who knows, I may need to update *How the Irish Saved Magic Civilization* as well."

"What? Turns out they didn't save it?" Corrine laughed at her own quip.

"Well, in fact, they did, but perhaps only for themselves. We always assumed they gave up meekly when we invaded their shores, but I've been finding records of a great battle and an underground system to thwart the English Magics."

"And no one knew about this?" asked Corrine, her voice now showing she was truly interested.

"Oh, I'm sure someone knew. It's all very fascinating. See, there was quite the skirmish led by the— Now here I am a little unsure of the translation, but I believe the name of the leader means *snow*. Anyway, this Snow Warrior led the final skirmish, and then we— Well, I hate to think of how we behaved then. Of course, many of the Tuatha died in that fight, as did the Snow Warrior. Or so we thought. Because according to these sources," he indicated a tattered collection of parchment held in plastic sleeves, "the warrior's body was never found and this raised the Tuatha's belief that the Snow Warrior would rise up and reclaim their power once more. As I said, very fascinating, and it's up to me to verify whether the historical documents can prove any of this or if it's all a far-fetched fable."

"Well, it is a good story." Corrine then pointed to the box. "So is that part of your research?"

"No, no. Those are for me. I absolutely adore the American Hershey chocolate bars, so I order them by the case. Don't tell the Queen I said this, but the ones you get here simply don't taste quite right."

After we bid him goodbye, Corrine jabbered the entire way out of the museum, along the City's streets, and through the myriad of passageways that led from the Museum-Tower portal to the London-Portland portal. Her chatter helped distract me from some of the misery at the memory that when I had last passed through a long-distance portal, I had been with Alastair and had gotten a good laugh at seeing Tobey taped to Mr. Tenpenny.

"I hear your new boss is doing well under Eugene's care. It must be so handy to have one of the Medi-Unit workers living right under you. Will he be helping you find where the Mauvais went? Eugene, I mean, not your new boss."

My "new" boss was Mr. Wood, who I'd been working for for about seven months. But since Corrine had been my previous employer, I guess she still thought of him as the new guy in town.

"Why would Morelli help me with the Mauvais?"

"He did some portal work in the past. He's been known to build a few, although they aren't regulated. But sometimes, well, we need to get certain packages to certain locations even when the official portals aren't open."

This was a whole aspect of magic culture I'd never considered. Covert postal operations? What next? Bootleg potions? Black market wing of bat? Which reminded me I still hadn't gotten Morelli's packet to Runa.

"Runa is supposed to be working on the portal side of things."

"Oh yes, I forgot. We do miss her being around all the time. I really need her to open up shop again so I can get my skin cream. I'm nearly out, you know. Ah good, Chester's on duty. Chester, how much longer?"

"Hello, Sir Corrigan, Mr. Cassie," he said in his dimwitted drawl. "Portal's opening in just a few minutes."

"I thought the portal was fully open now," I asked.

"Oh, it is," Corrine replied, "but it takes a few minutes to reset itself if someone's just gone through. It's far better than when we were having to wait for the temporary portal's two or three openings a day, I'll tell you that. You wouldn't believe the how terribly the packages backed up..."

CHAPTER THIRTEEN
ALONE AT THE PORTAL

Minutes have a habit of ticking by way too fast when you're taking a timed test, but when you're impatiently waiting for something like a bus or a traffic light, or say, the opening of a magic portal, a few minutes can feel like a lifetime.

That time stretches even longer when you're listening to a woman rambling on about packages and pastries, and a troll chiming in with random small talk. And given that Chester didn't have a wide range of interests, mostly focused on what he'd recently eaten. And trust me, you don't want to know about the things trolls will put in their mouths.

A rat scuttled by in mid-conversation. Chester didn't miss a beat in his recitation of what he'd had for breakfast. His heavy foot came down on the poor thing, and its ratty little vertebrae cracked under Chester's boot. The carcass then vanished in a puff of dust, which I have to admit was intriguing.

Finally, the portal clicked and Chester pulled it open. Not wanting to miss my chance, I grabbed hold of Corrine's arm and hurried her through. Since this was a regular portal, not one for mail delivery, it was far smoother than my first time through a long-distance portal. But thanks to Chester, my stomach was queasy with thoughts of deep-fried slugs served with pickle-flavored ice cream and garnished with a pinch of powdered rat.

We emerged at the end of a vibrant street lined with brightly painted houses that ranged from flamingo pink to emerald green. From the house to our left came the sound of a radio playing Caribbean-style music complete with the tinging of steel drums. Even at this early hour of the morning, the air was filled with the spicy scent of cooking.

"Are we on Lola's street?" I asked, my fingers itching to stroke Pablo's fur. A message from Lola had pinged its way through when we'd been on our way to see Professor Dodding. For her latest fashion shoot, Lola had dressed Pablo in a white and purple kimono and placed him in front of a Japanese tea set with the caption: *I just love sushi night.*

"Sure are. There's her house. Oh, you'll be wanting to stop by and see your kitty. He's become quite the celebrity in Rosaria."

We headed toward the familiar house I'd been made to clean for two weeks straight. Supposedly this had been part of my training, but I had a sneaking suspicion it had more to do with Lola's preference for doing crosswords and word searches over pushing a broom, magically or otherwise.

Pablo was sitting in the front window. When he saw me, he stood up on his hind legs and began pawing at the glass with his front feet as if he were on some sort of feline treadmill. And people say cats aren't loyal. I waggled my fingers at him as Corrine knocked on the door.

Lola answered, and before I could defend myself against it, I was being swaddled in another pair of arms and squeezed half to death. Seriously, I think I'd almost prefer going up against the Mauvais again over enduring all these invasions of my personal space.

Still, this was Lola LeMieux we're talking about. Before I'd gone missing as a child, she'd been my babysitter, and along with the cumin scent of her magic, she oozed a sense of comfort from her pores. Which makes it sound far grosser than it actually is. It's like if you could bottle the scent of freshly baked cookies, the feel of your own bed after a long day, and the pure, contented warmth of a candlelit soak in the tub, you'd have whatever it is that makes up Lola's aura. Probably pretty handy when you're someone who deals with fussy babies.

Lola gushed over me, asked about my parents, and attempted to kick a blanket over a pile of cat-sized costumes. I also noticed her eyeing the vacuum and forcing herself to snap back to attention, clearly deciding that now was not the time to rope me into chores. Pablo, meanwhile, was purring so loudly and deeply I worried he might hyperventilate as he nudged his cheeks against my chin.

"Are you taking him with you?" Lola asked, trying to put on a brave face.

"No, you can keep your fashionista for a little longer. I'm only allowed to visit."

"Back to HQ?" Lola said, a hint of worry in her voice. "You're being careful there, aren't you? The Mauvais isn't your only threat, you know."

"You mean the traitor?"

"I mean exactly that. They don't know who it is and a few of them once even suspected me for my, well, you know." Lola was supposed to have been watching me the day I disappeared. "It just seems odd that after all these years, they haven't sorted out who it is."

"You mean there was a traitor all the way back then?" Pablo flopped over so I could stroke his belly, and I got down on the floor to obey his demands.

"Of course. Devin Kilbride was a strong wizard, but nothing extraordinary. And sure, the watch enhanced that power, but as the Mauvais he had an unnatural strength from the very start, even before he had the watch. I don't think he could have performed or gotten away with half of what he did if he hadn't had help from inside. It's hard to say how much your parents knew, but I think they'd come close to figuring it out. Maybe they did figure it out and that's why he did what he did. You know, wipe their memory, keep them from testifying. If only they'd snap to, we might get the answers locked inside their heads."

"Busby told me if the Mauvais dies they will snap to."

"Don't you go after him, Cassie. Pablo doesn't look good in black and he will not appreciate attending your funeral."

We chatted a while longer and Lola made sure I was well stocked with her signature coconut cookies before Corrine said we had to get going, that she had an appointment to get to. Given that, with the time difference, it was only just seven in the morning, I'd have bet a six-pack of Terminal Gravity that this "appointment" was with the day's first batch of scones that would be coming out of the Spellbound ovens at any minute.

"I can take her," offered Lola. "It'll give us more time to chat."

"You'll get her to Eugene?" Corrine asked, suddenly serious. "You won't..." Like an elephant dressed in a ballerina costume paraded the unspoken criticism that Lola, having lost me once, might slip up again. "Actually, thanks, but I've got the time and I should probably see to it. After all, I do have rules about not leaving packages lying around. Come along, Cassie."

Lola wore a hurt expression on her round face and her dark eyes brimmed with tears of frustration. The look was a stab to my heart. I gave her hand a quick squeeze before Corrine yanked me by the other hand to get me moving.

As he'd told me once before, Morelli's portal that led from Rosaria into Real Portland was at the far end of Lola's block. Corrine, sniffing the air as if trying to detect any freshly emerging scones, rushed me down a narrow alley and to a slim side door in what looked like a garden shed.

She knocked, and when the sound of footsteps came from inside, she said, "He's on his way. I'll be off."

Despite her rules about not leaving deliveries unattended, Corrine couldn't get out of there quickly enough. After she had race-walked toward Main Street and turned in the direction of Spellbound Patisserie, I glanced around to see only rakes and empty terra cotta pots. I was completely alone. I could wander off wherever I chose. How soon before the gnome police were put on the alert? What was to stop me from going back to Lola's and playing with Pablo and eating coconut cookies all day?

Or what if the traitor in HQ had relayed the message that Cassie Black was on her way? Whose footsteps were on the other side of the door? What if Corrine had delivered me right into the hands of the Mauvais?

I know, I really needed an off switch for my brain. But since one hadn't been installed yet, when the knob began to rattle, my legs tensed, ready to flee.

CHAPTER FOURTEEN

INTERLOPER!

"What's wrong with your legs?" asked Morelli as he scrunched up his face in consternation.

"Nothing." I performed a quick squat, then stood up straight, hoping that some fake calisthenics would cover up my fight-or-flight response.

As with my own portal, Morelli's doorway to MagicLand opened onto his coat closet, which was obscenely tidy and had shelves stocked with various colors of yarn in plastic, shoebox-sized organizers.

"Cassie?" called a familiar voice from the kitchen.

"How is he?" I whispered. Mr. Wood was my employer, who might soon be my former employer if Daisy kept wowing him with her work ethic. He'd been beaten and left for dead because of me. Or rather, because of the watch. When his live-in nurses had refused to remain in a funeral home in which the dead kept waking up, my landlord, who had a surprising number of handy life skills for a guy I assumed to be nothing more than a TV addict, offered to take him in.

"With the cast removed, he's been managing a few steps at a time, and his appetite's impressive. I got tired of fetching him snacks, so I've given him a little extra boost to help him care for himself."

"A boost? What exactly did you give him?" I asked, barging past Morelli's bulk and marching toward the kitchen.

Mr. Wood was sitting at the kitchen table. My heart jumped with relief at the sight of his cast-free leg. Although the joy was tempered by seeing he still relied on his wheelchair. For his breakfast, he'd put together a sandwich that had a fried egg and several strips of bacon poking out the sides. When I walked in, that sandwich was levitating above the plate as Mr. Wood stared intently at it.

"Look, Cassie. Isn't that amazing?"

"Sure is. When did you learn how to do that?" I gave Morelli a look that was both questioning and accusatory.

"Oh, a few days ago. Eugene told me to give it a try with a medicine bottle I couldn't reach. It took a few tries, but I'm getting quite good at it." He grabbed the hovering sandwich and took a bite.

"I'll leave you to your breakfast." He waved his hand dismissively and chewed while the sandwich floated before him as if patiently waiting for the next bite to be taken from it. "Eugene, a word."

We went back into his front room with its sleek, modern furniture and hand-crafted, hand-crocheted embellishments.

"Before you say anything," said Morelli, "I only gave him a little bit. It's not like he can do anything more than levitate light objects. Plus, he's a Norm, so it won't stick."

"I didn't know you could give magic to non-Magics."

"Well, we're not really supposed to, but you know.... In the name of medicine..."

Morelli didn't mind bending a few rules now and then. Which made him exactly the kind of guy I needed. And please don't tell him I ever said that.

"Speaking of magic powers, I hear you build portals."

"A long time ago," he said. Which wasn't a lie. He had worked on portals years ago, according to Corrine. What he didn't add, what he didn't know I knew, was that he'd continued this hobby into the present day.

"So you could make one now if I needed you to?"

"You got a gnome with you, or something?" Morelli whispered, glancing toward his front window, outside of which I knew a gnome stood guard.

"Purely off the record."

"I've been known to make a portal in my time and maybe didn't register it."

"Register?"

"Portals have to be registered so they can be tracked and times set up for their use. It's kind of like air traffic controllers monitoring planes. Portals contain a magic that works as a trace. You know about orbs, right?"

I did. Some spells, like the Solas Charm, create a trace that makes it possible to find the witch or wizard performing the spell.

"Building a portal typically requires a small amount of the Solas Charm put into it. This makes them traceable and trackable, but you still register any portal you make if you don't want HQ raising a fuss. They get really annoyed when their tracking comes across an unregistered portal. The fines..." He trailed off as if he'd had personal experience with such matters.

"Can you track a portal that doesn't exist anymore, or re-create it?"

"It's not easy, but I might be able to manage it if—" And I swear the room got brighter as the light bulb of understanding clicked on over Morelli's head. "No, I see what this is about. You want to track where the Mauvais took Alastair, don't you?"

"You saying you can't? Are you afraid of the Mauvais?" I taunted.

"Of course I'm afraid of the Mauvais. Only a halfwit like you wouldn't be. But calling me chicken isn't going to suddenly make me capable of rebuilding that portal even if it could be found."

"Why can't it be found? I mean, you just said portals are trackable by their very nature."

"Some Magics have been known to experiment with portals that don't use the Solas Charm. Besides the trace, the Solas Charm component lends some stability. It also makes the portal last longer and the ride go more smoothly. If you only need a portal for a limited amount of time or for a quick escape, you don't need that stability."

I heard the suck of a refrigerator door being opened and craned my neck to see bread, ham, cheese, and mustard floating out. I arched an eyebrow at Morelli.

"I'm going to have to put a lock on that thing. I can't believe one person can eat so many pork products. Anyway, even if the Mauvais included the Solas Charm as part of his portal and didn't put any secrecy spells on the thing when he used it, he would have sealed the location to keep anyone from following him."

"But if he wanted to come back, he'd have to go through that portal, so it must still exist somewhere."

"Not necessarily. First off, why would he need to return to the same spot? Also, he could have built a series of secondary or even tertiary portals." I gave him a quizzical look. "It's like going from L.A. to New York with a quick layover in Denver. Even if the Denver airport closes down, you can still route through Chicago to get to your destination."

"So he could be anywhere," I said, dejection over this prospect gnawing a hole in my gut.

"He could be. I can work on tracking it, but if Runa hasn't found anything using the resources at HQ, I doubt I'm going to have much luck."

"Who else knows how to build portals? Would the Mauvais have known how himself or would he have needed help from someone inside HQ?"

"Hard to say. Portals have to be registered, not the people making them."

Just then, a crash came from the kitchen. Morelli's lips tightened and he sucked an angry breath through his nostrils.

"His magic must have worn off. I told him it only lasts an hour."

"Maybe best to concentrate on healing him rather than magicking him." Morelli scowled at me. "Just saying."

Once Mr. Wood finished his breakfast — Morelli told me it was actually the second breakfast he'd had — I offered to take my boss into the funeral home so he could catch up on some paperwork. Morelli was having none of it and saw this as some sort of escape attempt. You know, because pushing a guy in a wheelchair across town really boosts your ability to flee. So Morelli joined me and even gave a little salute to the gnome out front as if to say, "See what an excellent job I'm doing at keeping her under control. Now, go tell HQ so I can get a promotion or raise or whatever it is they're handing out for rewards."

The funeral home was surprisingly busy. As Mr. Wood told me on the way over, there were three clients lined up with more on the schedule. It was a huge improvement from before I left, and I wondered if Daisy might be murdering people to drum up business. I couldn't prove anything regarding that, but what Daisy had done was convince Mr. Wood to schedule the funerals back to back on the same day so he wouldn't have to come in more often than necessary.

"Won't you be tired after that long of a day?"

"Oh no, I've got so much energy these days. Healthy eating, exercise, it does wonders."

A little hit of magic now and then probably didn't hurt either, I thought as I gave Morelli a knowing look.

The interior of the funeral home looked no different, although I did notice Mr. Wood's belongings had all been moved back up into his living quarters now that he was shacking up with Morelli. But the moment I stepped into my workroom and saw the perfectly made up, perfectly blonde-haired Daisy with my cosmetics tray, well, I didn't shout, "Interloper!" but I was thinking it.

"Cassie," she said brightly, as if we were old bosom buddies meeting up for coffee.

"Daisy," I replied so drily you could have desiccated the person she was working on and called him Tutankhamen.

She made a tiny hand twist and a cosmetic sponge swiped across a pan of French Honey foundation, then proceeded to dab and dot its way across the skin of her victim. I'm sorry, her *client*.

"How's Tobey? He texted me and told me he was in the hospital. I've been worried, but I can't get portal privileges. I did send him a box of chocolates. Did he get them, do you know?"

He certainly did. They'd been delicious.

"He got them. He's on the mend." I pointed to an eyeliner pencil that was now drawing a smooth streak across the client's eyelid. "You shouldn't have to do this much longer. I'm sure I'll be back soon."

And that was my nice way of saying: *Get out.*

"Oh, I find I like it. Maybe we can be partners, or co-workers, or whatever you call it. I'm sure once Nino is out of his wheelchair and back on his feet full time, the work will just be rolling in." She paused. "Rolling in. Get it?"

"Nino?"

"Nino Wood. Short for Ninonodes, actually. Don't tell me you didn't know his first name."

109

"Of course I did."

Didn't I? I just never used it. He was always Mr. Wood. But Ninonodes? Was not expecting that.

Needless to say, after a couple hours of helping Mr. Wood with his paperwork (Daisy insisted she didn't need my help), I felt more than a little sullen on the return trip to Morelli's place.

I was being pushed out of the one job I had enjoyed, and it was my own fault. If I'd been able to deliver the watch for Corrine, I wouldn't have brought back the dead. If I hadn't brought back the dead, I wouldn't have had to get involved in my magic fiasco and I wouldn't have put Mr. Wood's business in jeopardy. If I'd learned to control my magic, I wouldn't have been sent to HQ and Mr. Wood wouldn't have needed a temporary replacement.

Daisy was temporary, right?

It was frustrating and disheartening. After all, I'd initially started on this magical adventure in an effort to save the very business I might soon be dismissed from. Assuming of course, that I didn't get captured by the Mauvais or extracted by HQ first. I couldn't blame Mr. Wood. He needed to keep up with his funereal work to pay his hospital bills and living expenses. He also needed, deserved, a reliable employee to help with that work. Unless business really went bonkers, he couldn't afford to take on two assistants. And since one was proving far more useful and far less hazardous than the other, I knew which of us would win out if push came to shove.

Once Mr. Wood had settled back in at Morelli's with a crochet needle and some creamy-yellow yarn, Morelli asked if I was ready to go back. I wasn't exactly, but I suddenly felt out of place. He allowed me a few minutes to go up to my apartment and grab some clean clothes and a couple new books, including a pictorial history of Portland I thought Nigel might be interested in — although I wasn't entirely sure it was a good idea to mix histories in an already mixed up mind.

Morelli then came up and, with many criticisms over the mess in my closet, escorted me through my portal.

As we stepped out, I felt a strong tug to go back and see Pablo, or maybe to be around Lola's comforting air, but Morelli told me at this time of day the London portal would soon be busy and we wanted to get there before the rush. While we waited, a strawberry blond-haired woman with round hips and slim shoulders came running up to us.

Fiona normally wore fairly casual attire — a sundress or a simple skirt with a plain blouse — but today she had put on a crisp, dark pink dress with tiny white dots and a sharp, white collar leading down to a V-neck that set off the slimness of her upper body. Despite the bright attire, her face was grim.

"We need to go through now," she said in a frantic command that was a jarring change from her usual stoic demeanor. "Something's happened. Or happening. Busby's just contacted me and told me to get Cassie back ASAP."

"Should I go with you?" Morelli asked.

"No, best to stay here. It may turn out to be nothing." But her tone and the way her eyes were darting around, implied that she didn't believe her own words. "Keep your phone on. If it is something, if we need you, I'll contact you. I don't know what this is, but try to act normal for now. We don't want to raise a panic if we can avoid it."

Morelli nodded his head sharply, as if taking instructions from a drill sergeant. "We still need to talk, Black," he said. Then, wringing his hands worriedly, he headed down Magic Main Street in the direction of the Sorcerer's Skein yarn shop.

CHAPTER FIFTEEN

THE TOWER TUMBLES

I went through the portal first. The moment I stepped out, I slammed into Chester's broad chest. He didn't seem a bit fazed by it, as if that sort of thing happened to him all the time. Instead of stepping back, he took hold of my upper arms, picked me up, and set me aside like a piece of furniture in the wrong place.

Fiona came through and joined us, then hurriedly asked, "What's going on, Chester? Is it really so urgent?"

"Go to Sir Olivia's office," he said, and now that I was looking into his face instead of his pectoral muscles, I could see distress furrowing his heavy brow.

"What's going on?" All I could think was Alastair had shown up. And I don't mean a living Alastair.

"Go to the office," Chester repeated. "I have to find the others."

I didn't know who *the others* were, but I didn't have time to ask as Chester was already thudding away.

"Come on, quick," said Fiona, moving confidently along the corridors and stairways with the rapid steps of someone familiar with a place. When we emerged on a hallway I recognized, sounds of horror came from Olivia's office.

We raced inside. In front of one of the unicorn tapestries that decorated the walls and insulated the stony room, hovered a large television. Or, I thought it was a television. It turned out to simply be a screen. No cords. No antenna. No cable box. Just a pamphlet-thick screen that I later learned could be rolled up and stored in Olivia's desk drawer.

Olivia, Busby, and Rafi were all watching the screen. On it was a scene instantly recognizable to any armchair traveler: a grassy plaza sprawling beneath the Leaning Tower of Pisa.

And like so many tourists' photos, next to the tilting tower was a hand held in a position against the side of the structure to make it appear as if the owner of that hand had the strength to push the tower over. Or to hold it up if you put the hand on the other side.

Although it hadn't even been lunchtime when Fiona and I left Portland, in Pisa it was early evening. The day trippers had mostly departed and the tour buses had rolled away long ago, but there were still plenty of tourists lingering around, enjoying the warmth of an Italian summer.

From the screen came a loud rumble. The area around the tower shook. It knocked a few people to the ground, but they didn't stay down long. They scrambled — some on hands and knees — to get out of the way. Others were being dragged away by braver bystanders.

Because the hand was pushing.

With the first couple shoves, the tower found a balance point and managed to teeter back into position. I held my breath, but the others in the room sighed with relief. On the third push, the tower traveled past this balance point, but somehow remained rooted to the ground. The room went silent, as if making any sound might create a butterfly effect that would be the last straw for the structure.

For a few moments, I thought maybe the Leaning Tower would just have a new angle of lean from now on.

But then the hand flicked the tower with its index finger.

And the tower fell.

The column crashed to the ground, the top third breaking completely apart. Dust puffed up and debris flew out from the shattered masonry.

The silence broke into angry chatter when words flashed across the screen. Words that nearly had my breakfast making a reappearance:

Send the girl so we can bridge this problem. You have two days.

And then the screen went blank.

Not because the Mauvais had control over Olivia's television, but because she had a remote. Not all things are magic, you know.

"This puts the Starlings one spell closer to being out of range," Busby said. "We need to come up with a plan."

Well, it would certainly be about time.

* * *

Thankfully, the plan was not to hand me over to the Mauvais. Not yet, anyway. The plan was to double down on tracking where the portal had gone. So, while Rafi and Olivia tended to issuing reassurances to the magic communities around the world, and especially to the Pisa Magics, I joined Runa, Fiona, and Mr. Tenpenny to dig deeper into portal probing.

"The trouble with a Magic vanishing is that they really do vanish with amazing efficiency," Runa said.

We were sitting in a small office she'd been given to use while she was at the White Tower. As she'd only moved in a couple days ago, the room had few personal touches other than her black doctor's bag and an alarm clock with Bugs Bunny in the center, his arms serving as the minute and hour hands.

"And the trouble with going back and forth between portals," I said, noting the time, "is that you end up missing out on afternoon tea." They looked at me like this was completely inappropriate to bring up. "Think about poor Fiona who's missed lunch to get here."

"Only for Fiona," said Runa. She then performed a little swish-and-flick maneuver with her index finger. The pleasing mint-and-honey perfume of her magic hit me just before a pot of tea, four cups, and a three-tier serving dish brimming with crustless sandwiches, tiny tarts, and fluffy scones appeared. "I have to admit, I'm starving. I've barely been off the ward for ten minutes today. Your parents," she said to me as I poured us each a cup of smoky-scented tea, "are proving tricky."

"I thought you figured that out," said Mr. T as he selected a flower-shaped sugar cookie. Despite the desperate situation in Olivia's office, his eyes had practically fallen out of his head when he saw Fiona in her dress. He'd now scooted his chair as close to Fiona's as possible, angling his body toward hers, and making sure her small plate was kept filled with whatever she craved.

It would seem love was cropping up everywhere in MagicLand these days, and I wondered bitterly what it was like to fully trust someone enough to enjoy your crush on them.

"It works," Runa said. "I know it works, but it's like the moment I get their levels up, they crash back down. I get these half-glimpses of them as they once were, only to see it whisked away a second later."

"Have they said anything?"

"No, it's too fleeting and I don't want to strain them with an interrogation. I just don't understand what's keeping the magic from sticking."

Three pairs of eyes turned to me.

"Don't look at me. I haven't even been in the country. Could there be another absorber in the ward?"

"There is one," Dr. D said. "She's only a weak absorber, but I've still placed her as far from the Starlings' room as possible."

"And the portal scans?" Busby asked.

"About as fruitful as my healing abilities. I swear, I'm so frustrated with failure. Now I know how Gwendolyn felt trying to teach Cassie potions." This jab earned her one of my you're-not-funny smirks. "I had a scan done of portal usage over the past week, but I've found nothing unusual. All usage has been for legitimate purposes. Well, except for the owner of the Burning Wand sneaking off to Mexico with his mistress. A Norm. Can you believe it?" she said, as if the woman's magic status was the most scandalous part of this piece of news. "If his wife finds out, his head is going straight through one of the saloon's plate-glass windows."

Given what Morelli had told me, this wasn't a surprise — the portal dead end, not the Burning Wand affair. The Mauvais may be a jerk, but he wasn't stupid enough to allow himself to be tracked as easily as a wayward husband.

"How have you had the time to do all this, Runa?" Fiona asked, setting down her bite-sized ham-and-egg tart. "You must be exhausted."

"This stuff is basically what's flowing in my veins now." Dr. D lifted her mug of tea, not the fine porcelain that had come with the tea things, but her own mug that featured a scene of Daffy Duck dressed as Duck Dodgers and standing next to his spaceship. "I can't take all the credit, though. I've looked over a few things, but it's been Banna who's gone over the majority of the scans. She volunteered to help out after seeing my frustration with the Starlings. I've read the reports she's generated, but neither of us has found a single suspicious thing."

116

"So it has to be an illegal portal," said Busby. He then nibbled on a strawberry tartlet after first offering it to Fiona.

"Illegal portal?" I asked, curious to hear their version of what Morelli had told me.

"Think of it like a burner phone," Runa said. "Something you use specifically because it can't be tracked. Meant to serve its purpose, then get tossed aside."

"But obviously even those can be traced on some level," said Fiona, as I selected a cranberry-studded, orange-scented scone. "It goes against all laws of physics for it not to have caused some ripple that can be detected. Even a slight disturbance should alert a sensitive surveillance gnome. Have Percival, Petunia, and, oh I can't recall all their names, but you know who I mean. Have they been trying?"

"Yes, they've been monitoring the area Tobey came through, but so far haven't caught wind of anything."

"But just because Tobey came through there, doesn't mean that's where the Mauvais is."

"Don't remind me," complained Runa. "Even if we do figure out where he's gone, there'll be a whole separate issue of where he went afterwards. I mean, surely he wouldn't just stick around. He'd want to get as far from the portal entry as possible, wouldn't he?"

"True. We need to think of areas he would feel safest in. Maybe focusing on the portal is a waste of time. We should be looking into your old records, Busby."

"Do you think I haven't been doing that very thing since arriving to the Tower? Every night I'm in bed and unable to sleep, I go over what I remember, begging my mind to see what I've missed. I haven't come up with anything we don't already know, but if I was going to divulge anything I might have discovered, I wouldn't do it in front of Cassie. Sorry, but I'd be in no end of trouble with HQ if I got you involved."

"Involved? Mr. T, I'm so involved I'm coated in involvement and will probably need an industrial solvent to clean off that involvement."

"You're dead, Busby," said Fiona. "They can't exactly reprimand you."

Apparently, I now had Fiona on my side. Perhaps with Mr. Tenpenny dazzled by the pink dress, this could work to my advantage.

Mr. Tenpenny took a long sip of tea, then toyed with a triangle of salmon and cream cheese on rye before taking a decisive bite. I guess the pink dress wasn't a miracle worker, after all.

"There are proper channels we must go through. We—"

Just then Bugs Bunny called out, "What's up, Doc?" The startling alarm that was as loud as someone trying to speak in a noisy restaurant sent my tea sloshing out of my cup as I flinched. Even Mr. T and Fiona tensed at the sound. But not Runa. Without batting an eye, she set her cup down, switched off the alarm, and stood up.

"I need to check on Tobey."

"We'll join you," said Fiona, and Mr. T looked appreciative of her I-won't-take-no-for-an-answer statement.

As we made our way from the office and through the ward, I could hear my parents singing their same tune. This time as a duet, but while my dad was humming, my mom was replacing whatever lyrics were in the lullaby with a single word: *white*. Over and over in melodic harmony. I wondered if maybe the Mauvais had previously been holed up somewhere snowy. Norway? Alaska? Antarctica? I shivered just thinking of having to travel to the tundra to track down Devin Kilbride.

When I glanced over, Fiona had a curious expression on her face, like she was trying to remember something, but simply couldn't grasp it from the air of memory. She gave up and fixed her attention on Mr. T.

"You were saying?" she asked Busby as we reached Tobey's curtained cubicle. He was conscious, but the doctor who'd last examined him still advised he not exert himself. Tobey did look good. Well, as good as someone can look in a hospital bed. He appeared in full health and had tried to greet us, but Fiona's question cut him off. "Channels?" she prodded.

"I was saying, there are proper channels we must go through. We know where Kilbride once lived and we know where he once operated from. I'm arguing that we start there, but I keep meeting resistance. It's ridiculous. We found him once using these very methods."

Mr. Tenpenny abruptly stopped speaking. He and Fiona both glanced at me from across the bed. I knew what the glance was about. My parents had been the ones to find the Mauvais's lair. They'd gone there to bring him in. They had warrants, not even magically forged ones. They'd gone through proper channels, but the Mauvais was one step ahead of those channels. He zapped them, sucked out nearly all their power and the majority of their comprehension of the world at large, then tucked them away in a nice, quiet place for a couple dozen years. And that's where doing things by the books gets you.

"Even so," Fiona said, as Runa flipped through Tobey's charts, "we can't just go barging in with guns blasting like an action movie."

"Magic guns," Tobey muttered, and I bit my lip, trying not to laugh.

"Fiona, a word," Mr. T said crisply. He and Fiona stepped out into the hall where I could hear words like "immature" and "needs trained" and "vulnerable" and "not ready."

"I think they're talking about you," Tobey said. He leaned

toward me and whispered, "Let me help you. I feel like this is my fault. If I hadn't followed you from the V & A, maybe you could have gotten in and saved Alastair. Then he could have helped you with the watch or whatever."

I didn't respond. Instead, I grabbed two more of Daisy's chocolates and went over to stare out the window.

"It's me, Cassie. I swear it."

"I believe you, but I— I just don't know. I mean, one, I don't work well with others. And two, he's already shown he can use you."

"Then let me do something in the background. I'm not feeble, you know. Granddad and Runa insist I keep resting, but..." He pointed to the floor. I looked to where he was pointing and saw the tips of a pair of maroon-red Doc Martins poking out. Unlike my scuffed and battered pair, which had been purchased on Half-Price Wednesday from the thrift store, his sported that brand-new sheen. "I've been going out and walking up and down the hallway while they're away and I feel totally fine."

"Walks? You think strolls along the corridor are training exercises for being whacked with Mauvais magic? He had you in a Binding Spell, he knocked you out to get you here. I can't trust that you'd be able to take another hit like that."

"Or is it that you just don't trust me?"

"Well, the Mauvais did impersonate you really well," I said, cringing at the idea that I had kissed my own cousin. Who had actually been the Mauvais. Double cringe.

"Then we set up a code word. You can ask for it every time you see me and if I don't know it, you'll know it's not me."

This wasn't entirely true. The Mauvais could get into Tobey's head with a Confounding Charm or BrainSweeping Charm, but the idea of an ally was strangely appealing. Especially one who had been wherever the Mauvais might currently be.

"I need to think about it. Busby would kill me if you got hurt."

"Thanks for the vote of confidence."

He turned away from me. I wanted to tell him I'd already lost Alastair because of the Mauvais, and I'd already essentially lost my parents. I'd lost so much because of one vile person. I was tired of losing and I wouldn't take the risk.

But I wasn't the sort of person who made those kinds of speeches. You know, emotional, showing vulnerability. Instead, I snagged another chocolate and left him to sulk.

CHAPTER SIXTEEN

A GOOD MORNING

I spent the next day feeling lost and a little pointless. Olivia and Rafi were still busy appeasing the magic communities around the world. I sat in on a few of these calls just to hear the reactions. That was a bad idea. I can't blame them and I tried not to take it personally, but nearly every community demanded HQ give the Mauvais what he wanted: me. Olivia tried to explain the consequences of me falling into his hands, how it would be far worse for everyone if that happened, and that all Magics must stay alert and report anything odd to HQ immediately.

After the third call, to the Toronto community — and yes, even those polite Canadians were willing to toss me to the wolves — I left Olivia and Rafi to it and climbed up to my room. I flopped on the bed and spent half an hour blindly flipping through the black-and-white pages of my Portland history book. Realizing I wasn't registering a damn thing, I let out a growl of irritation, slapped the book shut, and tossed it aside.

In the hospital ward, Runa was running herself ragged between trying to sort out my parents, hurriedly having me fill another batch of capsules, and racking her brain over the portal problem. Since I knew I wouldn't be allowed anywhere near my parents without Rafi nearby, I asked if I could help with the portal searches.

"Nice try," she said. "But if you find out where he's gone, you'll go after him, and then it'll be my head on a platter."

Fiona and Busby said pretty much the same thing: I couldn't help them go through Mr. Tenpenny's notes because I might do something rash. As if I'd ever do such a thing.

Frustrated and bored, I decided the only thing useful I could do would be to work with Nigel. Once I'd perused my messages that dinged through after stepping outside the White Tower, I guided Nigel along more of the twists and turns and highlights of royal history in the Tower of London.

Oh, and since you're probably curious, Lola's message was of Pablo dressed as the Easter Bunny, with the caption: *I'm hoppin' happy to have seen you.* Mr. Wood's message had said much the same thing about being glad to see I was okay. Although he hadn't donned rabbit ears in the selfie that accompanied his message. Instead, he was holding up a string of crocheted hearts in various shades of pink.

Neither photo did anything to ease my homesickness.

As sometimes happens in the White Tower (to me, anyway), the following day I was woken by someone pounding on my door. After shoving aside the books on magical theory I'd been studying when I fell asleep, I groggily answered the knocking, not once giving a second thought to whether or not it might be Banna. Luckily, since I'd left the curtains halfway open, it wasn't. Well, *luckily* might be stretching the term to its thinnest usage because instead of a diminutive Irish witch, it was a stout American doctor.

Wait, did that make Runa a witch doctor?

"Don't just stand there grinning like a moron," Dr. D said. "Get dressed. I think I've found a way for your parents' magic to stick."

I gestured her in and spoke from the bathroom as I got dressed.

"Are they better? Talking?"

"No, not talking, but they do seem more aware of their surroundings, which in my books is a huge improvement. If I can get more magic into them, who knows. I don't like to get my hopes up, but we may be rounding a corner."

"A bend."

"What?"

"You turn a corner. You round a bend."

"Oh, Merlin have mercy. Are you really going to lecture me on semantics?"

I stepped out from the bathroom and shrugged as if to say, *I just might.*

Breakfast popped into existence on my table, but Runa was already rushing me out the door before the scent of sausage ever had a chance to reach my nostrils. As I closed the door behind me, I noticed Winston arriving at my open window. Well, at least the food wouldn't go to waste.

"Are you sure it's okay for me to visit? Won't I suck their strength away?"

"I don't think so, not with this new technique. Besides, it will be a good test of how sticky the magic I've given them is."

Runa Dunwiddle normally speaks gruffly, sardonically, and in short sentences that are so sharp they leave you at risk of needing a tourniquet. So to hear her speaking with a hint of enthusiasm over my parents' health, had even me, a dyed-in-the-wool cynic, hopeful that we truly had rounded a bendy corner.

In their hospital room, Simon and Chloe Starling were sitting in cushioned dining chairs at a small, circular table.

And I'll just note here, those chairs looked far more comfortable than the back-breaking ones in my room. Just in case anyone wants to relay that to the White Tower's customer service department.

My parents weren't talking, they weren't humming their usual tune, they didn't seem to be looking at anything in particular, but they were both eating triangles of toast on their own. And, when eating twice-cooked bread is seen as a leap forward and a sign that you're on the mend, you really were in bad shape.

"How— I mean, what changed?" I whispered to Runa. Even though she'd told me I wouldn't absorb their new magic, I didn't want to get too close. Plus, they had the fragile appearance of a newborn deer or dwarf rabbit who would be easily frightened by any sudden movement. And, okay, if we're going to get all analytical, I suppose I was afraid they'd recognize me and reject me. What was I to them, anyway? Just another forgotten memory.

"I stopped treating them like they were Magics. I should have seen it all along. Instead of trying to restore their power so they could heal themselves, I treated them like Norms and used magic in a healing capacity."

"And now I'm out of a job," said Rafi's dancing voice from behind us.

"You're not out of a job, you elvish twat." There's the Runa I've come to know. "We'll still need you to be a conduit when they're stronger."

"So who's healing them?"

"I've had Chester come back in."

"*You* had Chester come in?" Rafi asked tartly.

"Fine," Runa conceded. "It was Chester's idea."

"Chester has ideas?" They both gave me that look that makes it very clear you've said something inappropriate. "Sorry, he just doesn't seem like an Idea Man, more of a Sure-I'll-Do-That Guy."

Several moments of silence followed. "Don't I have a lesson to get to, or portal to find?"

"You'll not be hunting down any portals," Runa asserted. "We're still looking for traces."

"I thought you said you already tried that."

"We tried one way. Then Fiona's comment reminded me that you can find illegal portals by analyzing what locations had signature disturbances. That night was a busy one for portal usage, but we can pick out which of those disturbances were from registered portals, eliminate them, and continue from there. All that's to say, Banna and I are working on it, not you. Got it?"

"Got it," I said gloomily.

"Come on, smooth talker," Rafi said, linking his arm with mine. "If I remember correctly, you have a lesson with me. How about a little sparring to start the day?"

"If you can handle it. Sure."

I gave one last glance at my parents. From where I stood, I wasn't certain, but it looked like my mom had eaten all but the crusts of two triangles of toast. She had placed the leftovers on the table where they stood out against the dark, laminated surface. The way she had set them down had formed a W, and I wondered if it stood for Winston. Or perhaps an upside-down mountain. Or maybe my mind was grasping for meaning and there was nothing more to it than some hard, discarded bread.

* * *

Even though it meant climbing to the rooftop recreation area, sparring with Rafi was just what I needed. Well, that and some scones, which he called up before we began when my growling belly told him I'd missed breakfast.

I don't know if it was simply the fact that I enjoyed practicing with Rafi, or if I was on a high from seeing my parents on the road to recovery, but over the course of that long practice session, my movements felt smooth, my defensive charms snapped readily into action, and my attack spells hit their mark every time. Without nearly killing my opponent, I even managed to block a Binding Spell and to stop Rafi's Vacuum Hex — the spell Banna had used on me during my last test.

"Are you going easy on me? If so, don't," I said as we stopped to finish off the last couple scones, which we heaped with strawberry jam.

"I'm not. You are improving. A week ago I wouldn't have thrown half the spells at you I just did."

"Why? Think I can't handle it?"

"No, because I'd have been afraid your counter spell would knock me off the roof. You struck back just now, but with control. A few seemed to go a bit wild, and with your first couple Shoving Charms, I could feel the magic wasn't entirely under your power, but for the most part, you really are improving."

My cheeks warmed and Rafi was polite enough to not comment on my inability to take praise.

Some time after the bells at St. Paul's chimed the one o'clock hour, Rafi called up a plate of sandwiches and a couple pints of ale. Once we polished off all but a few crumbs, we took our stances again and he worked me hard for another hour.

The practice session had challenged me, but it also left me buzzing with my success. I was in such a good mood, I decided to visit Tobey once it was done. I know, what kind of crazy, personality-altering potion was in that beer? Still, I'd kind of been a jerk to Tobey the last time I saw him, and thought I'd make it up to him. Since I had no idea how to make food appear out of thin air — which would have been a really good trick to have in my arsenal when I'd been on the brink of starvation the year before — I asked Rafi to conjure me a box of chocolates.

"You can't be hungry again," he said.

"Well, yes, I could be. But they're for Tobey. I might have eaten most of the ones Daisy sent him."

"Cassie Black being nice voluntarily. This is a bigger change than you getting a grip on your magic."

"Unicorns, Rafi. Unicorns."

At that, the teasing came to an abrupt halt and a robin's-egg blue box held shut with a sticker bearing the Fortnum & Mason emblem appeared.

"What's with all the Fortnum stuff you guys whip up?"

"We have a direct line to the store. Goes back to the day when we had one of our own on the throne."

"A Magic? Who?"

"Queen Anne, last of the Stuarts. Poor thing. She was so troubled by what people said about her, over her children's deaths, and by the petty little jealousies within her own court that it took a toll on her power. It didn't take long before she simply couldn't muster the confidence to tap into her magic, not even to relieve her gout. But," he said cheerily, "she did like her treats, so she formed a special relationship with Fortnum's, and we continue to benefit from that relationship to this very day." He handed the box over to me. "Enjoy your visit."

I circled my way round and round down the spiral staircase, wondering why, with all the Magics' abilities to conjure random corridors, an entire hospital ward, modern hotel rooms, and quite a number of floors that weren't in the original, or any, architectural plans, could they not whip up an elevator, an escalator, or at least a flight of normal stairs in the White Tower.

Tobey was sitting up in his bed, looking thoroughly bored. I handed over the chocolates as a peace offering. He scowled but was bored enough not to raise a fuss when I called a truce.

Although not bored enough to share a few of his chocolates. Which was really disappointing because I'd been smelling their rich scent through the box the entire way to his room and my mouth was drooling for a sample.

"What's got you in such a chipper mood?" I asked in response to his grumpy expression.

"I'm fine. Perfectly healthy." He threw the covers back and hopped out of bed. Thankfully, he was wearing a t-shirt and gym shorts, not a display-it-all hospital gown, because he danced a weird two-step jig to show just how fine and healthy he was. He then plunked back down on the bed. "But they," he gestured rudely at the curtain, "won't let me leave yet. I have to wait for Runa to come check on me since she's been my doctor since I was three years old. It's so stupid."

"It's for your own good," I said doubtfully. It did seem a little silly. Tobey was my age, healthy, and showing no signs of after-effects from his time with the Mauvais. And if there were going to be unexpected reactions, I didn't think lounging in a hospital bed would prevent them. "I mean, it's not like you had plans, did you?"

"Well," he said, dropping his voice to a whisper, "my grandad's pretty busy lately with Fiona, with this portal thing, and with all the other stuff going on. Which means I could easily get to his notebooks and see what they say about the Mauvais."

"He brought his journals with him?"

"No, he had them scanned before they were sent to be stored here. They're on his iPad."

I was just about to ask Tobey if he couldn't just tell me where the iPad was when someone cursed from the adjoining ward. The ward where my parents were.

And by *curse*, I don't mean the may-toads-spring-out-of-your-nose kind of way. This was in the things-have-just-gotten-way-worse genre of curses.

CHAPTER SEVENTEEN
BRIDGE TO NOWHERE

Tobey leapt from his bed and proved he was feeling tip-top by keeping up with me as I ran to my parents' room. I stopped in the doorway. Tobey only avoided slamming into me by catching onto the doorjamb.

Inside, Runa's cheeks flared as hotly as a contestant in a chili pepper-eating competition as she scanned the chart at the foot of my mother's bed. The bed in which my mother now rested, staring into the void, not even a hint of the awareness from earlier in the day on her face.

My dad remained in the same chair he'd been in that morning, clutching a half-eaten piece of toast. Presumably the same one he'd been gnawing on for breakfast. Drool dribbled from his mouth. His eyes stared as vacantly as those of one of Mr. Wood's clients. The ones we get ready for burial, that is, not the ones who pay us to arrange the funeral. Those clients tend to look fairly lively, for the most part.

The television on the wall was on, but muted.

"How did this happen? They were doing so well," Runa demanded of the nurse on duty. Not Jake, but a mousey-looking woman who crept back as if wishing there was a hole she could scurry into.

"I don't know. They just sort of faded back to this state."

"Who was in here?" Dr. D whipped to look in my direction. "You?"

"No, I've been with Rafi all morning. I only just came down to see Tobey."

"Then who did this?" Runa growled, as if I knew.

"Chester was in here about an hour ago looking for you," the nurse said tentatively, as if offering up any name that might serve to pacify the angry medicine lady. "He wanted to know if you needed him again."

"Well, I'm obviously going to need him now. Where is he?"

"Runa, what is this shouting? You're disturbing the other patients. You're disturbing the entire floor, in fact."

It was Olivia. Ever since Runa had arrived, the two had been shyly polite with one another. So, to hear Olivia scolding Runa— Well, first, I didn't think I'd ever hear anyone scold Runa, so that was shock enough, but for Olivia to be doing so was like a slap to the good doctor's face after it had already been rubbed raw with the harsh blast of a salty wind.

"I— I'm— I didn't mean to. It's just disappointing. Not to mention discouraging."

Olivia looked about to say something when the nurse squeaked, "Great Gandalf's ghost." She reached for the remote on the bedside table and clicked on the volume, but the words couldn't seep through my ears to reach my stunned brain.

On the screen was a scene that was perfectly familiar to anyone who has grown up in the Pacific Northwest. A bridge undulating, then twisting gently. The twisting then grows more and more violent until the bridge collapses into the water below.

It's the footage of the Tacoma Narrows Bridge, a suspension bridge that opened for business in 1940. Poorly engineered, the bridge shook and rumbled when it was hit with nothing more than a summer breeze. Barely four months after traffic began flowing over the span, a forty-mile-an-hour windstorm kicked up, the twisting began, and the deck of the bridge ripped apart.

But that familiar footage had been shot in the 1940s. It was black and white and grainy with age. What was on the screen before us came through in full color with high-definition clarity. And instead of one bridge, there were twin bridges: the first built as a replacement for the original in 1950; the second opened in 2007 to adapt to increased traffic needs.

Realizing their past mistakes, engineers had built these new bridges with strict attention to safety, stability, and the physics required to withstand wind sheer. But the bridges that had started with only a gentle sway when the nurse made her Gandalf gasp were now doing the same bucking, galloping, twisting dance as in the historic footage. Crawling repeatedly across the bottom of the screen were the words: *Hand her over, or from the tower to the pyramid, all will crumble.*

By the fourth time this had rolled across, the twin bridges swung out from each other. The nurse cried out, Runa swore, and Tobey shouted at the television like a crazy old man watching the news. But it did little good. Momentum paused the bridges at the crest of their swing. They then rushed back together.

The camera couldn't hold steady, and the view shuddered for several moments. When the cameraman regained focus (although it remained unsteady, possibly due to his hands shaking), the centers of the bridges were gone. The water beneath churned with the heavy crash of steel and concrete. Some cars, lucky enough to have been thrown out of the direct suck of the sinking decks, bobbed in the wake as their occupants tried to scramble out.

The scene panned up again, showing the towers that had supported the feats of engineering. Some cables had gone slack, but some still lashed out like the tails of angry cats. And then one supporting tower began to tilt. Slowly at first, as if not quite sure about what it was doing. Its partner tower had no such hesitation and tipped inward at a more confident pace.

Like a kid not wanting to be left out from something its friend was doing, the first tower's tumble rushed to catch up. The camera shook as the two structures crashed into one another, bringing to mind of a pair of clumsy dancers bonking heads. It took only minutes for the entirety of the bridges to disappear into the waters of the Puget Sound.

We all stared dumbfounded at the television as a blonde reporter in an overly tight blouse said, "Morning rush hour has turned into a rush of destruction and death. This breaking news story is still unfolding, and seismologists are still trying to understand the reason for this devastating start to the day. No earthquakes large enough to cause such destruction have been reported anywhere in the Pacific Northwest, and no terrorist groups have claimed credit for the collapse. The loss of life is currently unknown, but we will keep you updated."

Pause for collection of breath and she quickly threw on a smile to report about a litter of lion cubs born at the London Zoo the previous evening.

"Turn it off," Olivia ordered. Her voice was cool and unwavering, but her dark cheeks had drained of blood, leaving them unhealthily grey, like weathered cedar. She stared at me blankly, but behind the look I could see pity and regret. I didn't think this was regret over having to face another round of consoling and cajoling the world's magic communities. No, I had a strong feeling she was thinking of what the tribunal would have to say about this latest trouble. Olivia turned and left. I pushed past Tobey and hurried after her.

"He can't mean to destroy the world."

"What?" she asked, sounding truly confused.

"The crawler. It said from tower to pyramid. He can't mean from the Tower of London to the pyramids in Egypt, can he?"

"I don't know what he's capable of anymore. Please go, Cassie. Go find something to do. I need to think."

And with that, she disappeared down the stairs, leaving me standing in the hall, knowing I had to stop this before it went any further. Knowing my parents were yet another spell closer to being out of range. And knowing the time before the tribunal voted to extract me might have just shrunk from days to hours.

CHAPTER EIGHTEEN
HARSH REALITY

I wandered through the maze of the White Tower with my mind and body as numb as if they'd been dipped in a vat of Novocaine. Without realizing how I'd gotten myself there, I stood in front of the London-Portland portal. And no one else was around. The homesickness I'd felt earlier latched on with a ferocity I couldn't fight. I wasn't planning an escape. I just wanted to be around Lola, around Pablo, around Mr. Wood for an hour or two.

I reached for the handle. The instant I touched it, I was hit with the feeling of someone driving their hands into my chest and shoving me backward.

Either because I'm a slow learner or I'm just too stubborn for my own good, I tried the handle again. This time I was shoved away so hard, I fell back on my butt. On the door at eye level — well, eye level if you were standing — were the words: *You shall not pass, Cassie Black.*

Great. Not only was I trapped in the Tower, but I was trapped there by people who weren't very original.

After brushing myself off, I began my aimless roaming once more with my mind running on an infinity loop of thoughts. The tribunal might at that very moment have been making the decision to extract me, or to simply kill me outright to solve the problem once and for all.

Of course, it wasn't difficult to imagine my fate being determined in a dozen other ways. Perhaps to halt any further destruction, someone in the magic community might decide to play the vigilante and hand me over to the Mauvais. Or the Mauvais himself might cut a deal with HQ: me in exchange for Alastair. Then again, Alastair could always bargain with the Mauvais directly. I mean, why protect someone who doubted him, who flung accusations at him? He could save himself and few would blame him for doing so.

There was so much to worry about that my head couldn't take it all in. Which is why I failed to notice Fiona as I plodded down the corridor.

"Cassie," she said sharply, as if she'd already called my name a few times. I looked up and could tell from the ashen color of her skin that she had heard the news. Something in me crumpled at the sight of her. I couldn't speak and I began furiously blinking my eyes to hold back tears. "Inside." She pointed to a door. I hadn't realized where I was until I saw the familiar number. I unlocked the door to my room and we stepped in.

Fiona held up a canvas shopping bag. "I bought these for Busby, but I'm sure he won't mind if we sample them with some tea."

After putting the kettle on to boil, Fiona pulled out a tin of cookies from her bag. She opened the tin, placed it in front of me, poured the tea, then sat down at the table.

"You heard?" I said, the chocolate chip treat already having soothed my nerves a small degree. "About the bridges?"

"Yes."

"The Mauvais issued a threat. He said he would. And now..." As a lifelong Portlander, I don't even particularly like the Seattle area that much, but the thought of someone wiping out a vital bridge system just to prove a point left me feeling agitated, ready to fight, and helpless all at once. "What does he want?"

"What he always wanted. Control of us. Control of everyone."

"They can't destroy the watch. Not yet. We have to get Alastair back first."

"I know, but if it comes down to not being able to rescue Alastair when you can save thousands of people, they'll have to make a choice. The Mauvais," she said, shaking her head. "You just don't understand what it was like when he was throwing his power around. You see magic as a burden, or who knows, maybe now you see it as fun. But he sees it as a way to subjugate others. If he regains his position, magic will no longer be something that can be used to amuse, to heal, or to help. It will only be used to control and to hurt."

"I know. I understand."

"Do you? Do you really?" she asked, a challenging bitterness filled her words. "Then you know that Devin Kilbride didn't achieve what he wanted before your parents stopped him. Things were bad when he was in power. It was like hatred and corruption reined. If he has the chance to rule again, he won't begin where he left off, he will begin with what he most wanted to do."

"What does that mean?" I asked, the cookie suddenly tasting no better than a piece of roofing tile.

"That means," she said, her voice losing none of its bite, "that someone like Tobey, like your Mr. Wood, would no longer be allowed to exist if the Mauvais gets a hold of the strength within you. Shall I have Chester and Eugene tell you about what was done to the trolls by the Mauvais's minions? What they escaped and now live in fear of happening all over again? You may think you understand, but until you've seen how vicious he can be, you can't fully understand it."

I like to think she was only speaking to me so harshly because she was upset, but I'd already had a rough day and was sick of being treated like I was a moron.

"Then why do you only have one witch — who is already busting her butt to care for two very ill patients — searching the portal information for any sign of where he went? Olivia's getting in touch with other communities over what the Mauvais's doing, so why don't they band together to fight him? Why are you waiting for some prophecy to be fulfilled? You could have wiped him out long ago, but you've wasted your time expecting some half-trained witch to take on a man who seems to be the wickedest Magic in all of magical history. I'm the one you expect to save you all, but yet you act like I can't hold a concept in my head for more than ten seconds. You can't have it both ways."

Fiona's lips had tightened to a thin, white line of anger during my rant, but on my final sentence her eyes showed a hint of self-reproach. She glanced down at her tea cup. "You're right. We've put a lot on you. We should be more supportive."

"You should be, but instead you throw stupid tests and inconsistent lessons at me when you should have been showing me how to fight, how to defend myself, how to find the Mauvais. You want me to destroy him, but you also want me to stay away from him. You expect me to be able to thwart a wizard with no reservations for fighting dirty, while also expecting me to control my magic like some debutante taking etiquette lessons. As I said, you can't have it both ways. You can either teach me how to be nasty with my magic or you can produce a prim and proper witch. But I'll tell you which one is going to win in a fight against the Mauvais."

Fiona's lips were now curling into a sly grin, and a hint of her chalky aroma drifted over to me.

"You have won in a fight against the Mauvais," she said, toasting me with a chocolate chip cookie.

"Twice. No thanks to you guys," I said sourly, but I softened it with a grin and toasted her back.

"Let's go talk to Busby, shall we?"

* * *

Fiona's assumption was that Mr. Tenpenny would be more than willing to share his knowledge on the Mauvais's whereabouts if she argued in favor of the three of us working together. After all, wouldn't you want to see justice served to the person who killed you? Mr. T had firsthand information on where the Mauvais used to operate from and where his boltholes had been. It was Mr. T who had run the surveillance team on the Mauvais. And he was the one who sent my parents in at the head of Operation Winston.

But only a few minutes after Fiona and I had entered Busby's suite-sized room, I was receiving a stern lesson in just how stubborn Magics could be. No wonder I'd been beginning to feel such a connection with them.

"I know you want me to tell you, but I can't," Mr. T insisted.

"Can't?" I asked skeptically. "Maybe a month ago you couldn't, but you're stringing pretty long sentences together now."

"Not *can't* as in physically incapable," he said in a withering tone. "*Can't* as in, I don't think it's the wisest course of action."

"There are probably potions I could mix up to make you tell me the truth."

"There are, but you have no skill at potions and I'd be more at risk of being poisoned by one of your concoctions than of divulging any secrets to you."

139

"Busby," said Fiona evenly, "every minute you delay sharing what you know, every minute you think you're protecting Cassie, you're killing Alastair. You know she's capable, and she wouldn't have to face him alone this time if you assembled a team to go with her. You sent her parents in after the Mauvais. Why are you being so resistant to doing whatever it takes to let her go after him?"

"Precisely because I did send her parents after him." Mr. Tenpenny jerked up out of his seat and marched over to the window. After a few shaky breaths, he turned back to us. His eyes shining with restrained tears. "I thought I had gotten one step ahead of the Mauvais, but I was wrong. He knew of our plan and he was waiting for them."

"Because of the traitor?" I asked.

"Traitor?" asked Fiona. "Is that still a possibility? I thought it was only a rumor."

"It's not a rumor. Not only is someone within HQ passing him information, possibly alerting him to our every move, but they've also been delivering small packets of Cassie's magic to Kilbride. It's how he's gained enough power to do what he's doing."

"And you think this same Magic was helping him before?" I asked.

"Yes, I believe so. I hope so, in fact. The only other option is that he was somehow getting into my head and reading my thoughts, but that idea is no more appealing than the idea of one of my own colleagues betraying me, betraying us."

"So you're really going to tell Cassie nothing?"

"There's nothing I can share at the moment that could help."

"You know I'll just go blundering my way ahead with this." I spoke kindly, reasonably, hoping he'd see he was being foolish by withholding what he did or didn't know. Even eliminating where the Mauvais *wouldn't* go would be a start. "I will find the way to him, with or without your help."

"Please don't do that," said Mr. T. "Swear you won't. Be patient with Runa. She's clever and she knows what to look for with the portals. When the time is right I'll tell you more, but for now we can only hope Alastair will be okay. He is a powerful magic. He knows the Mauvais." I think this was supposed to be reassuring, but his voice carried more than a hint of doubt.

"Wait," said Fiona. Her face had tightened as her eyes squinted with criticism. "Do you think Alastair is the one who betrayed you? Is that why you're not rushing in to save him? Because you think he and the Mauvais are working together? Do you even—" She bit back her words as if knowing they'd do irreparable damage. Mr. T was smart enough to look shamefaced.

"All this time you told me to trust him," I said flatly.

"I don't know what to think. Maybe you've been right all along, Cassie. There's so many things pointing to Alastair's involvement. He's placed himself too often in the same location as the Mauvais for it to be coincidence. I promise you I want Alastair back, but I worry I only want him back to question him. Because of what Chloe told him, he's one of the few people who knew about the Starlings' raid that night. And he did once work with the Mauvais. It's hard not to doubt him."

"Is that why the tribunal…?" Fiona began, but trailed off as if rethinking the question. She and Busby exchanged a glance.

"Why the tribunal what?" Had they moved up their timeline? Had they already decided to extract me? Was I out of time? If so, then why was Mr. T being so dogged about not telling me anything? It's not as if I could do much rescuing without a functioning brain.

"The tribunal isn't just about you, Cassie. It's weighing the options with Alastair as well. From what Banna has been willing to share about the proceedings, they're leaning in favor of extracting you by destroying the watch. It would solve," and here Mr. T's chin shook as he choked on his words, "so many problems."

"We have to get Alastair," I insisted. Busby's words had tried to kick up the dirt of my suspicion again. I mean, if Busby Raven Tenpenny, a guy who'd known Alastair for years, couldn't trust him, what was I supposed to do with that?

But the kick just wouldn't swing through.

Up until that very moment, I might have held my own doubts about Alastair, but it was like I held those doubts out of habit, out of fear. Now a different fear took over. A fear I might never see him again. A fear I might never get the answers from him I craved. I couldn't fool myself any longer about Alastair's sincerity. My lips still tingled at the memory of that kiss after my first test. The *Shoop Shoop Song* was not lying: that kiss told me everything I needed to know about Alastair's true feelings for me. And yes, if I'd been forced to admit it, mine for him. Now, can we get over my sappy confessions and get back to my rousing speech?

"Even if you think I'm too much of a risk, even if you think he's done something wrong, you can't just let them execute him. It's barbaric."

"It's a sacrifice, Cassie," Mr. Tenpenny said cooly, "not an execution. Give the tribunal time. They still have a couple days to deliberate, and we can hope they'll take arguments. They might see reason."

"Time? The Mauvais is on a rampage of D.E.A.D. Magic. We need to get him. If nothing else, we need to stop him before the Extraction Hex on my parents can't be undone."

"And I need to think of the safest course for all of us." Busby shouted, startling Fiona who stared at him as if he'd just grown horns out of his ears. Mr. T took a breath to calm himself, apologized to Fiona, then continued. "As I said, there's many things pointing to Alastair's involvement with the Mauvais. From your going missing, to the Mauvais's sudden show of power he should no longer have. Banna has shared with me troubling information about each aspect of it."

Fiona had been shifting in her seat as Mr. T spoke his carefully chosen words, making a noise in her throat as if wanting to say something. When he paused, she seized the chance and said, "Busby, there's something you should know about Alast—"

But Busby, who didn't appear to have heard what she'd been trying to say, spoke over her. "I don't say this lightly. I would like to bring Alastair in for questioning, but if it comes down to it, I don't know if I can justify risking so many lives for a possible traitor. Is that understood?"

I didn't understand. I didn't understand how Busby could have defended Alastair whenever I'd had doubts, but now seemed more than willing to throw Alastair under a magic bus. I couldn't speak. If I did, I was afraid of what might come out. I glared at Busby. Angry confusion, painful indecision, fear for my parents and myself, and doubts of my own ability to judge people all washed over me.

I blamed Busby for that. I wished I had never met him, I wished my parents had never met him, I wished he had never existed. My thoughts must have been raging across my face because Mr. T could no longer meet my gaze. As soon as he looked away, I stormed out of the room.

CHAPTER NINETEEN
A CHAT WITH MORELLI

"Oy, where's the fire?"

In my haste to get away from Busby's room, I hadn't been paying attention as I stormed my way down the hall. As seems to be my habit with half-trolls, I bounced off the barrel chest of my landlord so hard I staggered backwards and tripped over an uneven stone in the flooring. Morelli's big hands reached out with surprising speed, grabbed my upper arms, and kept me from falling. Although I don't know why he did so — I'm sure he would have found it amusing to watch me land on my butt.

"What are you doing here?" I snapped. "You barely leave the building for six months, and now you're jaunting off to London every other hour."

"You know, maybe I'm here because of you. Ever think of that, you ungrateful brat?"

"Because of me?" I glanced around to see if anyone was in the hall. "I don't think Runa or the others should know I asked you about the whole portal thing."

"Yeah, duh. What kind of halfwit do you think I am? Don't answer that. I'm here because, as ever, I have to watch over you."

"What's 'as ever' supposed to mean?"

"You have no clue, do you?"

"Given that everyone speaks in half truths, half sentences, and half explanations, while expecting me to somehow know everything there is to know about magic spells, magic culture, and my magic-filled past, no, I don't have a clue. I live in a constant state of not knowing who to trust or what to believe. And now, just when I think I can maybe, just *maybe* trust Alastair Zeller, Busby Freakin' Tenpenny throws a big old monkey wrench into the works."

It was more than I'd meant to say, but the words had erupted from my mouth like some sort of verbal Vesuvius. Morelli clearly didn't know what to make of this. All totalled, it was probably more words than I'd spoken to him since I'd moved into his building. His face had gone slack as if stunned, but then his lips slowly tightened into a scowl and his eyes narrowed warningly. I stepped back a pace.

"It's time we talk."

Apparently this wasn't a request because Morelli snatched hold of my wrist and marched down the winding spiral stairs and out of the White Tower. We didn't stop until we got to The Keys, a pub open only to Yeoman Warders, their guests, and anyone involved with HQ. Morelli nodded to the barman, who pulled down two pint glasses and began filling them with a dark ale. As I tried to wrap my head around the fact that my landlord was such a regular here they knew his beverage of choice, he dragged me to the booth farthest from any other customers. He finally released me and ordered me to sit.

The bartender brought our drinks, glancing between me and Morelli with a look of concern. I nodded to show all was well and the small man headed back to his station. Morelli swallowed a third of his beer in one gulp, then began speaking.

"You owe your life to Alastair Zeller. Don't you ever forget that."

I didn't respond. I merely took a sip of my drink and waited for him to continue.

"You know he was in the park that day you went missing?" I nodded. "He kidnapped you."

Don't worry, I didn't pull the old comedy gag of spitting beer out of my mouth in shocked surprise, but I did choke on the sip I'd just been swallowing.

"Sorry, he what? I thought he was cleared of those charges."

"He explained to a few people. They pulled some strings, and there might have been a Confounding Charm or two involved. Anyway, he was cleared of the charges. But he did kidnap you."

"And what does this have to do with me owing him my life? Because it sounds like he should be the person I stay the farthest from."

"You had this curse on you. You know about that, right?" I did. Someone had cursed me on my third birthday. "If you were away from Rosaria, if you were unable to be found, the worst part of the curse would be avoided." That worst part being I would die. According to Banna, the curse stated that if I stayed in MagicLand, I'd be loved but I'd die young. If I left, I'd be treated like crap, but I'd survive. "Alastair couldn't get enough of you. Ever since you were born, he— I don't know, it was like the reverse of a baby duckling imprinting on its mother. He was very protective of you."

A group of three men in their early fifties came into the pub, gave us a cursory glance, then sat at the bar where they began comparing who'd had the most obnoxious tourist that morning.

"I don't understand. If he was protective of me, why would he kidnap me? Lola would have watched over me."

"She couldn't have. If you had stayed in the community, besides the curse, with your parents gone you would have lost your familial protection."

"What's that?"

Morelli, speaking like a teacher giving a favorite lesson, said, "Familial protection means that if its parents are alive, a child can't easily be touched. Their magic forms a sort of bubble around the kid until the kid reaches twelve years old and begins training. With your parents out of commission, that bubble burst. So the moment Alastair knew your parents had gone missing, presumed dead, he began plotting how to keep you safe."

I thought of what Alastair had said once. That he'd only ever wanted to protect me. Was this what he meant?

"And that plot involved kidnapping a four-year-old? Why not just tell Lola or Busby or Fiona that I needed to be hidden?"

"It had to be a secret. The Mauvais— Well, not just him, any Magic who learns how to do it can get into the heads of other human Magics."

"*Human* Magics?"

"He can't get into the heads of trolls, elves, or gnomes."

"Your skull is too thick to get through, anyway," I said, and raised my glass to him to show the comment was only in jest. He rolled his eyes, but returned the toast.

"You're one to talk. Anyway, so he starts asking me about how to go about stealing a kid. Yeah, that didn't sit well with me, so I asked him to explain. He does, and he was right. You couldn't stay in Rosaria. So I tell him to just make it look like he's talking to you, convince you to walk away with him, and to do it while other people might be distracted."

"It is disturbing you know so much about child abduction."

"I know so much because trolls have always been the magic world's most reliable and most sought-after guards. Which means we, even those of us who are only halfsies, get trained in many aspects of security. And one of those aspects is child protection. Anyway, one day Alastair sees his chance, takes you, and brings your scrawny ass to me."

"Why you?"

"Because the Mauvais can't get into my head and because Alastair's a kid himself. What was he—?" Morelli stopped, muttering to himself as he calculated. "You were four, so he would have been thirteen. As an adult, I could get you through town and to the Norm authorities. And as a Magic, I could do a little," he waggled his fingers, "paperwork adjustment, and have you in the foster system in no time. Course, I didn't know you'd end up in such terrible homes. I guess the part of the curse about you only being loved in Rosaria stuck, or maybe it was just your charming personality that got under people's skins. Or it could be because Alastair kept your mother's locket." Morelli took a large gulp of his beer, draining half the glass. "I told him he should keep it with you. I didn't understand at the time, I thought he just didn't want it stolen, but Alastair said it couldn't be near you. Not then, anyway. He kept saying one day he'd give it back to you."

Barely conscious I was doing so, my hand went to the spot under my shirt where the locket dangled.

"He told me my mom gave him the locket."

"She did, but he kept it. The locket itself has a protection charm on it, but the piece of baby hair inside is a trace. Trolls don't really use them, but I guess the hair inside is linked to the hair on the baby's head. It makes it so if a child gets lost, the kid can be located by using the hair as a sort of beacon."

Morelli paused to drink the remainder of his beer. My head reeling with this new information, I guzzled mine as well. But Morelli wasn't done overwhelming my poor brain.

"Because Alastair was given the locket by your mom, it created a bond between you two. It was a symbol of her binding him to you, making him part of the people, part of the magic that protected you. He was a smart kid. He knew, because of the trace, that if he kept the locket with you, you would have been found within days of going missing. And because of the prophecy— You at least know about that, don't you?" I nodded my head. "Well, because of that, the Mauvais was hunting you down like a madman after what he did to your parents. You took a few beatings as a kid, but it could have been worse."

"It was more than a few."

"It was good for you, kept your magic from growing. If you'd done any spell as a kid, the Mauvais would have known. Don't think he didn't have spies out looking for you."

I shuddered and stared at the lingering foam sliding down the inside edges of my glass. Magic took confidence, it took self-esteem. My foster parents, most of them anyway, had made sure to slap, scream, or starve any self-worth out of me. And as an adult, things didn't improve much. Morelli grabbed the two empty glasses, went up to the bar, and soon returned with two more pints and a bowl of potato chips.

"Wait," I said after eating a few of the salty treats, "so my moving into your place, was that part of the plan or just some weird happenstance?"

"Kind of both. I hadn't ever rented the place before because I didn't think anyone would want to live there, but then I kept hearing all these things about the housing problem in Portland, so I threw one apartment up for cheap. Didn't know what I'd attract with that, but I certainly didn't expect you. And that's not a compliment, by the way. But I've always kind of wondered if someone didn't interfere. I mean, do you remember exactly how you found the ad?"

"I never saw an ad. The Trimet bus I'd been on broke down one day. And there I was, being told by the driver to get off outside a sketchy quadplex with a garden gnome and a for-rent sign out front. I jotted down the number and called you while I was waiting for the replacement bus. Did you know who I was?"

"Not a clue. I smelled the magic on you, but figured maybe you were some out-of-state Magic, or wanted your privacy, or maybe had been kicked out of a community — which after getting to know you, I figured was the most likely explanation. Then one day, I'm checking in with Fiona about her leg—"

"Her leg?"

"Yeah, I'm the one who set it. She got into a fight with one of the Mauvais's people back when things were real bad. She won the fight, but the bastard shattered her leg before she got him. I set it, but it's never been quite right. You've seen the limp. Anyway, I'm at her place, we get to chatting, and I tell her I got a tenant who reeks of magic. She asks for a description and just as I'm trying to figure out how to describe your lanky, goth girl look, I see those photos she's got on her wall. The class photos, you know?" I nodded. "And there you were, sort of. Simon Starling in girl form. Although he didn't look half-starved like you always did."

"So Fiona knew I was living with you? What did she say? How come she didn't tell you to bring me in?"

"Because she didn't really know what good it might do." With surprising prissy-ness, Morelli delicately ate three chips, then brushed the salt off his hands. "I don't mean that as harsh as it sounds. I think she wanted to, but it was a risk to the community if they brought you to Rosaria. Fiona, while she sorted some things out, thought the best course of action would be to keep your magic down. So, I got to be mean to you. It was kind of fun, actually."

"I'm so glad you enjoyed your Oscar-winning role."

"I wasn't that mean to you, just hounded you for rent. Plus, monitoring your coming and going meant I was keeping to my bargain."

"What bargain would that be?" Huh, would you look at that? Half my beer had evaporated.

"The bargain I made with Alastair when he took you. The bargain that said if I ever came across you again, I would guard you. That's a troll's speciality. Guarding. He cast a Connecting Charm over us that day before I took you to the foster center, so I guess, in a way, you couldn't help but find me eventually."

"We were bound together? That is a disturbing thought."

"Suppose it is, but it's a good thing I did keep your magic down because not long after I met with Fiona, some strange characters began lingering around the apartment. Guildenstern alerted me to them."

"Guildenstern?" I asked through a mouthful of chips.

"The gnome out front. He and his twin brother Rosencrantz trade shifts. Anyway, it was maybe the day before or after you thought you were being clever with bringing Busby to stay with you that I got rid of them."

I swallowed hard. "Got rid of?"

"You really want to know the details?" Morelli asked over the rim of his glass.

"No, not really. Maybe a bedtime story for later. And only Fiona knew I was living with you?"

"Yeah, and she made sure I kept you around. That's why your rent was kept so low."

"And the day you threatened to raise it?"

"I was scared," he said with a shrug. "When your apartment got broken into, when I was attacked—"

"You were attacked?"

"Yeah, you had to have smelled it." I thought back to when I'd been attacked at my apartment, the night Pablo died. There had

151

been a stench near Morelli's door and that smell had lingered at least through the next day. "I don't know what genetic joke it is, but trolls let out a stink when we've been cursed. It's embarrassing. Anyway, I thought you'd been found and I wanted you to hightail it. Fiona worried her mind might have been read. But turns out it was just Vivian being right there in our midst." Morelli carefully selected a few more chips from the bowl. "Stupid of us not to have realized something wasn't right with her."

"And Alastair, did he know I was there? If he doted on me so much, why didn't he stop by to check in on me?"

"He didn't know. Fiona and I thought it was for the best. I almost slipped up and told him a few times, but if he had come to my place and Kilbride followed him and saw him talking to some girl who looks like she's got Starling blood, how long do you think you'd have survived? Alastair told me long ago never to tell him if I came across you again. Once Fiona was in on the secret, it made it easier to keep from him."

"A secret shared and all that?"

"Pretty much. It did feel like a big burden had been taken off my shoulders." Morelli fidgeted with his mug, then drained the rest of his beer. "So, anyhow, that's why you should trust Alastair. He's always done his best to protect you. He's the only reason you're alive today to annoy the bejesus out of me. He loves you. He always has. I will never fathom why, but there it is."

CHAPTER TWENTY
EAVESDROPPING AGAIN

With a whole new cluster of information to process, I headed back to the White Tower. Alastair's words played again through my mind. When he had told me he'd only ever wanted to protect me, no matter how clumsily he'd gone about it, I didn't have a clue what he meant.

But now I did.

Alastair wasn't evil. He wasn't a secret agent working against me. Alastair had cared for me. And the fact that that caring had never wavered hit me with full force, far more so than that first kiss had done. Maybe it wasn't "in his kiss" as the "Shoop Shoop Song" insisted. Maybe it was in a story told to you in a pub in the Tower of London by your half-troll landlord.

But I suppose that's not as catchy a lyric.

Alastair had to be saved. That's all there was to it. Did Mr. Tenpenny even know what Alastair had done? Was that what Fiona had been trying to tell him earlier? If all this was true — and I don't know why Morelli would make up such an elaborate lie — it was more imperative than ever that we find Alastair as soon as possible. He saved me. He saved Tobey. And as Tobey had said, that sort of behavior should be rewarded by not giving up on the person, by seeing that person to safety no matter how challenging it might be.

Trouble was, except for Morelli, Fiona, and perhaps Rafi, who'd also hinted he knew of Alastair's relationship to me, the others seemed to have written him off. Well, I was going to be damn sure they wrote him back on. I don't even know if that's a saying, but regardless, it would be pretty rude to leave to die the person who had done his best to save your life. Even I knew that, and I'm not known for having a stellar social IQ.

On the way to the stairwell, I passed by Olivia's office. She was speaking to someone. I know these accounts would have you believe otherwise, but I'm not normally the type of person who lurks at doorways to eavesdrop. But this time I couldn't help it. The tone of Olivia's voice was like a Stunning Spell that halted me in my tracks.

Olivia's a confident woman, a natural-born leader, who from what I had seen, could maintain a serious amount of grace under pressure. She was the kind of person you'd expect to stay calm just to keep other people from panicking. She'd have made an excellent president. Or flight attendant.

So, to hear her voice brimming high with anxiety and carrying a slight tremble, couldn't help but catch my attention.

"I think it's the only way to stop him," she said. "These threats, he won't stop until we do it."

The door was open just a crack. The room was dark but for a glowing arctic-blue orb casting a limited amount of light. Still, I could see Olivia coming in and out of view as she strode back and forth, waving a piece of paper. I couldn't see who she was talking to, but would have recognized Banna's Solas orb anywhere.

"He always issues threats. We can't give in to them."

"These are different." A smack echoed from the office as Olivia slapped the paper onto her desk, I assumed in front of Banna. "He is going to destroy everything if we don't comply."

"What do you mean by *everything*?" Banna asked calmly.

"I don't know," Olivia snapped. "Everything he plans to do if we give Cassie Black to him. With that much power, he'll easily gain the upper hand again."

"We survived him once before," said Banna, as if speaking of revisiting an old vacation spot.

"But this time his goal isn't just to have us under his control. Why do you think he's been so casual about destroying these places? He's getting a head start."

"Head start on what?" Banna asked.

"His same plans." Olivia's voice pitched a few notes higher on these words and she took several deep breaths to steady herself. "His plans to rid the world of all non-magics."

This finally grabbed the attention of a third person I hadn't noticed. I shifted my position and finally caught a glimpse of him. From the set of his shoulders and his steel-grey hair, it could only be Busby. He leaned forward, putting himself more in the orb's light, and looked at the paper. When he picked it up, the sheet shook.

"He cannot," he said in a forlorn whisper.

"He's gaining power by the day," said Olivia. "Somehow he's getting stronger. And even if we don't know who's passing it to him, we know which Magic he's getting power from."

"Cassie Black," said Mr. T, his voice cracking as if it hurt to say my name.

"Maybe we've judged her wrong," Olivia said. As she continued speaking, my skin went cold. "Maybe she hadn't planned to drain the watch that day at Vivian's boutique. Maybe she planned to help the Mauvais, then got greedy. She claims she was only tricking him, but what if she did it because Alastair showed up and ruined her plans? And what about her actions since she's been here? We've spent how long trying to find the

Mauvais and she just happens to encounter him with hardly any effort? But once again, Alastair ruined her plans. What really happened in that building, in that boutique? We have only her account of those events."

"And Tobey's," said Mr. Tenpenny, his voice defensive. "He corroborates everything Cassie has told us about that night she found Simon and Chloe."

"A BrainSweeping Charm would be no difficult matter for someone with her abilities. She could have been channeling power to the Mauvais ever since she arrived here. She may still be doing so. I've had my own worries about her. To lose Alastair like that. I can't help but wonder: Did she lose him or did she give him up? Doesn't it seem convenient to you that Alastair, who might be a threat to her plans, is still gone? But Tobey, who could have been charmed to back up her story, has returned? And then there's her stubborn resistance to destroying the watch to factor in. Busby, I know you have your reasons for not wanting to, but I think we ought to extract her. It would solve so many of our troubles."

How dare they accuse me of doing anything for the Mauvais? How many times had I told them I didn't even want this stupid magic? My legs shook from the anger coursing through me, and my hands rattled like I'd just developed a case of sudden-onset Parkinson's.

It's near impossible to hear yourself being insulted, accused, and practically convicted without barging in and defending yourself. Especially when one of the people talking wants to turn your brain into little more than a skull-bound cauliflower. I couldn't just stand there. I reached up, touching my hand to the heavy wooden door to push it open.

"But the tribunal," Banna reminded Olivia. "It's really not your decision to make."

I lowered my hand. A few ounces of the fifty-pound kettle ball that had been dumped into my gut lifted. The tribunal didn't sound like they were leaning in my favor, but at least they weren't unjustly accusing me of anything.

"And there's the prophecy," Busby said. "If we extract her we could be giving up our only chance at truly defeating him." Olivia said nothing in response. "You said the very same thing only a few days ago."

"I suppose you're right," Olivia said grudgingly.

Blessed prophecy! Did I ever say that prophecy was a farce? No, the prophecy was a most wondrous bit of poetry that all students should be forced to memorize and revere.

"But someone here is feeding him power," Olivia insisted. "I say if she doesn't truly show herself to be on our side, we consider other actions."

"She deserves some time," Mr. T said. "After all, she might lead us to Alastair and to the Mauvais."

Wait a tick. I was back to being used for bait? My heart dropped, but sadly I'd reached the point that being dangled like a worm for the fishy Mauvais sounded better than being completely useless to HQ.

"When will the tribunal make its decision?" Olivia asked.

"I've argued for an extension," replied Banna, and I instantly took back all the wicked thoughts I'd had of her. "I think it only fair given the seriousness of the sentence. They've granted another few days. If they decide against her, then we will extract her and destroy the watch. But not before. Agreed?"

"Agreed," Olivia said, although the reluctance in her voice did nothing to reassure me. And I can't say it didn't hurt to learn what she really thought of me. I hadn't liked Olivia at first, but I'd grown to respect her, to think she was on my side. So much for that.

But this knowledge ignited a certainty within me. Blazing with unflappable determination through my cells even more strongly than just a few moments previous, was the need to find Alastair. Because now, in addition to wanting to rescue him and apologize for all the suspicions and accusations, I needed him as a witness to what had happened that night the Mauvais took him through the portal. Tobey knew of course, but if even one single person was convinced I had him under a BrainSweeping Charm, how was I supposed to prove otherwise?

More than ever, I needed to find where that stupid portal had taken them.

CHAPTER TWENTY-ONE
BACK TO THE ARMORY

With Olivia's words and my own worries about what to do repeating through my head all night, I slept fretfully and my fraught nerves blazed through all my energy stores. Despite an extraction and whatever havoc the Mauvais might wreak next, I was famished the next morning as the sun streamed into my room, brightening the space as if everything were perfect in the world.

After enjoying a hearty breakfast of eggs, sausage links, and pancakes with Grade A maple syrup (apparently the kitchen staff had gone American that morning), I headed to the hospital ward. I wanted to check in on my parents, but I also wanted to grill Dr. Dunwiddle about her progress with the portal scans.

When I showed up, I peered into Runa's office. She was busy reading something on a tablet screen, so I knocked on the doorjamb to get her attention. When she glanced up, her brow was furrowed. Although that's often how she looks when she catches sight of me, so it might not have meant anything was amiss. She set down the device, signaled her glasses to zip into her pocket, and beckoned me in with a tilting nod of her head.

"Is it safe to see them?" I asked.

"Safe? I don't know." She shook her head and wore a dejected expression that was made worse by the dark circles hanging

159

under her eyes. Things were so bad even the frills on her shirt drooped under her lab coat. "I just don't know."

Except for the time I set her exam room on fire, I'd never seen Runa as anything but stalwartly pragmatic, so her defeated air hit me like a donkey kick to the chest.

"They're not, you know, getting worse?"

"No, not worse. The method works, really works. I get your magic from the absorbing capsules into them. They get better. Their power should do nothing but strengthen with the treatment. But I leave the room for a few hours to sort out this portal thing, and when I come back, they're back to zero again. I just don't get it. It's like unless someone tends to them twenty-four hours a day, the magic fades. If I or one of the nurses stays with them, they're fine, but we can't live in their room."

"So, the magic you're giving them is leaking out?"

"It can't. It's not that kind of magic. It's healing magic from a troll. Maybe Chester isn't as skilled as we thought."

"He fixed my hand."

"Exactly. And when he wasn't in your presence, did the hand go back to being broken? No. Because healing magic is sticky magic. It can take several doses in tricky cases like your parents, but it doesn't fade. It doesn't reverse, not to this extent." Runa dipped her head and rubbed her brow with her fingertips. "I just wanted to get this right for Olivia," she said, mostly to herself. "The idea she has is our best chance, but—" Runa peered between her fingers and abruptly cut her words off when she realized I was still there.

I didn't want to talk about Olivia, nor did I want to hear her name. The very fact that Runa would be doing anything to make Olivia happy made a petty little piece of me glad that whatever she was doing wasn't working.

"But what?" I prodded.

"Nothing. Never mind. Come on, you might as well stop in and see them now that you're here. No entering the room, though. This is challenging enough."

Expecting to see two people lying in bed staring into the void, I was surprised to see my mom seated in a chair, her back rigid, and her hands being held in Rafi's. He didn't glance over or acknowledge our presence in any way. He only stared into my mother's eyes like a very intense lover.

"What's he doing?" I whispered to Runa.

"His idea. Hypnotizing. Elves excel at it because they're so calming to be around."

"Calming? Wait, is Lola an—?"

"Yes. Obviously." Again, another fact of Rosaria that Cassie Black was just supposed to have known via osmosis or something. "She's a different breed of elf than Rafi. Her kind are more comforting than calming, but her line goes way back. Time with her was in high demand during the Mauvais's rise and it's a wonder he didn't try to wipe out the elves along with the trolls. Merlin forbid he allow anyone any sense of peace."

From the pair at the table came a noise. A groaning hum like someone doing a vocal exercise. Rafi's hands gripped tighter, his fingers digging into the skin of my mom's hands, and I worried her fragile bones might snap under the pressure. I started forward without thinking, but Runa stuck out an arm to hold me back.

The throaty rumble ceased and my mom opened her mouth.

"White. White. White. Tuhhh—"

And then her eyes closed and her head lolled until her chin dropped to her chest. Rafi let go of her hands and gently placed them in her lap.

"It's all I can get from her. It's the third time she said it. Just *white* and *tuh*."

"White Tower?" Runa inquired. "Does that mean she knows

where she is?"

"I don't know. I asked her to focus on the last thing she saw before her extraction, so it's possible she's confused. She may think I'm asking about what she sees now, but I doubt she knows where she is exactly."

"What about Tobey?" I asked. "Have you tried this on him?"

"I'd planned to start on him, but he made bail before I got here and is now roaming free once again."

"You'll try it, though? He might know something."

"Yes, Ms. Impatient, but it'll have to wait a few hours. I was really giving your mom all I could muster, and I need a bit to build up again. Which also means no sparring with your favorite teacher today."

"Does that mean I'm working with…?" I couldn't say the name. My stomach twisted in ways that would spark the jealousy of the most bendy contortionist.

"Yep, Banna's waiting for you in the armory."

"Why the armory?" I asked, picturing (and dreading) having to make the wooden horses march again.

"Because the Yeoman Warders and their spouses are using the practice room for a yoga class."

"A yoga—?"

Rafi nodded before I could finish the sentence, leaving me with a mental picture of a group of men and women in full Beefeater regalia doing their sun salutations.

* * *

The only good thing about a practice session in the armory was that it couldn't last long since we had to clear out before the tourists started trundling in. And yes, the armory was opening again to the public. The gnomes couldn't detect a damn thing, and after sixty hours of round-the-clock duty, had insisted their contracts specifically stated they could not be worked more than three days in a row.

Even with the limited time before the display's grand re-opening, I wasn't looking forward to my upcoming lesson. I mean, it was great that Banna seemed to be on my side in regards to not extracting me — or at least waiting for the tribunal to make that decision, not just jumping in all trigger happy with the extraction gun like Olivia — but after my last lesson with her, I imagined Banna would not go easy on me this time around.

Once I reached the armory, I peered in, hoping Banna might have changed her mind. But no such luck. The main lights had been fully dimmed, leaving only the small display lights glinting off suits of armor and the cold glow of her Solas orb to illuminate the space.

"Ah, you made it," said Banna, whose eyes, which were the same chilly color as her orb, showed genuine delight that I'd shown up. Maybe Banna was more tolerant of bitchy behavior and sandy screw ups than I gave her credit for. "Come on in, we don't have much time. I thought we'd go back to a little more practice on the membrane spell. Alastair had been working on that with you, correct?"

"Yes," I said cautiously. Cautious because I didn't dare hope there was more to this than met the eye. If the tribunal was leaning toward extracting me, they certainly wouldn't send one of their own to have me practice a spell that not only controlled my nasty habit of absorbing, but also reined in my giving tendencies. For an extraction they would want my magic flowing as freely as the long, luscious locks of a model in a shampoo ad.

Perhaps the tribunal was considering letting me off with a warning. Perhaps they could put a halt to Olivia's blood-thirsty, or rather magic-thirsty, craving for my extraction. I couldn't help but hope. Which meant I went into the session with a very un-

Cassie-like level of enthusiasm and positive thinking.

It's amazing what a good attitude can do. I guess I should have been taming my snarky cynicism all along because conjuring the membrane came easily. I didn't quite feel like I was doing it correctly, that maybe it was a little leakier than it should be, but Banna said she was sensing only the tiniest bits of magic emanating from me as she circled around, trying to pull power from me as she evaluated the membrane for any chinks in the armor.

"Quite good. Since you've done so well, it's your choice for how we use up the last ten minutes or so we've got. Sparring or giving the horses some exercise?"

To be honest, neither sounded like a good option. The armory was only just re-opening after days of closure, and I didn't have a good track record with preventing disasters in this room. But sparring with Banna scared me more than the possibility of making a mess of the armory and disappointing hundreds of tourists again.

"The horses," I said hesitantly.

"Good choice. That will let me see just how much control you're showing over your magic."

Was it too late to change my mind? If I sent the horses into a stampede, how soon would that get back to the tribunal? Plus, I worried I'd already overdone it. I felt tired, far more tired than I had in weeks from doing magic. If I'd known what I was going to be up to this morning, I would have drowned my pancakes with the entire bottle of syrup.

Just then a buzzer went off and the glass cases that protect the suits of armor from the hands of Norms lowered. (The Magics like to leave the cases open in the evening for any role-playing shenanigans they might want to get up to.)

Banna gave a disgruntled huff. "I could have sworn we had

more time. My internal clock's been completely thrown off lately." She then snapped her fingers to conjure a pair of sunglasses and an umbrella. She'd just gotten her shades on and the umbrella up when the full array of lights came on. "I better get going. Keep up the good work." With another snap of her fingers, the orb vanished and Banna dashed out of the armory.

My head ached and my eyelids felt like they had boulders weighing them down. I guess I hadn't realized how much effort I had been putting into the membrane. But it had worked and I'd impressed Banna, a feat almost as unlikely as impressing Runa. Still, I didn't think I had the energy to climb to my room for a nap. I needed sugar. I wasn't exactly sure how the food situation worked in the White Tower, but I figured it couldn't hurt to ask.

"Can I get some cookies?" Then, remembering this was the U.K., I added, "Or biscuits?"

Something popped only inches from my face and I flinched back, pinching my eyes shut. When I opened them, a plate of three chocolate chip cookies hovered before me. Talk about convenient. How did the Tower-dwelling Magics not turn into blimps? To keep the plate from refilling, I grabbed all but a small piece of the cookies. The dish then disappeared and I devoured the treats in about ten seconds, feeling more rejuvenated with each chocolatey morsel.

After strolling past the horses — they really were impressive — I exited the armory just as the sounds of voices with Germanic accents reached my ears from the display's entryway.

An odd sight met me when I came out into the hallway: Nigel. I mean, he looked the same as ever, but I'd always seen him outside on the Tower grounds; he seemed out of place inside.

"Hey Nigel, looking for a lesson?"

"What?" he asked distractedly, as he glanced down toward the end of the hallway. "Oh yes, I suppose it would be good if I could give a little speech about the White Tower. But was that Banna who just came from the armory?"

I couldn't imagine who else would be sporting an umbrella indoors, but I merely said it had been.

"I wonder what she's doing in there again. She and Olivia have been going into that area a lot recently. Maybe they're visiting the pool. Have they taken up swimming? Are they starting a Tower swim team?" he asked excitedly. "Do you think they'll let me join?"

"I think it's more to do with Tobey's reappearance. But if there's any talk of a swim team, I'll mention your interest."

"Oh, how splendid. Now, shall I start my speech?"

"Go for it," I said as we started our way toward the stairwell.

"Well, the White Tower was constructed by the Druids after they realized Stonehenge was a bit too drafty to live in." Nigel glanced at me as if waiting for my confirmation.

"That's absolutely incorrect, but I kind of like it. Might be a good test to see how gullible your tour group is."

"Then wait until you hear how the turrets at the four corners of the White Tower are topped with the hats of giants the Druids conquered."

"That might be going a bit far. Did you ever consider writing fiction instead of being a Yeoman Warder?"

"No, why would you ask that?"

"No reason," I replied as Nigel finally got on track and delivered a pared down and mostly accurate history of the White Tower, starting with William the Conqueror's invasion of 1066.

While he spoke, his news of Banna and Olivia in the armory wouldn't leave my head. But then again, why wouldn't they be in there? It was a common area of the Tower, not someone's room, not someone's office. Plus, this was Nigel we're talking about. He's not known for having a firm grip on the facts.

CHAPTER TWENTY-TWO
MID-MORNING ARGUMENT

After Nigel's ghostly brain had reached its limit for new information, we headed out of the White Tower and into the crush of early bird tourists wandering in a daze of history. Weaving through them with a determined stride was Olivia — her face grim and her braids looking tighter than normal.

The sight of her and her obvious foul mood forced me to abandon any concerns over where she and Banna chose to spend her time. Instead, my mind filled with worry over what city the Mauvais would hit next. And whether Olivia would take it upon herself to extract me to protect that city.

"Oh, there's a tour just starting," said Nigel as he noticed a group approaching the tiny St. Peter in Chains chapel. "I might be needed." Nigel sometimes helped the other Yeoman Warders lend credence to their tales of haunted crypts and spectral sightings. He enjoyed the role, and I figured his hearing the correct history of the Tower as often as possible couldn't hurt. Who knows, eventually it might even seep in.

I told him good luck, then made my own way to the raven enclosure. Most of the birds would be out and about at that time of day, but a couple might be lingering around. I truly liked the birds. Not only did their all-black attire show they had good fashion sense, but they had a clever intelligence that could get them in trouble and I couldn't help but admire that.

Winston was just waddling over to see me when someone, a male someone, called my name. He — Winston, that is — let out an annoyed *squawk* and turned his back on me. Who knew birds could be jealous?

I turned to see Tobey heading toward me. I then recalled Winston's earlier reactions to Tobey Tenpenny, namely the bird's seeming desire to thrash Tobey on the few occasions the two had been near each other. A shiver ran up my spine. Winston had attacked the window when he had seen me kissing Tobey (who, as I now knew, had actually been the Mauvais all morphed up to look like Tenpenny Junior). Had Winston's other freak-out sessions around Tobey been because he sensed the Mauvais's magic on him? If so, Winston merely giving Tobey the cold shoulder might be a good indication that Tobey was now Mauvais-free.

Still, you already know how far I reel out the trust line. I wasn't about to put my magical fate in the hands, or rather wings, of a dead bird. Probably good life advice for anyone, really.

"So you really did escape from the hospital?"

"Yeah, I kept telling them I'd gotten all the rest I needed, and they finally agreed there wasn't any reason to keep me there. Go for a walk?"

I eyed him warily.

"When you first met me, I gave you a paisley tie," he said, looking at me with impatience. I glanced over to Winston. He still wore a sightly put-out air, but he bobbed his head as if in approval.

"Fine. It's you. Along the walls?"

We climbed the stairs and joined the cluster of tourists shuffling their way along the walkway that overlooked the

Thames and from which they could get great shots of Tower Bridge. We squeezed past a crowd of selfie sticks that were threatening to tangle together, then walked in silence until we reached the chilly interior of Wakefield Tower. I was just pondering whether I should conjure my hoodie or perhaps a Warming Spell when Tobey finally spoke.

"So, here's the deal. Runa's borrowing Grandad's iPad to look over his information regarding the Mauvais. She's trying to match up any location the Mauvais might have been with the portal records Banna pulled up for her. I could go in for a quick check up. You know pretend that I'm feeling weird or something. Then, while I'm in there, I could get the info for you. Or go over what's there and tell you what I find out."

I was tempted. Really tempted. But I'd already gotten Alastair in a bad situation, and Tobey had just spent the past few days getting over a nasty concussion and was lucky he hadn't been killed. I also knew that if Tobey helped me uncover where the Mauvais was, he'd expect to go with me when I went after Mr. Evil. And I don't think Busby would be as forgiving if I lost his grandson a second time.

"Look, I appreciate it, but Runa isn't going to leave that stuff scattered around for any passerby to read. And, I don't know, the more I think about it, the more I feel like it's the wrong direction. Whatever we find in your grandad's journals isn't going to help. I'm sure he's told us all he knows."

"You're not even giving me a chance." Tobey's angry words bounced off the stone walls. "The Great Cassie who can do anything. Is that how you see yourself?"

"That's not what I was thinking at all."

"You're a snob, you know."

"*I'm* a snob? Exactly what aspect of my life do I have to be snobbish about?" I should have whipped up a Silencing Spell around us, because by now, people were snatching quick glances at us and looking away with smug grins on their faces as if they'd never had a public argument with someone. I lowered my voice, but my jaw ached with the tension of wanting to shout at Tobey. "Let me see, could it be my joyous upbringing? My brain-drained parents? My glamorous job at a funeral home? Yes, I can see how I might lord that over you."

"Your magic," Tobey hissed into my ear. "That's what you're a snob about. You think you're better than me because of it. You think Norms are losers. You're little better than the Mauvais in that respect."

"Do not compare me to him," I said with a seething grumble coming from behind my gritted teeth. I pulled him aside to make it look like we were checking out the coat of arms painted above the tower's fireplace. "Until a few weeks ago, I never even knew I had magic, so how in the world can I be snobbish about it? You know very well that I saw my magic as nothing but trouble, which it has been. I only decided to keep it so I could stay in your world and find my parents. And now I'm about to lose my stupid magic when I might need it to save Alastair."

"Then let me help you. Like you say, this is my world. I'm not completely useless. I want to help."

"No."

"Why?"

"Because you're no better. You think because you *don't* have magic that everyone in the community thinks less of you."

"You do think less of me," Tobey said as if this were as true as the fact that rain is wet.

"Since when?" Before he could retort, I added, "Besides the time I accused you of being the Mauvais. I got my due for that and I even apologized."

"Oh, thank you for gracing me with your humility."

"I wasn't too far off the mark, though, was I?" I asked as we strode away from the fireplace. "You did end up being the Mauvais. Sort of," I added lamely.

Tobey came to an immediate halt that was so sudden, a woman who was staring at her phone walked right into us. She scuttled aside, probably due to the scowl I fixed on her.

"I'm out of here. This was a stupid idea. Admit it, Cassie, you think you're better than me. Maybe once you can do that, we can be friends, but until then, leave me alone."

Leave *him* alone? As if I was the one who sought out his company? And with that, and with loads of people surreptitiously smirking over our little tiff, Tobey Tenpenny marched toward the door.

Wait, did he really think he could out-attitude me?

CHAPTER TWENTY-THREE

GIFT GIVING

"No, uh-uh, you do not get to walk away from me like that."

Before he could escape the tower, I had grabbed Tobey's arm. Now, he spun around on me. At the hurt and angry look on his face, I instantly took a step back.

"Don't tell me what to do," he snapped.

"Then don't tell me I think I'm better than you, Trust Fund Baby. You have no idea what I think."

"Assuming you think at all," he muttered and half-smiled. I couldn't help but laugh at the pure childish nature of the comeback.

The laughter serving as a truce, we wandered around the interior of Wakefield Tower, this time actually taking in the historic structure. I recalled it used to be the king's apartments. The vast space was cozy with the white stone being warmed by electric candles. But it had also been the place where, as he knelt in prayer, the ineffective King Henry VI had been murdered by the man who would become King Edward IV. I reminded myself to test Nigel soon on that bit of historical trivia.

When a tour bus crowd started cramming into the tower, I gestured for us to continue on in the direction of Bell Tower where both Thomas More, who had riled up Henry VIII; and Elizabeth I, who had riled up her sister Mary I, had been imprisoned. We then strolled along the small section of the ramparts between Bell Tower and Beauchamp Tower, the only area Elizabeth had been allowed outdoors.

Spreading below us was Tower Green, the place where Elizabeth's mom, Anne Boleyn, had been beheaded. And walking from the White Tower across that small expanse of fateful lawn was Rafi. The sight of him sparked an idea in my head. Tobey Tenpenny may not be pointless; he just needed a little work.

"Look, you're right. The main reason I don't want you getting involved in this is because you don't have magic. That's not an insult. But if you really want to help—"

"I do."

"You could start by not interrupting me. It's rude." He rolled his eyes. "If you want to help, we need to be on equal terms. You can't think I despise you because you're not magic, and I can't risk an Untrained going up against the Mauvais."

"So you're telling me I can't do anything."

"No, I'm saying there's a way we could work together," I said, picturing Mr. Wood assembling his ham and Swiss without laying a single finger on his slices of meat, cheese, or bread. "You can be given magic."

"It's illegal."

"It's only against the rules. It's not actually a law, is it?"

A conspirator's grin filled Tobey's face. Another surge of uncertainty went through me. If he was housing the Mauvais in his mind or body again, this would be the perfect setup for him to rob me of my magic. But he had known about the tie, Winston wasn't pecking his eyes out, and I was the one who brought up this whole transfer of power notion.

Tobey wanted a role, he wanted to feel useful. I knew how it felt to want to do more than sit on the sidelines while everyone plotted and planned. I wasn't sure what role Tobey could take, but having a little magic couldn't hurt. And who knows, maybe some magic would help if the Mauvais tried to worm his way into Tobey's head again.

"Can you really do that?" asked Tobey.

"If we can convince Rafi." Who happened to be retracing his steps across the Green at that very moment. "Quick, let's get down to him."

We were the targets of many dirty looks and angry words as we scrambled past people, most of them flowing in the opposite direction as we hurried back to the stairs. It was nearing eleven on a sun-filled June morning, and let me just say when you're in a rush to execute a cunning plan, it's really bad timing to come up with said cunning plan during the busiest tourist season, at one of London's busiest attractions, and at one of the busiest times of the day for tourists to be out touristing that attraction. By the time we got down to ground level, my ears were burning with peoples' curses and I'd lost sight of Rafi.

Luckily, I had a rapport with a certain raven who knew he had to keep me happy if he wanted his daily dose of blood sausage. Winston hopped up to me as if on cue when we reached the raven enclosure. Then I remembered that for some reason, only a few living beings could see the damn bird. And I didn't know if Rafi was one of those few.

"Can you get one of them to stop Rafi?" I asked, pointing to his companions, one of which was trying to figure out how to tear open a bag of potato chips he'd snagged from someone. Winston bobbed his head.

"Me?" Tobey asked as Winston fluttered over and chattered to another of the ravens.

"No, it's— Never mind. I'll explain some other time." Just then, Winston's feathered friend took off, heading toward the White Tower. "Let's go."

"Are we following that bird?"

"You wanted to be magic. This is your initiation rite."

Had Rafi's step been a little quicker, he would have made it to the White Tower without incident. But it hadn't been, and he was now standing with a raven perched on his head. With a beak that could snap off smaller body parts, and claws that could leave some nasty scars, Rafi didn't dare swat at the bird. Instead, he played it cool, standing nonchalantly as if everyone was wearing raven hats these days. Personally, I think he enjoyed the attention he was getting from passersby who couldn't resist taking his photo.

Soon after I stepped up to him, the raven gave a quick nod of his head and flew off.

"Did you have something to do with that?" Rafi asked, pretending to be angry.

"Don't complain. I probably just made you Instagram famous. Got time to talk?"

Rafi pointed toward the St. Peter in Chains chapel. "Will that do? It'll be empty for a bit." I said it would. We walked over and Rafi snapped his fingers over the lock. The door unlatched and he ushered us in.

"Is this a secret mission?" Rafi asked once we were inside.

"Kind of. I need Tobey to take some of my magic."

"That's not allowed," Rafi scolded with a mischievous glint to his dark eyes. "But I am intrigued enough to consider it. If you have a good reason."

I knew I couldn't tell him that Tobey was going to help me hunt down the Mauvais. That sort of thing would get straight to Olivia and I'd be thrown into even tighter lockdown. But there was one reason that might work.

"If Tobey has magic, the Mauvais can't use him like he did before. The BrainSweeping Charm only works on Norms and the

Untrained, right?" Rafi agreed. "And if Tobey has magic, he can thwart a Confounding Charm if he learns how. He could also be taught some defensive spells." I forced my voice to drop to a tone of sincere concern. "I only want my dear cousin to be safe."

Okay, maybe that was laying it on a bit thick.

"I like you, Cassie Black, and I'm telling you this as a friend: Whatever your plans are in life, you need to set aside any dreams of becoming an actress." Rafi then paused a moment, drumming his fingers against his chin in thought. "Any other time, I'd say no, but you're under so much surveillance I doubt even you could get into too much trouble."

"So you'll do it?" I asked, surprised it could be that easy.

"Yes, I'll do it. But mostly out of curiosity. I've never done a Magic-to-Untrained transfer."

"Will it stick?" Tobey asked. "Transfusions have never worked before."

"That's because you didn't have me. I'm the King of Sticky."

"You might want to rethink that title," I said.

"Yeah, probably. Still, my line of elves has always had the ability to get magic to stick, even in the toughest of cases. Your parents being the exception," he said with an apologetic shrug. "But that's a different situation altogether. Replacing magic into someone who's been extracted has always been a challenge. But an Untrained," Tobey grimaced at the name, "should be a cinch."

"So when should we do it?" I asked.

"Can't see any reason not to do it now."

"Really?" said Tobey, sounding excited, but also nervous as his fingers fidgeted at his side.

"Yes, really. Now let's do this before the next tour comes through." He held out his hand and I took it. Now that I was aware it should happen, as his warm, smooth fingers wrapped around mine, I recognized the sense of calm that elves were known for.

Rafi held out his other hand, palm up, for Tobey to take. Tobey reached for it, his own broad hand hovering over Rafi's slim fingers in hesitation.

"Go on. You're not scared, are you?" I said teasingly. Tobey sneered at me, then latched onto Rafi's hand.

"So, Cassie, I need you to imagine something flowing. And please don't make it someone going pee. I hate it when people do that."

I pictured pouring water from a glass jug into an empty cup. Since I only wanted to pour in enough magic to give Tobey a start, I imagined a small juice glass. It wasn't that I was being stingy — Merlin knows I had more than enough magic to spare — but I wasn't sure how much magic Tobey might need or how his cells would react to it. Knowing how troublesome an overdose of magic could be, I didn't want to risk overwhelming his system. Of course, Morelli had been dosing Mr. Wood with magic and he seemed okay, but levitating sandwiches and retrieving pill bottles wasn't quite the same as fighting evil wizards or locating magic portals.

Rafi's hand got warmer, and I don't know if it was magic flowing through us or just the heat trapped between our palms. When I'd filled my imaginary cup to its brim, Rafi said, "Okay, Cassie, release my hand slowly."

I did as he said. I expected the burning, itching pain to rush in and hoped Rafi would be able to call up a bucket of ice. Perhaps it was because I had pictured cool, crisp water, or maybe transfusing an Untrained was different, but I didn't experience any of the searing agony I had when we'd transfused my parents. Instead, there was a sensation of gently warmed honey flowing over my palm. My fingers tingled. That could have been the magic, or it could have simply been the frigid temperatures inside the stone chapel.

Rafi held Tobey's hand a moment longer. "I'm putting a lid on what Cassie has poured to hold it in," he said, his voice distant, like someone in deep thought. "Okay, Tobey, let go."

We stood there for a moment in complete silence, staring at each other.

"Did it work?" Tobey asked, his voice just a tad bit shaky.

"Let's find out," Rafi said.

CHAPTER TWENTY-FOUR
PROFESSOR CASSIE

"What do I do?" Tobey asked while waggling his fingers and jutting his hands forward. A Yeoman Warder had just allowed his tour group in (Nigel waved at me from the back), and many of his people stopped in their tracks. A few tried to back out and away from us.

"Not here," I hissed at Tobey. My vision swam and I fought the urge to put my head between my legs. Instead, I grabbed Tobey's fingers and pulled his hands down.

My head then suddenly felt like someone had scooped out my brain and replaced it with helium. I dropped into one of the wooden chairs facing the altar.

"Is she all right?" a slim woman with a Spanish accent asked. "Did he attack her?"

"No, it's fine," said Rafi. "Just a little low blood sugar."

I sat up, elbows on knees. To keep anyone from calling an ambulance, I propped my woozy head in my hands.

"Oh, well, here, I have just the thing," said a heavyset white woman with big hair and a thick, Texan accent. From a pink, sequined backpack she wore strapped across her expansive bosom, she pulled a packet of Twinkies.

I'm not known for being a picky eater, especially when it comes to sweets, but even I cringed at the sight of those yellow, nature-defying oblongs.

"Thanks," I said with as much polite curtesy as I could muster, "you keep them. I'm feeling better now."

I wasn't entirely. I hadn't expected so much magic to be pulled from me. Pain I'd expected, but not this overwhelming sense of naked fatigue. It hadn't been like this when I'd donated to my parents, but then again, Tobey was a completely empty vessel. Maybe it had created a sort of vacuum.

"Are you sure, sweetie?" asked the woman, even though she was already tucking the spongy treats back into her bag. "I've got plenty more back in the room. You just never know what kind of strange food you're gonna find in these foreign places."

"I'm sure. Thanks again."

I stood. My legs were still a little watery, but the worst had passed. I glanced at Rafi. How much had he taken from me? And more importantly, had he put it all into Tobey? Could Rafi be—

No, I warned myself, you will not go down that route again. Every time something odd happens does not mean the someone who was part of that odd something is working for the Mauvais.

We left the chapel and shut the door as the Yeoman Warder began explaining the age of the little church.

"Why do I feel so off kilter?" I asked Rafi, hoping that by coming straight out with it, the suspicion wouldn't fester like some medieval skin lesion.

"The magic takes a minute to stick in an Untrained, if it does at all. With your parents...how can I explain? Their cells are already primed for the pump. They've known magic before and should readily accept it. Tobey," who was still making strange finger movements, "has cells that have never known magic and are more likely to reject it. So, I wanted to give him a strong hit. I also kept some of your magic for myself, and this briefly drained you."

"You kept my magic? You drained me?" Okay, maybe my suspicion wasn't out of place this time.

"Only a little. If I hadn't, with your absorbing tendencies, you would have sucked all the magic back out of Tobey before it ever had a chance to set up shop in his cells. So, yes, I held onto some of your magic. You were closer to me than Tobey, so while you were busy re-absorbing your power from me, that gave his cells some time to introduce themselves to the new magic in town. Pretty clever, right? Oh, stop looking so put out. You're already feeling better, aren't you?"

I was actually. My legs felt like they were made of muscle and bone instead of elastic, and my head no longer felt like it was going to float off into the ether.

"You could have warned me," I grumbled.

"This isn't exactly something we do every day around here. I didn't know what I was going to do or how, so a little magic improv was required. Your quick recovery proves just how strong you are."

"I could still use some cake."

"I think we can manage that once we get inside."

We slipped into the White Tower through the ground level door that was only open to Magics. Like seeing Winston's change in behavior, I suddenly recalled Tobey passing through this door not long ago. On his own. As a person with no magic, he shouldn't have been able to do that. He should have only been able to get through the door with a Magic.

This brought on another memory of a plate of fries refilling itself when Tobey had taken the last one. The plates should have only refilled for Magics. How stupid was I not to see all these signs of something strange going on around me? Then again, I had been more occupied with doubting Alastair, finding my parents, and trying to pass magical placement exams than with fried potatoes and magic doorways.

"But won't I suck my power back out of him?" I asked Rafi. "Runa won't let me near my parents because she's worried about me absorbing the magic out of them."

"You probably will, which makes this a handy double lesson. Tobey learns magic, you learn control over your absorbing side."

"Why is everything a lesson with you people?"

Tobey, walking faster than us in his eager hurry to get to some magicking, started heading straight to the practice room situated only a few doors down from Olivia's office.

"No, not there," Rafi said, rushing forward and grabbing Tobey's t-shirt. Personally, I would have thrown a Binding Spell at him, but to each their own. "We don't want the others to see. My office."

"You have an office?" I asked, bewildered.

"Of course I do. Did you think I worked out of one of Olivia's desk drawers?"

I did briefly think he might live in Olivia's tea-lephone, but didn't mention this as we continued down the hallway.

From the outside, the White Tower doesn't look all that big. Bigger than your average home, sure, but when compared to your standard medieval castle or French palace, it's on the small side of royal residences. But once you get inside — assuming you're part of a magic community, that is — the place is enormous. I still didn't have a grasp on how many floors there were, but the corridors are long, the rooms uncountable, and the spiral staircases just go on and on and on. As my thigh muscles will be glad to tell you. And it seemed nearly everything (including Rafi's office) was up, not down, at least one flight of those staircases.

Rafi's office was, well, to be honest, a cluttered disaster. Olivia's workspace was open and sparse, with only a modern desk and some chairs to fill the space. Her one concession to decoration were the tapestries on the walls, but I'd bet those were in place long before she ever moved in. Rafi's work area, on the other hand, looked more like an oversized storage closet where every bit of unwanted junk had been thrown. From stacks of stationery to clumps of cast-off clothing, and mounds of magical textbooks to boxes of beetle legs (according to the labels on the sides), it made even my messy apartment look tidy.

"It's in a little disarray," he said, having noticed me staring at a jumble of feathers. "I just organized everything and haven't quite found a place for it all."

"This is organized?" asked Tobey.

"Well, yes," replied Rafi, as if this should be obvious, as if these heaps were the model of how everyone should arrange their belongings. He lifted a pile of papers and placed it on top of another stack of crates that looked about as stable as someone who had guzzled ten shots of vodka. This cleared some space on his desk. "Sacher Torte?" he offered.

I agreed enthusiastically and Rafi called up the decadent dessert along with a pot of tea, milk, and a large packet of the simple cookies known as digestive biscuits on his side of the pond. While Tobey took only a cup of tea, I didn't hesitate to eat half of a large slice of the chocolate torte. After the head swoon from giving magic to Tobey, I'd been mostly feeling better, but the rich treat was just the thing to leave me buzzing with a burst of magic health.

"So, Cassie, since you've done this recently, where do you think Tobey should begin?"

"This is another lesson, isn't it?" Rafi raised his fork to agree that, indeed, it was.

"You're going to teach, but you're also going to have to concentrate on controlling your magic. Tobey," he said, reaching out his hand, "give me your arm for a sec." Rafi wrapped his long fingers around Tobey's wrist as if taking his pulse. After a few seconds he let go and said, "He's about as full as he can get right now. We'll see where his levels are when you're done. That'll show how well you've controlled yourself."

I thought of my own first use of magic. My first intentional use, that is. My actual first use had been bringing back the dead, but I didn't think reviving one of the boxes of beetles would be the best way to kick off Tobey's magical career. Dr. Dunwiddle had set up a series of objects for me to move. I hunted around and collected a long, sleek raven feather, a discarded candy wrapper, a broken piece of pottery, and a small stone on which someone had painted a smiley face. I lined them up on the desk in front of Tobey.

"Try to move them," I said. "Any of them."

"How?"

A good question, and one no one had bothered to answer when I asked it. I don't know if that's just the standard teaching method in MagicLand, but I wasn't going to be that kind of teacher.

"Hold on." I moved each object one by one, concentrating on what I was thinking, what I was imagining at each step. It didn't help. I guess I'll just cross Magic Teacher off my possible career list if I lose my job at Mr. Wood's. "Look, I don't know how to do it, it just happens."

"Oh well, lucky you."

"Attitude," I warned. "You do remember, I could suck that magic right back out of you." Which reminded me to throw the membrane around myself that was meant to keep my magic from seeping out. It was difficult to do while I was considering how to put Tobey through his paces, but I knew that was part of the lesson: for me to be able to control my magic without a second thought, for it to simply happen in the background as I went about my business. "So, are you going to listen?"

"It's hard. I feel like everything in me is buzzing right now."

I hoped I hadn't given him too much.

"Can an Untrained overdose on magic?" I asked Rafi.

He shook his head no, then said, "It would overwhelm me first. Besides, he's more likely to reject magic than overdose on it."

"Okay, well, I'm sure that buzzing will go away," I said doubtfully, and when I looked to Rafi for confirmation he simply took a forkful of cake and popped it in his mouth. "Um, so, I guess every object is made of atoms. Atoms barely held together. With magic, you can break an object apart and re-form it elsewhere. It happens so fast that it appears as if the object is moving as a whole, but it's really not. So, just imagine all the little feather atoms or stone atoms moving apart and then back together a few inches over."

"Okay," Tobey said excitedly. "This is so cool."

He rubbed his hands together, then stared at the feather, squinting his eyes and scrunching up his face as if that would direct the magic better. "Relax," I told him. "You're doing magic, not taking a poo."

He shook out his shoulders, tilted his head from side to side which caused his neck to make a disturbing popping sound, took a deep breath, and stared at the feather.

Which promptly burst apart.

"Well, at least that shows you've got magic in you," said Rafi. "Cassie's magic, to be exact."

"I just blew something up with magic!"

"That was not the goal," I said, suddenly understanding Dr. Dunwiddle's frustration in her efforts to teach me. "Okay, whatever you did, do that again, just maybe a bit less. Try the wrapper this time." I was scared to have him try the rock. Sending tiny fragments of stone exploding through the confined space would not be safe.

Tobey did his stare again, but I noticed his eyes looked a little softer as he focused on the wrapper. He pursed his lips like he was going to whistle. I was about to tell him to relax again when the wrapper rose up and settled down six inches to the left. Tobey grinned as gleefully as a serial killer with a new set of knives.

"I imagined blowing it. I mean, I did the atom thing too, but I think it was the blowing thing that worked."

I wasn't sure if that was the right approach to the spell. I mean, if Tobey didn't learn spells as they were meant to be performed from the very start, what were the consequences? Had I just created a monster, I wondered as Tobey pursed his lips and moved the wrapper back and forth with little puffs of air.

I glanced to Rafi for some advice.

"He might hyperventilate, but if it works, it works." Tobey stopped blowing and turned to Rafi. "You'll hone your technique with time, but that's a good start. Cassie, how's the membrane going?"

"Still in place, Professor."

"Why am I so tired?" Tobey asked, his voice suddenly as groggy as mine first thing in the morning.

"You need sugar," said Rafi. "It's like magic fuel."

"No, sorry, I'm sugar-free. That stuff is terrible for you."

Rafi's eyes went wide, as if Tobey had just admitted his favorite pastime was kicking puppies.

"For normal people," Rafi said sternly. "Not for Magics. You need it to keep yourself charged. Now eat the damn cake."

Tobey hesitated at first, lifting a bite of Sacher Torte on his fork like a child being forced to eat Brussels sprouts. Then the fork went into his mouth and a look of pure bliss lit his face.

For someone who has sworn off sugar, Tobey put away a lot of the stuff in a short period of time. As if making up for lost chances, he ate two large slices of torte and a third of the package of digestive biscuits. All washed down with several cups of tea that were — at a guess from how much he'd spooned in — half sugar by weight.

Rafi then placed his hand on Tobey's arm.

"Magic levels only slightly depleted. You get a B+ for the day, Miss Black."

I thanked Rafi for his help, then Tobey and I left him to work a little more on his concept of organizing.

"Feel better?" I asked as Tobey and I headed down the hall.

"I'd forgotten how good sugar tastes."

"When were you planning to play the invalid act for Runa?"

"Do we have time for a pastry?" he asked.

Merlin's beard, he'd gone from stringent abstainer to complete junkie in under an hour.

"Better wait until some of the five pounds of sugar you just consumed clears your system."

"Then I could do it now. Man, I feel amazing!" Wired on enough sugar to kill an elephant, Tobey chattered the entire way down the hall, down a flight of stairs, and over to the stairwell that led to the hospital ward. "I'll meet you in your room once I get the notes."

"Don't try any magic on them. We can't risk you blowing them up."

"Got it," he said with a salute and bounced off like his shoes were made of trampolines.

CHAPTER TWENTY-FIVE
NOTHING TO CELEBRATE

Once Tobey and I parted ways, I wasn't exactly sure what to do. I was full of cake and cookies, so there was no need to visit the cafe. There was Nigel, of course. Even though I'd just spent the morning with him, the walk with Tobey had left me full of ideas of what history I could quiz the ghostly warden on next. Still, it was midday, the busiest time for the Tower and I didn't feel like enduring the stares of hundreds of tourists who would likely wonder why the tall, skinny girl was talking to herself. Befriending ghosts can be terribly inconvenient.

I then remembered, yet again, the stupid pouch Morelli had told me to give to Runa. I figured it was as good a time as any to finally take care of that chore. Besides, dropping off the pouch would also give me a chance to see if she'd made any headway with my parents.

Once I'd returned to my room to fetch the pouch, I made the climb up to the hospital ward. As I started down the hallway that smelled of sanitizer and disinfectant, I caught sight of Banna, sunglasses on, a small satchel over one shoulder, and umbrella in hand. She was just finishing up telling Chester something, and he bumbled off as I approached.

"It's wonderful news, isn't it?" Banna asked when I reached her.

My heart skipped a few beats. Had my parents come to their senses? Were they in there right now performing Shoving Charms and levitating their bed pans?

"What is? Are my parents better?" I picked up my pace, eager to see them. Banna hastened along beside me.

"Well, no," she said. Did you hear that crash? That was my hopes slamming into the tiled floor and bursting apart. "But Runa thinks she's come up with a breakthrough."

"What is it?"

"She was just about to explain. She's with them now."

Inside their room, my parents sat propped up in their chairs, looking like creepily realistic mannequins someone had arranged for a low-budget furniture ad. But there was a brighter aspect to their eyes and their skin no longer had the dull, dry appearance of an empty corn husk.

I paused, unsure if it was safe for me to enter the room. Olivia stood next to a beaming Runa. The doctor's pride seemed to be spilling over onto Olivia, who was sporting a broader smile than I'd ever seen on her face. Mr. Tenpenny, with Fiona at his side, was dotting an emerald green handkerchief to his eyes. As he tucked the silky cloth back into his breast pocket, he caught sight of me.

"Come in, Cassie. Runa was just telling us what she's discovered. It's all right for her to be here, isn't it?" he asked Dr. D. She said it was and I stepped forward. "Runa, you genius," Busby went on, his voice catching with emotion, "tell her, tell us."

"I don't know why I didn't think of it before," she gushed. "I needed Rafi, yes, but I also needed a little extra push. This is really good news because Olivia has the idea to— Oops." Runa bit her lip and grinned like a child who's almost spilled a naughty secret. "I'm not supposed to say anything about that. Where's Chester? Oh yes, off to get champagne. We don't conjure food in the hospital ward," she said in a silly voice, as if reciting a rule even she found illogical. "He's a big part of it, and not just because he's a troll. Big. Troll. Get it?"

Perhaps realizing her bubbly enthusiasm and stupid jokes weren't exactly professional behavior, Dr. D took a deep breath, then spoke more calmly. Or tried to. The thrill of her discovery had built a momentum behind her words and she was soon rambling with excitement again.

"Chester was doing his healing work and I was thinking I could use a cup of coffee. Sorry, I just can't get used to tea. And—"

Just then Chester came in, carefully balancing a tray on which there were five flutes of fizzing, blonde liquid. He offered a drink to Banna, but she corrected him, saying since Runa was the reason for the celebration, she should be offered hers first.

Chester did as he was told. Runa took her glass, then the others followed suit. Unfortunately, they were one glass short since I hadn't been in the room when the drinks were ordered.

"You can have mine, Mr. Cassie," Chester offered. "I don't like it much, anyway."

"Grog more of a troll thing?" I asked as I accepted the slim glass and set Morelli's pouch on the table next to me.

Chester grinned in reply. "Yeah, especially me mum's brew."

Mr. Tenpenny toasted Runa, and we each took a sip. With the chocolate taste still lingering in my mouth from the torte, the champagne tasted especially good. Not as good as beer and chocolate, but a very close second.

I was just wondering if the glasses would magically refill themselves like plates of food did in the White Tower when someone's glass crashed to the floor and shattered against the crisp white tiles.

"Runa!" Olivia shouted and snapped her fingers to make her own glass disappear.

I thought Runa was choking. Her hands went to her throat and her cheeks flushed red, but she was able to suck in rasping gasps of air. Olivia flittered around her, asking if she was okay, panicking, and making things worse.

Runa collapsed to the floor. Fiona eased a distraught Olivia out of the way as Mr. Tenpenny bent down and sniffed the doctor. It seemed like the same way Magics will sniff one another to pick up the scent of magic, but Mr. Tenpenny stopped, looked up at us, his eyes wide with fear.

"She's been poisoned. Get a nurse now."

"I'll do it," Banna said and hurried out of the room as quickly as her short legs could carry her.

"Poisoned with what?" Fiona asked, jumping out of the way as Olivia hurled herself across the room.

"Who did this?" Olivia shrieked. Then in a frantic, pleading tone she said, "Come on, Runa. Not now. We don't know what you did."

It was only then I realized Runa hadn't told anyone how she'd helped my parents. If she died now, her discovery would go with her. My parents' progress would die with her. I couldn't move, which was probably for the best. With everyone scattering like leaves in the wind and fussing over Runa, I'd have probably tripped over someone and made things worse. My gaze went from Runa, whose face was now a worrying shade of purple, to my parents, before drifting over to the table.

And to what I'd placed on that table.

I grabbed the pouch and fumbled open the leather thong holding it shut. Once open, I spread out the wallet and ran my fingers along the tiny packets inside. One flickered between shades of green and blue and brown. Jumping over Runa's body, I took my dad's cup of water and shredded the chameleon skin into it, using my fingernails to pick apart the tough skin.

Spinning around with the cup of liquid, I pushed it past Mr. T's shoulder.

"Give her this."

Runa's eyes went wide. A moment ago I didn't think she could look any more frightened, but apparently she could.

"No," she fought to say, "not one of hers. Potions."

But Mr. Tenpenny was having none of it. He took the cup from me. Jake had come in at some point and Mr. T commanded him to help.

"Open her mouth," Mr. T told no one in particular. "Jake, Cassie, hold her down."

Knowing Runa would never forgive me for doing so, I pinned her legs to the floor. Jake, who was burly but moved with surprising grace, slipped down between everyone and placed his knees on Runa's shoulders. Runa stopped struggling then. And not because we had her locked down.

"She's slipping away," Jake said, then grabbed Runa roughly by the nose and jaw and pulled her mouth open.

Mr. Tenpenny's hands were shaking too much to control how much of my potion went into Runa's mouth. Some spilled onto the floor, but most found its target. Jake pushed Dr. D's mouth shut, propped her up a little, and Mr. T massaged Runa's throat. Some of the liquid dribbled out of her lips. And still she remained unmoving. Maybe I should have just shoved the chameleon skin up her nose.

Mr. Tenpenny continued to massage. Olivia at this point had knelt beside me and was patting Runa's leg, begging her to swallow.

"Isn't there a spell to make her drink?" I asked.

Mr. T and Olivia looked at one another, dawning realization on both their faces.

"The drinking game," they said as one.

Olivia pointed two fingers at Runa and, through a trembling voice, said, "Chug-a-Lug."

Okay, that was really not what I was expecting to ever hear come out of Olivia's mouth, but as they say, needs must. I also made a mental note to learn this drinking game.

Runa twitched. Mr. T removed his hand from her throat. Her trachea lifted, paused a moment, then lowered as the sound of swallowing filled the now-silent room. Dr. D gasped, choked, then sucked in several ragged breaths of air.

Once she'd caught her breath, she glared at me.

"You," she said, her voice raw. "Potion. Tasted like crap." Then a stream of tears fell from her eyes. Sheesh, my cooking wasn't that bad, was it? "Thank you."

Mr. Tenpenny helped Runa to her feet, but it was Olivia who remained by her side, supporting the doctor despite Runa seeming quite steady on her feet. Olivia then directed her attention to Chester, who still held the empty tray.

"Chester, you are under arrest for trying to kill another Magic." The words were barely out of her mouth when glowing, Wonder Woman-like ropes threw themselves around Chester's wrists. He struggled against them.

"But I was only—"

Olivia snapped her fingers, casting a Silencing Spell on Chester.

"I've always had my doubts about letting trolls do more than guard. You remember their uprising in 1896?" Banna commented in a regretful tone.

"I do. I thought they'd changed," replied Olivia brusquely.

I worried for Chester. He'd always acted as if he loved his job, as if enjoyed working with us humans, but maybe I'd misread him. I'm not exactly the best person to gauge other people's intentions.

Still, Chester a murderer? It just didn't fit. Olivia was grasping at straws in her panic, and this was yet another example of her judging people unfairly. Just as she was doing with me, she was assuming the worst about Chester and seemed more than willing to be rid of him—

My heart stopped. Did they still execute people at the Tower? Would Chester be taken to the execution block he feared?

"Come Chester," Olivia said in a voice as cold as the champagne had been, "to the lower levels. A cell will be made ready for you."

I don't know what spell she placed on him, or if Chester had just given up, but he followed after her without putting up any fuss.

CHAPTER TWENTY-SIX
MISSING SCANS

"Cassie," Tobey whispered as I stepped into the hallway. His unexpected lurking unnerved me and I squeaked out a noise of surprise.

"Do not do that. Until you know what it's like having an evil wizard stalking you, never *ever* do that."

"Sorry, I— Come on, to your room. I've got news." I eyed him warily. "Knock it off. It's only me in here." I still watched him. "Paisley tie," he said with exasperation. "Now, can we go?"

I told him about Chester on the way up the stairs. And yes, I was pretty certain we should have been going down.

"That doesn't make any sense," Tobey said. At first I thought he was referring to the nonsensical stairways. "Trolls, even half-trolls are bound by their promises."

"Well, I doubt Chester was ever made to promise he wouldn't poison Runa Dunwiddle."

"No, it doesn't have to be specific like that. Once a troll gets enrolled in the security forces, he's promise-bound to do nothing to betray anything or anyone in the place he's meant to guard. It's why Chester's so enthusiastic about stomping rats. It's just one more way he protects the White Tower."

I thought of Morelli promising to protect me. Even if he went about it in some really weird ways, he had kept that promise.

Then again, Chester didn't seem like the sharpest troll under the bridge.

"Maybe he forgot his promise," I suggested.

Tobey shook his head. "They can't forget unless they're released. I can't remember what spell it is exactly, but it makes a promise binding. Magically binding."

We climbed the rest of the way in silence, then made our way down the familiar, hotel-like hallway and into my room.

"So, what's up?" I asked as I flicked on the electric kettle.

"Well," began Tobey, looking quite proud of himself, "while everyone was tending to Runa and arresting an innocent troll, I did a little snooping."

"You didn't. There were people everywhere."

"But they were busy. I'm not glad Dr. Dunwiddle was poisoned, but it did provide a great distraction."

The water boiled, and I poured two cups of tea. I handed one to Tobey, who immediately stepped over, then tore open and dumped four packets of sugar into the cup.

"And..." I prodded as I took a seat at the table.

"The portal scans were gone."

"You probably just didn't find them."

"No, there's a folder in there labeled, 'Portal scans' and inside was a note stating the date and who had ordered them. There's also a sheet with signatures to keep track of who had accepted the folder as it got passed along. Runa's was the last signature. It was pretty clear the file was meant to stay as a whole. She wouldn't have removed the paperwork and placed it elsewhere."

"Where are they?"

"Do I know?"

"Well, they'll have to run them again. I know Runa wasn't done going over them."

"Can't be done." Tobey took a sip of his tea, decided it wasn't

THE UNTANGLED CASSIE BLACK

sweet enough, and dumped in another two packets of sugar. "From what I've gathered from Grandad over the years, once a scan has been done, those records get filed away. It can't be repeated. That's why they're only run if it's really important."

"So, we have nothing. Even if any weird portal activity had been detected and registered, we can't retrieve it?"

"Pretty much. But the real question is, who took them?"

"You just better hope no one saw you in there. With the way accusations are flying around this place, you'll be next on Olivia's List of Doom." I eyed the packet of cookies by the kettle, but my appetite was gone. Plus, I didn't want to send Tobey into diabetic shock by adding more sucrose into his system. "So your little spy session was fruitless. Thanks for trying, anyway."

"No, I did get into the tablet."

"There's no way you had time to read anything."

"I didn't need to. We're trying to figure out where the Mauvais might be, right?" I nodded. "And we think he might be where he worked from before, right?"

"Yes," I said and rotated my hand in a get-along-with-it gesture.

"Grandad had in the appendix—"

"Wait, his journals have an appendix?"

"Sure. He's crazy organized. There's an index too. He put them together when he was converting everything into the digital version. Which is why I didn't need to read everything. With the appendix and the index, the info is right there. Now, do you want to know what I found? Or, well, didn't find?"

"That doesn't sound good."

"No, it is good. In the appendix, there was a list of places the Mauvais had worked from. He's only ever set up shop in Portland and in London. That really narrows it down for us," he said as if he'd just translated the Rosetta Stone, unearthed King Tut's tomb, and discovered the polio vaccine.

"It does," I said, hoping to burst his bubble as gently as possible. I mean, he was trying and really did seem excited by his efforts. Although, that may have also been the sugar high he was riding. "But London is a huge city that's expanding ever outward. Nailing down one spot would be like finding a needle in the mess of Rafi's office. And Portland isn't that big of a city, but it's big enough to provide hundreds of places to hide. Besides, I don't think we should assume he's gone to either of those cities. It's a big world out there, ripe for the evil pickings."

Tobey threw back his tea, probably rotting off a couple layers of enamel with the hasty action. I hoped his dental insurance was paid up.

Something nibbled at the back of my head. A memory of the night I found my parents. A sound or a smell. It was one of those thoughts you can't pinpoint and one that could drive you mad as you fought to sort it out. I tried to put it out of my mind, which was about as easy as telling someone not to think about penguins because then all that person is going to think about are flightless birds dressed in tuxedos.

"Can you make a portal to where he is? If we located him, that is," Tobey said, interrupting my thoughts.

I shook my head. "I don't know how."

"But you're supposed to be Miss Super Magic. Couldn't you figure it out?"

"I give you a little magic and suddenly you have all this confidence in my power? What happened to Cassie the Halfwit?"

"I'm sure she's still in there somewhere."

"This isn't helping," I said, pushing my cup away and standing up from the chair. "I need some air."

"Want me to come along?"

"No, stay here and practice."

Tobey's face lit up like a kid who's just been told he can open a Christmas present early. "Really? What should I do?"

I conjured my inner Lola and said, "Clean the room. Use Shoving Charms at various levels to make the bed, tidy the counters, that sort of thing."

"Great!"

And the weird thing? He didn't say that sarcastically. He really was excited to do housework. More power to him.

As for me, I needed some time to myself. I needed to think about what to do next, about what I could do. Before Tobey got started, I sifted through the bag of clothes I'd grabbed when I'd gone back to my apartment. Gandalf's gonads, had that only been a few days ago? It seemed like months.

Shifting aside some shirts, skirts, and the pictorial history book of Portland I'd brought to show Nigel, I pulled out a small, rarely used garment from the bottom of the bag. I ducked into the bathroom, undressed and slipped on the swimsuit, then put the clothes I'd been wearing back on over it.

I know. Leaving Tobey to do chores while I went off for a bit of recreation? I really was tapping into my inner Lola.

CHAPTER TWENTY-SEVEN

SWIMMING WITH GHOSTS

I headed down to the main floor of the White Tower. From Nigel's comments and from the state of Rafi's undress and his dripping hair on the day Tobey had been found, I knew the pool had to be somewhere beyond the armory. Or perhaps there was a secret staircase within the armory that led down to a dungeon-themed swimming hole. Which, I have to admit, would be worth the stair work to see.

It being only early afternoon, the Tower was still open for business. The armory itself remained busy, but the biggest crush of tourists had already swarmed through the room's displays of armor, weapons, and wooden horses. As I passed through without too much jostling from the remaining gawkers, something nagged at me that there might be some sort of clue here the gnomes had missed. Tobey had been dumped in this room. Was there a reason for that or was it—

"Henry the," said a familiar voice, pausing and making clicking sounds with his tongue as if that would stir up his ghostly brain cells, "eighth. Right?"

Nigel appeared in front of the king's enormous suit of armor. To avoid the questioning gazes of holiday-makers who couldn't hear or see my phantom companion, I fished out my phone to look as if I was having a chat with someone other than myself.

"Impressive," I said. Two weeks ago, Nigel didn't even know the Henrys numbered all the way up to eight. "And the wives?"

Nigel counted on his fingers as he said, "Divorced, beheaded, died, divorced, beheaded..." He paused. "Liquefied?"

"Definitely not. The last one survived." Although, I guess after she died, under the right conditions, she might have liquefied, but it was best not to confuse Nigel with speculation. "Alright, how many wives named Anne did he have?"

"Two. And they were two different people, not the same wife recycled," he said proudly. "So how is your day going?"

"It's been better." I told him about Chester and Runa, to which Nigel scoffed and, repeating Tobey, said no troll would ever forsake his duty of protecting others. "I know, it's strange. I thought I'd have a swim to mull it over. Do you know anything about where the pool is?" It was madness to ask Nigel for directions, but it had been a weird day.

"Ah, yes, there's a maintenance door just behind that display of swords." He pointed toward a case to our left. "Mind if I join you? I haven't been swimming in ages."

"Maybe next time. I could really use some time alone to think."

"So I should..." He made a walking motion with the first two fingers of his left hand.

"If you don't mind. I'll catch up with you in a bit."

"Looking forward to it," he said without a hint of being disgruntled over my dismissal.

Nigel disappeared once more. Surprisingly, he hadn't been wrong, and I did find the pool behind the maintenance door. And down a long set of stairs.

Rather than being dungeon-themed (slightly disappointing), the pool's low-lit, windowless, underground room had a Roman vibe going on. The side walls were painted with trompe l'oeil columns, and the far wall featured Roman mosaics depicting Neptune hanging out with dolphins and mermaids. The pool itself, lit with underwater lights that made the water sparkle, was large enough to have held Kensington Palace with room to spare.

I was relieved to see no one else was bobbing around, leaving me the chance to ponder in peace about what Tobey had suggested. Could I build a portal? Obviously, I'd never tried, but why shouldn't I be able to? If a feather could be moved by imagining its atoms drifting apart, couldn't you just imagine your own atoms drifting away from each other and ending up somewhere else?

And if all the atoms don't make it? a voice warned in my head.

A shiver ran through me. Loosening a feather's atoms briefly enough to shift them from one end of a table to the other was nowhere near the same as hurtling a human from one country to another, or even one building to another. No, regrouping an entire human in the proper arrangement wasn't something to go experimenting with.

But if others knew how, then it had to be something you could learn. Which meant there must be information on building a portal somewhere. And where do people go who need information? Well, people who need information that can't be found with a well-worded Internet search.

"Is there a library here?" I called. Nigel gives off a certain presence. It's a slight chill, but not a miserable, wintry one, more like the refreshing coolness of a summer breeze. I knew he'd followed me to the pool area. I suppose that should be creepy, but with traitors and evil wizards in the world, it did provide a sense of calm knowing someone was watching out for me. Although, if push came to shove, I did worry if Nigel might not get confused as to who he was meant to protect and who he was meant to fight.

"Yes, there is," Nigel said enthusiastically just before he popped into view in the pool's water about twenty feet away from me. His grey hair was tucked up in a rubbery swim cap, and instead of his typical Beefeaters' uniform, he had on a striped tank top tucked into high-waisted swim trunks that reminded me of something from a Sears catalog circa 1932. He dog paddled up to me. "It's in the part where they keep the crown jewels."

"Seriously? Are you sure that's right, Nigel?" It was a fair question. I mean, the guy had recently been certain Druids built the White Tower, and had marveled that Henry the Eighth was more than just a song that got easily stuck in your head. "You really think all that security is for jewelry? Fake jewelry at that."

"It's fake?" I asked doubtfully, swimming a lazy breaststroke to the side of the pool as Nigel paddled alongside me. Being a ghost, his movements never stirred the water; his upper torso and head just sort of floated through, which I have to say looked really disturbing.

"Mostly. And before you start doubting old Nigel, this information is correct because I heard it from the other Yeoman Warders. There are a few real pieces and the metal is actually gold and silver, but most of the stones are nothing more than colored glass given an extra little—" he waggled his fingers, "— sparkle."

"You know we don't waggle our fingers like that, right?" He shrugged. "So why the security if they're fake?"

"Well, it does give people the sense that they're seeing something extraordinary, doesn't it? But the security's really in place to watch over the library located behind the display. Some of the books are far more valuable than those silly crowns."

"Can I go in?"

"Certainly, you're a Magic. It's only off limits to Norms. Are you looking for something in particular?"

"I need to research something," I said as I pulled myself out of the pool, then used a Drying Spell to evaporate the water from my suit and hair. "Speaking of libraries, I've got a book to show you, if you're interested. Later, though."

"Yes, later, it's a nice overcast day and I'll be needed."

"What's the weather have to do with it?"

Nigel floated out of the pool. As he did, the swim cap, top, and trunks morphed back into his Yeoman Warder regalia. At least he wouldn't be wandering around in wet clothes, I thought as I pulled my skirt up over my now-dry swimsuit.

"My haunting tasks with the other Yeoman Warders, of course. Sunny days are never scary, but the dark clouds lend a certain atmosphere to the rooms that's just perfect for a spot of fun with the tourists. In fact, Thomas still owes me a beer for that group of Japanese tourists who—"

"Wait," I said, stopping in mid-stroke as I brushed my hair. "You can drink beer?"

"Thank goodness, yes."

CHAPTER TWENTY-EIGHT
IN THE LIBRARY

The Waterloo Barracks, where the Crown Jewels are housed, are situated almost directly across from where the Magics' door into the White Tower stands. Despite my time in the Tower of London, I'd yet to take a peek at the sparkly royal wonders. I suppose getting tricked by an evil wizard and rescuing a pair of parental units really does eat into your time.

The entrance, above which was a large clock, was flanked by a pair of crenellated towers and watched over by two Tower Guards, complete with red jackets and tall, black, furry hats. The line to get in was predictably long, but as it was already past midday and the clouds were rolling in, the line wasn't as thick as I'd seen it at other times. Most visitors had likely already "done" the Tower and were now cramming in five more must-see London sights before the day was through.

When I finally stepped up to the entrance, both guards — without breaking their rigid stance — pulled a quick intake of breath through their nostrils. They looked at me, turning their heads less than a millimeter to do so. The one on the left gave the smallest nod.

"The library?" I asked.

"Behind the coronation robe. You'll see a door," he said through tight lips that barely moved. Wondering if the guard might find future work as a ventriloquist, I entered into a darkened display room where I moved with the group ahead of me past a glassed-in, strategically lit exhibit of crowns and necklaces and loads of shiny objects I'd bet the ravens would love to get their talons on.

Once past the main bit of bling, I headed toward a tall display case that held a bulky, goldenrod, cloak-like garment that was elaborately embroidered with gold thread. I walked around to the back of the glass display case as if taking in the coronation robe from all angles. Then, instead of looping back around to the front, I dragged my fingers along the wall, feeling for a knob or a latch. My hand discovered a small indentation similar to a handhold for a sliding closet door.

I gave a little tug and discovered it was a pocket door that slid into a recess in the wall. I ducked in before anyone else came along. Closing the door behind me, I found myself in a cavernous room lined with books on shelves that stretched at least, I'm not kidding, seven stories high. As there were no ladders to slide along the stacks, I wondered if this was where I'd finally discover that, yes, Magics do use broomsticks to get about.

"Holy hell," I muttered, taking it all in.

"Shhh," hissed a voice. I glanced down to see a very round, very lumpy person (and I use the term *person* in the loosest manner possible). It was staring up at me. *Dwarf* was the first thing that came to mind. *Tricksy hobbit* was the second. "They can hear you in here even if they can't see you," it whispered sharply. "Are you looking for something?"

"A book," I said, because I simply can't resist a bit of sarcasm.

"Oh good, American wit."

It watched me impatiently.

"I'm supposed to do a paper on portals. Got anything about them?"

"Of course I do," it said, as if these books were the creature's own possessions. "But are you studying portal geography, a history of portals, portals in magic literature? You can't just say you need a book on portals and expect me to know what you're after."

"Is there a card catalog?" I asked because clearly I'd disturbed this being who probably didn't know the words *customer service* existed.

"I *am* the card catalog," it said haughtily.

"Maybe the physics of portals? The nitty gritty of how portals function."

"Yes, you'll want the technical section. One moment."

And then the tricksy hobbit/dwarf thing stretched out and wriggled a long, segmented body up and along one of the support posts to a spot on the third level where it snatched five books. Then, moving head first, it slithered back down, squished itself into its original squat and lumpy form, and waddled up to me, clutching the books like newly discovered treasure.

I couldn't help it. I gaped at the thing.

"Are you a—"

"A bookworm, yes. From a very long line."

The creature prodding me with the books was the only thing that kept me from snorting with laughter at the unintended pun.

"You may take these to the tables there." It pointed to an open area where a single long table with green-shaded reading lamps stood.

"I can't check them out?"

"Were you granted a special card to do so?"

"Can I apply for one?"

It gave a long, exasperated sigh.

"The tables. Bring the books to my desk when you're done. And no eating or drinking in this room."

207

I know I should have been jumping right into my research, but for at least the first ten minutes I was too distracted by the bookworm's movements to look at a single page. When it wasn't getting books, the thing walked on two very stubby legs, dragging a stumpy tail behind it. When it was retrieving and shelving books, its body stretched and lengthened as it wriggled upward and downward amongst the stacks. It was an off-putting sight and I could see why bookworms might have been kept behind locked magical doors.

I studied the books for a couple hours, jotting down notes, occasionally being disturbed (mentally) by the whispering sound of the bookworm's actions, and getting a general idea of how portals were made. A very general idea. Like reading a recipe for bread that included the ingredients but no instructions.

Unable to focus, my thoughts drifted to the Mauvais. And for some reason to the cities he'd targeted. On my notepad, I kept writing the names of the cities.

Pisa.

Tacoma.

Were those the places he'd gone? It didn't make sense. He wouldn't be so obvious, would he? But they couldn't just be random. There had to be meaning behind what he was doing. Or maybe that was just wishful thinking.

Pisa.

Tacoma.

And then the world from the pyramids to the tower. Which was annoyingly vague.

As I flipped through a book on the history of the physics of portals (written in academically dull language), I scribbled the letters P and T. Pisa. Tacoma. Did P and T mean anything?

P.T.

Barnum? Was Devin Kilbride going to strike a circus?

T.P.

Toilet paper? Were all port-a-potties in danger?

The frustration with my brain's inability to have a *Eureka!* moment was compounded by the lack of a portal recipe spelled out for me step by step on the pages before me. I gave up and put the books back on the worm's desk.

Hoping to avoid speaking to the odd librarian again, I'd waited to make my move until it had been slithering around. But the moment it saw me at the desk, its body snapped together, zipping itself back to me. After telling me to wait, it rubbed its squat, knobby hands over each book.

"All looks in order. You may go."

I made my way out of the building, thinking I'd never been so happy to leave a library. The Tower grounds now sat under a heavy bank of clouds as steely grey as Mr. Tenpenny's hair. Despite the clouds, the outside world was intensely brighter than either the bookworm's realm or the gallery that held the crown jewels. As such, I stood a moment, blinking my eyes.

A moment later, when my eyes finally adjusted, my happiness died.

It was the shirt. A stupid t-shirt that sent me rushing toward the White Tower.

CHAPTER TWENTY-NINE
CONNECTING THE DOTS

See, when my eyes had adjusted, a tour group was being guided along by a Yeoman Warder who looked like he'd had just about enough of humans for the day. Sauntering along at the back of the herd and wearing a look of utter boredom was a teenage girl with straight, bleached-to-white hair streaked with blue. She wore a black t-shirt with a pair of dice placed strategically across her flat chest and the words *Viva Las Vegas* underneath.

She must have sensed me staring because she turned her face toward me, then rolled her eyes before continuing to trail along.

Vegas.

From tower to pyramid.

He was going to hit Las Vegas. Specifically, the Strip from the Luxor's pyramid to the Paris! Paris! casino's scaled down Eiffel Tower. How had we missed such an obvious clue?

That's when I started running toward the White Tower. I don't know what I thought the Magics could do. Stop time? Send up an emergency evacuation order for Sin City? Actually go after the Mauvais? Oh gee, there's an idea.

I'd barely taken three steps when Mr. Tenpenny came rushing up to me.

"He's going to hit—" I blurted, but Mr. T was already talking over me.

"Nigel told me you'd be here. It's—" Only then did I notice how drawn and ashen his face was. "I can't believe even he would do this. Come, get inside."

He placed his hand in the small of my back and nudged me forward as if I wouldn't get moving unless he gave me a boost. He then, in stuttering sentences, half of which were cut off by declarations of indignant disbelief, told me what had happened.

I'd been right. But I'd been right too late.

The Strip, that long line of casinos, some of which take up more real estate than an entire city block, had collapsed into what reporters were calling a sinkhole, but what Mr. T swore, from the footage he'd seen, had been a fissure created by the ground pulling apart.

"That could be natural, couldn't it? Earthquake territory and all that?" I asked, making stupid excuses even I didn't believe.

"It's too perfect. The line of destruction is too straight and it goes exactly from the Luxor to the Paris. It's him."

"But that's awfully strong magic, isn't it? I mean, we're talking about ripping apart the earth itself. You said he wasn't that strong."

"He's not. Or at least, he shouldn't be. It's got to be someone here. Olivia is fuming," he said as we entered the White Tower. A chill that had nothing to do with ghosts or clouds or stony interiors crept over my skin.

"She's going to push for my extraction, isn't she? I mean, she can't possibly let this continue."

"I don't know, Cassie. Keep in mind, while you're the prize, he also wants us all to submit to him. If we extract you, is that any guarantee he'll stop, or will he keep striking out of revenge? No, we have to find him. We have to stop him for good this time. But without the portal scans— Oh, I'm not supposed to tell you that." He was speaking in the quick, choppy sentences of someone who was clearly flustered. "But what's it matter if I tell you now? The scans may have gone missing. They're our best clue to where he might be. If they are gone, I honestly don't know how we're going to find him," he said with pained irritability.

"But the traitor? Find that person and they have to know where Kilbride is."

"Yes, but we're running out of time. If Kilbride casts three more D-spells, Simon and Chloe..." He trailed off, but I knew what he meant. The Mauvais had now cast eleven D-spells. Only thirteen could be reversed. Two more spells, and there'd still be a chance, but three more spells meant my parents would be out of range. There would be no easy recovery for them. And with Runa's continued setbacks, possibly no recovery at all. As we turned onto the hallway that led to Olivia's office, he switched to a whisper. "She's making a decision tomorrow."

"But the tribunal."

"She's dug up a little-used rule that says, in an emergency situation, she has the authority to override the tribunal. I'm sorry. I have argued your case, but with Pisa, Tacoma, and now Las Vegas, if he plans to strike again in two days, she's going to want to act before that."

We remained silent as we continued down the hall, but my mind was racing, repeating the cities over and over again. What would be next? Had he delivered a clue with this one? Was there a pattern?

"I just can't imagine what the people of Las Vegas must think. The loss of—" Fiona was saying as we stepped into Olivia's vast office. Since she hadn't brought any bags with her, Fiona must have returned home to change. She was now dressed in a casual denim skirt with a lavender t-shirt with the words *Keep Portland Wyrd* stitched across the front.

And something in my rattled brain snapped into place.

"Las Vegas! The cities!" I cried out excitedly. Banna, Fiona, Runa, and Olivia whipped their heads in my direction and gave me reproachful looks. I bit my lip even though I was buzzing with the thrill of Dr. Watson when he thinks he's figured out a scrap of evidence that Sherlock Holmes has missed (which he never has). "They're clues," I said in a more reasonable tone of voice.

"What are?" asked Runa.

"Pisa. Tacoma. Las Vegas. P. T. L."

"Port Armstrong?" said Fiona.

"What?"

"PTL, it's the airport code for Port Armstrong."

"I don't know why you know that, but no. The letters PTLD used to be the abbreviation that Portlanders used for their return address on mail, or just as shorthand in general. PTL. I bet his next target is going to be a city that starts with D. Duluth, Des Moines, Dubai," I said, rattling off the first cities that came to mind as a dozen other places fought a geographic battle with each other on the tip of my tongue.

"I suppose that's some help in warning them," Olivia said without any sign she thought I was a genius. "But what does that have to do with anything?"

"Don't you see? It's a clue. He's in Portland. He has to be."

"That's quite a stretch, Cassie," said Fiona. "The hits could just be random. It's human instinct to search for patterns."

"And what are we supposed to do with this idea of yours?" Runa asked. "Wait for him to spell out his entire street address with destruction?"

"I think we need Tobey and we need Rafi," I said, practically leaping out of my shoes, ready to go.

"What do you need Tobey for?" Mr. T asked cautiously, no doubt worried I'd lose his grandson down a portal again.

"It's well past time to hypnotize your grandson. He may not know exactly where he was, but if he can visualize it, maybe we can figure it out." Mr. T looked skeptical. "Look, it's either that or I get my brain drained. And I'd really rather experiment on Tobey, if you don't mind."

"I don't think it will provide anything new," Banna said almost apologetically. Since Olivia had barely dimmed the lights, Banna was fully wrapped in clothing and wore the largest pair of sunglasses I'd ever seen. "He's already told us he saw nothing but an interior space with no windows."

"No, she's right," said Fiona. "It might provide a clue. It can't hurt." She shifted to face Olivia. "Since you're insisting on overriding the tribunal, you should at least give her this chance."

"Fine," said Olivia, "but if it turns up nothing, we're going to have to set things up for the extraction to take place some time tomorrow. This can't continue. Cassie, fill these capsules for Runa, then please leave," she said curtly, then turned her back on us.

Knowing Olivia was in no mood to be trifled with, I scooped up the packet of capsules she'd indicated. I hurriedly filled them, wondering if my parents would taste the bitterness in my magic. We then left without a word. Banna, as if wanting to get away from the light in the room as quickly as possible, hadn't lingered around and had been the first out the door. Fiona and Busby walked out together. I trailed along, but glanced back when I got to the office's door. Runa had remained behind. She and Olivia were whispering, but their gaze briefly met mine. A knowing smile lifted both their lips as they went back to whatever they were plotting.

So Runa would be part of my extraction. After all her talk of me not giving up my magic. What a way to repay the person who'd just saved your life a few hours ago.

CHAPTER THIRTY
PREVIOUS WHAT?

Not wanting Fiona or Busby to talk me out of what I thought was a brilliant idea, while they were distracted with one another at the end of the hallway, I dashed to get Tobey who, having cleaned my entire room, was currently using his magic to coax the wrinkles out of my t-shirts. With hardly any explanation, I marched him down the stairs to Rafi's cluttered office. Which was empty. Of humans, that is. It was still crammed full of Rafi refuse.

I poked around the clutter a bit just to make sure Rafi hadn't gotten trapped under a heavy box or perhaps a fallen bookshelf. He hadn't. I scanned the mess scattered across his desk. On top of a stack of binders from which tufts of fur and feather stuck out was a spiral-bound day planner. I checked it, a gnawing worry growing in my belly. Not a worry that Rafi might be off on important HQ business, but a knowing worry regarding my luck within the White Tower. And there, jotted into the current time slot, was what I'd suspected.

"Come on," I grumbled.

"What is it? What are we doing?"

"Climbing to the roof," I said, my legs already aching at the prospect. "Rafi's doing his laps."

"Do I need another infusion of magic? Because I feel great. Did you see your room?"

"Yes, good job. You get a gold star for the day. Now," I said, pointing to the stairwell, "get up the stairs."

After the first couple flights, Tobey again asked why we needed to see Rafi.

"Because he can hypnotize you to see if you can remember more about where you were."

"I told you all I can remember."

"All your waking mind can remember."

Rafi was whipping his slim frame around the small, rooftop track when we stepped out. When he saw us, he slowed to a jog to cool down.

"We don't have a lesson for another hour," he said, barely breathing faster than normal as he wiped from his brow the three drops of sweat he'd produced. Fit people are so annoying.

"Can you hypnotize Tobey?" I explained what I'd been thinking. That since I had a clue where the Mauvais might be, maybe a little subconscious memory tapping could seal the deal.

"I was thinking the exact same thing, but Olivia doesn't see any reason for the hypnosis. And Runa agreed that, since Tobey doesn't seem to have any memory problems after his little trip, we'd only be wasting our time." Runa again. It's not like we were best friends or anything, but it was still disheartening to have her siding so strongly with Olivia. From what I'd seen, Runa had never been opposed to trying any method that might work. I knew the two had something going on between them, but it seemed as if Runa was no longer thinking for herself. "But," Rafi continued, "I still think hypnotizing him might help draw us a clearer picture."

"Exactly." I watched Rafi impatiently. "So do it."

"Am I allowed to drink some water first?"

"If you must," I said as we walked over to the side table where a pitcher of water with lemon slices floating inside

216

waited. Rafi drank two glasses, then told Tobey to sit on the bench.

"Shouldn't I lay down?"

"Why? Are you sleepy? Don't worry, if you start to topple over, you'll catch yourself. If you don't catch yourself and end up falling to the floor, we'll be sure to take pictures and share them on Instagram." Tobey, protesting, started to stand, but Rafi pushed him back down. "I'm kidding. You'll be fine. Now, close your eyes and be quiet."

Tobey obeyed. Rafi then took Tobey's hands in his and closed his own eyes, muttering something that did not sound like English. Tobey's head drooped, but soon lifted again. His eyes had a creepy, far-away look that reminded me of my parents' vacant expressions.

"Tell us where you were, Tobey. Before you came to the White Tower most recently, you were somewhere. Describe it."

Tobey went on, telling of the same wood beams and hard-packed dirt floor. But as Rafi prodded with more precise questions while tightening his squeeze on Tobey's hands, Tobey began to fill in more detail. His subconscious mind dug up images of a stone- and brick-lined room and, of all things, a dentist chair. Perhaps his teeth were sending him a message after his recent sugar overload.

"He wants Alastair to do something with the chair," Tobey said groggily. "Alastair doesn't want to, but he's being made to."

"Compulsion Hex," Rafi mouthed to me and I wondered what else Alastair might be made to do under that spell. Was he being made to destroy the cities? The thought made my stomach ache.

Tobey droned on. "There's something cold and bright. I can't figure it out. The floor isn't a floor. It's dirt, but hard. There's wooden beams on the ceiling. Lots of spider webs. I'm reminded of the sea." Rafi and I exchanged a look and we both shrugged. Who knew what random things Tobey's brain was dredging up.

"There's a door. Oh, we came in that door," Tobey said as if just remembering. Rafi remained silent and passed me a look that told me I shouldn't interrupt. I pinched my lips to hold back the questions bubbling in me. "It's like a hall, sort of arched though, like a tunnel. And there's doors off to the sides. At the end. That's where we came in. Where we popped through. A smaller room than the first. Lots of shelves."

"Is this a new place, Tobey, or an old one?" Rafi asked, speaking quietly.

"Old. Nothing's new, but there's some dim lights, so maybe it's used for something."

I tapped Rafi's shoulder and pointed to my nose when he glanced up at me.

"Is there a smell to the place?"

Tobey sniffed as if he were there. "Musty. And like stale beer. Dusty too, but also like it had once been wet."

Rafi looked to me and mouthed, "More?" I shook my head. It hadn't rung any bells of familiarity and it seemed Tobey really had only been in a small, possibly underground area with no windows. He had no clue where exactly he'd gone.

"Okay, Tobey, good job. You're going to wake up, but first, don't forget to drool a little because we think that's funny."

A small trickle of drool dribbled out the side of Tobey's mouth. His eyes cleared and he immediately wiped his face. "Did I fall asleep?"

And, as childish as it was, the drooling was funny. Except to Tobey, of course.

* * *

218

The next morning I woke to rain lashing against my window and a breakfast that was little more than toast and tea. Placed between the plate and the teapot was a crisply folded (and worded) note ordering me to go to Olivia's office the instant I was dressed.

Would this be when she said, *Sod it all,* and extracted me to save the Magics of the world? Or maybe the tribunal had made their ruling. Had they decided I was never going to fully tame my magic and that I was too much of a threat to keep around? At least I knew Pablo would have a happy home full of sartorial splendor.

At the thought of Lola and Pablo, I suddenly, urgently, needed something familiar. I craved a kind word, a cat in a silly costume, even a crocheted creation would do. If this office visit didn't result in an immediate brain drain, I swore to get outside to check my messages.

Or I could just go out now and—

No, I had to face whatever horrible music was waiting for me in Olivia's office. And I had a feeling I knew what tune would be playing.

See, Tobey hadn't been wrong. Mr. T hadn't been wrong. Not long after the Tobey hypnosis session, Fiona had told me they'd confirmed the portal scans for the night I'd recovered my parents had completely vanished. And I'll give you one guess as to who was going to get the Blanket of Blame piled on top of her.

"Did you take the scans?" Olivia asked the moment I stepped into her tapestry-lined realm. Mr. Tenpenny and Fiona were there with cups of steaming tea before them. They at least had the decency to look shamefaced at Olivia's harsh accusation.

"No, I wouldn't have any idea how to read them, anyway."

"Your arm." With her palm up, Olivia flicked her fingers in a get-over-here-now gesture. I took a step back.

"She's not going to extract you," Mr. T said, reading my mind as easily as a child's primer. "She only wants to check on something."

I strode up to the desk, feigning confidence even as my legs urged me to turn and run. When I held out my arm, it would take a blind person not to see the limb trembling.

"Olivia, maybe you could explain?" said Fiona. "You're frightening her for no reason."

"I need to check what you've done recently." Olivia's voice was sharp and far from comforting. She wrapped her long, cool fingers around my wrist, then said more gently, "It won't hurt. *Previous non persona.*"

I was about to ask, *Previous what?* when half the tea in Fiona and Busby's cups evaporated.

"Only a Drying Spell," Mr. T said in a tone that implied, *Please release her, you're being ridiculous.* Or at least that's what I hoped the tone implied.

"Why did you perform a Drying Spell?" asked Olivia without letting go of my arm.

"Because I went swimming and didn't want to drip all over the stonework." I thought it best not to tell her it was also because I'd been in a hurry to get to the library to study up on how to build portals.

"When was this? When did you go swimming?"

"Just after you arrested Chester," I said evenly.

"I told you Olivia," said Busby, "it would have been impossible. The scans had to have been taken from Runa's office soon before or after she was poisoned. Cassie was right there with us."

"I suppose you're right. It was best to check, though. We can't rule anyone out these days." Olivia released my arm, and it was only then I noticed the dark circles under her eyes, the drawn pallor of her normally vibrant skin. I might have sympathized with the strain she was under. You know, if she wasn't itching for my extraction. That kind of thing does lessen your empathy for a person. "You may go. I believe Rafi has something planned for you. He should be in his office. No detours on the way, please." Olivia dropped into her chair, then looked up at me, a sincere expression of understanding softened her face slightly. "I do apologize for your lessons being in such a shambles lately. I hope you're practicing."

I hesitantly said I was, while trying to grasp the incongruity of it all. Why would Olivia care one lick if I was practicing or not? Was the strain getting to her? Was she trying to keep me busy to keep me out of her hair? Why show concern about my lessons at the same time she was clamoring for my extraction? As I've said more than once and will likely have made into a bumper sticker: Magics are impossible to figure out.

With a quick nod to Fiona and Busby, I cleared out before Olivia went back to accusing me of magical crimes.

CHAPTER THIRTY-ONE

ORBS & EXPLANATIONS

When I got to Rafi's workspace, I knocked on the door. In response, a bright pink sticky note appeared at eye level. Words wrote themselves in black ink: *Rafi is in the Practice Room.* This took up most of the space on the note. These words vanished and new ones appeared: *Meet me there, Cassie.* Then the note faded away as if melting into the door's woodwork.

Of course I should have known he'd be in the practice room. First, as I'd seen while cramming toast into my mouth that morning, the grey clouds from the day before had dragged in an angry squall. And although the netting around the rooftop rec area had a Camouflage Charm on it, HQ hadn't bothered to treat it with any type of waterproofing. As such, each gust would lash rain straight through, soaking anyone up there.

Second, what would a day in the White Tower be without having to climb an endless number of stairs? I devised several new curse words as I trudged back down to the practice room. You know, the room that was barely twenty steps from where I'd just been.

"Ah, you got my note."

"You could have told Olivia I was to meet you here." I pointed to Tobey, who had been chatting with Rafi when I entered. "Is it safe for him to be here with the others so close?"

"One: the exercise is good for those skinny legs of yours. Two: if anyone comes in, we'll just say he was bored and wanted to watch. But I doubt they'll be stopping by."

I said nothing to this. After some debate, and because the weather was making the room depressingly gloomy, we decided orbs would be a good place to start.

"You're not going to burn any holes in the door, are you?" Rafi asked, referring to a little problem I had when I first came to the White Tower.

"No, but that doesn't mean I can't light your hair on fire if you annoy me."

"Point taken: Do not annoy Cassie Black."

"Good luck with that," Tobey chimed in. Rafi high-fived him and I rolled my eyes. Rafi then took Tobey's arm, grasped my hand, and gave Tobey what he called, "A little top up."

"He barely needs it, though. His magic levels are staying pretty steady. It's unusual. Didn't you say it never stuck before?"

"Sure. Grandad tried in the past, and I've had infusions from other Magics just as an experiment, but none worked. Of course, we didn't have a conduit. You think that's the difference?"

"Could be. My breed of elf, the kind that can conduct, are rare these days and we're nearly absent in American communities, so that's not surprising. But I think it's more to do with Cassie's strength."

"So why doesn't it work on my parents?"

Rafi shrugged one shoulder. "Don't know. Like Dr. Dunwiddle said, it could be that their cells have forgotten how to hold onto magic. Some is getting in, though, from what I hear."

"Yeah, it's sticking, then vanishing. Like it's just being sucked out of them."

Tobey and Rafi looked at me.

"I haven't been near them except when Dr. D has allowed it. I want them better." I could still feel where Rafi's fingers had gripped my arm. It reminded me of the question I'd been too afraid to ask Olivia.

"What's *previous non persona* mean?"

"That's a bit advanced, even for you," said Rafi.

"That's not an answer. I'm not planning on doing it. It was done to me."

"Ah, so she went through with accusing you. For the record, I did tell her it was pointless. Anyway, the Previous Spell on its own makes the last spell a Magic performed happen back on him or herself. It's one of the few spells you do while touching someone."

"What do you mean by that?" I asked.

"With any other spell, touching someone while you're casting it causes the spell to happen to both of you. Say you're doing a Stunning Spell while grabbing someone's arm. Well, you'll stun them, but unless you've been trained to resist it, you'll also stun yourself.

"But a Previous Spell only affects your victim by, like I said, re-casting the last spell they performed back onto them. So, if you grab my arm and say, 'Previous,' I'll—" He thought a moment. "I'll end up with the words from the note I left you written across my forehead. Make sense?"

"Yeah, but the *non persona* bit. What's that about?"

"It conjures the Previous Spell, but deflects the Magic's last incantation onto some nearby object rather than on the Magic himself. You know, just in case the last spell was a dangerous one. So, going back to my Note Charm, if you took hold of my arm and said '*Previous non persona,*' the words would write themselves on the wall instead of my forehead.

"It's a quick and clumsy way of finding out what spells a Magic has done. It certainly wouldn't stand up in a court of law; the records of spells the gnomes keep make a far stronger case. So," he said, clearly ready for a change of subject, "orbs?"

Rafi twisted his hand in the same motion you use when putting in a light bulb. A Magic's Solas Charm typically reflects their eye color — for example, mine produces a hazel orb, while Banna's creates a blue one. However, despite Rafi's deep brown eyes, an orangish-yellow orb appeared before him. He said it had taken months to perfect. Months during which he'd accidentally conjured quite a few black holes — only tiny ones, he assured me.

To show off his Solas prowess, Rafi spread his hands to enlarge his orb. He next brought his hands together to shrink it down to a pinpoint, which he then, with his index finger bobbing and twirling, made the pinpoint dance in loops in midair, leaving behind a trail of light that spelled out his name.

"I forgot how fun these things can be. Your turn," he said, shutting down his orb and facing Tobey.

"How?" Tobey tried twisting his hand as Rafi had, but nothing happened.

"I believe that's Cassie's job." I gave him a sour look. "Your magic, your student."

I thought of what Banna had told me when she had first shown me the spell. Basically, you come up with a good memory and focus that memory into a point of light. I told Tobey to think of a good memory. He stood there for several moments looking up at the ceiling as if hunting for an idea in the rafters. His lips twisted and he shook his head a few times, as if casting off a few candidates.

"It doesn't have to be you winning the Nobel Prize or anything," I said. "Just something good. Happy."

"Yeah, I know, but I keep coming up with doing things with you. I was hoping for something better than that."

Rafi snorted a laugh.

"You're not helping," I told him.

"Look, Tobey," said Rafi, "like she says, it doesn't have to be anything stellar, just not something miserable. I do find it hard to believe you have any memory of Cassie that isn't miserable, though."

I threw a gentle Shoving Charm at Rafi's upper arm. He cried out more in surprise than pain, after which he promised to keep his comments to a minimum.

"Okay, I think I've got one," said Tobey.

"About time. Now concentrate on that while picturing a light. A small light, like no more than a fifteen-watt nightlight. I don't want you blinding us."

Tobey's face tightened. We were really going to have to work on his presentation if he wasn't going to look like he was in constipated agony every time he did magic. Slowly, a swirling, wispy cloud of light appeared. Banna had said most beginners produce orbs that aren't tight. This must have been what she meant.

I told Tobey he was doing well, then looked to Rafi for guidance. He made back-and-forth cupping motions with his two hands.

"Now, imagine compacting it, like you're making a snowball."

The light cloud got looser. "How about a snowball you're going to aim at my head. Do the hand motions."

Tobey's face tensed, showing his frustration, but he did as I suggested and moved his hands in a cupping motion around an imaginary snowball. It took some time, but the cloud slowly came together into a circle of light with only a loose corona around it.

"Not perfect, but nearly so," I said encouragingly.

"Now, move it," Rafi said.

Tobey, who was sweating with concentration by this point, got a worried look on his face. "How?"

"Yes, Cassie, how?" chimed in Rafi.

"A Shoving Charm, I guess. A gentle one. This isn't a heavy object; it won't need much."

"Two spells at once?" Tobey's orb began to loosen.

"Go on, you can do it," I said. "Tighten that back up and make it move. An orb's not going to do you much good if you can't get it to cast light where you need."

Tobey inhaled deeply through his nostrils, made the poopy face, then made the cupping motions. The orb formed more tightly this time. There was no corona, just a sphere of light the size of a golf ball. "Good," I said quietly. "Now a little push." Tobey moved his hands up, extended his index finger, and made a motion like he was poking something.

The orb shifted. Only about three centimeters, but it was a start.

"Take a break," I told him. "Can we get donuts?" I asked Rafi.

"Not until you show us yours. You're still learning this too, you know."

Since I'd done the spell a few times, I didn't have to go through the steps of conjuring a memory, focusing it, or any of that novice stuff. What I did have to do, what I kind of had issues with, was to stop the orb from radiating heat. An orb is supposed to be nothing but light. More efficient than an LED bulb, it should give off no warmth. Mine, well, they tended to be a little toasty.

I closed my eyes and pictured the orb. It appeared without any problem, but the instant I made it, I could feel the heat on my face. The center of the thing was the same rich green Tobey's had been, reflecting the hazel of my eyes. But it also had sparks of red jumping from it.

"Think of ice," Rafi suggested. I tried, but only ended up producing puffs of steam as the ice sizzled from my sparks.

"Not working."

"Maybe your memory is too warm?" Rafi suggested. He had a point. When I'd first done the Solas Charm, I'd produced an orb even Banna was impressed by. It was compact and emitted no heat. The memory I'd used had been of Tobey helping me clean up my apartment. A good memory of unexpected friendship, but a rather neutral one that was made good only in relation to the terrible stuff that had happened just before.

But I couldn't get that memory to stick during my latest efforts. The memory that kept rising first in my mind was of Alastair, of the kiss he'd surprised me with after I passed my first magic test. As Rafi had guessed, the image was far too warm.

I tried to come up with a different memory, but ones of Alastair wouldn't stay away. The orb grew warmer. His voice becoming more worried than encouraging, Rafi offered tips. Then the thought broke through of what the Mauvais might be doing to Alastair while I was playing around teaching Tobey. My orb disappeared entirely.

"I can't do this," I said.

Rafi stood up and strode over to stand face to face with me. He took my hands and stared into my eyes.

"Ah, now I see why your orbs are so fiery," Rafi teased. He then spoke more gently, "He'll be okay. We'll get to him."

"You can't know that," I said, tears pricking the corners of my eyes.

"No, I can't. But you found your parents against all odds. We'll find Alastair. Am I guessing that you no longer think he's a fiend?" I nodded. "Good. Now, chin up." He let go of my hands and chucked me lightly on the chin. "Let's make an orb that won't burn the place down, shall we? A little cooler memory, perhaps."

I pulled through the files in my head and came up with a recent one of Pablo nudging me with his chin and purring louder than a leaf blower.

The orb appeared. A tight cluster of hazel green that seemed to pulse in time to the rhythm of Pablo's purrs.

"And the Teacher of the Year Award goes to Rafi," Rafi said, mocking the overly enthusiastic voice of a sports announcer. He walked up to the orb, holding his hands out. "Hardly any heat. Better. Much better. Now, let's have some fun with these things."

It took some practice with Tobey, but after about an hour, he could move his orb around with a fair amount of efficiency. My orb was staying relatively cool even as I experimented with bringing in *warmer* memories, as Rafi called them.

After a plate of donuts was summoned and consumed, we tried a game of follow-the-leader with the three orbs in which we had to follow the front orb's every motion. This was difficult for Tobey, as he didn't have the same control as Rafi or I did and his orb kept charging past ours.

We finished up with both Rafi and me making a second orb, pulling all of our orbs into tight balls, lining up the five points of light with Tobey's in the middle, and swinging out the end orb to send a wave that made the orb at the opposite end swing out while the middle three stayed in place.

"Just what the bored CEO needs for his desk," Rafi said.

I didn't respond. Watching those balls swinging back and forth, seeing that they had a connection even without any visible ties, gave me an idea of how I might get to the Mauvais.

CHAPTER THIRTY-TWO
SHORT CONNECTIONS

The clacking orbs, plus everything I'd read at the library the previous day, had filled my head with an image of portals connecting together, influencing each other without ever touching. And that image might just get me around the problem of creating a long-distance portal to the Mauvais.

A long-distance portal, also referred to as a deep portal, essentially required taking a person apart in one place and putting them back together in another. Not something I wanted to attempt. But short-distance portals were different. As Morelli had told me, instead of taking one big leap, you could link shorter portals together to hop your way to a destination. Even better, these shallower portals involved a separate principle of magical physics that didn't involve dismantling a human down to the molecular level.

And if I could create a string of short-distance portals, I could get to wherever the Mauvais was.

Okay, granted, I still didn't know where that might be exactly, but at least I was getting a plan ready just in case. Which is more than any of the others seemed to be doing. After all, even with their combined power, their experience, and their access to magical information, HQ wasn't exactly rallying the troops with any sense of urgency.

And they wondered why I kept taking matters into my own hands.

I mean, look who figured out — in only a couple weeks, mind you — that Vivian wasn't on the up and up. Sure, I hadn't exactly realized she was the Mauvais before I confronted her, but I'd also found my parents on the slimmest of clues. Again, there'd been complications I hadn't exactly foreseen, but at least I had solved these problems while the other Magics had been doing little more than twiddling their thumbs.

So while Olivia and the others went about things in their usual slow and plodding way, perhaps stopping along the way for a lengthy lunch and a nap, I was more than ready to jump into a fighter jet and speed my way toward figuring out where the Mauvais was holed up with Alastair.

There was just the minor problem that, just as I didn't know how to fly a fighter jet, I didn't know how to make any type of portal — short- or long-distance. Well, and the fact I might be extracted at any moment. Details, details.

Unable to keep my ideas to myself, as soon as Tobey and I began heading up the stairs and were well out of earshot of Olivia's office, I told him my theory of connecting up a series of short-distance portals.

"We should try it out," he said excitedly. His enthusiasm was a change from his previous prickly attitude toward me, but at that moment I wasn't sure it was a change for the better. Theory was one thing. Putting it into practice was another. Especially when one wrong move could have Olivia rushing up to my room and whipping the magic out of my neurons.

"But I don't know how to make one portal let alone several of them."

"I think you should just try the deep portal."

"Brilliant idea. Do you want to be the lab rat for that

experiment?" Tobey didn't answer. "I thought not. A deep portal is out of the question."

"But you think shallow ones are possible?"

"Maybe. From what I read, creating a portal basically involves using the physics side of magic to bring the two areas as close together as possible. The portal itself serves as a connector. But that connector is different based on the depth of the portal. That's why when you step from MagicLand— sorry, from Rosaria to regular Portland, it's not much different than walking from one room to another. But when you travel from Portland to London, you feel it more keenly."

"Yeah, and if you do it too often, it messes up your sense of time," Tobey said as we entered my room. "Fiona's been going back and forth, and she keeps complaining about feeling like everything's twenty minutes off." This sounded vaguely familiar, but Tobey didn't give me time to dwell on it. "So, can you do a short one?"

"Maybe. I mean, it's worth a try, right? All I need to do is fold the two places together."

"You lost me."

I grabbed a piece of paper from my nightstand. On one half of the paper I wrote *British Museum*. On the other half I wrote *Tower of London*. "We have two places. A shallow portal joins them like so." I folded the sheet in half so the words met. "A deep portal is way more complicated, but if we add in another place," I jotted *Buckingham Palace* at the bottom of the sheet and folded that up so it overlapped the other words, "we've added another layer. And if I thread a string through these places, they'd be connected. Just like a portal."

"And you're able to do that?"

"Nope. Not that I know of, anyway. But from what I've seen, half of doing magic involves visualizing what you mean to do."

I held up the paper. "I've got my visual guide."

"Then let's do this," Tobey said, hopping up from the bed and slapping his hands together like we were about to run outside and toss the old pigskin around. Despite my phobia of all team sports, playing football sounded like the more appealing option compared to experimenting with portal creation. But, there was Tobey, egging me on. "Come on, Cassie, let's try a shallow portal."

"I think I liked you better when you despised me." I paused, thinking of how to go about this, and regretting mentioning anything to Tobey. "All right, you go in the bathroom and shut the door. I'll see if I can get there."

Tobey went into the bathroom and latched the door. I concentrated on folding my room, imagining a straw between the two areas as I drew my hand in a circle. I know I'd admonished Tobey numerous times for it, but apparently there is some finger waggling in more advanced magic spells. Then, recalling a note jotted in the margins of one of the books in the library, I said, "*Locus unitus.*"

On the eighth circle, a glowing ring formed in front of me. One of the books had said it should only take three circles, but maybe that came with practice. I wasn't sure about sticking any body parts into my creation, so I took the piece of paper, wadded it into a ball, and chucked it through the portal.

It disappeared. It actually worked.

"What the hell, Cassie!" Tobey yelled, cutting off my *whoop* of success before it ever reached my lips.

I heard running water and splashing. I whisked away my portal and rushed to the bathroom. Tobey yanked open the door and pointed at the floor where a blackened wad of sodden paper lay smoldering.

And that's why you run tests.

"Let me give it another go. At least I know how to magically incinerate trash now."

Tobey closed the door again. I tried the spell again. A glowing ring appeared again. I tried another piece of paper.

It went through the ring, but rather than disappearing into the bathroom, the paper merely fell to the floor on the opposite side of the ring. The following attempt had the paper bouncing right off the portal's surface. On the next try, I got the paper to go through. Before any sense of pride could bloom in me, Tobey opened the bathroom door and pointed to the floor. The paper had scattered in a confetti blast of tattered shreds as if Pablo had gone wild on it after too many hits from his bag of catnip. That put a stop to my experiments right there.

"I can't use one of these things. Even if I could get through, even I could travel farther than one room to another, I do not want to end up shredded for recycling. I'm not going to be able to learn this on my own," I said, staring at the ragged bits of paper and imagining my skin and bones being run through a meat grinder. "I need someone who knows portals."

"Runa knows them, and Banna probably invented them."

"Yeah, but it's not like they're going to help me break any rules." Just then, my stomach growled, demanding to be refueled after such an intense use of magic. I was wondering if lunch might appear soon or if Tobey and I should go down to The Keys when my head filled with a picture of Mr. Wood assembling his sandwich. Morelli knew portals. "I need to make another trip to Portland."

"I could—" I think Tobey was about to invite himself, but the pounding at my door stopped his words.

"Cassie. Cassie, are you in there?"

I hurried over to the door. Instinctively, I took a quick sniff before turning the handle. The bergamot scent of Earl Grey.

When I pulled open the door, Busby had his fist raised, about to knock again. "Oh good," he said when his eyes caught sight of Tobey, "you're here as well." Mr. T's nose then wrinkled. "Has something been burning?"

"What's going on?" I asked, avoiding his question.

"Another city has been hit," he said, anger ringing through his smooth accent.

"Dublin?" I said, grabbing at the first city that came to mind.

"Yes. St. Patrick's Cathedral. It just collapsed in on itself like an implosion, and there's no sign of any seismic activity in the area. How did you know?"

"I told you the next one would start with a D. But this is too soon. Las Vegas was only yesterday. He said every two days," I complained, as if you could really expect an evil wizard to stick to schedule.

"Yes, well," he glanced down to his shoes, took a steadying breath, then met my eyes. "That's why Olivia has made her decision."

CHAPTER THIRTY-THREE

TOBEY APPRECIATION DAY

Mr. T walked with me back down to Olivia's office. Tobey trailed close behind, even though Mr. T had told him he wouldn't be allowed in. It was a silent descent of doom, not only because I knew what was coming, but because what could possibly be said in my defense in the face of the utter destruction the Mauvais was causing? I couldn't blame Olivia for her choice. If I was a cold-hearted witch faced with such a problem, I might make the same decision. I was a risk. My magic was a danger.

Granted, I would have preferred to find Alastair first. One last goodbye kiss wouldn't have gone amiss. And it would have been worth everything to see my parents back to health. But that wasn't in the cards for Cassie Black.

At the door to Olivia's office, Tobey tugged me aside and pulled me into a tight, completely awkward hug. When he wished me luck, my throat tightened and my eyes burnt with the tears I needed to fight back. I would not let Olivia see me cry.

"Thanks," I said, pushing back from the embrace. Turning quickly on my heels, I followed Mr. Tenpenny into the stony space I'd become too familiar with.

"Have a seat," Olivia offered. Fiona was there, as was Runa. Rafi, whose calming influence I could have used, was absent. Figures.

"Busby has told you of the latest development?" I nodded, afraid to speak. "The Mauvais is showing his strength as well as his impatience, and we have to assume that some of that is due to someone passing him your power. He's growing stronger as a result of your magic still making its way to him. Because of that, I've decided the only way to keep other Magics, and all the world, safe is to extract you. The tribunal does not fully agree with my assessment, but that is the way it is. I know you may find this unfair, you didn't ask to be—"

"It's fine. I understand."

I didn't fully. Not even a week ago, Olivia said it was too dangerous to extract me. That having my power collected into convenient takeaway packages would make it easy for the Mauvais or his traitorous partner to snatch up those packets of Cassie goodness. But there was no point in arguing. If all of Mr. Tenpenny's, Morelli's, and Fiona's pleas couldn't sway Olivia, there was nothing my tongue could produce that would change her mind.

My acceptance threw the normally unflappable Olivia. She literally did a double take at my response. It was obvious she'd been ready for an argument, for complaints at the very least. As such, she staggered over a few words before saying, "I— that is, I appreciate your cooperation. It will be recorded as part of your character."

I didn't know or care what this meant. I assumed she was talking about the book that each community kept to note the events that took place within their realm. But I was going to be turned into a magical moron. What did I care what some book said about me?

Almost as if reading my thoughts, Fiona pulled a large hardback from the small, daisy-patterned purse she had on the floor beside her chair. She handed the hefty tome to me. I didn't need to look at the title. It's hard to forget a book you've flung across the room. The spine had been repaired, but it was the same copy of *An Enchanted History of the Portland Community* in which I'd first seen an image of my parents. They'd been standing with Devin Kilbride's arms draped chummily over their shoulders.

"If you'd like to add your own story in there, it would be an honor," said Fiona, her voice raspy with emotion.

"When?" I asked. Fiona started to respond, likely thinking I meant when I should do my scribbling, but I clarified. "When will I be extracted? How long do I have?"

Olivia looked to Runa as if for confirmation. Runa gave a small nod and Olivia said, "Tomorrow morning. The same time we'll be taking care of Chester. The hour before dawn is the optimal time for such matters. That should also give you time to say your goodbyes."

"My goodbyes wouldn't only be to people here. I'd like to go home."

"That can't be allowed. It's too dangerous."

"I won't run, if that's what you're thinking."

"No, that's not it. Until we know who the traitor is and where the Mauvais is, we can't risk you being out in the world unguarded. You will have to make do with phone calls."

This hurt more than the knowledge I'd be extracted. I think I'd pretty much known Olivia or the tribunal would come to that decision, but to not say goodbye in person to Mr. Wood, to Lola, to Pablo? I couldn't help it; tears burned their way down my cheeks.

"I understand," I said through tight lips, then stood and marched out of the room.

238

Seeing my face, Tobey was wise enough not to say a word. I didn't want to sulk in my room. After the following morning, I was sure I'd be confined to tight quarters, perhaps a padded cell, for the rest of my life. I wanted fresh air. I wanted to be away from the White Tower. Tobey followed me outside.

No messages came through my phone. I can't explain the utter disappointment this drove into me even more strongly than the news of my sentencing. It pulled every ounce of energy from me and I knew I couldn't walk any farther. Sensing something was wrong, Tobey gripped me by the arm and guided me to the nearest bench.

After a few moments of sitting there in silence, I started thumbing through the book with Tobey watching the pages go by. My brain was too numb to come up with words about myself, but the feel of a book in my hands, the action of turning the pages was somehow familiar and comforting. Tobey pointed out a few images of places from his childhood and a few friends from his youth who had gone on to other communities. His chatter was pointless, but it did provide a distraction, and I appreciated him for that.

It wasn't long before Winston found us. He gave Tobey a calculating glance, then jumped onto my shoulder and rubbed his smooth head against my cheek, which nearly had me sobbing again. The bird then hopped down to the arm of the bench and tilted his head at the book. Crouching down, he wedged his beak into the front pages I'd already flipped through.

"What's he doing?" asked Tobey.

"Wait, you can see him?"

"Of course I can see him. Why shouldn't I?"

"Because you've never seen him before. Remember when the raven went to stop Rafi?" Tobey gave a single nod, but looked at me like I was nuts. "And you were wondering who I was talking to?" Again, the wary nod. I pointed to Winston. "This is who I was talking to. Tobey meet Winston. Winston meet Tobey." Like mirror images of one another, the two both tilted their heads in greeting. I then explained to Tobey about Winston.

"But why can I see him now if I couldn't before?"

I thought for a moment. Tobey wasn't dead like Nigel. He wasn't undead like Mr. Tenpenny. He was too young and nowhere near clever enough to have become a Yeoman Warder without telling us. It had to be—

"My magic," I said, my misery momentarily pushed aside by magical wonder. "That's what allows me to be one of the few living people who can see Winston. And since you have my magic—"

"I can see him too. That's kind of cool." By now, Winston had returned his attention to the book. "Still doesn't explain what he's doing."

"Maybe there's a picture of a girl raven on that page."

Tobey gave me a look that said, *Yeah, right.* But I turned to the page anyway.

"See," said Tobey when there was nothing but text on the pages. I didn't even know it was possible for birds to do so, but I would swear Winston scowled at Tobey with a look of pure disdain. He then tapped his beak on the fourth paragraph on the left-hand page, looked at me, then tapped the paragraph again.

"Maybe he wants a story read to him?" I scanned the paragraph. I couldn't stop my mouth from gaping open in surprise. Looking at Winston, I asked, "Are you—? Winston, you are very creepy. Wonderful, but creepy. How could you know that?"

"What are you talking about?" Tobey asked irritably.

I read him the paragraph.

"Adneta Walls was arrested today, the fifteenth of March, 1861, for building a person-to-person portal. Adneta, known for her ability to foretell the future, saw a great battle coming. Her brother, Arnold Walls, lives in the Manassas Community in the state of Virginia. Adneta stated she only wanted to get her brother to the safety of Rosaria and that she should not be punished for such an act.'

"And then there's a side note dated May 1861, stating Arnold was killed following the Battle of Bull Run. Arnold didn't fight, but Norm locals accused him of collaborating with the north, of using witchcraft to try to thwart the Confederate army."

"But the Confederates won that battle."

I was terrible with my American history, so I took Tobey at his word and pointed to a note in the side margin.

"It's dated June 1902, and says person-to-person portals hadn't been illegal during Adneta's time. She was posthumously pardoned, but such portals have been banned due to the inability to regulate or register their activity. Don't you see? This is the key. Build a portal to the Mauvais himself, not to where he is."

"Yeah, but how did Winston know that was there?"

I stroked the bird's back. "Because he's a good boy, aren't you?" Winston held his head even prouder than normal. I shut the book. "I need to go to Portland."

"They said you couldn't."

"Tobey Tenpenny, were you eavesdropping?" He shrugged. "I don't care. I'm going anyway. This could be the only way I get to Alastair. I can at least do that before they turn me into a moron."

"Not that that'll be hard."

"Oh, har har." I started to head back to the White Tower, then remembered my last attempt to sneak home. "Damn it!" I nearly threw down the book in frustration.

TAMMIE PAINTER

Tobey was by my side in an instant. "What?" he asked worriedly as he bent over to pick up the book. "What's happened?"

"Nothing's happened. And nothing's going to happen. I can't get through the portal. They've closed it to me." I quickly told him of my earlier attempt to get through the Portland-London portal on my own. "I need another Magic to chaperone me."

I let out a growl of irritation. More than a few heads turned my way, and more than a few tourists scuttled away from me. I swatted the book away when Tobey held it out to me. Then, of all the inappropriate things to do, Tobey grinned, looking stupidly pleased with himself.

"What?" I snapped.

"I'm kind of a Magic now, aren't I?"

I couldn't help it. I laughed. Then, experiencing a lapse of my normal personality, I threw my arms around Tobey in a delighted hug. I know, two hugs in one day. Just goes to show what stress can do to a person.

"Tobey, for once you are not completely useless."

CHAPTER THIRTY-FOUR
ILLEGAL PORTALS

Despite my initial joy, reality quickly settled in.

"It's not going to work," I said and slumped down on a low stone wall.

"Why do you always have to be so negative? Is it because it was my idea?"

"No." I pulled out my phone. "It's because of that." I showed him the clock on the home screen. "It's too early. Olivia told me the Portland portal doesn't open until after dawn unless it's urgent. Somehow, I don't think she's going to see my exploring the possibilities of an illegal portal as urgent." My frustration, my feeling of being trapped was made worse by Tobey's gleeful expression. "And why are you grinning?"

"Because I know things you don't," he said in the taunting tone of an eight-year-old. I crossed my arms over my chest and stared at him, feeling very tempted to set his eyebrows on fire. "On Sundays, which would be today, the international portals open early and stay open later than normal. It allows Magics to enjoy a weekend out of town, but to still get back to their home community in time to get their Sunday chores done before the workweek begins." He raised his chin, looking immensely proud of himself.

"And what about the troll on duty, Super Genius? Don't you

think they're going to be told not to let me leave?"

"Nope. There's no actual troll duty on the portals."

"But Chester," I said, hoping the big oaf was doing okay in his imprisonment.

"Chester just likes to meet people. He does it for fun, not as part of his job. Unless of course, he's been told to meet someone like he was when he came and got us from the delivery portal that first time."

"So you're saying this really could work?" I stood up, energized by a tiny speck of hope that was growing bigger by the millisecond. "That I could really get to Morelli?"

Tobey patted me on the head. "It's amazing there's any room for a brain up there with how thick your skull is. Yes, it's going to work. Now let's go."

I went. The closer we got to the London-Portland portal, the more my cynical pessimism took over and the more convinced I became that the scheme wouldn't work. After all, Tobey had my magic. The portal might not be closed to me personally, but to my brand of power. By the time we got to the portal, I almost told Tobey not to bother. It might set off alarms, it might bring the wrath of Olivia down on me, it might—

"Hurry up, go through." Tobey stood at a very open and a very no-alarms-going-off portal. "I'll stay here. They might get suspicious if we're both gone."

"Thanks, Tobey. I owe you one."

"You already gave me magic. I was the one who owed you."

Before things got too gushy, I rushed through the portal, crossing my fingers that any magical sirens would remain silent.

It was still dark when I entered Portland. That pre-dawn hour in summer when the sky is still painted an inky blue, but crawling up from the horizon is a splash of color signaling the warm day to come.

Crikey, don't I sound poetic? Basically, the streets were empty and everyone was still snoring in their beds (although a sweet and yeasty scent on the air told me the day had already begun at Spellbound).

Since MagicLand doesn't use street lamps, I had to pull in some photons to avoid tripping over anything as I strode down the Caribbean-themed street the London-Portland portal opened on. I felt a strong pull to peer into Lola's windows to see what Pablo was up to, but I couldn't risk wasting the time. I needed to act. I needed help or I'd lose everything — my mental faculties, my parents' recovery, Alastair. It just really sucked that that help had to come from Morelli. If I survived this, he would never let me live it down.

I slipped through the door in the building beside Fiona's house and into the familiar mess of my coat closet. I nearly hugged my winter jacket for the joy of being home, but again, this was no time for nostalgic nonsense. Stepping carefully over a couple pairs of knock-off Keds, I turned the knob and entered my apartment. The smell, the sight, the feel of my junky little place all hit me at once. Like a kid who wants to show off her room, I suddenly wanted to bring my parents here. I'd never felt any sense of pride over this place. It wasn't much, but it was mine. Okay, yes, technically it was Morelli's. Just shut up and allow me my moment.

I tiptoed downstairs. I don't know why since I planned to wake up my landlord anyway. But when I got to the door, I could already hear someone inside rustling around and humming the theme song to *I Dream of Jeannie*. It could only be Morelli.

I tapped on the door, loud enough to be heard, but hopefully not so loud it would wake Mr. Wood if he was still asleep. The humming stopped, followed by the distinctive whisper of a blade being pulled from a knife block.

Careful footsteps approached the door and I said as quietly as possible, "It's me. Don't come out stabbing."

The door opened a crack, the chain of the interior lock still in place. Morelli's nose appeared first. He sniffed, then his dark eyes peered at me. Once he realized it really was me and not some clever Cassie impersonator, he slid back the chain and let me in, gesturing me to the kitchen. He put his index finger to his lips and pointed toward the hall where, if his apartment was of the same layout as mine, the bedrooms would be. Like any sane person at this time of day, Mr. Wood was still asleep.

"What are you doing here?" Morelli asked.

"I live here."

"At this hour, I mean." He held up the knife in mock threat before putting it away.

"I'm probably going to regret admitting this, but I need your help."

"Oh, that *is* good," Morelli said as he stifled a chortle. "What? Need a tax document altered or something? Maybe a fake will that leaves you a million dollars from some mysterious aunt."

"No," I said, fully serious. Something in my eyes stopped his teasing. "I need you to build me a portal."

"No way. We already discussed this. First, you don't even know where you need to go. Second, I'm a trusted member of the community, and building portals without first registering them is a huge no-no."

"Part of why you're a trusted member of this community is because you know how to detect underhanded things. You're telling me you didn't gain that knowledge without some firsthand experience?"

"Those days are long behind me," he said, the slight hesitation in his voice making it clear that not every dealing he'd had in recent years was on the up and up.

"And as to your first point," I continued, "there's a different kind of portal, isn't there? Not to a place, but to a person."

"Where'd you learn that?" He glanced around as if the walls might be listening.

"A little birdie told me."

"It's arcane knowledge. Alastair and I discussed person-to-person portals on a few occasions, just hypothetically," he emphasized when I was about to ask what this portal was going to be used for. "I was surprised he knew about them. They fell out of favor over a hundred years ago, mainly because of their limitations."

"Limitations?" I asked, worried they couldn't span long distances, worried what I'd thought was a brilliant idea was just another dead end.

"Yeah, limitations. They don't last all that long, a few hours at most. It reduces the chance of them getting noticed by the authorities. These days, not many people even know about person-to-person portals, let alone how to make them."

"Exactly, or how to detect them, I'd bet." I fixed a goading stare on him.

"You know, I am trying to live my life by the book." I looked to the direction of Mr. Wood's room and back to Morelli with an eyebrow arched. Giving Norms magic wasn't exactly keeping your nose clean. "It's only a little, and he needed the magic to heal," he said defensively. "It's nothing like making the type of portal you're talking about."

"Do you know what's happening out there because of the Mauvais?" I grabbed the remote before he could answer and clicked on the TV, quickly hitting the mute button to keep the sound down. I flipped channels until I found a news station. On screen was a reporter with dark hair that looked like it had been styled after a comic book pane of Clark Kent. I turned the volume up just enough for us to hear him speaking in the lightest of Irish accents.

"...the cause is still unknown for the collapse of St. Patrick's Cathedral, adding to the mystery of why this building has gone down. The tragedy only made worse by it being a Sunday. Some people suggest the formation of a new tectonic plate may be to blame, others are stating the Irish government is at fault for too much cost cutting. The only thing for certain is today we all mourn for the great city of Dublin. Jim, do you have the footage? Okay, folks, this was just sent to us from a survivor. I warn you, what you are about to see may be upsetting to some viewers."

The shot changed to a cell phone video of the great cathedral not so much collapsing as being swallowed by the ground underneath. One second, the building was standing. The next, it was a pile of rubble.

The camera turned back on the reporter, who was picking something from his teeth. He hurriedly brushed his hand over his hair to hide what he'd been doing, then cleared his throat and shook his head remorsefully.

"I've been told rescue dogs are searching for survivors, but officials worry about the ground's stability after—"

I clicked off the TV.

"That was the Mauvais."

"You're sure it's him? He wasn't supposed to do another one until—"

"Yes, I'm sure. And the next hit is not going to be a building or a bridge. It's going to be me. Olivia wants to extract me to make me worth nothing to the Mauvais."

"Not Olivia." Morelli spoke the name as if shocked. "But she—"

"Yes, Olivia. Tomorrow, at dawn. Bye bye Cassie brain. So I don't have a lot of time here. My guess is the Mauvais's in Portland somewhere, but that doesn't narrow it down much. A person-to-person portal is the only way to get to him."

Morelli scratched the back of his head in thought.

"I promised to keep you safe."

"The only way you can keep me safe is to get me to the Mauvais. Once he's taken care of, I'll be super safe." And still, Morelli hesitated. "If I don't do this, my brain will be turned to mush. I've beat the Mauvais twice before. I have a far better chance of surviving a showdown with him again than surviving an extraction. You swore to do whatever it took to keep me safe. You've never been released from that obligation, have you?"

"Damn you, girl. You're too smart for your own good. And too stupid at the same time."

"So you'll do it?"

Morelli gave a heavy sigh of defeat, then his face brightened in a way that told me he'd figured out a possible loophole.

"The only way I can build it is if you have an object that once belonged to the person." He crossed his arms over his chest and put on a smug grin. "Somehow I doubt you've got anything of the Mauvais's in that mess you call an apartment."

Well, doesn't that figure? Six months the Mauvais's damn watch had been in my coat closet, but when I needed it most, it was locked away somewhere in the Tower of London. I toyed with the chain around my neck, trying to think of anything in MagicLand that had belonged to the Mauvais. Vivian's shop likely still had its winter display of clothing in the window, but had any of that really to belonged the Mauvais? Probably not.

The locket shifted under my shirt. The feel of it stirred up the memory of Alastair on the night he'd given it to me. The memory soon shifted to my first lesson with Alastair. The shy glances, my first taste of Sacher Torte, the beetle timer trundling across the table—

The timer!

"Hold on," I blurted, then dashed out of Morelli's apartment, up the stairs, and to my front room. I scrambled through a pile of books on the coffee table that sat in front of the couch. Nothing. Damn it. Maybe Alastair had taken it with him. I didn't think he had, but with my luck, you never knew. I scanned the room, eyeing the bookshelf, an end table, then the wingback chair. A flash of Pablo perched on the back of that chair, of him jumping down, and of him—

I dropped to my knees and pulled my phone out of my back pocket. About a hundred messages had pinged through when I'd stepped from MagicLand into my apartment. I ignored them, turned on the flashlight function, then pressed my cheek to the floor and peered under the couch.

It took several passes back and forth with the phone. It was hard to believe how many scraps of paper, cat toys, battered paperbacks, and fur clumps had migrated underneath a single piece of furniture. I was about to get up and shift the couch out of the way when the light of the phone glinted off a metal surface.

I couldn't help it, I let out a cry of triumph. Well, I also cursed Pablo for being such a rascal. And then, because I was on quite the roller coaster of emotions for one day, I suddenly wanted to cry at the memory of the day Alastair had brought this little trinket, of him sharing HQ's letter with me, of him telling me why I should go to London. It seemed like a dozen years ago.

I stretched my arm out under the couch, my fingers dancing across the shag carpet. I shifted my shoulder to get just a slightly longer reach. My hand touched something cool, metallic. I latched onto it and pulled out Alastair's timer. Joy and heartache filled me as I held the small penguin that was designed to flap his wings and clack his beak when time was up.

I ran back down to Morelli, practically jumping from the top step to the bottom landing in my excitement.

"Here." I shoved the timer at him.

"This is Devin Kilbride's?" he asked, turning it over and admiring the handiwork.

"No, Alastair's. He builds them."

"But you need to get to the Mauvais."

"Who I'm sure still has Alastair."

"Kind of gamble there."

"Can you do it?"

"Yeah, I can," he said reluctantly. "But you can't tell anyone I'm doing this."

"Despite what you think, I'm not that big of an idiot."

Morelli did nothing.

"What?" he asked in response to my impatient stare.

"So make it." I made a flapping, go-ahead gesture with my hands.

"Making a black market portal is not just a snap-your-fingers thing. To keep it hidden from the detectors, I'll need a few hours."

"So what time should I come back? You'll get on it straight away, right?"

"You've sure gotten pushy. You used to be so quiet."

"I guess having the fate of the world on my shoulders has its side effects."

"Don't worry. I'll get it to you. Now get going and let me concentrate."

"You really can do it?"

"Yeah, and I'll add the fee for it to your rent. Which is due in two weeks, six days, and ten hours," he added, with a slight catch to his voice.

I nodded, afraid to speak through the lump in my own throat. We both knew that if he made this portal, he risked never getting to harass me for rent again.

CHAPTER THIRTY-FIVE

CAUGHT IN THE ACT

Knowing Guildenstern (or was Rosencrantz currently on duty?) would be on high alert, I couldn't risk waiting around the building for Morelli to build my portal.

I went back up to my apartment, waded through my closet, and returned to the streets of MagicLand. It was early morning, prime time for a patisserie to be baking their wares for the day, and I can't tell you how tempting the smells wafting from the Spellbound kitchens were.

Actually, I can tell you exactly how tempting they were: tempting enough, despite my intention to head straight for the London portal, to pull me in and force me to order two lemon-ginger scones.

I had just paid for my order and was eyeing some fresh apple chaussons when Gwendolyn emerged from the kitchen. At the sight of me, her face — already rosy red from the heat of the ovens — lit up.

"If it isn't my star Potions student."

And yeah, she said that without any hint of sarcasm or irony. I nearly dropped my sack of scones.

"No, it's me. Cassie Black." Maybe the hot kitchen and early hours had finally gotten to her.

"But you saved Runa with a potion. You're my first student

this year to use potion knowledge in a life-saving capacity. I'm so proud."

This from the woman who had been in existential doubt over her ability to teach because of my inability to mix even the most basic potion without destroying life and property? It was like I'd stepped into an alternate universe's version of Spellbound Patisserie.

"It really wasn't a potion. Just a bit of chameleon skin. You told me about what it could do in my first lesson."

"And you remembered," she gushed, clapping her hands together and gripping them with glee.

The bell of the shop door chimed. Gwendolyn's bright gaze lifted from my face to greet her customer.

"Fiona, it's not often we see you. Some orange-cranberry tea bread just came out of the oven." She indicated several small, golden loaves on a cooling rack behind her.

My heart sank like an overcooked dumpling. I wasn't supposed to be here. I'd come on a whim and hadn't given a single thought to the possibility of Fiona coming home, or of Busby or any of the others from the Tower popping by MagicLand for a visit at this time of day.

"Thank you, Gwendolyn, but I really shouldn't," Fiona said, patting her hips. "I came here because I noticed Cassie stopping by." And believe me, these words were delivered *very* meaningfully.

"Through the hole?" I asked with true curiosity, even though my delightful moment of pastry procurement had just gone tits up. Oh, and that hole would be the one I made when my magic (and a book) got away from me a few weeks previous.

"Yes, through the hole," Fiona said testily. "Why are you here, Cassie?"

I held up my bag. Obviously, I couldn't tell her I'd been hiring

Morelli to create an illegal portal. "Scones. I had a craving."

Fiona arched a skeptical eyebrow. "Yes, I know how they've been experiencing a scone shortage in London. You're heading back soon." This was not a question.

Gwendolyn, ignoring Fiona's denial, wrapped one of the breads in wax paper, sealed it with a Spellbound sticker, and popped the loaf into a paper sack. Fiona grudgingly accepted the bag, whose contents smelled of tart berries and fragrant orange zest. I wouldn't have minded waiting around for whatever might be rolling out of the oven next, then stopping in to see what Pablo was wearing these days, but with Fiona's eagle eye fixed on me, I merely said I was indeed on my way back to London.

"Then I'll join you."

Understanding, or maybe just hoping, that Fiona wasn't going to rat me out, I said goodbye to a glowing Gwendolyn and left the shop with Fiona.

"It's kind of early in the day for a trip home, isn't it?" I asked.

"It is. Luckily, it's a Sunday because something occurred to me after Olivia's judgement," she said in a tone that made it clear she did not agree with Olivia's decision. "The library at the Tower of London, it's well-stocked, but that librarian..." She shuddered. I wanted to tell her I knew exactly what she meant, but then she might ask why I'd gone to the library, and I didn't want to dig the hole I'd found myself in any deeper. "Anyway, I looked through my books and came across some information that might help with this Mauvais problem. It's not really a concrete idea, but I think if I can talk it out with the others, we might be able to come up with a clue of how to use it. And hopefully we can keep you from being extracted."

"Thank you," I said sincerely.

When we passed Lola's, that magnetic tug again pulled on me to stop in and cuddle Pablo. But Lola's curtains (dust- and wrinkle-free, thanks to yours truly) were drawn. Not surprising since at that hour on a Sunday morning, I would have still been tucked into my bed as well.

After only a short wait, Fiona and I went through the portal. A heavy weight hung over me at the thought that I might not be coming back. The squeezing and jostling sensation of the portal was uncomfortable, but bearable relative to the pain of leaving MagicLand. Still, I did hope my scones weren't getting mangled.

The moment we re-entered the White Tower, I checked inside the bag and was relieved to see the pastries still intact.

"So am I allowed to know about this information?"

"We've gone over it a little. Remember when I had you read about the Light Capture Charm, how entanglement allows you to do it?"

"Sure. The particles are tied together because they have a history together. What happens to one, happens to the other."

"Very good," said Fiona, switching to teacher mode. "Even though there's some debate about whether what happens is the opposite effect or the same effect, we do know that somehow those particles have a bond no matter how far apart they are. I just feel like we could use that somehow."

"Like if something happens to me, the opposite happens to the Mauvais?"

"Yes, but we can't be certain. What we do to you might also happen to him."

I took a heavenly bite of one of my scones as we turned onto an unfamiliar corridor. The walls, ceiling, and floor were all made of stone, and the route was lit by small lights at foot level and a few recessed lights overhead. Still, I didn't need light to sense the pathway was gently sloping up as it zigzagged back and forth. I couldn't believe it. Was I actually changing levels in the White Tower without climbing stairs? My thrill over this discovery was tempered as I grasped what Fiona was implying.

"So, if you extract me, you might extract him," I said right after taking another bite of my treat. "Or you might make him all that more powerful."

"Precisely," Fiona said after chastising me for speaking with my mouth full. "And that's what I want to talk to the others about. Banna especially, she might recall something from her histories about just such a thing. And Rafi, he's co-authored some papers on magical physics with Alastair. He might be a good one to bounce ideas off of."

Speaking of bouncing, Fiona was practically bouncing in her excitement over this. Her speech was animated, and her hands were waving about so much as she spoke that I worried she might cast a spell by accident. But, being a little self-centered, I saw my own advantage in this news.

"So if there's a risk, then you'll argue against extracting me?"

Fiona's hands dropped to her sides and her voice fell to a graver tone when she said, "We'll see, Cassie. As with Chester, Olivia has made her decision about you. And she's not one to go back on something once she's made her mind up about it."

"Chester?"

"He's been convicted. He's scheduled to be extracted on the same day as you. It's what she meant when—"

"But that's not right. Did he even get a trial?"

"Busby is still pleading both your cases. I will argue the entanglement matter, and point out that extraction is a cruel thing to do no matter what the circumstances, but I can't fight her decision. I'm sorry I can't be more definite on that."

"Thanks anyway." Suddenly losing all my hunger, I dropped my scone back in the bag. We'd reached the end of the hall down which Olivia's office was situated. "And if you could maybe leave out telling them you saw me in MagicLand…"

"Will I regret not telling them?"

"No. I don't think so."

I left Fiona to explain her theory to Olivia. Not knowing what to do with myself, I was about to head outside when Tobey came jogging down the stairs. He only barely stopped from crashing into me. Once he'd stepped back a pace, he caught sight of the bag in my hand.

"Spellbound?"

"Want one?" I asked, removing my nibbled-on scone and handing him the bag. Tobey pulled out the other one and eyed the scone like a dog who's just caught sight of a hunk of prime rib.

"Dear Gandalf, I haven't had one of these in years." He bit into the pastry and his eyes rolled up into his head. "Oh man, that is good. Did you want to practice or anything?"

"I don't know. Rafi's not around and—"

"Wait," he mumbled through a mouthful of crumbs, "what did Morelli say?"

"Shut up," I hissed. "Come on. My room."

CHAPTER THIRTY-SIX
THE GHOST KNOWS

I know. Me voluntarily going up stairs? Without complaint? Goes to show you how much my mind was occupied with matters other than my burning thighs.

Inside my room, I told Tobey that Morelli had agreed to help. Maybe I should have kept my mouth shut, but Tobey had been some help, or at least he had tried, and I was no longer in the mood to keep secrets from people who were on my side.

"Can he do it?" he asked.

"He seems to think so."

"And you'll let the others know about it? Grandad I'm sure could have a team together in under an hour. Maybe we should tell them now."

Did I say I would no longer keep secrets? Okay, maybe I'd been a little hasty in that resolution because I had no intention of getting Mr. T and the others involved in this. Hey, don't judge. I was just getting used to this playing-well-with-others thing and it was weird enough allying with Tobey. As they say, baby steps.

"No, let's wait to see if he can do it. We'll both be in trouble if it doesn't pan out. You for helping a convicted felon through an international portal; me for, well, everything. Besides, Busby's pleading my case, and Fiona is down there right now trying to work out another idea. I don't want to jeopardize their efforts if Morelli can't get the portal to work."

Tobey seemed to accept this, and soon after, a late lunch appeared for both of us on my table. There was no cake or cookies for Tobey the Sugar Junkie, just two six-inch tall portobello mushroom burgers and a mound of fries. Besides snagging a couple fries off his plate, Tobey ignored the food. He was too eager to play with different spells, including a Shoving Charm to make my bed. Can't complain about that. I did complain, however, when he tried a Binding Spell on my pillow that sent feathers and fluff everywhere.

"Too tight," I scolded. "If that had been a person, you'd have sent their head popping off."

"I get the idea of binding, but I keep doing that. Grandad is starting to think I have anger issues and am taking it out on the pillows."

"What are you picturing when you're doing the spell?"

"Ropes. What else would you bind someone with?"

"Well, since I haven't ventured into any kidnapping schemes—"

"Except for being the victim of one," Tobey added helpfully, then took a large bite of his burger.

A stab of worry for Alastair hit me right in the gut, followed by another stab of desperate hope that Morelli really could build this portal. If he did, I'd see Alastair soon. And if we survived, I'd drown Alastair Zeller in apologies for how I'd behaved toward him.

"Except for that," I said. "And yes, you'd normally use ropes, but since you seem to be a bit overzealous with your binding, maybe try visualizing something that's more stretchy instead. Bungee cords might do the trick. Go on," I pointed to the second bed pillow, "there's another pillow in the closet if you kill that one."

Tobey set down his now-half-eaten burger, then — again with the poopy face — concentrated on the pillow. It began to cinch in the middle, then the constriction stopped, giving the pillow an enviable hourglass figure.

"I did it!"

"Try bringing it to you." I wasn't sure if this would work. If Tobey was picturing bungee cords to manage this spell, the cords might be too bouncy to reel anything in. Tobey made a hand-over-hand motion just like someone pulling in a rope. The pillow slid across the bed toward him.

"Look at that. I did it!"

"Yes, the world of pillows will forever be under your power."

"Very funny. What next?"

"Next, we eat this food before it gets cold. Then we clean up these feathers."

I'll admit, I was a little worried about this chore. Since taking on the watch's power, I hadn't exactly been in reliable control of any of my magical abilities, especially when it came to delicate work. The feathers might seem harmless, but if one of my Shoving Charms got a little too much 'Cassie' behind it, the feathers could go flying out the window and right into the eyes of the tourists below.

So it was with a tentative hand that I began, along with Tobey, to shift the feathers back into the pillow casing. Tobey struggled at first. Light objects can be tricky to move because it's easy to apply too much force, but he was soon lifting feathers one by one and — without causing a single speck of downy fluff to explode — flicking them into the pillow casing that I'd propped up like a garbage can with a Rigidity Spell.

As for me, one or two feathers missed their mark, but that might have just been Tobey's cheers of his own triumph disturbing the air and pushing my feathers off their course. Still, no feathers went piercing through the walls, none burst into flames, and no tourist had his eye gouged out that day. Or at least not by me. I can't verify what the ravens might have gotten up to.

Once all the feathers had been collected, I tried something I'd never done before, by magic or by hand: sewing the pillow closed. It didn't go quite as well as I'd hoped. Threading a needle, by hand or by magic, is just something I'll never have a talent for, and I soon gave up on that tactic. But who needs needles when you're a witch? I visualized the tattered edge of the pillowcase and the small threads poking out. With little pinches of my fingers, those threads knotted themselves together in a way that looked as good as the finest couture stitchery.

"Nice," said Tobey, and to hear him praising me was really, *really* weird. Even weirder? The sense of pride in what I'd just done allowing me to accept that praise.

Bizarre, right?

"I'm going to go grab a pint," Tobey said. "And maybe some ice cream. And have you seen those chocolate chip cookies at the cafe? Maybe one of those too."

I'd created a sugar-craving monster.

"I'll go down with you, but I think I'd prefer to get some fresh air over getting sugared up."

We left the White Tower, and Tobey made a beeline for the cafe, saying if I changed my mind to meet him at the pub in half an hour. I wasn't sure exactly where I wanted to go. The walls were crowded at this time of day and the line to the crown jewels was jammed tighter than an L.A. freeway at rush hour. However, from what I'd seen with Rafi, there was one spot that would be quiet if no tour groups were being shown through it. I strolled up to the St. Peter in Chains chapel and peered in the window. Empty. Making sure no one was looking,

261

I magicked open the lock on the door and ducked in before anyone noticed.

Or at least I thought I'd gone unnoticed. I'd just started roaming around, looking at the decorations around the altar, when I sensed the breezy chill of Nigel's presence.

"Hey, Nigel," I said, and he materialized beside me.

"Thought that was you coming in here. I've just been to see your parents. They're doing—" He paused, searching for a good word. "Well, they seem to have decent appetites. And you, how are you progressing with your missing person search?"

"Like someone trying to wade through frozen molasses."

Nigel's eyes lit up and a hopeful smile beamed across his face. "Maybe he's hidden in one of the Tower's many chambers," he said with complete conviction in the idea. You got to give the guy credit: self-doubt never plagued him. Still, I eyed him questioningly. "Well, you do know the White Tower was once a place of exile? That's how it got its name. From the word *banishment,* which shares the same root as the French word *blanc.*"

"In what language?"

"William the Conqueror's." Nigel twisted his face, pondering something. He then whispered, "He's the one who founded the Tower, right?"

"He is, and he did come from France, from Normandy. But I'm not sure if *banishment* is related to the word *blanc,* even in Norman French."

"No? I could have sworn there was some sort of tie between the two words. Do you think I should cut that out of the speech?"

"Probably for the best."

"Good to note," Nigel said, not for a moment daunted by my constructive criticism.

"How's your other history coming along?" I asked as I strolled down the central aisle of the chapel with Nigel floating alongside me. "Who ruled after Charles I?"

"Not Charles II." I gave no hint as to whether this was correct or not. "It was an angry guy. Liked killing." Nigel clicked his tongue as he struggled to find the information. "Cromwell!"

"Very good, Nigel."

I had no idea where this education was leading. Sure, Nigel would have a more robust knowledge about the place he'd chosen to haunt, but would they really let him lead tours even if he passed his exams without a single error? I mean, he was a ghost. Who would be able to see him besides a tour bus full of clairvoyants? Still, learning, being tested, and reciting his knowledge seemed to please him, and you can't fault that.

I stopped near the altar, and Nigel began reciting the tour guide spiel about the chapel.

"That's where Anne Boleyn is buried. Or is assumed to be buried, we're unsure if those are really her bones that were discovered in a small case at the base of the altar. See, although her husband, Henry VIII," he emphasized the name as if showing off his new historical prowess, "had planned every last detail of her execution, he hadn't planned for her burial, so her headless remains were tucked into a box and tossed aside without ceremony."

I watched Nigel, impressed with what was the longest string of accurate historical facts he'd ever recited. "But," he continued, "at least we have hope that Anne's bones are here, unlike Catherine Howard, Henry's other beheaded wife, whose remains are forever lost. When we move to the armory, we will see the block where young Catherine, ever the performer, practiced placing her neck the night before her demise."

And cue giant cartoon light bulb over my head.

"The execution block!"

"Oh, did I get the wives wrong again?" asked a dejected Nigel.

"No, Nigel, you were perfect. Surprisingly perfect. But the block in the armory. Chester was deathly afraid of that block. He would never go into the armory alone."

"No, of course not. Our Chester might love the suits of armor, but he hates the room they're in. Don't know why they don't move that bloody block to the torture exhibit, anyway. Even I know it has nothing to do with knights and jousting and all that."

"And if Chester doesn't go into the armory alone, he couldn't have been in there by himself when Tobey came back. Someone else found Tobey. Maybe that person gave Chester the note to bring to us, but it wasn't Chester who found Tobey. Or brought him through," I said as an afterthought.

"Brought him through?"

"Tobey had no magic at the time, he couldn't have gotten through any portal on his own. And I don't think handing him an absorbing capsule would have done it," I said, mostly to myself since Nigel knew nothing about Alastair supposedly giving up the capsule's power to get Tobey back to London. "Someone had to bring him. Whoever did is the person HQ is looking for."

"But Chester did poison Runa."

"I don't know. Does Chester seem the type to poison someone? I mean, if he wanted someone dead, he'd just stomp on them or something," I said, thinking of the many rats bones I'd heard crushed under Chester's heavy boots.

"You have a point there."

"Look, good job on the tour, but I've got to tell the others this," I said, taking long strides toward the door.

Some other idea, something about Chester, was trying to rise in the waters of my memory, but my sense of urgency wouldn't let it surface.

CHAPTER THIRTY-SEVEN
MESSAGE FROM BEYOND

I ran from the chapel and toward the White Tower, planning to go straight to Olivia's office to tell her about Chester, about the rats, about Tobey going through the portal on his own, about a troll's promise of loyalty, about— Arrghh! What was the other thing? But just as I reached the door, a dark shadow swooped overhead. Winston perched on me, his heavy claws gently gripping my shoulder. In his beak he held a scrap of paper.

It wasn't writing paper or newspaper or even a food wrapper pulled from one of the trash bins, but brown paper like the kind used to make lunch sacks or grocery bags.

"I give you sausage and you bring me recycling? Not a very fair trade."

But Winston shook his head, then jutted the paper at me. The movement was accompanied by the scent of chocolate. And raspberries. My heart jumped.

I took the scrap from Winston and turned it over several times as if it had more than two sides. But no matter how many times I flipped it over, both sides remained blank. My heart leapt again, but this time straight into the Thames to drown itself for being so stupidly hopeful. The paper was likely nothing more than a piece of a bag Alastair had carried a sandwich in at some point. Winston must have picked it up from a bin that hadn't been dumped yet.

"Thanks, but it's not exactly what I want."

Winston snapped his beak, and let me tell you when a bird — even a ghost one — the size of a raven with a beak that can tear flesh off bone snaps at you, you pay attention.

"I don't know what you want me to do with this."

Just then, the door to the White Tower opened and Mr. Tenpenny, who had started to step out, took a step back in surprise.

"Ah, hello, Cassie. And Winston." The raven tilted his head in greeting. "Any reason you're standing here?"

"Winston has brought me what he thinks is quite the treasure." I handed it to Mr. T. "It smells like—"

"Alastair," Mr. T said immediately upon taking the scrap. "Very good, Winston. Come on, Cassie. Inside so we can read this."

"It's blank."

"It's not. Go on, Winston. I'll bring you some steak in a bit."

Only after the bird eyed Busby as if making it very clear he would hold him to that promise, did Winston fly off.

Mr. Tenpenny wouldn't answer any of my questions about what significance a small, torn piece of lunch sack might have as he raced toward Olivia's office.

Olivia was at her desk, calculating something by swiping rows of beads that hung in the air like a floating abacus. Mr. T slapped the paper down on her desk, breaking her concentration and sending the beads scattering. Of course, these were magic beads so they only rolled a few feet before vanishing in a puff of mist.

"What is this?" Olivia asked, looking at the paper with distaste.

"It's from Alastair. I think he's managed to project a Communication Charm."

"Are you sure?" Olivia asked. She sat up straighter and examined the paper. "It could just be garbage."

"Winston brought it to Cassie. It carries the scent of Alastair's magic. It has to be a message from him."

"Can someone explain to me what's going on?" I asked.

"A Communication Charm allows you to write with magic remotely. It's been ages since I've seen it used. Let's see if I can still manage it." After a moment's concentration, Olivia demonstrated by making some odd motions with her index finger, almost as if she was listening to a symphony and imagining herself as the conductor. The smell of smoldering came from a side table where a tidy stack of stationery sat. Mr. Tenpenny went over, picked up the top sheet, then handed it to me. On it was written: *Cassie has much to learn.*

"Cute," I said drolly.

"That's just the basic spell," Olivia explained. "It takes a Concealing Spell layered over it to make the words invisible. Unfortunately, that combination of spells has fallen out of usage."

"But how did the paper get from where Alastair is to here?"

"That's the whole point," said Mr. T. "It's a way to send a message remotely without anyone knowing you're doing so. All Alastair had to do was move a single finger in the shape of the words. Well, and be able to muster the magical strength to send and conceal those words. It takes a great deal of concentration and proves Alastair is still in good shape. The spell was a marvel before the telegraph. Now, as Olivia said, it's rarely used. Mobiles, what you call cell phones, have mostly replaced the need for the Communication Charm."

"Even if the Mauvais had allowed Alastair to keep his phone," Olivia mused, "the battery would have died days ago. Modern technology is convenient, but it's far from perfect."

Given my own phone's quirks with cell service in MagicLand and in the magic-altered White Tower, I had to agree.

"It's very clever of Alastair to send it, but we need someone who can undo the concealment portion of the charm to reveal the message. Corrine and other messenger service workers used to be well-trained in such spells, but I'm afraid we've all gotten a bit lazy with them. Busby, do you still know how to do it?"

Before Mr. T could answer, Banna, swathed in her layers of clothing and dark sunglasses, stepped into the office. "Ah, good, you're all here. I thought I should inform you the tribunal—"

Mr. Tenpenny's face had brightened the instant Banna entered the room. As she'd been speaking, he'd double-timed it over to her. In his excitement, I half expected Mr. T to lift the tiny woman up and carry her over to the desk. Instead, he grabbed her by the hand and hurried her across the stone floor, her short legs nearly tripping over themselves to keep up with his long strides. Once to the desk, he pointed excitedly to the paper.

"A concealed Communication Charm. Can you read it? You of all Magics must still know the Revealing Spell."

Banna glanced at the paper, then brushed her fingers along it. "It's recent." My heart went leaping like a caffeinated frog. *Recent* meant Alastair was still alive. This wasn't some three-week old message lost by the magic postal service. Banna held the paper down with one hand while making circular motions over it with the other, almost like she was massaging the thing.

Faint words began to appear under her fingertips. At one point, she jerked her hand back and her jaw tensed. She glanced up to see if anyone had noticed. Of course we had. We were watching her every move.

"Sorry, I've gotten out of practice with this spell. It got a wee bit carried away from me." She gave a self-deprecating shrug, pinched her first two fingers to her thumb, then continued. "That should do it," she said when she stopped her hand motions. I leaned over her shoulder to read what she'd revealed:

I'm alive. Underground somewhere, Portland I think.
Find me soon. Attacks won't stop. Talk to Morelli.

My throat went very dry. Morelli had said he and Alastair had discussed person-to-person portals. Was *Talk to Morelli* in reference to that? What if HQ found out about his extracurricular portal activity? I mean, if Olivia herself asked my landlord to make a portal, that would be one thing, but if she caught him making one, namely one I'd commissioned... I just had to hope Morelli was quick with his excuses. Or with covering up evidence.

"What does that mean, 'Talk to Morelli?' You don't think he's the traitor, do you?" asked Busby.

"It's possible," said Banna. "The trolls, you know they've always born a grudge. Just look at what Chester—"

"Chester is innocent," I blurted, causing Banna to flinch.

"What did you say?" she asked.

I went on to explain about Chester and the armory, and the rats, and just Chester in general. He wasn't exactly the shrewdest half-troll, so how could he conspire against the likes of Olivia and Banna? I'm not even sure if he could outwit Pablo.

"This is mostly conjecture," said Banna.

"But we will consider it," Olivia added. I stood there waiting for more, waiting for one of them to act. "Well, we're not going to do it this very second. We need to sort this out." Olivia tapped the paper.

"Have you finished your entry for the book?" Mr. Tenpenny asked. I said I hadn't, annoyed at the change of subject, at how easily they were ignoring Chester's possible innocence. "Perhaps you should go work on that." Talk about your not-so-subtle dismissals.

I left, wanting to take the paper, wanting to have something of Alastair's with me. I didn't feel like holing up in my room and adding my crappy life story to some stupid book, so I headed to the hospital ward, grumpily wondering what the point was since I couldn't be near my parents.

When I got there, Dr. D was nowhere to be seen, so I took my chances and peered in to see my mom vacantly but willingly accepting from Jake spoonfuls of what looked like mashed potatoes. My dad sat at the table, staring out across the grounds. It was an improvement, but nothing to celebrate. It was clear they still had no idea who or where they were.

I counted on my fingers. Pisa. The bridges. Vegas. Dublin. Two more spells. Two more spells and they would be pushed out of the running for any chance at an easy recovery. If the Mauvais stayed on his path of destruction, and if Runa couldn't figure out the transfusion thing, my parents faced years of slow infusions of magic to return them to normal, assuming they could ever return to normal. And so far, no one had given me any guarantee of that.

As another spoonful of potato neared my mom's mouth, she mumbled, "White."

My dad echoed the word.

"Yes, good job, both of you," Jake said with oddly pure delight. I mean, how excited could you get over a word they'd been saying since they'd been brought in? "The potatoes are indeed white. Very good, Chloe."

Leaving them to their starchy white wonderland, I wandered around the hospital, but couldn't find Runa to ask her about my parents' progress. Seeing little else to do, I headed back to my room to wait for Morelli to finish his task.

Tobey was lingering outside my door.

"Hey, I wanted to show you this spell—"

Just then, someone came around the corner. I unlatched my door and pulled Tobey in.

"Shut up and get in here." I wanted to slam the door closed, but the pneumatic hinges meant it took the damn thing what felt like ten minutes to click shut. "You can't talk about spells in the open. You're not supposed to have magic, remember?"

"Right, sorry, I just got an idea in my head and wanted to try it out."

"Okay," I said warily. "Let's see it."

Tobey shook out his shoulders, then tipped his head side to side, sending disturbing popping sounds from his neck. He then squinted his eyes and tightened his face in that same look of constipation he always wore when doing magic.

And then it began to snow. The room didn't grow any colder, but fluffy, glittering snowflakes drifted down around us. Unfortunately, when they landed on the floor, they immediately melted, leaving a dark puddle on the carpet.

"Nice," I said, as I performed a Drying Spell on the carpet. I really was impressed, not just being sarcastic. "Did Rafi teach you that?"

"Nope, I read about the principle in one of grandad's books, but I put my own spin on it. That was the glittering."

"Not too bad for an Untrained," I said with forced encouragement, trying to hide my jealousy. I could barely control my magic and here he was mastering spells after only reading a few pages? So much for my status as the magical prodigy.

After this wintry demonstration, we went over a few other spells for practice. My mind kept returning to Alastair, to what he might be doing, to how he was holding up, to whether or not I could get to him in time. Still, the work with Tobey helped distract me from overthinking and gave me something to do with my nervous energy. After about an hour, two coronation chicken sandwiches and an entire apple cake appeared. Once three-quarters of the cake had gone down Tobey's gullet, a raven (not Winston) landed at my window. It tapped on the glass with its thick beak.

"I heard a tapping gently rapping at my chamber door," I said as I went over to open the window. The bird hopped in carrying a square box that measured about five inches on each side. It was tied with string that the raven clutched in its claws. "Hand it over."

It shook its head. I went over to the plate of food and picked up a piece of chicken that had fallen from my sandwich. It seemed a little cannibalistic to me, but the raven didn't hesitate to gobble up his avian cousin in exchange for the package.

"What is it?" Tobey asked.

I turned over the tag. In purple ink and block letters, it read: *This should take you wherever he is. Snack first, then be careful.*

"It's the portal."

"Are you going now? I'll go with you."

"No, we should rest. It's going to come down to a fight and we should give the cake time to charge our magic. Besides, if we leave now, it might be noticed. We'll go once everyone else is asleep. Meet me back here in a few hours."

"Alright. Midnight, then?"

"That's the witching hour," I said and ushered him out the door.

The moment he was gone, I opened the box.

CHAPTER THIRTY-EIGHT

THE PORTAL

Inside the box, nestled in shredded paper, was a black ball about the size of a baseball.

I felt like a heel for tricking Tobey. He wanted to go, to help, and in some ways I did want him along, but I couldn't take the chance. He had magic now. My magic. And if the Mauvais sensed that on him, he would drain Tobey for everything he could take.

I wasn't sure what that would do to Tobey. After all, he wasn't truly a Magic, but he was also no longer an Untrained. Would draining him simply pull the plug on his power, leaving him as before? Or would he end up like my parents? It wasn't an experiment I was willing to run.

I lifted the portal from the box. It had almost no weight, but felt as cold as dry ice. Once out of its confines, it expanded to the diameter of a sewer pipe but with none of the pungent sewer-y smell.

Sewage! That was what I'd been trying to recall. The armory had had a foul smell lingering in the air when Tobey had been returned. Morelli told me trolls, even half-trolls, give off a stink when they're cursed. Chester had to have been cursed before we got there. But cursed to do what? To bring Tobey through? To bring us that note? To poison Runa at some specified date? I needed to tell Olivia this new revelation.

But how long might I get stuck in Olivia's office explaining and arguing?

I looked at the portal. Morelli said the illegal ones didn't last longer than a few hours. How long was a few? Did I have three hours or twelve? Either way, the thing would deliver me to Alastair, and that meant to the Mauvais. Even if the portal stayed open for a week, I might not return. I had to make sure Chester wasn't punished for something he didn't do, or at least didn't do of his own free will.

I jotted a note to Olivia and Busby about the timing of the smell in the armory, about my theory that it could be a sign of Chester having been cursed. I propped the message on my table. Then, with my hands shaking, I wadded up some of the box's paper lining and tossed it in. It vanished just as the stapler had done when I'd thrown it into the portal Alastair and Tobey had been pulled into by the Mauvais.

My belly twisted. The tiny bit of optimistic self-delusion I allow myself now and then wanted to say that maybe the Mauvais, worn out from all his evil-doing, would be in bed taking a nap. That maybe I could go in and rescue Alastair without the Mauvais noticing a thing. Once back, I'd tell the others about the portal and they could go in and wrangle Devin Kilbride into non-existence.

But I'd never gotten the hang of fooling myself, and I knew the truth. Someone was going to die. Or be made into a human battery. Whatever happened, it wasn't going to be sunshine and rainbows on the other side of this portal.

I closed my eyes, gathered my strength, focused my magic, then, wondering where I'd end up, stepped through.

And immediately cursed Morelli.

This was nothing like the portals I'd been in before. It wasn't like walking through an open door into another room. It wasn't even like being treated like an uninsured package. This was more like bashing head first into a screened patio door, then feeling my skin and muscles and bones squishing through like straining berries through cheesecloth to make jam. I just hoped everything stayed together and that I wasn't leaving behind a liver or kidney or some other vital tidbit. This is what you get for ordering quickly made, illegal portals.

The strained-berry feeling intensified as I suddenly slammed against a hard surface. An electrical smell pierced my nostrils and a crackling noise filled my ears. My neck hairs prickled. I tensed, fearing the crash and spark of a lightning storm.

CHAPTER THIRTY-NINE

IN THE TUNNELS

The storm never came, and the electrical sizzle subsided. Once the strained-berry sensation eased, I checked myself. Everything seemed like it had made it through, but if I survived this, I swore to schedule an exam with Dr. Dunwiddle as soon as possible to make sure all my internal bits and pieces were still where they should be.

The portal had let me out into a cramped room with shelf-lined walls like a basement storage pantry. I caught the scent of hops, not fresh ones being dumped into a batch of beer, but musty, like ones discarded decades ago. I recalled Tobey's hypnosis session. He'd mentioned the same smell.

A faint amount of light trickled in from whatever was beyond the room. I glanced around. Yep. There was the wood-beamed ceiling. Looking around a bit more as I gathered my nerve, I noticed the walls were brick, not stone as Tobey had described. However, the floor was hard-packed dirt, and the only exit from the room, other than going back through the portal, was an arched doorway.

And it was that archway that struck a memory. I'd seen this place. In my picture book of Portland history, the very book I'd been flipping through only a few nights previous, had been the archway I now faced.

The portal had taken me to the Shanghai Tunnels, located in Portland's downtown barely a few miles from my apartment. Not having extra cash to play tourist in my own hometown, I'd never visited the Tunnels. They'd been used during the late 1800s and even into the early 1900s for illegally moving newly (and often unwittingly) recruited men to waiting ships. Taken most often from taverns where the men had been knocked out thanks to a little something extra in their beers, the men would then be tricked into signing on to become the lowest of the low on board a ship. By the time they came to, they were far out to sea. Portland once had the worst reputation in the world for this naval trickery.

I tiptoed toward the arch, my fingers tingling with pulses of magic ready to zap out and wallop whatever might be beyond it.

Peering around the edge, the room led out onto a long tunnel, rough-hewn as if it had been carved out of the bedrock. Doors were set at regular intervals, giving the impression I was loitering in the corridor of a hotel of horrors.

Which, come to think of it, I might very well be.

Unlike the dark room where I'd come out at, this tunnel was faintly lit by a string of white Christmas lights whose tiny bulbs were as faded as a pair of designer jeans from the 1980s. But one room at the end of the hallway glowed with the unnatural brightness of a flood light.

As I crept closer, I began to make out the sound of men's voices and a chill of *deja vu* ran up my spine. One voice, haughty and cocksure, belonged to the Mauvais. I couldn't quite make out the words, but the tone was enough for me to know he was gloating about something.

I reached the doorway, halted, and caught my breath. My heart raced in my chest like that of a high-strung Chihuahua who's just been given a syringe full of pure adrenaline.

Alastair had spoken.

Alastair was alive.

"She'll never fall for it," he said. He sounded awful. Tired, in pain, and as if he could use a large glass of water. Or maybe gin. Still, the voice carried a sense of defiance, a sense that he still had some fight in him. My first instinct was to run in, throw my arms around him, and tell him I'd been an absolute idiot for ever doubting him.

My legs twitched. They were ready. They wanted to go in and do some rescuing. But Sergeant Brain was in command and ordered my limbs to take only the smallest, most cautious steps. My legs, although itching for the signal to charge, obeyed and moved only far enough to allow me to peek into the room.

The Mauvais's back was to me. Hey, a girl's got to have some luck now and then, right? Alastair, facing the direction of the doorway, was bound to a slim concrete post that didn't look sturdy enough to hold up a starved kitten, let alone provide support for the wood-beamed ceiling and all the ground above us. Perhaps feeling my heavy stare, Alastair glanced up and met my eye. He immediately looked away.

But not quickly enough.

"So she's here, is she?" the Mauvais purred.

The second the taunting words came out of the Mauvais's mouth, I knew I shouldn't have hesitated. I should have come in with spells a'blazing and taken him out. Stupid caution.

From down the tunnel, I picked up a crackling sound. My distraction was just enough for the Mauvais to have his chance. A Binding Spell tighter than any of the ones Alastair had ever used on me slapped my arms to my sides. The invisible rope then jerked me forward. I struggled back, not because I thought I could escape, but because it was the only way to maintain my balance.

278

Just as my feet figured out how to follow along with the demanding tug, something like a cold, sweaty hand pressed over my mouth. There was nothing there. There was no true pressure against my skin, but I couldn't move my lips. Clever that. Magics can use arm or hand motions to perform a spell, or we can speak the name of the charm. I was now unable to do either.

With my arms and mouth stifled, a sense of powerlessness washed over me. Magics can of course, mentally conjure a spell, but there's nothing like fearing for your life to really mess with your focus in that regard. Somewhere deep inside I knew if I could just concentrate, I could work up a hex. But the binding shook my confidence and eroded away my magical dexterity.

The Mauvais — pretending he was reeling in an imaginary leash as he strode up to me — wore a casual air, as if we were two friends and this was just a chance encounter on the city street.

"So good to see you again, Miss Black. I was told you'd come today. I said, 'She won't fall for it', but you did."

And there it was. Realization hit me like an elephant's trunk smacking me across the head.

"The portal wasn't from Morelli, was it?" I asked, just to confirm what a fool I was.

Devin Kilbride laughed as if truly amused by my stupidity.

"Hardly. Oh, he can make one, but not that quick. Takes real magic for such speedy work. I suppose you've come to fulfill that prophecy." I hadn't. Not really. I'd come for Alastair. I'd hoped to get him, get out, and send in the troops. "How charming of you."

On the final words, the Mauvais's face changed from that of someone doling out pleasantries to a hyena about ready to dip his muzzle into a fallen antelope. Without any warning, he yanked me to him. I staggered, not only from the sudden motion, but because of the odd slope to the floor. My captor then gave a snap of his fingers and his Binding Spell wrapped around my legs. The only thing that kept me from toppling over was the Mauvais snatching his hand out and grabbing me by the hair.

With my legs hobbled, I couldn't kick out, I couldn't find purchase with my feet which scraped across the dirt floor of the uneven, unfinished underground space as he dragged me across the room.

On my unwilling journey, during which my scalp felt like every strand of hair might snap, I passed Alastair. I could barely move my head, but out of the corner of my eye I caught a brief glimpse of him, feebly fighting against his own bonds and shouting my name in his hoarse, in-need-of-a-drink voice.

I don't know what I expected. Death? Torture? My mind was running a marathon race of possible scenarios. With my head restrained by the Mauvais's grip on my hair and the position he'd thrown me in, I could see little of where I'd landed myself.

What I can tell you is the room was bigger than the one I'd entered. If these tunnels held storage spaces, this must have been the main loading area. It was vast, and once past the main area where Alastair was still grinding my name through his throat, the ceiling arched up like an airplane hangar. Not that big, of course, but tall enough that if the Mauvais, a big man who was at least ten inches taller than me, stretched his arms up, his fingers would only just scrape the ceiling.

Finally, the Mauvais threw me out of his grasp. My follicles screamed with joy at the sudden release, and my hair felt six inches longer from his pulling on it. My eyes had teared up from the sheer agony, but with my arms still bound, I could only wipe the moisture away by tucking my face into my shoulder and scrubbing my cheeks against my shirt.

The sense of relief abruptly halted when the Mauvais called off his Binding Spell. Normally, that would have been a good thing, but before I could register my release, before I could whip up a Stunning Spell, before the blood could fully return to my fingertips, the Mauvais jerked me to my feet and spun me around.

It was only then I realized I wasn't fully free of his Binding Spell. He'd only loosened it. It had been so tight, even a slight easing had seemed like freedom.

But I didn't have time to dwell on whether or not I could punch with my arms or kick with my legs. My entire core had filled with ice because I knew the object he'd turned me toward was meant for me.

CHAPTER FORTY
THE CONTRAPTION

The contraption — for lack of a better term — looked like something straight out of an old sci-fi comic in which the mad scientist plans to employ various evil experiments to alter his victim's brain.

It was a sort of chair, like a cross between an electric chair and the dentist's chair Tobey had mentioned. Above it dangled a metal skull cap with electrodes poking out. At the arm rests and at the front legs, from which metal foot plates stuck out, were thick leather cuffs with heavy buckles.

From the cuffs, which were positioned to fit around the wrist, sprouted a twisting tangle of electrodes. These wires and the wires from the skull cap snaked up to two coils behind the chair that twined a double-helix around one another. One of the coils was black, the other bright red. The black one had a minus symbol on it. The red bore a plus symbol. And, bizarrely innocent, next to and attached to the machine with a thick cord was what looked like a gumball dispenser complete with a round, glass top and red metal base.

With the Binding Spell eased, the Mauvais grabbed me by the upper arm and threw me into the chair. My spine slammed against the stiff back rest, sending jolts of pain into my already sensitive scalp.

I squirmed like a lizard. I fought against his magic. I kicked, landing a good blow somewhere to the Mauvais's body. The Mauvais cried out, then glowered at me. With a flick of his fingers, the leather straps slapped over my wrists and ankles, and the buckles cinched those damn cuffs down so tight that any amount of struggle — or water retention — risked cutting off my circulation.

"Let her go," Alastair protested. He was breathing hard with the effort of speech.

"Or what?" the Mauvais asked Alastair, then turned back to me. "Don't expect any help from your knight in dirt-stained armor over there. He's been a wonderful partner in all this." The Mauvais flicked his fingers, creating a few sparks that he sent flying at my face. They smelled of chocolate. Of raspberries.

So Devin had taken some of Alastair's power. What had he done with it? Simply given the contraption a jump start? Or worse?

"Did you use his magic for those attacks?" I seethed. The very idea that Alastair's magic had been the power behind the destruction of any of those cities stoked the fire of fury within me.

"Of course not," the Mauvais scoffed, as if offended. "That was all thanks to the packets of your power my colleague has brought me. But you know how good Allie is at tinkering. He's been instrumental in the creation of this beauty." He swept his arm out toward the chair like someone presenting a prize package on a game show.

"And what exactly does this thing do?"

"Draining the conventional way requires too much cooperation. This," he said, tapping the skull cap so it rang, "is so much more efficient. And it works well for extractions too." He glanced over and grinned at Alastair. Had the Mauvais extracted

Alastair? That would explain why he hadn't attempted a single spell since I'd arrived. But no, Alastair recognized me. He'd spoken in complete sentences.

"You didn't extract him. If you had, he'd be a magical moron."

"Like your parents? I know girls like men who remind them of their fathers, but that's taking it a bit far, don't you think?" He glanced over his shoulder. "No, you're right. He's not extracted, but I've drained him to the point that it will take years for him to regain his magic. And it is a good magic." He smacked his lips like a sommelier salivating over a fine vintage.

The Mauvais leaned over me, both hands on the arm rests. Even though the ankle straps were pressing my calves into the chair, I jerked my leg in a vain attempt to knee him in the groin. He laughed at my efforts. And on the breath carrying that laugh I caught another whiff of chocolate and raspberries underneath his smoky cinnamon aroma.

"Why did you need his magic if you had mine?"

"Delivery schedules were unreliable. Then Runa started having you fill all those absorbing capsules and I've been receiving a steady supply of power ever since." Runa? Runa was the traitor? Even if she wasn't my best friend, I couldn't believe it was her. But hadn't she encouraged me to fill capsule after capsule? Capsules that soon went missing?

Oh, hold that thought. The evil wizard is still blathering.

"The capsules were delightful, but before that, I needed top ups, and Alastair kindly provided them. Now I hear a big hit of your magic is on the way. I wasn't sure about an extraction, but my colleague thinks it's the best course. Just rip it right out of you and bring it to me to play with. I wonder if she would have gift-wrapped it," he mused. "But you've come to me. Even better. Now, watch."

And before I could ask, "Watch what?" the Mauvais snapped

his fingers and my body went rigid. Holy hell, this *is* an electric chair, was my first thought. But then I recognized the buzzing, sucking sensation. The switch went off and my body relaxed. Until Kilbride turned a dial and the fluid in the coils began bubbling along. Something flowed through me, giving the feeling of being filled with warm liquid on one side of my body and cold liquid on the other as the coils began to glow.

A tugging and pulling sensation screeched across my skin. I knew the feeling from my test with Banna. Magic was being yanked from me through my very pores. I tried to conjure a membrane. No, not tried, I *did* manage a membrane, but whatever made the chair work was too strong. I could slow the flow, but I couldn't stop it.

Fiona, Runa, and Mr. Tenpenny would be thrilled to know their theory had been right on the mark.

See, not long after I'd found out I was Magic, they'd warned me that if the Mauvais ever caught me, he might turn me into a magic battery.

Thanks to my ability to absorb and to give, as well as my magic's super-charged ability to rapidly regenerate itself within my cells, I wasn't your standard, landfill-polluting battery, but an eco-friendly, rechargeable one. Even if I did start to wear down — if you weren't the kind of wizard who handed out cake, that is — all you would need to do to recharge me is put another Magic near me and I'd be able to suck his or her power dry and make it my own. Do that on a regular cycle and I'd become a superconductor. I suppose that would have been nice if I was being used to power a third world village, but I don't think the Mauvais was much for humanitarian efforts.

I don't quite know how the chair worked or how it could be so powerful. I mean, it's not like anyone gave me an instruction manual or schematic so I could read about the mechanical marvel that was to be my doom. What I do know is the Mauvais soon shut it off, and a moment later something plinked against the gumball machine's metal downspout.

The Mauvais reached over then showed me his prize. An absorbing capsule, pulsating with a purple glow. He clasped the capsule in his hand, squeezing tight, a good old, evil-villain grin on his lips, and when he next held up the capsule, the purple glow had faded to red. He'd taken in my magic. This must have been how he had taken Alastair's magic. Alastair had been the guinea pig for the contraption.

"You can't keep that up. You'll eventually drain me. To the point of no return, like you did to Alastair." I had to hope the Mauvais didn't know just how strong my magic was and how quickly it could replenish itself.

"Oh, I can. As soon as you start to tire, I've got an IV with a sugar solution ready for you. And if you resist that procedure, I will bring in any Magic who refuses to kneel to me. Maybe I'll start with that landlord of yours. Hook him up, throw the right switch on this little treasure, and your absorbing trait will have you taking in any power within a ten-foot radius. "Want a demonstration?"

The Mauvais took a single step toward Alastair. Alastair was already drained. If I took any more of his magic, it risked leaving him extracted.

"No, I believe you. Why are you doing this?" I spit out the question, hoping to buy a little time. For what, I had no idea, but if movies and books were anything to go by, evil folks just loved to talk about themselves. Devin Kilbride proved to be no exception.

"Because I want control. I want everyone to acknowledge my importance, my destiny to lead all Magics. The best way to do that is to create chaos. Because if you churn up things, cause instability, spread fear, people turn to whoever will take charge. I," he said magnanimously, "will take that charge. I will demand respect."

"So, all this is an ego boost?" I asked.

"Ego fuels magic. Fear saps it. The more fear I generate in the world, the more they need me, and the stronger I become. It's an amazing high, I'll tell you that. You will serve to feed that high. Doesn't that make you feel important? Useful?" he said with a rather maniacal gleam in his eye.

"Prophecy," Alastair breathed. The word barely audible.

"Prophecy?" the Mauvais said with a chuckle. "You think this is your savior? Well, I'm certainly shaking in my boots. Let's see what she can do. I hadn't really planned on my next strike, but shall we make Portland next?" Alastair and I both remained silent. "Yes, what a lovely idea. You know, if I want to have an intelligent conversation these days, I have to talk to myself. The Portland community has refused to agree to my terms, and," he glanced down at the non-existent watch on his wrist, "it seems they've reached their deadline."

The Mauvais closed his eyes in concentration, and from somewhere above the underground lair, something rumbled.

"What was that?" I asked, my voice quiet with worry as dirt cascaded from the ceiling just behind Alastair.

"The Steel Bridge has just collapsed."

"But we're not far from there." My eyes darted around the storage room. That support beam would not hold up if he hit a nearer target like the Burnside Bridge. "We're in the Shanghai Tunnels, aren't we?"

"Very clever of you. Not the tourist bits of the Tunnels, obviously, but the darker sections. The Magics' sections." The Mauvais strolled around, speaking almost wistfully. "They really were the perfect hideaway for those of us who believe the Magic

Morality Code is little more than a suggestion. Allie, you used to spend time here, didn't you?"

"Only to spy on you."

The Mauvais's face twitched. It was only a slight, subconscious movement, but that little tell revealed he honestly thought Alastair had been a true-blue convert to his cause. Hubris certainly does breed stupidity.

Again, from somewhere in the tunnels came that crackling sound. I glanced up, uncertain how long these wooden beams could hold up the weight of the world above us. Portland was known for its fair share of wet weather, and the area of downtown Portland where the Shanghai Tunnels were located had regularly flooded in the city's early days. Where did these tunnels lead out at? Was there another way to escape if I couldn't get back to the portal? Or if the portal timed out. Would Alastair and I make it before the tunnels caved in from the rumbling above? I had a very sudden, very strong, very claustrophobic-filled urge to be out of the contraption. Well, stronger than it already had been.

"If that's what you want to tell yourself," the Mauvais said through tight lips. "But you, Cassie Black, will lend me the power to turn the City of Roses into the City of Rubble. Prophecy my ass. You know what I prophesy? Your magic soon filling every absorbing capsule in that container behind you. I'll have enough of your magic for a lifetime. It might turn you into a moron, but maybe I'll keep you around. You know, like keeping a stupid pet."

This couldn't happen. Not just because I didn't want to see my hometown turned into the latest natural disaster, not just because it would mean the deaths of thousands, including Mr. Wood. I even worried for Morelli. Those things mattered, but if Olivia's count was correct, the Steel Bridge damage was the Mauvais's thirteenth D-spell. If Devin Kilbride called for one more destructive hex, my parents would be pushed out of range. My parents would only have an instant recovery if he died—

When he died, I corrected myself.

He had to die. The only way any of this would be worth the trouble and the only way to return the magic world to safety would be if the Mauvais died. You know, take no prisoners, and all that.

But at that moment, I couldn't see how on earth that was going to happen. I was the prisoner, so my whole heroic thing wasn't going any farther than my own imagination. And while I do have a rather vivid imagination, it's never done much to save my butt from a life-threatening situation.

The Mauvais reached for the switch. My body tensed. How bad would it hurt for all my power to be turned into magic gumballs?

I wasn't ready to find out.

"The City of Roses to the City of Rubble. Really?" I jeered. The Mauvais whipped around, pure hatred on his face. I guess Mr. Evil didn't like being heckled. "That's the best you've got? You've had over twenty years to come up with plenty of wicked wizard witticisms and yet you continue to disappoint."

"Cassie, don't antagonize him," Alastair pleaded.

I flicked my gaze toward Alastair. I hated the sound of defeat in his voice. I hated that I felt that same defeat in my own heart.

Just as I started my stroll down Mopey Lane, from the entryway to the Mauvais's chamber of torture, something caught my eye. But before I could process what I'd seen, there came a metallic *snap*.

The Mauvais had hit the switch.

CHAPTER FORTY-ONE
BECOMING THE BATTERY

I grit my teeth. I tried to picture a wall around my magic, a cork crammed into my magic bottle, my magic turning into solid rock that wouldn't flow. None of it helped. Plinking sounds kept coming from the gumball machine as fully charged absorbing capsules rolled into the dispenser.

Eventually — after what felt like days of needle-pricking, razor blade-slicing, cat-scratching agony — the Mauvais turned back the dial.

My veins hurt as if they'd been stretched too far by the magic surging through them. I wanted to fight back, I wanted to demand he at least let Alastair go, but the only thing that came out of my mouth was a groan of misery and despair. Tears flowed from my eyes, both from the pain and from the sheer exhaustion of so much of my power being pulled from me so quickly.

At the sight of my waterworks, the Mauvais got a good laugh. Really, if this guy wasn't trying to enslave every non-magic in existence, he seemed like an easily amused fellow who'd be a real hoot to hang out with. But, you know, circumstances being what they were, I didn't think we'd be sharing a table and having a few beers at the comedy club any time soon.

The Mauvais made some snide joke again about the prophecy.

Banna had been wrong. I would not be his end. I would be his new beginning. There was no way I could destroy him. Even if I got out of the chair's bindings, I was too weak to do anything. Alastair, he'd been the guinea pig for this thing, and now look at him. I could still smell the magic on him, but it was faint, like a whisper of a scent.

As the Mauvais chuckled, enjoying his own cleverness, he moved over to the gumball machine. From the corner of my eye, I could see a pile of absorbing capsules that glowed purple like a brand of grape-flavored candies that would stain your tongue for days after eating them.

Kilbride might take one, he might take ten, but it really didn't matter. His next destructive spell would be the one that would put my parents out of range. I had to get out of the contraption. I had to stop him. But at his promise of a break, all I wanted to do was curl up into a ball and cry myself to sleep.

But even that was too much to ask for. The Mauvais moved in front of me. With a snap of his wrist, he whipped my head back. It was then — with that quick, forceful action of my chin being magically jerked up — that I caught movement over the Mauvais's shoulder.

My eyes couldn't focus, but I recognized his walk, his height, and even the smell of my magic on him. It was like my life was a music track stuck on repeat.

Tobey had found the portal. Then, just as the idiot had done the last time I was trying to have a little one-on-one time with Devin Kilbride, he'd followed me into the fray.

Only this time, I was actually glad to see Tobey Tenpenny. And if you ever tell him I said that, I will magic your hair into a crown of earwig-infested pine cones.

Tobey inched toward us. The Mauvais, tumbling a cluster of absorbing capsules from his left hand into his right then back to the left again, was too distracted by his own success to notice.

"We'll give Little Miss Savior a break, shall we? I mean, it's only fair I allow HQ one more chance to meet my demands. Or should I take down the Hawthorne Bridge too, just to show them I'm serious? What do you think? Too much? Or would it send just the right message?"

I was exhausted, but I had to keep him talking. I only needed Tobey to release the straps. He could do that with either a Breaking Charm or a Shoving Charm applied with the right finesse. He had that finesse, but there would be no second chance if he missed. I needed him to get closer to have a clear shot.

"Why would they give in?" I asked groggily. "Like you said, they want to extract me. You know why? Because we're entangled. The quickest way to destroy you is to destroy me."

"You don't understand a thing about how this works, do you?"

"Since we're taking a break, why don't you explain it to me? Be better than hearing more of your lame jokes."

The Mauvais, the person who had wreaked havoc on how many magic communities, actually looked hurt and taken aback that I thought his jokes were lame. Everyone's got a weakness, I suppose.

As Kilbride searched for a snappy retort, Tobey made four chopping motions in the air.

At that very instant, all I could think was, "Oh dear Merlin, he's going for the Slicing Spell," and expected to spend my final moments of life with stumps instead of hands and feet.

Unfair, I know, but what can I say?

Still, surprises are like dogs. Some will bite your ankles, poo on your lawn, and make a nuisance of themselves. Others will come up to you with their tongue lolling and turn your day for the better.

This surprise was of the tongue-lolling variety. The straps slashed down the middle and fell open. I did later find superficial cuts at my wrists and ankles, but I wasn't about to complain.

I was, however, about to kick. I jerked my legs up and shoved out as hard as I could with my feet against the Mauvais's knees. The capsules he'd been playing with skittered across the floor as my nemesis staggered back, grunting with pain.

"Tobey, quick, give Alastair some of those capsules," I shouted as I dropped from the chair — my unexpected freedom might have given me a boost of happy chemicals, but it hadn't offset my Mauvais-induced weariness. I scrambled for a few of the capsules, which were easy to find thanks to their purple glow. The moment I had three of them in my hand, I squeezed tight, pulling my own magic back into myself.

Or so I'd hoped.

Before the magic could do, well, its magic, the Mauvais's foot connected with my ribs. I screamed, but he'd already done some damage and the cry sent electric pulses of pain through my chest. Still, I'd spent my life taking a beating, and that kick wasn't enough to make me drop the capsules. My fingers tingled as magic pulsed into me.

And then his foot came down on the fist clutching the capsules. Seriously, why did my life have to keep repeating itself? And what was it with this guy and my hands?

Thankfully, the Mauvais had on rubber-soled athletic shoes, so that first stomp didn't break anything. Nevertheless, it was enough to flatten my hand, send more shocks of pain through my body, and force me to drop the capsules. Then the foot came down again. This time the bones of my hand crunched like a rat under Chester's boot.

"I should have never agreed to send you back," the Mauvais

growled, but not at me. On my knees now, barely holding myself up with one arm, I turned my head to see Tobey backing away from the Mauvais's wrath. Kilbride's legs tensed, ready to spring.

"Get out of here, Tobey," I grunted.

But it wasn't Tobey the Mauvais lunged for.

CHAPTER FORTY-TWO
THE FINAL SPELL

Like a classic-movie version of Count Dracula, the Mauvais flew toward Alastair. It was probably nothing more than some form of Floating Charm, but it was fast enough and sudden enough that Tobey hadn't had time to pass the absorbing capsules he'd gathered to Alastair.

With a snap of his fingers, Alastair's bindings came loose and the Mauvais, using a Compulsion Hex, forced Alastair to stand.

"Get back in that chair," the Mauvais ordered me. "Rosaria, all the magic communities have had their chance. No more toying around."

One more spell, I thought. One more spell and my parents might never be who they once were. I needed time. I needed to throw the Mauvais off his game just long enough. If Tobey had made it through the portal, surely someone else would find it and be curious enough to wander through.

Unless it had closed itself off. As Morelli had told me, person-to-person portals had limited usage and lifespan. Which meant the portal may have already stopped working. Help might not be on the way. The cavalry might never ride in. The Mauvais would cast spell after spell until, even if I managed to finish him off, he would leave irreparable damage to millions of people across the world.

Look at me caring about the plight of others. I've come quite a long way, haven't I?

I had to stop him. I had to do whatever it took. I'd known it the moment I stepped through the portal, didn't I? Whatever happened between me and Devin Kilbride, one of us was not leaving this underground den alive. And I really wanted to keep that "one" from being me.

If there was going to be any possibility of me getting my magic back and getting out of here alive, I had to distract the Mauvais. An idea formed in my head. A crazy idea, but goading him into performing a D-spell might throw him off his game. Even if it was only for the briefest moment, it would give me the chance I needed. But if I failed to act quickly enough, I'd put my parents out of range and achieve nothing in return.

One more spell. Save the world or save my parents?

"You've got enough magic in you now," I said, each word sending a small stab of agony through my ribs. "So, go ahead and destroy Portland. Why would I care what you do to the place?"

It didn't work. Kilbride only stood there, watching me with bewilderment in his eyes.

"Because it's what people do," he said, as if explaining to a toddler that you needed to put on clothes before going outside. "You're supposed to care. Empathy? Heard of it?"

"Tried it once. It didn't stick."

I'll confess, I had no idea how I maintained this cool detachment. My pain receptors were on overdrive. I was more scared than I'd ever been in my life — and that's saying something. My plan hadn't worked, but as long as the Mauvais was talking, he wasn't doing any damage.

"You must care about something," Kilbride prodded, "or you wouldn't be here."

My eyes, my damn betraying eyes flicked for only the briefest nanosecond to Alastair. The Mauvais, seemingly perpetually entertained by me, laughed again.

"Oh, that's too sweet. You really came here for Allie? Although I am a little hurt," he said, his tone a mocking pout. "I thought you came here for me." With his lower lip jutting out petulantly, the Mauvais raised his left arm then squeezed his hand as if gripping a rope for dear life. Alastair instantly began gasping for air. The frightened, desperate sound proved breath was not making it beyond his trachea. "Love is so charming."

The final two words were delivered with patronizing glee. They were spoken by a man, a wizard, who knows just where to hit the hardest.

And there I found my chance. The risk I had to take.

His left hand still clenched, the Mauvais pointed the thumb and forefinger of his right hand at Alastair's head like a child's make-believe gun.

"Shall I?" Kilbride asked.

Alastair struggled, his reddening, swelling face looking for all the world like that of a man who'd just been strung up at the gallows. The gasping noise turned to something that sounded like a plea. I couldn't meet his eyes. I couldn't look at his face.

One more spell. One tiny distraction.

A sacrifice was the only way.

So, to the Mauvais's smug sneer and questioning expression, I merely shrugged.

The dismissive body language wasn't enough to break the Mauvais's full concentration, but he knew there was something between me and Alastair. As such, he'd expected me to plead for Alastair's life. He'd expected me to beg him not to kill Alastair. Which meant my disinterest in Alastair's survival crumbled a small section of the Mauvais's rocky focus. The chokehold he had on Alastair's throat loosened.

Alastair sucked in a great gulp of air as he blurted, "Cassie, please."

The words and the pain behind them hurt. More than the contraption's surging power ripping my magical cells to shreds, it hurt. If this didn't work—

No, the capsules were right there. Right at my feet. The slope of the floor had sent them rolling to me. It would only take an instant to grab them and reabsorb my power. I needed the distraction. I just hoped it would last long enough.

"Cassie, please," the Mauvais mocked, looking at me as if asking whether I was sure about this.

I shrugged again. "Go for it. He's practically dead anyway, isn't he? No magic in him. What's the point?"

Saying those words stirred a rancid bile in me that surged into my throat. It burned as I swallowed back both it and the wrenching that went deep into my heart. I didn't look to Alastair, knowing that if I did, I would not be able to hide my desire for him to understand.

"Are you sure you don't want to join me?" Devin made the offer with complete sincerity. "You're the coldest bitch I ever met." I glared at him, wishing his head might explode. It didn't. Wish in one hand, and all that, right? "No? Well, if you insist."

The Mauvais looked at Alastair. With his attention distracted, I dared to glance in the same direction. Alastair's stare was fixed on me. Wounded regret filled his eyes. I mouthed, "I'm sorry."

I don't know if Alastair saw or registered my words before the Mauvais shouted a command. Like lightning from the sky, a flash of light momentarily brightened the room.

Light that struck Alastair in the side of the head.

CHAPTER FORTY-THREE
THE PROPHECY

Momentarily blinded by the burst of light, I didn't see Alastair go limp. But I did hear the *thud* of his body hitting the dirt floor. I was already bent down, my throat tight with remorse. I crawled toward him, my good fingers stretched out to rake up the absorbing capsules nearest to me as I went.

"Cassie, watch out!" shouted Tobey. Knowing what body parts of mine the Mauvais liked best, I snatched my hands to my chest just as the Mauvais's foot came down.

Still gripping the capsules I'd picked up, feeling my magic inside them flowing back into me, I flung my arm out. I threw a Shoving Charm that should have been strong enough to hurl the Mauvais across the room, but he only staggered backward, knocked slightly off balance. I glanced at my hand. From between my fingers, I could still see the pulsing purple light of the capsules. The magic was entering me, my palms buzzed with the energy seeping in, but it wasn't shifting quickly enough.

It didn't stop me. I jerked my hand out again, trying a Binding Spell this time. Even if it might only be strong enough to tangle his feet up a bit, I needed to keep the Mauvais back. Tobey might have the strength to slow the Mauvais, but I doubted he had enough power to kill him. Hell, he might not even know any killing spells. We certainly hadn't gone over them in our lessons. Besides, if I was meant to believe some stupid prophecy, seeing Devin Kilbride sent to his grave was all on me.

But first, I needed to get out of the Mauvais's reach. As much as I hated being anywhere near the thing, I ducked behind the chair and scooped up the absorbing capsules that had rolled into the furrow behind the rear legs.

Once in position, I peered around the contraption. I couldn't see Tobey. Had he fled? Had he gone to tell the others I'd let Kilbride kill Alastair? The Mauvais, for his part, was bending over to collect his own crop of purple capsules.

Relying on my old favorite, I let a Shoving Charm fly. It didn't have its usual force, but it was enough to smack the Mauvais in the back of the knees, forcing his legs to bend. Thrown off balance by desperately trying to keep hold of his violet treasures, my hit sent him toppling to the floor. He hit his head when he landed, but Merlin be damned, it didn't knock him out. In fact, the tenacious bastard still held tight to the absorbing capsules. If he pulled in all the power contained within that cluster of magic pills, he would have enough strength not only to do in Portland, but all of the Pacific Northwest with the snap of his fingers.

Not knowing my reach, fearing my magic wasn't charged up enough, I dragged myself toward the Mauvais, hoping proximity would make up for any loss of magical *oomph*. I readied a Stunning Spell. Dear Merlin, let it do more than my Shoving Charms had.

But before I could act, I heard footsteps running in my direction. Everything in me demanded I cast the spell before it was too late, but I hesitated. Then, blocking my direct line of sight and spell to the Mauvais, were a pair of maroon-red Doc Martins. The left one lifted then came down hard, lifted again, and came down once more. And with both of these heavy-soled stomps came a gut-wrenching scream of pain.

Did I ever say I couldn't stand Tobey Tenpenny? You must have misheard. He had crushed first the Mauvais's right hand, then his left. Knowing exactly how that felt, the Mauvais's squeal gave me far too much satisfaction. I wasn't lying when I said I wasn't great at empathy. Especially not when it came to murderers.

"The prophecy," grunted the Mauvais.

I stood up and aimed my Stunning Spell at Kilbride's head. His hair stood on end briefly and he swatted at the air like someone batting away a fly. I looked again at my hand. The purple still refused to fully fade. Gandalf's beard on a stick! What were these? Bargain basement absorbing capsules?

But just as the pills weren't returning my power to me with any sort of haste, neither had they boosted the Mauvais's magic. And his hands could no longer hold the capsules to gain more. Plus, I'd bet that pain was really throwing him off. I know mine was.

I stepped out from my mad scientist shelter. Tobey might know how to break hands and perform a few spells, but he wouldn't have the power to do an Exploding Heart Charm or anything handy like that. At this point, I wasn't sure if I did either, nor did I have any idea how to perform a killing spell, but I had to at least try to fulfill that poorly rhymed prophecy.

I hadn't taken two steps before Tobey, my idiot cousin, bent down and grabbed the Mauvais's hand.

"Tobey, get back!" If he was touching the Mauvais when I attempted the Exploding Heart Charm, the spell would affect him too. Even if it didn't kill him, it would leave him with permanent cardiac damage.

But Tobey wasn't listening. From the wood-beamed ceiling cascaded chunky flakes of glittering snow. Tobey glared at the Mauvais with a scowl that was both fiery with hatred and icy with determination. Was that what was making it snow? I mean, the look was sending shivers through me, and I wasn't even the object of his scorn. First time for everything, right?

"You?" the Mauvais muttered.

I don't know what Tobey was doing. Was he trying to freeze the Mauvais? Had he learned the Confounding Charm? I hadn't taught him it, but he'd had it performed on him so many times recently maybe that left him with some residual knowledge of how to use it. Regardless, something had frozen the Mauvais in place. He wasn't struggling to get away. He wasn't lifting his free hand to throw a spell. He was just staring back into Tobey's eyes and muttering, "You?"

Tobey nodded. He wrenched the Mauvais's arm until it bent at the elbow, then forced the Mauvais to push his own hand against his forehead.

My cousin, my Untrained cousin, in a voice that was full of primal anger growled, "Previous."

The Mauvais screeched. A flash of light flared from his hand, giving his head a momentary halo-like glow. His body went limp. Tobey Tenpenny then flung Devin Kilbride out of his grasp like a dirty tissue.

I strode over. Awed shock doesn't even begin to describe how I felt. The black bird. Not me. Not a starling. A raven. Tobey Raven Tenpenny. I didn't know whether to laugh or cry. Instead, I just remained stunned with admiration.

"When did you learn how to do the Previous Charm?"

Tobey, breathing heavily, but wearing the beginning of a proud grin, said, "Grandad used to let me do it as a kid to give me the impression I could do magic. I mean, not with a killing spell, just with like a Floating Charm to make a banana levitate or something simple like that. I completely forgot about it until you asked Rafi about it. Is he—?" He gestured toward Kilbride's body.

There was no reason to ask. The Mauvais was at our feet, not moving, not breathing. Just as the Previous Spell Olivia used on me had re-enacted the Drying Spell and evaporated a few cups of tea, the last charm the Mauvais had performed was to kill Alastair.

But unlike the Drying Spell, Tobey had not added the words *non persona*, which meant the Mauvais's last magical deed reverberated back on himself. It was a good thing he'd been so willing to kill Alastair, I mused with morbid cynicism.

"Alastair," I said, my senses snapping back together as I whipped around.

Alastair's body remained at the base of the support column. His chest didn't rise. His fingers didn't twitch.

What had I done?

CHAPTER FORTY-FOUR

AFTER THE FALL

D-spells don't reverse, after all, I thought numbly. How had Mr. Tenpenny been so wrong?

A hand rested on my shoulder.

I turned around and buried my face in Tobey's chest. He tightened his arms around me. I'd completely forgotten my broken ribs and the pressure made me cry out. Tobey eased his hold. A good sob was just working its way up into my throat when Tobey's arms tensed again.

I pushed back and punched my good fist into his chest.

"That hurts, you idiot. Ribs?"

But Tobey wasn't paying any attention. He was looking in the direction of the support column.

"Cassie, look."

I didn't want to look. All I could think was that, like the hydra of Greek mythology sprouting seven heads for each head Hercules chopped off, seven new evil wizards had sprung to life to take the Mauvais's place.

Tobey gripped me by the shoulders and turned me around. Tired of fighting, not wanting to face the Mauvais again, I resisted at first. Then the scent of chocolate wafted over me. And of raspberries.

"I can't believe you let him kill me," said a groggy voice.

I surged forward, each rib feeling like it was breaking into a couple hundred more pieces. Despite the pain, I threw my arms around Alastair. His arms went around me, one at my waist, the other around my upper back. Instead of hurting, it energized me. And when his lips met mine, well, that worked far better than the strongest dose of ibuprofen.

Tobey cleared his throat. Alastair and I broke the kiss.

"You killed me. You really let him kill me," Alastair said, keeping hold of my good hand. His voice was still weak, but during the kiss, I'd pushed some of my magic into him and his eyes now bore a glimmer of strength they hadn't had before. You know, before I murdered him.

"Only for a little while," I said. "I wasn't about to let the Mauvais leave this room alive. I needed to distract him if I was going to have any chance of achieving that."

"Please don't use me as a distraction ever again."

"I'll keep it in mind."

"Does this mean your parents—?" Tobey asked.

I nodded. The Mauvais using that D-spell to kill Alastair had put my parents out of range. The killing spell on Alastair had reversed, the cities would rebuild, but my parents would remain in their stupor unless Runa could whip up some miraculous magical healing. Alastair squeezed my hand, his eyes glistening with gratitude and sympathy in equal measure.

From above us, the city rumbled, sending vibrations through the dirt floor and up my legs. In the distance, barely audible through the layers of brick and soil, came the sound of heavy pieces of metal clanging against one another, reminding me of box car hitches knocking together in a train yard. I tensed. The Pacific Northwest was prime earthquake territory and we were continually warned about the possibility of The Big One.

"What was that?" I asked in a whisper as if, like speaking too loudly in an avalanche zone, my voice might trigger an aftershock.

No one answered. When another crash of metal sounded, Alastair said, "The bridge. It's rebuilding. Devin's spells are undoing themselves."

"How are they going to explain that one?" Tobey asked.

"He's right," I said. "People are dumb, but even the most unobservant are bound to notice a bridge being collapsed one minute, then structurally sound the next."

"We should get back to HQ," Alastair said. "Are you okay?" He indicated my ribs.

"As long as I don't have to run, I should be fine. This, however," I raised my hand, "is going to need attention." Adrenaline was holding back the majority of the pain, but the hand had already puffed up like an angry blowfish.

Despite having a mangled appendage (again), I felt amazing. And I didn't think it was just the surge of gooey feelings I was having for Alastair.

I glanced around. Absorbing capsules were scattered everywhere, but they'd lost their purple glow. My magic had found its way back to me. As I've said before, there's nothing like the boost you get from the return of your own magic. Although, the gooey feelings were nice too.

Without a word to one another that it was time to hightail it, we turned our backs on the contraption, left the room, and hurried down the tunnel to the portal. I begged the magic gods for it to still be open. And at the same time, I worried what would happen if it was.

Recalling the Mauvais's pleasure at seeing me, at knowing I would come to him, I knew it was the traitor, not Morelli who'd made the portal. As such, I was hesitant about using it to get back. Would it even take us back, or would it send us into the hands of whoever had made it? I then cursed myself for not getting the Mauvais to tell us who the traitor was before Tobey killed him.

Tobey killed the Mauvais, I marveled. Did not expect that.

I explained my worries to Alastair, and he assured me person-to-person portals had to go back to the original location. That still didn't stop the nervous gurgling in my gut. Even if they didn't expect me to make the return trip, whoever had made the portal was a strong magic. Surely they could have figured their way around tweaking the normal portal rules. As we stood before the cold, dark hole, Alastair took my unbroken hand.

"Trust me?" he asked, and I'm not the best at reading other people, but I was pretty sure he wasn't only referring to the portal.

I nodded.

We entered the portal.

CHAPTER FORTY-FIVE
LANGUAGE LESSONS

We didn't end up in tattered shreds, we didn't end up in a desert wasteland, and we didn't end up in a vat of hazardous biomedical waste. I just knew I was going to have to pay for this string of good luck soon.

After the jostling and straining of the portal, we were back in my room. I could have flopped into bed and slept for a week, but as soon as Tobey joined us, we raced down to Olivia's office. The instant we stepped in, we were thrown into a scene right out of a book on witches' covens. Runa, Olivia, Mr. Tenpenny, Fiona, and Rafi stood a circle and were calling out charms. Although I wasn't sure exactly what the circle of Magics was up to, I could feel the electric tingle of an astounding amount of power humming through the space.

Working with the careful attention of someone arranging a bake sale display, Gwendolyn was piling cakes, cookies, and other mouth-watering treats from Spellbound onto Olivia's desk. As if impatiently waiting for the snacks to be ready, Banna stood to one side, the line of her thin lips firm as if she was resolutely focused on all that was happening.

Alastair froze in place, his grip tensing on my hand.

"You got the note I sent through?" he whispered. I said I did and some of the tension eased. Without having noticed our entry,

Banna slipped out a side door. "They must know what they're doing, then."

Moving quietly to not distract the others, we made our way over to Gwendolyn.

"What's going on?" I asked her, keeping my voice to a whisper.

"They're enacting various memory charms across the globe. The cities," she said with awe, "they're rebuilding. Does that mean—?" She cut herself off, as if speaking the words might jinx her high hopes.

I nodded.

Her chin wavered and her eyes brimmed with tears, but the smile on her face brightened the room.

"With their combined strength, this shouldn't take long, but they'll be starving when they finish. You probably want to stay out of the way of that."

She signaled us to follow her and we stepped out of the room.

"So the cities are really rebuilding? Just like that?" I asked.

"Well, not exactly *just like that*. Reversing a spell works most easily, most quickly, if nothing that was affected has been moved. But most of the cities had already started their clean up work, which means a few bricks and beams might be flying as they return to their rightful place."

"That doesn't sound safe," said Tobey.

"It should be safe enough. Every city under construction had a Knock Out Draft sent through the air. That was my contribution," she added proudly. "When they wake, they'll think they had a very vivid and very odd dream. And the rest of the world who saw it on the news will have simply forgotten about that particular bit of programming."

"But newspapers, websites, Instagram accounts. They'll all have registered it."

"Morelli has his team in place for that."

"Morelli has a—?" I shook my head at the wonder of it all. "Never mind."

From inside, the sounds of the incantations stopped. When we entered, I caught a glimpse of Runa leaving out a side door with a plate of what looked like cookies. As Fiona popped an entire pink cupcake into her mouth, I briefly told them what had happened. Olivia's brow furrowed, but she didn't scold, didn't tell me I'd been an overconfident moron, and didn't call for my immediate extraction. Instead, she went on to explain just how vast this cover up and reconstruction plan extended. From HQ, a network of repair work had started the instant they saw the Steel Bridge's girders rising up from the rubble.

"You're pretty damn organized for a group who couldn't even sort out my class schedule," I said.

"Don't think that wasn't organized," said Olivia. Then, as these Magics seem prone to do, she left that vague comment dangling in the air.

"We've also been expecting for this for many years," said Mr. T, who had pistachio-green macaron crumbs on his jacket's lapel. "Perhaps not this exactly, but we took what he'd done in the past and planned for contingencies based on that."

There was something different about him. A warmer glow, like he'd been given a potent vitamin injection. My first thought was that it was Fiona's influence. A man in love, and all that. That might have had something to do with it, but then it dawned on me.

"Are you alive? Like, really alive, not just Cassie Black-induced alive."

He put his first two fingers to his neck just under his jawline. His foot tapped along with the beat.

"Haven't felt that in a while."

Just then, a black bird landed on the railing outside the window.

"Is that Winston?" Olivia asked.

"You can see him?" Mr. Tenpenny and I said as one.

"What's going on? Who's Winston?" asked Rafi.

"Winston is a Tower raven who was killed by the Mauvais. Only the dead, or those with certain powers," Busby said, indicating me, "should be able to see him. For him to be visible must mean... But he should have been well out of range since he was killed before— It makes no sense."

"You're making no sense, Mr. T," I said. "You spoke more eloquently as a zombie."

"You see it, right? The Mauvais killed Winston before he captured and extracted Simon and Chloe. The only way for the rest of you to see Winston is either for all of you to be dead, which I don't think you are, or for Winston to have been returned back to life. And if he's alive, that means our count of Devin Kilbride's D-spells had to have been off. Correct?" he asked Olivia, who was now scanning a sheet on her desk.

"Yes, with the D-spells he's done within the past week and that stunt with Alastair, Winston's death should have been pushed out of range after Kilbride hit Las Vegas. That means the Starlings might be—"

"We need to get to the hospital wing," I said. Ignoring the streaks of pain being painted from my hand all the way across my torso, I raced out of the office.

Alastair caught up with me and we sprinted through the corridors, up the stairs, and to the room where my parents were recuperating. He whisked the door open and swept his arm to gesture me in.

What greeted me shot all the pain I'd tried to ignore back into my body.

* * *

I had expected Runa and Nurse Jake to be buzzing about, thrilling over their patients' recovery, and marveling at what must have just happened. But there was none of that. The nurse on staff — the mousey one again — was checking something off on her chart. Another staff member was wheeling a snack cart to those in the ward who could eat solid foods, and no one was showing any hint that this was anything more than another shift to get through.

Mr. Tenpenny joined us. His look of confused disappointment matched my own sentiments.

"But Winston was killed before your parents. I don't understand. They should be better."

"Not if the Mauvais didn't put them in this state," I said flatly. I turned to Alastair. He jerked back, as if my look was a slap.

"Cassie, you can't think I did this. Not after—"

"No, you dolt. You weren't even on the same continent at the time. But someone Kilbride was allied with at the time was."

Just then, Alastair's gaze flicked to the hallway. His face went paler than an igloo and his eyes narrowed. I shifted to see what had upset him, but the hallway was empty except for a cart of supplies.

"You said you got my note," he said, his eyes still focused on the hallway. Runa entered and looked about to scold me for being in my parents' room, but the look on Alastair's face stopped her words.

"We did," I replied. Alastair's gaze, stony and determined, darted to me. I wondered if his brief time as a corpse had affected his mind.

From her bed, my mother muttered the word *white*. She'd

said this so many times, no one paid much attention. Except for Alastair.

"She said *'white'*."

"Yeah, she does that," I said impatiently. "Alastair, what's got you so worked up?"

"My note. I told you." His voice seething, fierce tension flicked across Alastair's jaw. "Why is she still allowed to wander around? Who read the note?"

"I did, we all did."

"I don't think you read the whole thing." He switched his attention to Olivia, then pointed at my mother. "She's been telling you all along."

"Alastair," said Runa gently, "did you hit your head at any point?"

"No, shush, Runa," Olivia said, her voice barely above a whisper as her eyes showed a realization that hadn't quite dawned yet. "Alastair, go on."

"I know what you are, Olivia. And I know what land your people come from originally. Do you know your people's language? The old language?"

"A word here or there," she replied cautiously. "Not fluently."

"But do you know the word for *white*?" Alastair asked through lips that were tight with tension.

Olivia played some syllables over her tongue. Then seemed to catch the one she was after as her eyes darkened.

"Bán," she said, the word rhyming with *gone*. Then I recalled Banna recoiling as she worked her spell to reveal what Alastair had written.

"Banna," Runa growled.

But by then, I was already charging out the door.

CHAPTER FORTY-SIX

THE SCREAM

Following in my wake of rage, Alastair, Tobey and Busby shouted repeated orders for me to stop. I ignored them.

I would kill her.

Sure, it was a ridiculous thought. She'd already proven herself far more powerful than me, she had a few centuries of experience compared to my few weeks, and she wasn't going into a fight after having been strapped to an evil, magic-sucking chair or having her hand stomped on.

But I would kill her.

The hallway was empty. Oh, great galloping Gandalf's ghost! Of course I would have to face a set of stairs before jumping into this battle. The fates in charge of the White Tower were determined that I would have well-developed quads and calves by the time I left here. Whether that leaving was done dead or alive.

Charging down the steps, I caught a cold blue light shifting from the stairwell to the hallway of the floor below. When I reached the landing, the glow disappeared into a room. I raced toward it, nearly slamming into the door in my haste.

My fingers fumbled for the knob, then shoved the door open. The room was dark, but its only occupant was easy to find under the harsh gleam of that icy orb. Sunglasses perched jauntily on her head, Banna stood at the edge of the light. And I took a great deal of satisfaction in her shock at seeing me.

Taking advantage of her moment of surprise, I knocked her back with my magic head butt. How closely had she worked with the Mauvais? What D-spells had she cast? Then, like molasses in winter, the understanding finally came to me that she was the one who had extracted my parents.

I know, you probably figured that out several pages ago, but I was operating under a keg's worth of stress hormones, so cut me some slack.

But how many destructive spells had she cast since? I didn't care. I didn't give a flying rat's behind if she'd already put my parents out of range. I wanted her dead.

Trouble was, I didn't exactly know any killing charms.

I knew of the Exploding Heart Charm, but had no idea how to perform it. I'd heard the incantation the Mauvais used to kill Alastair, but that was another spell my lessons had failed to cover. I could have given either one a try, but I had no room for error. This wasn't the time for experiments. Instead, I threw a Stunning Spell at her head, hoping to daze Banna enough to keep her from fighting back. If it came down to it, I would strangle the witch to be rid of her.

As Banna's sunglasses clattered to the stone floor, the others piled into the room. They begged me to get away, to get out of Banna's line of attack, but I ignored them.

"Did you do that to my parents?" I demanded. "Did you ruin their lives, destroy their minds?"

Banna lifted her chin, a smirk on her tiny face.

"They had to be stopped. We were so close."

"You weren't close. The watch had been taken, safeguarded."

"And I knew we would get it again. As long as we stayed low for a time, I knew security would eventually get lax. And if I kept passing Devin Kilbride power, he would have the strength he needed once we stumbled onto it. I couldn't ask around. I did try out a few Confounding Charms, but someone," she darted a glare over my shoulder, "had already set up countermeasures to that. Still, at my age, you've learned patience. The watch would come around. And it did. Unfortunately, you did too."

And that was it, our pleasant little chat was over. There was no formality this time. There was no silly bowing to acknowledge one another. There was only sparring.

Banna raised her arm and launched a Binding Spell my way. But this time was different than my test with her in the arena. This time, I'd gotten my magic ducks in a row. I immediately threw up a membrane, then a Shield Spell for extra measure. Her Binding Spell sparked as it hit my magical barrier.

Banna grunted in fury. Then, perhaps wanting this to be just between us girls, she hurled three spells over my shoulder in quick succession. Tobey, Busby, then Alastair fell to the ground. I didn't know what spells she'd used. I had to hope she'd only stunned them. Although, two of the three did have experience with coming back from the dead, so…

As the bodies dropped to the ground, I sent a Flaming Arrow Charm straight toward Banna's chest. She ducked aside, but not before she shrieked and pinched her eyes shut. Light, I realized. Not normally a weapon, but this fight was definitely not normal.

An image of Alastair filled my mind, of the delight in his eyes at seeing me, of the kiss after he came back from the dead. A tight, hazel-colored orb as bright as a spotlight for a professional theater popped into being. My eyes squinted under the glare. Unfortunately, other than making her squint as well, the light was having no effect on Banna.

She started laughing.

316

"Control. You've been taught to control your magic, so that little trick no longer works."

"It works. Look at that thing."

"There's no heat to it. Not anymore. Because you've learned control."

"But the light," I said, stubbornly refusing to see her point as I made the orb shine a little brighter.

"You think the light will send me to my grave? Light's little more than annoying. I told you in our first meeting: it takes heat to do me in, you stupid girl, not light."

Banna lifted her hands. The way she held them was oddly familiar. I'd seen it before, but as I said, I'd never been taught this spell. Time seemed to slow as her fingers splayed out in one sharp motion. And that's when I recognized the spell. When Busby had tried to explain he'd been murdered, he'd shown me this very hand motion.

The Exploding Heart Charm.

I was going to die. I had lost.

"Cassie, cover your ears," a woman shouted.

In case you hadn't noticed, I'm not one who takes orders very well. I don't like people telling me what to do, and when someone does make demands of me, my first instinct is to question that demand.

But it's never too late to change, right? Even when you've only got about three milliseconds of your life left.

I slapped my hands to my ears and pressed them tight against my head. Yes, pain throbbed from the broken one, but something told me to ignore it and to keep my hands firmly in place.

Olivia flicked one hand back. From the corner of my eye, I saw a faint glow settle over Tobey, Busby, and Alastair. Olivia marched past me, her hand held out, generating her own shield.

Her mouth was open, and all I could think of was Edvard Munch's painting "The Scream".

A muffled cry found its way through the bones and tissue of my hands. I felt dizzy, nauseous. I thought perhaps this was due to the agony of squeezing a recently damaged hand to my head, but when I looked to Banna, well, she wasn't looking too hot either.

Her face had turned grey and had broken out in a furious sweat, bringing to mind a perspiring heap of old wax. She tried to open her mouth, she tried to lift her hands for a spell, but any motion was halted by whatever Olivia was doing.

Olivia kept approaching Banna, her mouth open the entire time. And that muffled cry, even though my ears were blocked as fiercely as I could manage, turned into a muffled screech. My head throbbed, my hand throbbed, my gut throbbed, but I kept my hands firmly glued to my ears as I watched Banna's orb flaring, then shrinking, then glowing once more as if fighting to remain in existence.

Olivia's torso jutted forward with the strength of her scream. In a sudden flash of blinding light, the orb burst apart then winked out. Like a dying star, I thought, as Banna collapsed to the floor.

Olivia, gasping for air and rubbing her stomach muscles, signaled me to lower my hands.

"What the hell was that?" I asked. Or rather, grunted. I was in a lot of pain at this point.

"Banshee blood," Olivia replied, struggling to bring her breathing back to normal. "I've only got a drop of it. A full banshee, even a half one, would have killed her in an instant. But I guess a drop's all I needed."

"What about—?" I whipped around. Alastair, Tobey, and Busby had been knocked out. They wouldn't have been able to cover their ears. But when I looked at them, they were groggily coming to.

"I conjured a Stoppering Spell over their ears. I almost didn't finish it in time before that Exploding Heart Charm got to you."

"You killed her," I said, still not fully believing it.

"A banshee's scream is deadly."

"She was the one who extracted my parents, not the Mauvais."

"She did it for the Mauvais," Busby said, rubbing his ears.

Alastair, shaking his head like a cat with ear mites, strode up to me and tried to wrap me in his arms, but I stepped back, holding my hands up in front of me.

"No offense, but I could really use a troll."

CHAPTER FORTY-SEVEN
SOME EXPLANATION

Olivia gave one last look at the crumpled form of Banna before turning her back on it and leaving the room.

"Let's get you to Chester," she said, shutting the door behind her once we were all out. "He'll probably be glad to get out of his room."

"Chester? He's not in the dungeon?" Olivia gave me an odd look, like she had no idea what I was talking about. "Or prison, or wherever you stick people when you arrest them."

"Chester was never arrested. Well, he was, in a way. He's been kept in one of the hospital's quarantine rooms since Runa was poisoned, but only for his own protection. I considered putting him in his own room, but no one would think or dare to look for him in the quarantine ward."

"I don't understand."

"It was when you mentioned the stink in the armory after finding Tobey. I knew something was wrong then. Trolls give off an odor that's *distinctive*, shall we say, when they've been put under a curse. A Confounding Charm, a Mirage Hex, any negative type of spell."

"Morelli told me about that. It was on the tip of my tongue when I was explaining why Chester had to be innocent, but I couldn't quite remember until—"

Until I was about to step through a portal I thought was the illegal portal I'd asked Morelli to make, is what I did not say.

"Anyway," Olivia said as we wound our way up the spiral stairs, "I'd put my money on a Coercion Spell. Banna likely put it on him the day Tobey came back. And after speaking with Chester, I'm convinced he was still under Banna's spell when he slipped poison into Runa's champagne."

"So he did do it," I said. "But why Runa?"

"Runa had just figured out how to recuperate your parents. The extraction reversal process was a success, and Banna couldn't risk your parents bearing witness to her role in their imprisonment. Plus, it provided her a distraction to put a Concealment Charm on the portal scans."

"And you've known this how long?" I asked.

"For a while now we've been certain it had to be Banna who brought Tobey through," said Mr. T. "Chester was likely tricked into finding him and bringing us that note."

"Tobey mentioned a bright light," I said, also recalling his mention of the ground rumbling, which had probably been Chester's heavy footsteps. "It was Banna's orb he saw, wasn't it?"

"Yes," said Olivia gravely, "and I was never more glad to see that orb go dark. I hate revealing my banshee heritage, but I suppose sometimes it comes in handy."

"Is that why you try so hard to control your temper?" I asked.

"That, and the fact that it wouldn't do for one of the senior members of HQ to go around shouting at everyone," she said wryly. "Leadership requires working together, not creating discord."

"But why would she help the Mauvais? Why betray all of you?"

"I'm sure more answers will come, but I think Banna carried a hatred for the Magics since the time of her capture after she'd led the fight against us all those centuries ago. Because of her name, we called her the White Warrior — mockingly so after we defeated her. We ruined her people to gain our own strength, but I thought she'd come to terms with that after all these years. I thought she wanted to move forward. Clearly, I thought wrong.

"My guess is she saw in Devin Kilbride a wicked, selfish determination she'd been looking for. But she wasn't truly allying with him. She was using him to do her dirty work. He would start the ball rolling to subjugate the Magics. If he failed, he would take the blame and face the consequences, but if he succeeded, she would have done away with him and assumed her role as the White Warrior once more. She would take back the magic we stole from her people and use it to bring them back to power."

This didn't exactly sound like a speech Olivia had come up with on the spur of the moment.

"You knew all this and didn't stop her?"

"I've had my suspicions. Things she's said, ways she's behaved, but I had no concrete evidence." We were on the final few steps that led to the hospital wing. "She kept her nose clean, she became one of the group, and she didn't perform any D-spells. Which means if my records are correct, and if she was the one who extracted your parents—"

Before she could finish, we stepped out from the stairs and into the hospital area. All was chaos. Happy chaos, but it was a sharp contrast to the ward's earlier calm serenity. Runa caught sight of us first. The joy and relief in her eyes at seeing Olivia reminded me of the looks I'd often seen on Alastair's face. It warmed my heart for these two.

I know, I'm turning sappy in my old age, aren't I?

"They're back. It's—" Runa's face glowed with good cheer. "I've never seen anything like it. What happened?"

322

"Banna's dead. The Extraction Hex was done by her, not the Mauvais."

"So your theory about the tribunal—" She then pulled her eyes off Olivia and turned to me. I was feeling woozy with pain at this point and cold sweat chilled my brow. "Great goblins, what has happened to you?"

I held up my hand.

"Again?"

"Should be the last time. I think my ribs might be broken too."

Runa looked to Olivia, who nodded.

"Chester!" Runa shouted. The ward went silent for a moment, then the happy chatter resumed when Chester came thudding up to us.

"Yes, Mr. Dr. Dunwiddle?" Chester lifted his hand as if to salute, then seemed to remember this wasn't necessary and clamped the hand back to his side.

"It's just Dr. Dunwiddle, Chester. Now fix Miss Black. Ribs and hand."

"The ribs? But I'd have to—"

"It's medical, Chester."

"Yes, sir."

Chester blushed and muttered some apologies, then placed his large hands to my sides as if he was going to lift me in the air. His fingers acted like a push-up bra for my breasts, and the poor troll's cheeks turned an alarming shade of red. There was none of the strange bone-sliding sensation, but under his warm palms my chest instantly felt better and when he asked me to take a deep breath, there was no stinging pain.

"Not broken, just bruised," Chester said as he released me. "Easy fix." He then held out his hands to take mine, which even swollen like a Macy's Day Parade balloon, looked tiny in his

323

grasp. He closed his hands over mine and, as before, I could feel the bones shifting, the tissues deflating, the bits and pieces returning to their proper place.

"Better?" Runa asked. I nodded. "Now, would you like to meet your parents?"

"After which, we have something to discuss," said Olivia.

So, with that storm cloud looming over me, I followed Runa into the adjoining room.

"They're better," she said as we walked. "As in, their magic has returned, but it will still take time to fully recover from the starvation and dehydration. That should resolve itself more quickly now that they have their magic back, but they'll tire easily."

When I took a tentative step into their room, Simon and Chloe Starling were awake. Although the droopy eyelids proved they might not remain so much longer.

"Cassie?" And that's all it took to turn me into a blubbering mess. Hearing my mom speak my name broke the dam of strength, of hard-headedness, of toughness I'd built up over the past couple decades. Tears of relief and happiness spilled over as I nodded.

His voice weak and dry, my dad asked, "Is it really her?"

"Of course it's her," my mom chided, her own voice raspy. "Look at that face."

I didn't know what to do, but when my mom held out her stick-thin arms, I accepted the embrace, being careful not to squeeze her skeletal frame. She was too weak to tighten her hug, but it was enough. I'd waited twenty-four years for a hug from my mom, and even a gentle one felt like being wrapped in a world of love. My dad then asked when it was his turn and I was soon taking another dose of parental warmth.

"They say you saved us," he said, pride filling his scratchy voice.

I wiped my eyes and shrugged.

"I didn't have much else going on."

I sat with them for about half an hour, catching them up on who I'd met in MagicLand, telling them about Mr. Wood being the best boss in the world, and regaling them with the delectable desserts at Spellbound Patisserie, which had apparently been started by Gwendolyn's grandfather who, it turns out, was a distant cousin of my father's grandmother.

"The height, it runs in the family," he said.

I didn't tell them about any of the bad stuff. The abusive string of foster homes, the times of near starvation, the lack of funds to finish my schooling, nor the battles against the Mauvais. There would be time for that when they were better, and I feared any bad news would slow their recovery.

By the time I got around to showing them a picture of Pablo on my phone, they were fighting to keep their eyes open, so I made my goodbyes and promised I'd be back soon. I think they were snoring before I left the room.

Alastair waited for me outside.

"How was it?"

"Emotional, that's for sure."

"Did you tell them about us?" he asked with a hopeful grin.

"What about us?" I teased. "Is there something going on?"

With a smile, he took my hand. As we headed down to Olivia's office, he said, "I still can't believe you let him kill me."

"It was just for a little while."

"What if I hadn't come back?"

"I'd have made sure you came back," I said and waggled the fingers of my free hand at him. "This meeting, it's about the watch, isn't it?"

"It is."

Except for the hand Alastair held, my entire body went cold.

CHAPTER FORTY-EIGHT

A FAREWELL TO MAGIC

Alastair and I remained silent the rest of the way through the corridors and stairways. When we reached Olivia's office, he kept hold of my hand. Inside were Runa, Morelli, Mr. Tenpenny, Tobey, Rafi, Fiona, and of course, Olivia. On her desk sat the watch, still ticking away the time, or whatever it was those gears tracked.

I didn't wait for the hammer to drop. I knew exactly what this was about. Despite everything, my magic was still a threat and it was still entangled with the watch's power. Even if the Mauvais and Banna were dead, who else might come up with the cunning plan of using Cassie Black as a weapon?

"You're going to extract me, aren't you?" I fixed my stare on Olivia. On the way to the hospital ward, she'd been talking to me like we were equals, like we were comrades, like I was going to have a happy life amongst the Magics. How stupid could I have been? "It's what you've wanted all along, what you've been pushing for for days, so go on, get to it."

"Cassie, you've got it wrong," Runa said, her face grim as she scowled at my insolence.

"Then maybe you could explain it to me."

Runa and Olivia exchanged a look, then Olivia gestured to Runa as if she were giving the doctor the floor.

"Olivia did want to extract you. But not out of malice or spite or punishment. She knew the Mauvais wanted you, well, wanted your magic. So we, her and I, came up with a plan."

"What plan?" Rafi and Busby asked at the same time, sounding more than a little offended at not being included on this scheme.

"We'll explain everything, but first, let's have a seat," Olivia offered as she conjured some tea to go with Gwendolyn's desserts. We all settled into chairs and Fiona placed a slice of Victoria sponge in front of each of us.

The fights, the healing, and the emotional ride had left me starving, so I dug into mine. I'd already polished off half the slice before I noticed everyone else had remained politely poised, waiting for Olivia's explanation. I carefully placed my plate back on the desk. But really, why hand out cake if you're not going to eat it?

"Does this have to do with her lessons?" Mr. T asked, his perplexed expression declaring he wasn't used to being out of the loop.

"Wait, what about my lessons?"

"You didn't think it odd that we kept making you take classes and kept insisting you practice and study, even though you might be extracted by the tribunal?"

"You wouldn't believe how many times I thought that."

"We wanted to keep you busy," Mr. T said. "We also wanted to keep your schedule unpredictable. We hoped it would leave you too distracted to meddle in our efforts to find the Mauvais. And yes, we were actively searching for him, so please don't think we weren't.

"The other reason was so, if we did find anything, you wouldn't know. That way, if the Mauvais got into your head, he wouldn't be able to read your thoughts regarding our progress.

But," and here he fixed an accusing stare on Olivia, "apparently there was another layer of subterfuge going on?"

"We didn't want to tell you," Olivia explained to him. "You knew about the distraction tactics with Cassie's lessons, but the more people who knew what Runa and I were planning increased the risk of discovery if the Mauvais attempted any form of mind reading charm. That's why we kept it to ourselves. Even if it meant all of you thought I was being unfairly harsh on Cassie."

"I'll withhold my apology for now," quipped Busby.

"So you weren't going to extract me?" I said, thinking of how she'd hidden Chester away to keep him safe from any further curses.

"No, we absolutely were," Olivia said cheerily, as if I should be delighted to hear that news.

"I think you might want to explain a little better," said Rafi, who I noticed had ignored the others' behavior and had already eaten most of his piece of cake. "Because right now, neither of you are making any sense." He then, in a show of camaraderie, cut and placed another large slice of the spongy dessert on both our plates.

"We need to start with the tribunal. I have a feeling the reason Banna kept their proceedings so secretive was because she was the sole member. At first she would have been keen to use a tribunal ruling as an excuse to legally extract you and hand your power over to Kilbride," said Olivia. "But once you started filling absorbing capsules for your parents, well, she didn't dare slaughter the cow that could keep on giving. Especially a magic one that would give large, consistent doses of power."

"Each time Cassie would fill a bundle of those capsules, they'd go missing," said Runa. "I thought it was Jake not paying attention to the dosage, but he swore he followed my instructions to the letter. We should have realized that not long after Cassie filled a new batch, the Mauvais would attack a city. It had to be Banna taking them to him. It's the only way he would have had the strength for that much destruction."

"I tried to tell you that in the note I sent with the Communication Charm," Alastair said. "I saw her giving capsules to him one day, and I could smell Cassie's magic on him soon after Banna's visits."

"Yes, well, we will now insist everyone practice sending and receiving messages via the Communication Charm. Banna was the only one of us who remembered the revealing spell. I think she saw what you'd written and quickly concealed it again, giving us only half your message." Olivia took a deep drink of her tea.

"And this whole Extract Cassie idea?" I prodded.

"As I've told you before, I was worried about your magic being given to the Mauvais if you were extracted. Our plan was to get the magic out of you before anyone else could." When I didn't applaud this wonderful plan, she added, "We were going to give it back."

"Time was running out before the tribunal made its decision," said Runa. "That's why I was working so hard and getting so frustrated with my lack of progress at undoing your parents' extraction. Turns out my procedure did work, but Banna — or perhaps Chester under Banna's influence — was undoing it and setting the Starlings back to zero."

"She would have wanted to keep them too far gone to tell us what really happened to them," said Rafi.

"Exactly. Anyway," said Runa, addressing me, "the plan was to extract you. That would make you useless to the Mauvais and keep you safe until we took care of him."

"Then," Olivia added, "once Runa perfected her extraction reversal technique, we would put your magic back into you."

329

"Remind me to stay away from both of you if you're ever in research mode again," Rafi said before shoveling a massive bite of cake into his mouth.

"I still can't believe Banna's prophecy was wrong," said Fiona. "Or was that a ruse as well?"

"It wasn't wrong," I said. "It was spot on, but you just assumed it was about me." I gestured toward Tobey. "Tobey *Raven* Tenpenny. He's the black bird. The line about reversing must have referred to the Previous Spell he used. Tobey. Not me. Every line fits."

And I will admit I felt a little bitter about this realization. The Mauvais had made my life miserable. He'd had a curse placed on me because of that prophecy when he should have taken out his frustration on Tobey Tenpenny. All I can say is my dear cousin owed me one. More than one.

"She's right," said Fiona. "But the problem is solved, isn't it? The Mauvais and Banna are both gone. We don't need to go through with the extraction now, do we?"

I appreciated her concern, but while this chat to figure stuff out and make sense of it all was a great delaying tactic, I knew I'd have to face the inevitable. It was too dangerous to keep both me and the watch magically chugging along.

"We are," said Olivia. "Alastair, I think you can explain this best. The strands are different now, aren't they?"

Alastair pondered a moment before beginning. "When I asked for the watch to be sent to Rosaria," he said hesitantly as if still working out the ideas he needed to convey, "I'd come up with the theory that the magic in the watch had been woven together like threads. Two threads teased apart the right way are easy to separate, so I thought I could undo my magic from the Mauvais's. Then Cassie came along, her magic mixed in as well, and a braid was created. A braid is less easily untangled."

330

"But now the Mauvais is dead," Mr. Tenpenny said.

"Exactly. His strand within the braid was removed when he died. And, thanks to Cassie's unique form of strategy against the Mauvais, I died as well. When I died, my strand disappeared. I haven't touched the watch since, which means only Cassie's magic should be left in there."

"That's good, right?" I asked. "We can just drain my magic from the watch to shut it down." The apologetic looks on their faces were like fly swatters coming down hard on my pixie of hope. "The watch, because of the entanglement, it won't let go of my magic, will it?"

"Something like that," said Olivia. "It does have to be destroyed to keep everyone safe, but your magic has become intrinsic to the watch. Your magic is the only thing keeping it active."

"What does that mean exactly?"

"It won't leave you with the same mental after effects as an extraction, but if we destroy the watch, you will lose all your magic," Alastair said, trying to sound as matter-of-fact as possible, but regret came through in his voice.

I felt that regret too as I stared at the watch. I'd grown to like being Magic. I also liked — and this was really hard for me to admit — being part of the community. I even liked Runa. Plus, who could complain about having to eat vast quantities of sugar to stay in shape? Being de-magicked also meant I would only be given limited access to MagicLand, if I was given any access at all.

But they were right, the risk of keeping the watch active was too great. And my parents deserved to know the object that had ruined them, that had broken our family to pieces, was no more.

I looked up from the watch.

"Okay. Do it."

"Cassie, are you sure?" Rafi asked. "We could safeguard the watch again. We can, can't we?" He passed a questioning look between Mr. T and Olivia.

"Thanks, Rafi," I said, "but it's too dangerous. I'm right, aren't I?" Olivia nodded. "Will I still be able to see my parents?"

"Of course. The portals will be inaccessible to you, but we wouldn't stop you from seeing Simon and Chloe."

The hidden subtext was that I wouldn't be seeing them within MagicLand. Which also meant other relationships in MagicLand were going to suddenly be long distance ones. If they continued at all.

"Let's get this over with," I said gloomily.

Alastair, his voice shaking with emotion, instructed me to grasp the watch and to imagine it breaking, rusting, falling apart, to picture all magic cascading out of it and flowing away.

I expected it to hurt. I expected it to feel like the contraption the Mauvais had me in or Banna's Vacuum Hex from my second test. But instead, as I visualized the watch tarnishing and its gears locking tight, it simply felt like any sense of importance and belonging was dribbling away from me. There was no pain, but there was dismay, loneliness, and discontent.

Alastair had been talking me through the process, encouraging me and providing a focal point, but at some point it must have gotten to be too much. His voice trembled, then cut off, and Mr. Tenpenny stepped in.

As I followed the guidance from Mr. T, the watch glowed with a brilliant golden light that slowly faded until the light extinguished. The gears jammed to a halt and the ticking hands fell silent and still. To my eyes, the object that had always appeared highly polished and worth at least a thousand bucks now looked like a hunk of rusted refuse you'd pass by if you found it discarded on the side of the road. A broken thing ready for the scrap heap.

"Set it down, Cassie," Runa said. Was that a slight catch in her voice? I like to think so.

I placed the watch on Olivia's desk. What my mind had seen had only been an illusion. Although it had stopped ticking, the timepiece still looked in perfect condition. But whereas before it had hummed with an electric energy, it now sat there cold and lifeless, nothing but a pretty collectible.

"Try something, Cassie. Anything," Rafi said.

Returning to my old favorite, I tried a Shoving Charm on the watch. There was no tingle in my fingertips, there was no sense of power, and not even a cupcake wrapper rustled on Olivia's desk. Like the watch, I was out of commission.

CHAPTER FORTY-NINE

PARTING GIFT

A disengaged numbness took over me. Despite the group around me, I felt alone. Other than that, I felt nothing. I knew the loss of both the new world I'd found, and possibly my relationship with Alastair, would hit me soon enough, but for now I just wanted to go home, pour a beer, and receive chin rubs from Pablo.

"If someone could take me through the portal, I'd like to go home now."

"If you could just wait outside a moment," Olivia said with cool detachment.

I'd expected, or at least hoped for, a little resistance. Perhaps someone saying, "Oh no, you don't have to leave right away. Stay and finish your cake."

But it would seem a non-magic wasn't even welcome in the same room as them. Were these people so different from the Mauvais? At least he had made no effort to hide his prejudice.

I strode down the hall to stare out the window. The tourists had gone for the day, but two Yeoman Warders were walking together. One held a clipboard, while the other — judging by his hand gestures — was giving a tour. Someone must be taking a test, I thought, and again a wave of loneliness hit me. Everyone seemed to have their purpose except me. I swore when I returned to Portland, I would get my full license to work with the dead. But was that what I really wanted? Would Mr. Wood even keep me on after seeing Daisy's handiwork?

I thought of my parents. Could I follow in their footsteps and work at chasing down bad guys? Given my methods, I doubted any police force would allow me on the payroll.

The office door creaked open, startling me from my morose reverie.

"Cassie, if you could," Rafi said, crooking a finger to signal me back inside.

"What is this about?" I asked once I reached him.

"They've got a little going away gift for you."

Despite everything, my mouth watered. A big basket of Fortnum & Mason treats would make a fair dent in my sullen mood.

I followed Rafi into the office. It seemed ages since I'd first entered this room. And just as on that first day, there was no Fortnum & Mason basket waiting for me. Talk about disappointing.

Mr. T stepped up to me. Like, he was really close, and with neither of us comfortable with infringements on our personal space, it was more than a little awkward. I shifted back a pace.

"You've touched a lot of lives in the short time you've been with us, Cassie," he said. "I can definitely say I wouldn't be alive without you."

"Twice."

"Twice," he said, a delighted glint in his steely eyes.

Next, Tobey came up to me. This was getting more than a little creepy.

"You're still the biggest pain in the butt I've ever met, but you've done a lot for me." He flicked his fingers and a cluster of glittering snowflakes danced in the air.

"And you know I've been touched by you," Alastair said, approaching me with a knowingly coy grin that made my cheeks blush.

"Thanks, I guess. That means a lot." As far as gifts go, though, it was a little lame. Maybe they'd at least let me take the rest of that Victoria sandwich. "But what the hell is going on here?"

Runa stepped up. "Your magic is in these three people. Your parents too, but they're weak and I think we can manage this without them."

"I thought my magic was destroyed with the watch."

"The magic that was within you and the watch, yes," Runa continued with that annoyed tone she took on when I hadn't quite grasped whatever lesson she was trying to teach me. "But you can't kill off the magic that's twined itself within the fabric of others' cells. Your magic has been in Busby since you first woke him. And the magic in Tobey is purely yours."

"By the way," Olivia said, "we will be discussing that later."

"And?" I prodded. This was a nice trip down memory lane, but I failed to see the point.

"Are you always going to be so thick-headed?" said Runa with mock exasperation. "Boys, do what you will, I can't keep having this conversation."

Busby took hold of my right hand and Tobey grabbed my left. Rafi stepped up and gripped onto our clenched hands with his. I honestly had no idea what was going on and flinched at their touch, but the three of them held tight. My first thought was: *If one or both of my hands end up broken, someone is getting kicked.* Just as I pictured whose shins would feel the toe of my boot first, something that felt like warm honey flowed from their palms and into my skin.

They were giving a non-magic magic.

"Are you? I thought— Isn't this illegal?"

"We're only giving you a little of the magic you gave us," Mr. T said, as if this was something that happened every day in MagicLand. "Returning a borrowed item isn't against the rules, is it, Olivia?"

"Not that I'm aware of."

"And since you're relatives, it should stick quite nicely," said Runa.

After several very awkward moments, the flowing feeling stopped. Rafi let go, then Tobey and Busby released my hands. The air on the skin of my palms was cool, but underneath the surface was a familiar tingling sensation. Tobey leaned forward and sniffed. When he leaned back, he wore a satisfied grin and I just knew he was going to lord this gift over me for the rest of my life. A nuisance I could live with.

"Thank you." I didn't know what else to say. Well, other than, *Can we have cake now?*

After passing a knowing glance between me and Alastair, Rafi took it on himself to call the meeting to an end. "Let's leave these two. Probably a lot to discuss. Shoo, shoo."

"This is my office, Rafi," Olivia said.

"Well, I don't think they're going to steal anything. Are you?"

Alastair had come up beside me and taken my hand, adding a buzzing thrill on top of the dancing tingle of my magic charging back into my cells.

"I can't guarantee that cake will still be here when you get back," I told them.

The others left, Mr. T giving an approving glance back at us before he departed.

Alastair stepped around to face me.

"You know, thanks to all those absorbing capsules, I've pulled in a fair amount of your magic." He grinned. "Would you like it back?"

I shrugged with feigned nonchalance. "It would probably be the polite thing to do."

Alastair moved in closer, his free hand slipped up to caress my cheek. He hesitated just a moment, then leaned in.

From the desk, I swore I heard a tick.

"Did you—?"

Before I could finish my question, Alastair's lips were on mine. And there was more than one kind of magic in that kiss.

CHAPTER FIFTY

THE END?

That Yeoman Warder I'd seen from the window? Turns out it was Nigel. He'd been killed by Banna when he tried to fight the Mauvais out of vengeance for killing Winston. So, when Banna died, the killing spell she'd used on Nigel had reversed.

Giving way to the unusual circumstances, the Tower powers-that-be allowed Nigel to retake the test he'd failed over twenty years ago. Thanks to my constant work with him, he'd learned his Tower of London history front and back. Nigel, I am proud to say, is now a fully fledged Yeomen Warder of Her Majesty's Royal Palace and Fortress the Tower of London. Good luck, trying to fit that onto a business card, Nigel.

My parents regained their strength. It took time, but they have now returned to MagicLand and live in a small house next to Lola, who dotes on them like two new pets. Although, she doesn't dress them in silly costumes. That I'm aware of.

Catching up has been a long process and only once they were in full health did I tell them of the childhood I'd had. They blamed themselves, then they blamed Alastair and Morelli, but eventually, with Mr. Tenpenny's help and a lot of cake from Spellbound, they were brought around to accept it had kept me alive. Still, I think the new phone (which actually works in MagicLand!) for me and the elaborate cat tree for Pablo that showed up from them a couple days later was a bit of a guilt gift. Pablo's not complaining.

Morelli, now that he doesn't have to make me feel like a pile of fly attractant, has fully renovated the apartment building. It currently boasts a blooming garden complete with vegetable beds and a chicken coop. The first floor beyond his apartment has been turned into his crafting studio/workout room. I've been given full ownership of the entire upper floor.

As for Alastair, we're stupidly happy. As in, we make people gag with our happiness. He's joined me in my new spacious penthouse — hey, it's the top floor, so it counts as a penthouse, right? When I helped him unpack his belongings, I swear to you I never came across a single matching pair of shoes or socks. In a fit of making a home together, we've spent far too much time magically changing the color of the interior paint, the kitchen style, and the furniture. Pablo is so confused.

Alastair has turned his old studio in MagicLand into a craftsman's workshop where he specializes in magical timers in the shape of various animals and people, while also constructing larger works on commission. He is under strict Cassie Rules to never, ever make a watch.

Mr. Wood, thanks to Morelli, was back on his feet in record time and astounded his physical therapists with his quick recuperation. He still claims, to anyone who will listen, it was all the bacon that helped speed his recovery. As a housewarming gift, he gave me and Alastair a hand-crocheted granny-square blanket. Or at least I think that's what it is.

The funeral home is doing well, but my job is now being performed by Daisy. It was hard to pass the torch to her, but I needed to free up some time for training. Yes, more lessons, more classes. But this time they're part of joining the Magical Detective Squad, Rosaria Division. Mr. Tenpenny is serving as mentor to me and one other new recruit: Tobey Tenpenny. Mr. T insists our styles and approaches compliment one another and has threatened to propose Tobey be my partner when we graduate. Is it too late to change my mind about this career choice?

As for the other MagicLand love lives, Mr. Tenpenny and Fiona finally wed in a small, late summer ceremony. Olivia and Runa are making full and regular use of the Portland-London portal. I know every time I see Runa strolling toward the portal in one of her frilly, pastel shirts, she's heading off for another date. She insists Olivia says the delicate colors suit her, but there's never any mention of what Olivia thinks of those god-awful frills.

And Tobey's love life? Merlin's beard, I swear if he asks me one more time which ring would suit Daisy or the best way to make a memorable proposal (unicorns have been mentioned), I will slip him one of Gwendolyn's color-changing potions to turn his hair purple and his skin blue with green polka dots. I mean, he wants a memorable proposal, right?

I didn't tell anyone what I heard before that kiss in Olivia's office. When Alastair and I had spent a very thorough amount of time making sure he'd returned my magic that day, I had checked the watch's hands. Was there a slight tremble in the minute hand, or had it merely been a trick of my kiss-drunk eyes?

I can't say. No one else showed any concern, nor felt any magic coming off the thing, so I let HQ take care of it. Rather than smashing it to bits, they put it on display in a magic-proof case as a reminder of the danger they'd allowed themselves to fall into.

I pass that case whenever I report to HQ for an exam. It doesn't happen every time, and perhaps it's only my overactive imagination, but every now and then I detect the click of a turning gear.

THE STORY
BEHIND THE STORY

With the wrap up of this trilogy, it's time to look back on what inspired this book.

Several things. But namely, my grandma's funeral.

What? You don't get inspired to write dark humor that includes the waking dead and an entire magical world while facing down familial grief? Hmm...I may need to re-examine how my brain works.

Anyway, it took a fair while for the funeral to start and I'd brought with me a notepad, pencil, and one of my first line story prompts and thought I'd play with it. I'm not sure exactly what that first line was, but I think it was, "We need to talk."

I jotted down a quick dialogue in which a funeral home worker had to confess to her boss that she kept accidentally waking the dead. The tidbit wasn't all that great. It had way too much attitude, the funeral home worker came across as a big jerk, but it did plant a seed of an idea.

At the time, I was working through the final few books of my Osteria Chronicles series. I was bored with the series and feeling unmotivated to work on those books. But knew I had to get them done or I would never do them.

As I worked through those books, I had a few breaks in between drafts to play with this funeral home idea that kept growing in my mind even though I was trying to hold it back.

As part of trying to play a little looser with my writing, I was also doing writing exercises for 10 - 15 minutes one day a week. Using a prompt from the very fun book *Take Ten for Writers*, I ended up with the beginnings of a story set in World War II in which a bike messenger delivers what she thinks is a normal package, but turns out to contain a magic object that if it falls into the wrong hands could mean doom for the Allies.

I loved this idea and thought it could work into a novel. But damn it! There were still two books of The Osteria Chronicles (a six-book series) to get through, after which I *really* wanted to get out and play with my funeral home worker.

Let me tell you, slogging through the first few drafts of books five and six of the Osteria Chronicles was a HUGE exercise in discipline. But the good thing about drafts? You're recommended to take breaks in between them.

Okay, I may have looked forward to those breaks a bit too much. Because during one of these breaks I let myself loose on that funeral home story.

But wait, my funeral home worker (the future Cassie Black) is waking the dead. How? A magical object, perhaps? What if Cassie hadn't had the best luck in her life? What if she'd worked as a bike messenger to make ends meet? What if she happened to be unable to deliver a magic object that ends up changing the course of her life...and the dead people she's meant to be tending to?

Yes, I may have let out a squeal of joy at this point. I not only could get to work on the funeral home story, but I could also use the bike messenger concept without having to dedicate/find time to write a whole different novel.

Hoorah, indeed!

The first draft of *The Undead Mr. Tenpenny* came together within a couple weeks. I don't think words have flowed so freely from my pen as with that draft and I loved what I'd come up with.

But of course, there were those two Osteria books to complete. Which I did. Cheers to me for sticking with it...and I have to say, for all the grumbling, I think those final two books proved a strong and satisfying finish for the series.

While the core events stayed the same from that first Cassie Black draft, plenty changed as I began to plan how the trilogy might play out, how the original characters could have a role throughout the trilogy, and how I could dribble in hints and foreshadowing throughout the story.

And, thankfully, my early readers have told me it worked out and came together marvelously. I hope you've thought so too.

Thanks so much for reading these books. I'd love to stay in touch, so please be sure to sign up for my newsletter at *www.subscribepage.com/mrsmorris* (all lower case) to get a free story and to find out what's coming next from my overactive imagination!

—*Tammie Painter, May 2021*

THE PART WHERE I BEG FOR A REVIEW
IF YOU ENJOYED THIS BOOK....

You may think your opinion doesn't matter, but believe me, it does...at least as far as this book is concerned. I can't guarantee it mattering in any other aspect of your life. Sorry.

See, reviews are vital to help indie authors (like me) get the word out about our books.

Your kind words not only let other readers know this book is worth spending their hard-earned money and valuable reading time on, but are a vital component for me to join in on some pretty influential promotional opportunities.

Basically, you're a superhero who can help launch this book into stardom!

I know! You're feeling pretty powerful, aren't you?

Well, don't waste that power trip. Head over to your favorite book retailer, Goodreads, and/or Bookbub and share a sentence or two (or more if you're ambitious). Even a star rating would be appreciated.

And if you could tell just one other person about Cassie Black's story, your superhero powers will absolutely skyrocket.

Thanks!!

By the way, if you didn't like this book, please contact me and let me know what didn't work. I'm always looking to improve.

MY NEXT BOOK
IS COMING SOON!

In fact, it might already be here by the time you read this, and there's probably been loads of exciting stuff you've missed out on. You know, like photos of my cats.

Anyway, I love staying in touch with my readers, so if you'd like to...

- Keep up-to-date with my writing news,

- Chat with me about books you love (and maybe those you hate),

- Receive the random free short story or exclusive discount now and then,

- And be among the first to learn about my new releases

    ...then please do sign up for my monthly newsletter.

As a thank you for signing up, you'll get my short story *Mrs. Morris Meets Death* — a humorously, death-defying tale of time management, mistaken identities, cruise ships.... and romance novels.

Join in on the fun today by heading to www.subscribepage.com/mrsmorris

ALSO BY TAMMIE PAINTER

THE CIRCUS OF UNUSUAL CREATURES

It's not every day you meet an amateur sleuth with fangs.

If you like paranormal, cozy mysteries that mix in laughs in with murderous mayhem and mythical beasts, you'll love The Circus of Unusual Creatures.

Hoard It All Before, Tipping the Scales, Fangs a Million

THE OSTERIA CHRONICLES

A Six-Book Mythological Fantasy Adventure

Myths and heroes may be reborn, but the whims of the gods never change.

Perfect for fans of the mythological adventure of *Clash of the Titans* and *300*, as well as historical fantasy fiction by Madeline Miller and David Gemmel, the Osteria Chronicles are a captivating fantasy series in which the myths, gods, and heroes of Ancient Greece come to life as you've never seen them before.

The Trials of Hercules, The Voyage of Heroes, The Maze of Minos, The Bonds of Osteria, The Battle of Ares, The Return of Odysseus

THE CASSIE BLACK TRILOGY

Work at a funeral home can be mundane. Until you start accidentally bringing the dead to life.

The Undead Mr. Tenpenny, The Uncanny Raven Winston, The Untangled Cassie Black

DOMNA

Destiny isn't given. It's made by cunning, endurance, and, at times, bloodshed.

If you like the political intrigue, adventure, and love triangles of historical fiction by Philippa Gregory and Bernard Cornwell, or the mythological world-building of fantasy fiction by Madeline Miller and Simon Scarrow, you'll love this exciting story of desire, betrayal and rivalry.

Part One: The Sun God's Daughter, Part Two: The Solon's Son, Part Three: The Centaur's Gamble, Part Four: The Regent's Edict, Part Five: The Forgotten Heir, Part Six: The Solon's Wife

AND MORE...

To see all my currently available books and short stories, just scan the QR code or visit books.bookfunnel.com/tammiepainterbooks

ABOUT THE AUTHOR
THAT'S ME...TAMMIE PAINTER

Many moons ago I was a scientist in a neuroscience lab where I got to play with brains and illegal drugs. Now, I'm an award-winning author who turns wickedly strong tea into imaginative fiction (so, basically still playing with brains and drugs).

My fascination for myths, history, and how they interweave inspired my flagship series, The Osteria Chronicles.

But that all got a bit too serious for someone with a strange sense of humor and odd way of looking at the world. So, while sitting at my grandmother's funeral, my brain came up with an idea for a contemporary fantasy trilogy that's filled with magic, mystery, snarky humor, and the dead who just won't stay dead. That idea turned into The Cassie Black Trilogy.

I keep the laughs and the paranormal antics coming in my latest series, The Circus of Unusual Creatures, which is filled with detecting dragons, murder mysteries, and...omelets.

When I'm not creating worlds or killing off characters, I can be found gardening, planning my next travel adventure, working as an unpaid servant to three cats and two guinea pigs, or wrangling my backyard hive of honeybees.

You can learn more at *TammiePainter.com* or at that QR code, where you'll find probably more info than you could ever want or need.

Printed in Great Britain
by Amazon

37903107R00199